THE TERRORS OF WONDER

A tragicomedy about truth, identity, and leadership
by

- [Daniel Strasel] -

Published by Daniel Strasel

Synopsis:

*A prominent young child with disturbing visions
must overcome an intimate enemy or be lost forever.*

 HTTP://www.Mirroranium.com 

ISBN-13: 978-0-9859964-4-4

          - [The Terrors of Wonder] -

From The Back Cover

A tragicomedy ∆ rife with symbols, savants, and satire,
The Terrors of Wonder reads in the spirit of science fiction.

* * *

One of the world's most prominent heiresses is about to celebrate her 3rd birthday. A well-mannered and very precocious child, she is a delight to her parents and their entire household.

Every year a party of historic proportions is thrown, this year the largest celebration yet. The party, now as before, is being held in the statistically safest country in the world. As many gather from around the globe, however, a series of curious crimes slowly begin to disrupt the regular tranquility.

These crimes have been designed to–among other things–rob this girl of her inheritance, placing enough power to rattle the world into eager and willing hands.

Yet, as a consequence of these crimes, someone *else* begins stalking the girl…someone with an even darker purpose.

* * *

A plateful of truth, leadership, and identity, all seasoned with tragedy; served with a glass of comedy to wash it down.

This 316 page volume includes maps, art, footnotes, appendices, and more.

∆ **Tra·gi·com·e·dy**
  A style of literature or play that blends aspects of both tragic and comic forms.

TABLE OF

CONTENTS

PROLOGUE

"I'll be waiting for you," she said.

The way that she spoke was always alluring, always enticing, and so his mind often drifted back to *her.*

He always wanted to be closer, but he knew he couldn't be. He knew, because she *told* him that if he ever came any closer she would kill him. She told him this, *because,* she said, she needed a friend–and friends tell each other the truth.

She said she would tell him everything.

"But," she warned him teasingly, "if you listen to my story, you will fall in love with me."

He had laughed as she said it. Yet, it had been such a long time since he laughed or smiled, so he listened. She told him all about her nature, and all about her life, and when she was done he had indeed fallen in love with her.

He wanted to help her, and he knew he was the only person that could.

He remembered the meeting where she gave him *the amulet.*

"*This*," she said, outlining a small silver rod, "will conceal you *and* the contents of the room you are in from any outside surveillance. When it is unenclosed, you may act as freely as you dare."

"*Any* room?" He asked, his mind immediately considering the various possibilities.

"Well," she drawled, "any room that does not, at any point, exceed a radius of 200 feet."

"So then it would work, like, in a car…"

"Yes, certainly in a *car.*"

"But…then what if the windows are open? Will it still work? Would the car and the road disappear too? That could be awkward."

"No, *no*," she said, hesitating momentarily before resuming. "You're already over-thinking it. The algorithm uses the device *itself* as its point of reference. Don't worry: it's programmed to refrain from doing anything that might give itself away. Technically, it's smarter than you are. It will clean up the details you overlook.

"Also, bring me two Agents who trust you and who you trust. They must not be conscious when they arrive; they will not be conscious when they leave.

"Oh, and bring me a woman," she continued. "of sufficient proportion and early age. Someone from *the Company*. Someone you can *pretend* was never abducted. Someone that is an adult. I do not care if she is awake or asleep…she will not leave until *I* do."

▲

His short, black hair was always meticulously kempt - the current moment of no exception. His unlit pipe clacked a bit noisily as he unconsciously shifted it around in his mouth. Sweat beaded his forehead, which he intermittently sopped up with his handkerchief.

Despite a few slight variances in intensity, however, he never dropped his constant smile. It was the smile he wore since he met her - a goldilocks kind of smile: neither too large nor too small, bearing perfect teeth perfectly.

Today was the day. Today was the day he had been anticipating for *all* this time.

In a room concealed from any outside, unwanted observation, the man set to work repacking the satchel that he had unpacked and repacked more than several times before. He knew that it would be irrational to think that anything might be missing, yet it set him at ease to exercise the verification. Plus, he had just finished his letter.

The first "item" was actually a set of 5 identical silver tickets. Apart from the words "Admit One" and a set of numbers, they were inflexible and almost sharp. He placed them carefully into the satchel, so as to not carelessly cut himself in the handling.

The second item was a 6 inch black cube, which he gingerly placed back into the bag.

"Never mind the interior," She had instructed him when he first picked it up. "It's not a present for *you*, and I would hate for you to spoil the surprise. Of any instructions or tasks that I have given you, however, consider this the *most* important. If you must fail at anything, *do **not** fail in delivering **this***."

Although he never betrayed that charge, it did not stop him from wondering about it almost constantly.

The third item was a dull bronze ring, just under a foot in circumference and about a centimeter thick. He turned it on and off, rewarded momentarily with lights that signaled its effective operation.

"I dare not hope," she said when he held it for the first time, "but succeed in placing *this*, and you will save the world."
"I thought you said the *box* was the most important-"
"I did. I'll say it again. Of these things, the *box* is the *most* important."

The fourth and fifth items were envelopes - *paper* envelopes. One contained a purchase receipt for an American bus.

I still need to get rid of that, he thought to himself.

The other envelope contained a *paper* letter that he had just finished writing. It was addressed "For The Rook."

The last item to go into the bag was the anti-surveillance device, *the amulet.* After replacing it, he closed the satchel.

Slinging the bag over his shoulder, he grabbed his cane and left the restroom where he had been writing his letter. He slowly hobbled his way back down the mirrored hallway to finally relax at his desk.

Lighting his pipe, his thoughts drifted to replaying the entirety of his instructions and itinerary.

- [The Terrors of Wonder] -

HISTORY OF THE COMPANY

Serter Company, also known as "SerterCo", is easily recognized as one of the largest companies in the world come the year 2070–*this* year.

The Company began almost 2 hundred years ago in Stockholm, Sweden by a passionate Jewish baker named Parsifal Planer who had an otherwise intense love for ring bagels and bread making.

Word of his technique and expertise eventually made its way to the ears of the local magistrate. Having sampled Parsifal's products, the magistrate quickly declared him the finest baker in the region and extended to Parsifal a modest (although rather ad hoc) award.

Inspired, Parsifal transformed his modest home into a storefront bakery. "My Lord's Bagels" opened on February 13, 1883. The bakery was successful enough to last through the end of Parsifal's days.

Parsifal died never having a son, although he left 2 daughters. The elder of the pair died at a fairly early age of diabetes. [1Δ] The younger daughter, Isolde, had been married to an unsuccessful artist named Seigfried Serter several years prior to Parsifal's death.

Mostly penniless, the Serters moved back to Stockholm to operate the bakery and care for Isolde's birth mother, who incidentally passed away shortly after Parsifal. Do not let your imagination take you to dark places, however: the instance was coincidental–the Serters were neither complicit nor neglectful.

Seigfried did *not* love bagels *or* bread making, and so his primary contribution to the bakery was in his decoration of the interior. Isolde took almost all of the work of maintaining "My Lord's Bagels" upon herself while her husband spent a considerable amount of their earnings at the nearby pubs.

Isolde had a son, Richard, who, rather opposite his father, *delighted* in helping his mother maintain the bakery.

[1Δ] Naturally her cause of death was misdiagnosed at the time.

As Seigfried became more and more dispassionate and distant, Richard and Isolde grew closer and closer. Although they enjoyed their partnership for many years, Isolde rather sadly died of rödsot (or dysentery) a week before Richard turned 20.

Richard did not care much for Seigfried, and offered him an appropriate sum of money in exchange for sole ownership rights to the business. Seigfried eagerly accepted the money and ran off with another man's wife, whom he had apparently been entertaining for some time.

As he could not afford to enlist any help, alone in his bakery, Richard worked hard. Left without the distractions or obligations of family or friends, Richard became completely absorbed in the business. It was all he focused on, and his attention and dedication were well rewarded.

Richard proved to be a man of vision. He used some of his earnings to remodel the bakery by incorporating interior and exterior tables, and eventually a respectable wine selection. Richard's bistro was a tremendous success.

No room or time for romantic love in his heart or life, Richard started conscripting orphans from local workhouses that were of suitable age to assist him.

In 1912 Richard changed the name of the bistro to "Bagel Lord," and then spent the next several years purchasing and transforming some of the other less successful bakeries into copies of his already successful model.

The orphans that showed the most amount of dedication with little supervision he eventually adopted in full and placed them in charge of his outlying operations.

"Only a *Serter* can run a Bagel Lord, for only a *Serter* will be invested enough to protect the family business name. If there is no new Serter, there will be no new Bagel Lord."

True to his vision, if Richard did not develop and adopt a suitable orphan, he would simply purchase and close rival businesses.

After Richard passed his adopted descendants continued to propagate the business, eventually taking on several wealthy backers and changing the primary entity of the business to "Serter Company."

Serter Company quickly strayed from the "adopt-and-place" technique of Richard Serter, mostly because it grew exponentially, making it otherwise impossible to maintain such a stratagem. Serter Company started buying *other* companies. Initially it bought companies that produced the materials that "Bagel Lord" used in its daily operations, but as the profitability continued to escalate, Serter Company started buying anything that looked overly promising or possibly threatening.

By 1970 Bagel Lord was a leading international chain restaurant, and Serter Company easily one of the wealthiest and influential companies in the world. One thing never changed, however: a *Serter* has always been in charge of Serter Company.

In 2038 a very powerful and influential American company located on private land in New York-Axel Industries-declared itself as an independent *nation,* thereafter known as the nation of Silverberg.

At the point that Silverberg declared its independence, Axel Industries had grown to be the most profitable company in the world. SerterCo had been trying to gain control over Axel Industries for awhile, and now felt that something more needed to be done.

Tristan Serter, the head of Serter Company at the time, felt *personally* threatened by Axel Industries. He eventually went so far as to directly pledge assistance to America [2A] *if* it should try to seize control of seditious Silverberg.

In 2039 America launched attacks at Silverberg, only to be completely rebuffed and shamed. Tristan, disgusted, withdrew his pledge.

In 2043 Tristan died. Franklin Serter, his son and successor, knew that any idea of controlling Axel Industries (nee Silverberg) was stupid. Franklin also felt that Tristan was foolish, and sought to *build* relations with Axel Industries.

Franklin spent several years moving the primary headquarters of SerterCo from Sweden to Silverberg, although mostly to take advantage of Silverberg's Tax Law (The law that states that there are *no* regular taxes). SerterCo saved millions.

By 2048 the move was complete. Many in the financial and political world feared that Serter Company and Axel Industries were on the brink of a merger. There was never cause for fear. Axel Industries cared as much about SerterCo as it did about any company or person in Silverberg–neither more nor less.

[2A] Pledged assistance, which is to say, gave a great deal of money to a nation that desperately needed it, along with weapons of warfare and promises of future collaboration.

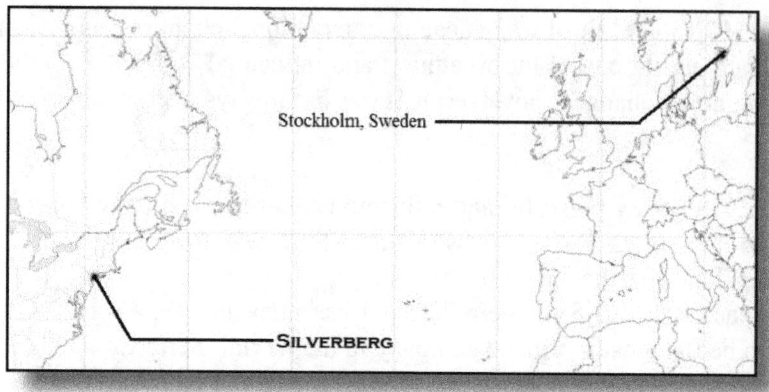

In 2060 Franklin died. Frank had twin (not identical) sons named Jason and Jacob. When their father died, Jason assumed the leadership of the company and Jacob went abroad to…well, mostly play.

Jason was a bit of an megalomaniac, however, and silently considered himself and his company at *war* with Axel Industries. What seemed like a joke at first was made sober reality when Jason unilaterally changed the titles of every position in Serter Company to reflect military designations–such as private, sergeant, et al.

Title	# of Employees	Name	Constituents
Private	Self		
Sergeant	8-12	Squad (Team)	
Lieutenant	26-55	Platoon (Department)	2+ Squads
Major	80-225	Company (Store)	2-8 Platoons
Colonel	300-1300	Battalion (Area)	2-6 Companies
General	1500-3000	Regiment (Region)	2+ Battalions
CEO	All		

Curiously, this actually had a very *positive* effect on the "Bagel Lord" portion of the Company, whose workers already felt like they were at war with every patron who came through their doors. Management teams and hourly employees solidified better in their roles, and although already prominent and considerable, Bagel Lord rose to become *the* single most successful restaurant chain in the world.

In 2066 Jason Serter died in some kind of explosion within the walls of the SerterCo Headquarters in Silverberg. Jacob, having been alerted to his brother's fate, was back in Silverberg and in control of the Company in the span of a few hours.

Jacob has spent the last few years operating SerterCo in a very different fashion than his recent predecessors. SerterCo, under Jacob Serter, has embraced addressing world poverty and hunger, funding research, encouraging sustainable business and agricultural practices, and educating the world abroad.

Every step Axel Industries makes, Serter Company takes a similar step to "be the better of the two," by offering alternate, possibly superior, services.

In the wake of Jacob's direction Serter Company has lost a considerable sum of money, yet Jacob Serter is–without any sense of doubt–one of the most respected and cherished men on the planet.

SILVERBERG

On the second day of September in the year 1973, an eruption of an unknown quantity and type of energy burst outward from its epicenter of New Rochelle, New York. At the radius of 15 miles, it abruptly terminated. Within its fifteen mile wake laid a land completely devoid of its earlier characteristics.

What *replaced* the landscape was a completely smooth, silver-looking substance later known as "mirroranium". [3△] Although numerous companies (SerterCo included) experimented with it, only 1 managed any utilizable success: that company was Axel Industries.

Axel Industries found a way to make mirroranium somehow *unbreakable*. Axel, founder and owner of Axel Industries, referred to the final product as "**tempered**" mirroranium. Thus far, there has never been an instance of it breaking… *or even bending*.

Already one of the larger companies, with no rivals able to replicate the process of making "tempered" mirroranium, Axel Industries quickly became the most powerful and wealthiest company in the world, foremost in *every* respect.

As much as worthless to anybody else, in 1984 Axel Industries purchased the land rights to the 30 mile diameter deposit of mirroranium from the United States of America. Axel moved the company directly *onto* the mirroranium deposit, transforming part of the land into a small city of employees.

From that time until it declared itself an independent country in 2038, Axel Industries continued to expand, eventually creating enough industry centers to have 5 well-populated and exponentially growing cities. People were migrating from all over the world, eager to be employed with or near Axel Industries in some capacity–immigration incidentally being one of the attributable reasons Silverberg left America.

Silverberg is now the most technologically advanced area on the planet. Those that come to Silverberg are often amazed (if not completely overwhelmed) by its inconceivable advancements.

Yet, possibly the most alien, unnerving aspect of Silverberg is that every original building and almost all the surfaces are apparently made out of mirroranium, acting as mirrors. The effect can be overwhelming, some places more so than others.

SerterCo is one entity (amongst several) within Silverberg that has gone to great lengths to cover its walls, ceilings, and floors with alternate materials in order to decrease the unsettling, mirrored effect.

[3△] △M SYMBOL
Mirroranium is depicted mathematically (scientifically) as a Delta encasing the letter "M"

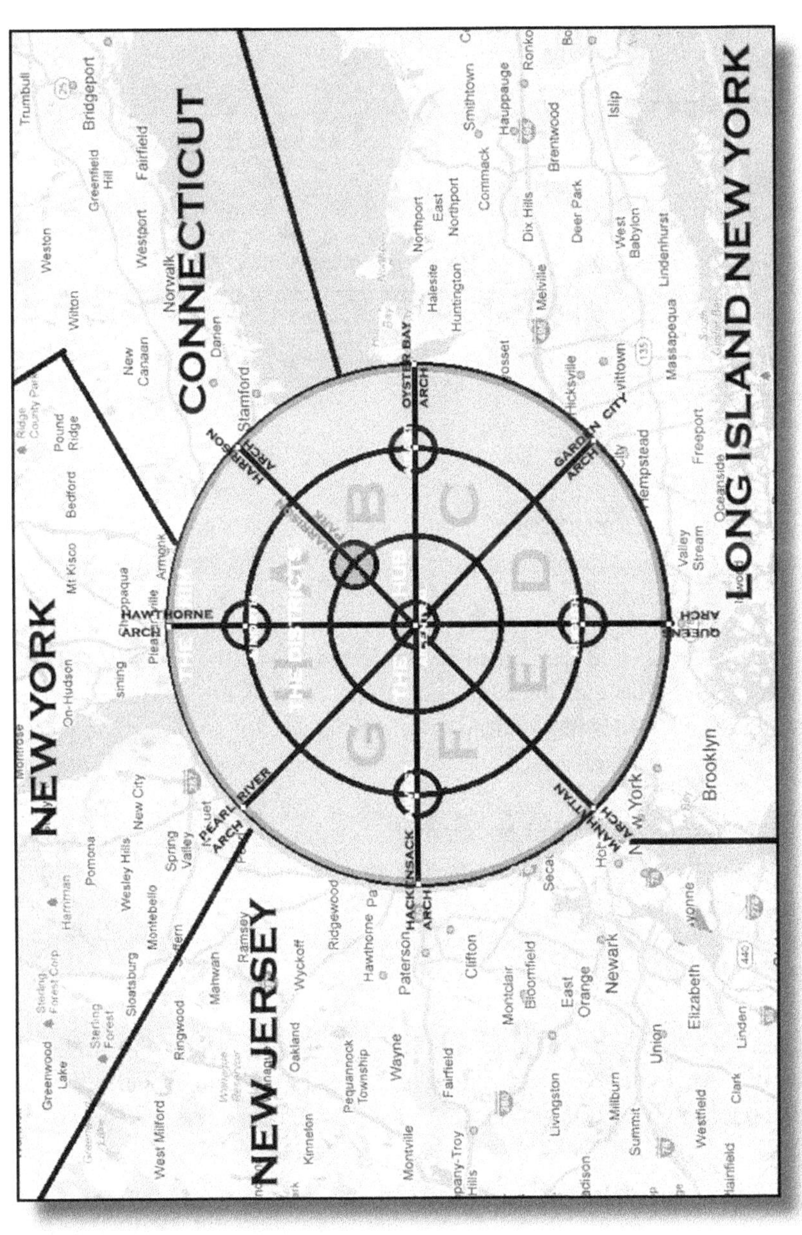
CONNECTICUT
Trumbull
Bridgeport
Weston
Greenfield Hill
Fairfield
Westport
Norwalk
New Canaan
Wilton
Danen
Stamford
Pound Ridge
Ridge
County Park
Bedford
Mt Kisco
Armonk
Chappaqua
Pleasantville
HAWTHORNE ARCH
Spring
On-Hudson
Montrose
NEW YORK
West Milford
Greenwood Lake
Sterling Forest Corp
Sterling Forest
Ringwood
Wesley Hills
Montebello
Suffern
Pomona
Harriman
Sloatsburg
Mahwah
Ramsey
Wyckoff
New City
Spring Valley
Pearl River
PEARL RIVER ARCH
Ridgewood
Hawthorne Pa
Paterson
HACKENSACK ARCH
Clifton
NEW JERSEY
Kinnelon
Oakland
Pequannock Township
Wayne
Fairfield
Montville
pany-Troy Hills
adison
Livingston
Millburn
Summit
Westfield
Clark
ainfield
Linden
Union
Elizabeth
Newark
East Orange
Bloomfield
Montclair
Bayonne
Secau
Hob
N. York
MANHATTAN ARCH
Brooklyn
N. York
OYSTER BAY
ARCH
HARRISON ARCH
GARDEN ARCH
QUEEN ARCH
A
B
C
D
E
F
G
H
THE HUB
THE DISTRICT
LONG ISLAND NEW YORK
Smithtown
Hauppauge
Ronko
Bo
Commack
Brentwood
Islip
Dix Hills
Deer Park
West Babylon
Lindenhurst
Melville
Massapequa
Freeport
Hempstead
Valley Stream
Oceanside
vittown
GARDEN CITY
Hicksville
osset
Huntington
East Northport
Northport
Halesite
Oyster Bay

Chapter 1:

The Lord and Lady

JUNE *2070 EST*

Fri 13	Sat 14	Sun 15
06:00		

Jacob did not like dialogue.

It's not that he didn't like *speaking* with others, *that* he genuinely enjoyed.
None should take from such a statement, either, that Jacob was an unlikable man; most people liked him, many even loved him. Rather, it was the concept of *frivolous* dialogue that he could not abide. Jacob never spoke without *some* purpose, you see, either transparent or otherwise, and it summarily unsaddled him whenever he was so victimized.

"*Banter's* for the *bored*," he often said. "I am *never* bored. If my job does not keep my attention otherwise occupied, then I assure you my household demands the remainder."
Now, Jacob was fairly young–young enough to have the energy and naivety to make such a statement *and* be genuine. He was important enough that anyone cared.
Jacob was, after all, a *very* important, *very* busy man. He was not always such a man, however. No, before he took control of SerterCo, he seldom committed himself to any form of promise, and most of his conversations were of content ephemeral.

It was just after his assumption of the Company that Jacob suddenly found himself to be a man possessed of a new mindset. From that moment on, for Jacob, each and every moment was precious. From that point forward, Jacob would commit himself to leadership.

 - [The Terrors of Wonder] -

"I needed an opportunity," he said in reflection of his past. "I needed the resolute trust of my peers. *I needed a purpose*...that's it! In short, I simply had no real *purpose* before taking over SerterCo. I was nothing more than an adult child, living in a world of celebrities and wealth, gravitating only towards that which tickled my current passion. I had become common, and common men are willfully and easily distracted."

Jacob thus surrounded himself with *un*common men. Men who were *not* so easily distracted, that were unquestionably loyal, and who were considered upstanding by their neighbors and peers.

"Be an individual," Jacob would often instruct those around him. "Have an opinion. I certainly don't need *copies of myself* running around. If I ask you your perspective, I should find it somewhat different than my own. A difference of opinion need not be an *insult*. Besides, I assure you, you cannot insult me–but you'll have much to answer for if you should try."

Neither menacing nor timid, Jacob Serter was a man who need not be either underestimated or feared.

Jacob was not ultimately attractive, although whatever he lacked in aesthetic, he compensated for in expression. His eyes were alert, yet soft–the same might be said of his voice. Jacob's face always wore a semblance of assurance, knowledge...which was suitable, for Jacob was unquestionably intelligent.

For some people, Jacob's intelligence was suspicious. Many speculated that he was augmented in some way: either by drug, implant, or both.

Despite ridicule or suspicion, however, Jacob freely gave his intellect to the world, offering remedy and actually *helping*–helping the impoverished, the broken, the lost, the unfortunate, the needy, the diseased, the hurt, the hungry, the sick, the abused.

SerterCo seemed like it was suddenly everywhere, attending to those who dare not hope of such a miracle.

Now millions of people throughout the world hold a certain softness and reverence for the name Jacob Serter.

A

Jacob arose this morning at 6 AM, as he did every day, no alarm required. The lights came on automatically, as they did every day, no command necessary. While he dressed, he reviewed the prior day and week-to-date results for the Bagel Lord component of SerterCo–as he did every Friday.

At 6:30 AM, (like every Friday) in a room not too far removed from his bedroom, Jacob initiated a virtual meeting with all of the Majors (or Unit Managers, of which there were 17), Colonels (or Area Supervisors, of which there were 4), and Generals (Or Regional Directors, of which there were 2) of the Silverberg Division of Bagel Lord.

"Welcome," Jacob announced to the images of the "officers" that had come into existence around the professionally decorated room. [4]

"The weekend is upon us. *Many* of you have experienced a considerable spike in volume this week–most of you have done well in response.

"Before we proceed, I would like to impress upon all of you that when we deal with tourists–such as right now–remember that *many* of them are from very wealthy, very significant families. Please be sure that this weekend you are all making your best impressions. Remember, you *represent* SerterCo. I don't want to ask the impossible, however; Majors, you are all welcome to add two additional bodies to every shift for the next six shifts, starting with this one...*if* you can find them on such notice. Of course, the shrewder of you have already developed soldiers who will present themselves whenever so necessary–isn't that correct, Major Tohm?"

One of the officers nodded accordingly.

"Now let's go over the week-to-date results of the operation and stratagems for this weekend."

Jacob spoke to his subordinates, praising those with positive results, and offering suggestions and assistance to those that were struggling. Never was there an implication or hint of disdain or belittling: only sincere empathy and a genuine desire for mutual success.

Jacob's Bagel Lord "officers" often looked forward to their Friday morning conference with their leader.

---

[4] "come into existence," which is to say via projection.

"Well, it is now 6:54, and our doors open for business in 66 minutes. Colonel, proceed with your food cost commentary."

"Thank you, Jacob," Colonel Nill began. "There are 3 basics that will help you get your food costs under control.

"First, Majors, you must verify all of your deliveries personally. If you have your lieutenants or sergeants in charge of receiving, stop this practice immediately. I am sympathetic to the need to delegate, but your deliveries must be monitored *personally* for integrity, temperature, accuracy...and presence.

"Second, monitor your prep and waste lists. Make sure you are only preparing the amount of food you are using for the same day, four week average, modified by your sales trend accordingly. *Run out of product* if you must...just make a note to increase the production of that item. It will balance out.

"On that note, if you *do* happen to run out of product, do not simply tell the guest that they should 'come back tomorrow;' explain the circumstance, apologize, and give them a free something on their next visit. I know that guests can be pretty unforgiving, but there is *nothing* in this industry more irresponsible than throwing away or serving substandard food. *Food is money*."

Colonel Nill coughed for a moment before resuming.

"Finally, watch everyone–suspect *everyone*. If you don't already, your soldiers are probably eating your food–your *money*. Oh, they're not trying to hurt *you;* they're not doing it to be seditious. They don't think of it as taking from *people*, they think of it as taking from the *Company* something that is already owed them, or should be. We all self-justify our actions.

"Now, at heart, *everyone's* a thief; do n-"

"*Stop*," Jacob interrupted.

Nill, as abruptly, stopped speaking. He was confused, yet compliant.

The momentary lack of sound was slightly unsettling.

"Colonel Nill, I am afraid you are suspended from duty. I will speak with you about this later. Dismissed."

"What?" Colonel Nill asked, shocked–but Jacob had already shut off Nill's image.

"I do not wish to leave any of you upset," Jacob said, turning to address the remaining images. "Second guessing your every move and word for fear you will suffer a similar fate. As stores open in roughly 61 minutes from now, I will hastily explain that such mentality, professional or otherwise, is *pernicious*; left unaddressed, it will spread.

"Anyone who says that *everyone's* a thief must be a thief themselves, for *only* a thief imagines that *everyone* steals. While he is hunting for thieves, he is looking for ways to steal.

"*Listen*: not everyone is a thief.

"Such a man cannot be left in a position where he might be *tempted* to steal, however, so Mr. Nill will have to either assume an alternate position within SerterCo or be terminated. Fear not, though. I am not without compassion: I will find Nill an otherwise lateral role.

"The message that the former Colonel *should* have delivered to you is that you should not *create an environment* where stealing is *possible*. Don't set your men up simply to knock them back down. Don't leave your treasure unattended. Do not tolerate unacceptable behavior. This is your job.

"Major Tohm," Jacob turned to the familiar image. "Congratulations on your pending promotion to Colonel. I will see you at your unit…Sunday morning to discuss your new assignment."

Major Tohm nodded, a slight smile on his lips.

"Ladies and gentlemen, it is now after 7:00, and you have less than an hour to get your stores ready. For those of you that I do not speak with otherwise, I will see you all tomorrow at one for the 2nd Leadership Summit at the Regency in the Ace. [5Δ]

"Banter's for the bored, people; let's go make some money."

One by one the images disappeared from the room as the officers ended their sessions. Jacob went on working, addressing concerns involving other aspects of SerterCo, and preparing for this evening.

[5Δ] The Regency is a hotel located within the walls of the titanic Axel Industries Central Building–a building known more colloquially as "the Ace."

Certainly, Jacob has changed considerably since assuming leadership of the company. *Now* he might be considered the hope of humankind, but prior to his "promotion," he was better known as "Serter's brother"–a philandering playboy who had a taste for parties, celebrities, and the limelight in many countries abroad.

Although Jacob has suggested that his transformation was as sudden as his inheritance, several skeptics assert that Jacob's behavior did not change so immediately.

It is at least true that he was seen carousing with *several* Silverberg celebrities just before his rather sudden marriage in October of '66–a full 2 months after taking over the company.

Following his marriage, however, *none* would contest that there was an observable change of behavior in Jacob Serter. As immediate as his marriage, Jacob was no longer the carefree playboy–he was instead the caring husband, fawning over his new wife, exclusively devoted to her.

Ayn Serter, formerly known as Ayn McNally, was neither brilliant nor beautiful. Do not conjure that she was then to the other extremes, however; she was simply average in appearance and generally more angry than stupid.

At least, she *was* angry.
…before she met Jacob.
Well, angr*ier*, anyway.

Ayn had all but lost her ability to love. Of the relationships she had, she suffered within and without during each and every one–the last perhaps the most damaging of them all.

But then came Jacob. He was obviously attracted to Ayn right from the moment they met. Initially, she thought that she might use this to her advantage somehow, but then Jacob turned out to be so honest, so caring, so…*genuine*.

They immediately started spending all of their free time together. For Ayn, this was nothing short of a miracle. She never dreamt she could be capable of trusting and loving anyone again, and now, as suddenly–here was this sweet, sensitive, honest man.

Who was so well spoken
…and presentable.
Who always made eye contact.
Who was friendly, who smiled.
Who was a perfect listener, always waiting for the speaker to finish.
Who was confident: an individual secure in his identity.
A man who was engaging, one who asked questions.
Who had *direction.*
Who was responsible.
…and knowledgeable.
…and powerful.
…*and* rich.

Not to imply that Ayn was *poor.* Ayn Serter, you see, is actually *much* better known as "Anthem", the primary vocalist for the popular music [6Δ] group *The Valentine Relics.*

The group, despite awkward origins, became considerably popular throughout Silverberg and several countries abroad.

Although not nearly as noteworthy as Jacob's, Anthem had a considerable fan base herself.

Anthem's sudden marriage to Jacob was not well received by her band associates. Her thoughts were always on "that man". Without her regular anger, depression, and consternation, *The Valentine Relics* almost stopped performing. When Anthem announced she wanted to write a love song, the group told her to go make a solo album.

And so, *The Valentine Relics* stopped performing with Anthem.

Exiting the honeymoon period of her marriage, Anthem eventually came to a

---

[6Δ] "As to whether or not *The Valentine Relics* make *music* is certainly debatable," said Essence Templeton, music critic and aficionado. "All that screaming and anger and sadness; *The Relics* seem only capable of writing songs that attack everything while saying nothing. The melodies are persuasive enough, but the lyrics are just ambiguous rants. Just. Depressing. *Blark*" ("Blark" being a fairly popular genre of music at the time).

                      - [The Terrors of Wonder] -

personal epiphany that performing was an otherwise integral part of her character. To further deny it would threaten her identity.

So strange that all of her needs were being met, and yet there was still something somehow missing in her life! She discovered she needed to *perform* in order to feel *complete.*

Pulling on her inner skeptic, and looking for a good source of anger, [7] Anthem drafted a few songs and contacted her old associates. With renewed energy and dedication, Anthem suggested that *The Valentine Relics* band together and make a new album…and start touring again.

At first *The Relics* laughed and refused–although once they collectively sobered up long enough to genuinely consider the idea, they agreed–albeit begrudgingly.

Within a very short period of time, Anthem really started to feel…functional again.

It felt so *good*, to be herself. Anthem did not realize how much of her identity went aside with her marriage! She wasn't angry, however–at least not about *that.* If anything, she was elated that she could be *both* Mrs. Serter *and* Anthem of *The Valentine Relics.*

---

[7] …which was not overly difficult. Many journalists and reporters had taken to labeling her as "The Bagel *Lady*" after she married Jacob Serter. More than several editorial cartoons pictured her as an anthropomorphic Bagel with horns and a tail. Nothing elicited a rise out of Anthem as quickly as someone referring to her as "The Bagel Lady."

She started exercising a bit more and even managed to find a way into her old wardrobe.

Years ago, Anthem developed her own stage presence. When she performed, she always appeared as a caricature devil, wearing horns on her head and a devil's tail. Her microphone looked like a pitchfork. To complete the effect, she would dye (sometimes paint) her skin various colors (although usually red), depending on her mood.

Far before her marriage, as *The Valentine Relics* enjoyed greater and greater success, Anthem had herself *permanently* augmented with a functional (and slightly prehensile) devil's tail and additionally had two horns surgically screwed into her skull.

Now these horns were of just the right size that they could be hidden beneath her hair easily enough, and her tail of such a size that a long dress would be sufficient to conceal it.

But *Anthem* was back, and the horns were out.

No more baggy bottoms and hats to disguise her stage persona, Anthem once again barely fit into her armless and legless tuxedo [8Δ] that was the trademark outfit of *The Relics*.

In this last collaboration with Anthem, *The Valentine Relics* have produced the most successful album of their careers: <u>One Fool Makes Many</u>. The album is currently under consideration for award, and *The Relics* have not only revived their old fans, but have attracted new ones as well.

Yet, because of the overwhelming success of the new album, and because of Jacob's philanthropist and businesslike demeanor, Anthem and her husband have been spending progressively less time together…well, because of these things, and then also because of their daughter.

[8Δ] She barely fit into it *before* her marriage.

Chapter 2:

The Daughter of the Devil

Fri 13	Sat 14	Sun 15
07:38		

In a plush white chair, sitting in the center of a circular white room, lay a young white girl who was wearing shining white clothes; she had radiant white hair and soft white skin.

She also had the brightest blue eyes.

There were a few trappings strewn about the room–a stuffed pig, a pair of black glasses, a few pillows, and several other items that need no description[9Δ]–and a large imagescreen which hung suspended near the wall opposite the chair.

The girl watched the screen, smiling wistfully at the intermittent images of herself playing with her mother and father.

There were several portals that offered exit from the round chamber, disappearing into twisting and turning mirrored hallways whose ends could not be seen, only experienced by travelling down them proper.

Although the girl was happy enough to watch herself play with her parents, she could not help but wonder what lay down the hallways.

Then she noticed *another* young girl standing just outside one of the doorways. The strange girl might have been identical to herself, except her eyes were completely white, and her smile was perhaps a bit more cynical than kind.

9Δ But, as I hate to be left in any kind of suspense myself: a silver circlet, a mirrored calculator, a black blanket, 2 letter blocks made of wood, and a paper book.

"Come play with me," the stranger beckoned.

The little girl in the chair hesitated.

"*Come*, play with me," the strange girl said with more authority.

The little girl with blue eyes felt she should probably go. As she left her cozy, fluffy chair, the imagescreen disappeared, and the room fell mostly silent.

She walked up to the strange girl, who then, quite to her surprise, hugged her. The two of them hugged for a moment, and suddenly the strange girl didn't seem so odd.

"This will be fun!" The stranger said with glee. Grabbing the girl's hand, she practically pulled her running down the hallway.

They ran, hand in hand, down the twists and turns of the mirrored hallways. After a short time, however, the girl with blue eyes could not remember how to get back.

"Where are we going?" She asked, starting to feel confused.

"Here we *are*!" The girl with white eyes cried, turning a corner and entering an alternate room.

The room was square, mostly devoid of furnishings other than a large recliner, a few glass cases (which neither of the girls were tall enough to properly see into), and some rugs that were hanging on the wall. The rugs had some pictures on them, but there was no time to look closely for the strange girl ushered her over and into the large reclining chair.

"What are we doing?" The girl asked, starting to feel a bit alarmed.

"We're going to play *doctor*," the strange girl said, strapping her almost-twin into the chair.

"I-I don't think I *want* to play doctor," The girl said, almost unable to move.

She might have protested further, but several spider-like arms abruptly sprung out from under the chair and started quickly touching her from head to foot. The girl with blue eyes found herself unable to struggle or speak at all.

She looked at the strange girl, helplessly waiting.

The strange girl just stared.

*I don't **like** this!* The helpless girl thought, panicking. *I want my Daddy! I want my Mommy!*

The strange girl continued to stare with her disinterested expression and blank, white eyes.

Finally, perhaps sensing the other girl's dismay, the strange girl spoke.

"Don't worry, *this* will make you better."

Then the pain erupted, overwhelming her. Her head felt like it was going to explode. Every pulse of her heartbeat pounded throughout her skull–boom, *boom,* ***boom****–*each new pulse more unbearable than the last. ***BOOM***.

The restrained girl started screaming, her voice suddenly returning. She screamed and screamed as hard and as loud as she was capable: *screaming* in pain, howling in desperation of this unspeakable torment–

Then, *mommy* was there, holding her and rocking. Everything was all right–she couldn't even remember what was wrong.

There was no pain, not even so much as the memory of pain. There was merely mommy and the last part of her scream already tugging at the fringes of her memory.

...what was I crying about? She thought to herself. *Shh,* she thought back to herself.

Slightly damp from holding her sweating child, Anthem pulled away just far enough to wipe both of their eyes.

"Everything okay now, baby?" Anthem asked genuinely.

"I'm fine, mommy." The girl answered, realizing she must have had another bad dream.

"Try and get some more sleep, okay? I'm going to try and do the same. I love you honey."

"I love *you,* mommy!"

Anthem laid down next to her daughter rather than return to her own bed, and both of them soon returned to sleep.

In a nearby room, Jacob continued to work.

Three years ago *today*, Anthem gave birth to her daughter.

Anthem never thought she would have any children, or rather, Anthem never thought she would ever *want* any children. Things change however, Anthem discovered, as she *additionally* discovered that it's okay to change your mind.[10A]

Three years ago today, Anthem marveled at Jacob's beaming delight as he received his new daughter into his arms.
"She's…she's *wonderful*!" he gasped, tears rolling down his thoughtful face.

And so, her name was Wonderful.

Wonderful Serter—Anthem had quickly taken to simply calling her "Wonder." It was one of the very few points that Anthem and Jacob differed on. Jacob was not overly fond of the nickname; whenever it came up, he would insist Anthem refer to her as "Wonderful".
"That's her *name*," he would often complain, slightly growling.
Now from another man, this might have seemed threatening; from Jacob, however, it was simply endearing.

Wonder has always been an alert, precocious child. People who meet her are often amazed to discover how young she is—although more for her manners and discipline than for her intelligence or skill.
For the last few months Wonder has shown a considerable jump in comprehension, learning, and retention…*and* for the last few months, Wonder has been suffering from *night terrors*.
Upon investigation, the Mainframe assured Jacob and Anthem that night terrors are common enough in children Wonder's age, and would pass in time—yet, nothing is worse for a parent than having to watch their child suffer. Anxious and feeling powerless, Anthem insisted her daughter be examined professionally.

The Serters were then *humanly* reassured that the terrors would pass.

10A At least about *this*. On *multiple* other subjects Anthem is resolutely incorrigible.

"We *could* put her on Hypnizium," Dr. Ryan [11△] suggested at their initial meeting. "This would help her with the terrors…at least when the long term effects kick in, at which point she should be able to wake up from any dream and will herself to sleep. But it does take a while, and if we're going to pursue this route, we need to begin medicating her now."

Both Jacob and Anthem agreed.

"In the meantime, just try to be comforting," Dr. Ryan counseled. "Also, don't try to wake the child; her eyes may be wide open, but she will likely be confused, and may not even recognize you. She may scream for a few minutes…up to a half an hour. Once the episode has passed, however, she should go right back to sleep."

Despite Dr. Ryan's professional commentary and reassurance, the situation was nerve-racking for Anthem. Every time Wonder started screaming, Anthem was reduced to helplessness. There was no way to treat or even *console* her child. It simply had to be endured.

For Anthem, however, *her* feelings of helplessness typically manifested as anger and accusation, and although Jacob had absolutely gained her love and respect, [12▲] he was generally the only person available to externalize on. Jacob regularly bore the brunt of Anthem's outbursts.

If any man were capable of withstanding Anthem's rage until it subsided into *"what was I thinking?,"* it was certainly Jacob Serter. Tolerant and patient, Jacob was not easily upset and he was quick to forgive. It was never hard for Anthem to remember why she loved him.

"We're only human," Jacob would say, smiling and winking. "If *this* is the worst we have to endure during our marriage, then we are pretty fortunate; our circumstance is nothing more than annoying when compared with others who have real problems such as disease, poverty, or those who must endure the vicissitudes of war. Soon, this will all be over; it will require effort to remember she ever suffered from it at all."

11△ Hypnizium: a medication exclusive to Silverberg. Hypnizium is typically prescribed to address mental health issues, such as anxiety or depression (although there are a great many reasons Hypnizium is prescribed).

Dr. Otto Ryan, employed at DivTree Associates, a Silverberg-based medical practice owned by SerterCo.

12▲ As much as any wife is capable of respecting her husband, which is to say that although it is certainly true in her heart, her mouth did not always speak accordingly.

Having finished his morning work, Jacob came and kissed his wife awake. Anthem's tail patted the bed in fond appreciation.

"I'm going to take the daughter now. You're welcome to sleep in; I believe you have nothing earlier than noon on your itinerary."

"Wait," Anthem yawned…then she seemed to think the better of his suggestion, and plopped her smiling head back down on the pillow. "Okay. Love you, baby."

"I love you too, my devilish darling. Good luck at the concert–I'll grab some slang [13Δ] merchandise I happen across at the park; we can make fun of it together tonight."

"The *Wonderful Bagel Bonnet!*" Anthem chuckled somewhat sleepily, rolling over. "Oh god, that was awful. I doubt anything will ever beat that."

Jacob lifted Wonder from the bed and took her into the other room.

*I **have** to get up,* Anthem thought. *I need to spend as much time with Wonder as I **can**.*

Anthem rolled back over and stretched out.

…and I better make sure The Relics are going to make the awards ceremony.

*…not that we're going to **win** any awards,* she thought as she lifted herself from her daughter's bed, *but it's good to show up anyway.*

I just hate the fake crap.

***And** the Queen's going to be there; oh, I cannot stand that man…I just hope he's far away.*

Anthem started down the hallway after Jacob. *Alright, I need to go back to happy thoughts.*

"Hey baby, wait for *me!*" Anthem called, quickening her pace. Then, as temptingly as possible, she said "I've got some *birthday* kisses for my sweet *Wonder!*"

"She's Wonder*ful,*" Jacob corrected, mimicking Anthem's tone.

13Δ The word "slang," employed by the culture of Silverberg, implies a derogatory meaning – something undesirable, unintelligent, or in poor taste. In essence, *slang* is slang for bad.

Chapter 3:

Secrets and Slaves

JUNE *2070 EST*

Fri 13	Sat 14	Sun 15
08:22		

There is nothing more reprehensible, nothing more horrible than the savage violation or willful destruction of purity. Despite this, most people perform such atrocities at some point during their lives.

Wonder's speech, and also her terrors, began within days of her secret surgery...a surgery in which Dr. Ryan augmented Wonder with "Thinking Cap" technology. [14Δ]

Now, Thinking Cap technology is such that it allows a person to communicate with another person *mentally*. Thoughts, or at least impressions, are willfully sent directly from one person to an intended recipient.   Impressions are subject to interpretation, however, much like with dialogue, and thus the "listener" may occasionally fail to interpret the "speaker" correctly. This may be either by personal misunderstanding, or should the speaker fail to reasonably or accurately "describe" the topic at hand.

The longer people are paired by a set of Thinking Caps (or at least Thinking Cap technology), the easier it becomes for them to communicate.

Nobody so young has ever had this surgery before, and while the surgery itself is not unlawful, it *is* criminal to refrain from reporting such an augmentation to the Mainframe.

Wonder's augmentation remains undisclosed.

[14Δ] A technology developed and researched by SerterCo, it has endured many setbacks over the years–although generally because of misuse rather than by product failure. Much of the Silverberg public is wary of it, as there have been grievous side effects on occasion.

Few doctors therefore would be *easily* persuaded to perform such a surgery, but many were ultimately vulnerable to the influence of a man with such wealth as Jacob Serter. Jacob's persuasive dogma–and the correct sum of money–convinced Dr. Ryan, for instance, that *he* should have the honor of assisting Mr. Serter in this endeavor.

*"It's the only way to protect her; it must be done," Jacob explained to Ryan. "**I** must be the person to educate my daughter. I will make sure she is learning the **proper** lessons. I will spare her the unnecessary curriculum–the waste of memory.*

"I will not live forever. I need to know that when she inherits the company, she will be capable and commanding, knowledgeable, honest, integral, compassionate–she must be an excellent leader.

*"The world needs it. The world **deserves** it. Governing Serter Company is a tremendous responsibility; would a king have his son raised by his foe?"*

Ⓜ

As Anthem, Jacob, and Wonder all sat around the table finishing their respective breakfasts, servants and slaves [15△] busied themselves with operating and maintaining the private Serter household.

Curtains were tied back to allow more sunlight to illuminate the immense dining room. Furniture was polished and dusted, drawers inspected and closed. This was all done as silently as possible, as to not interrupt the family. The mirroranium walls that were not covered with tapestries or obstructed otherwise, reflected the room trappings and sunlight perfectly.

Serter's servants knew something about mirroranium that most people did not: mirroranium never needed to be polished or wiped–it never stayed dirty or spotted. Now, most people simply never think about it, and the few people that *do* gain the knowledge eventually take it for granted; for although when one first learns this information it is genuinely curious and stokes the imagination, as time passes it is simply regarded as a welcome respite from all the other things that regularly need to be cleaned.

15△ Slavery is legal in Silverberg. Most of the citizens of Silverberg do not consider it offensive in any way–many Silverbergites, in fact, champion it.

The slave caste in Silverberg is comprised *exclusively* of volunteers and criminals convicted of crimes of a *physical* nature. Owners of slaves are responsible for their upkeep, treatment, and maintenance.

Slaves neither enter nor leave Silverberg.

"Mommy?" Wonder asked just before finishing her meal. "Can I go play with *toys*?"

"Oh, I don't know sweetie…well, maybe you *could* play for just a *little* bit while we finish getting ready."

"Getting weddy for what?" Wonder asked, spooning the last of her crepes into her mouth.

"Don't you remember what we talked about last night?"

"Oh yeah!" Wonder's face lit up. She jumped out of her chair and ran over to hug her mother. "So, I have more birfday presents today?"

"You sure do! *Today* is your birthday; *yesterday* was just for you and me since I can't be at your party."

Wonder pouted, but Anthem nuzzled Wonder's head with her nose.[16△]

"You get the biggest and best presents today, for today they are from your *daddy*–and he does love you so very much!" Seeing Wonder's smile widen, she added hastily, "but presents *later*. Right now go ahead and play, I suppose."

Wonder started climbing off of her mother.

"Remember, though: you're going to the Silverberg Amusement Park in just a little bit."

"Bemusement Park?" Wonder asked, hesitating.

Anthem sighed and smiled. "We talked about it last night. It's a huge place with lots of fun stuff and toys and games and rides. You're going to get lots of presents and see shows and try new, delicious foods–it's gonna be the best day of your life!"

I shouldn't bother mommy with more questions, Wonder thought to herself. *She said it's a busy day. She did? Yes. Right now I should go play with toys and wait for daddy to come get me.*

"Okay!" Wonder said aloud, smiling, answering her own thoughts–although it sounded like she was responding to Anthem's description of the amusement park.

Wonder ran back to her room.

[16△] Anthem was careful not to accidentally scratch her daughter with one of her horns, as she had once before–an otherwise traumatic episode for Anthem. For Jacob the instance was minor.

"It's so funny," Anthem said reflectively.

"What is?" Jacob asked.

"Well, like, she can label the staff lines on a music sheet, but she can't remember what we talked about last night. It's just odd, don't you think? What people remember and what they don't?"

"It *is* curious," Jacob said with a mischievous look. "But I'll bet she doesn't have any trouble remembering the '*Bemusement*' park after today. Now…are you gonna come over her and snuggle me or what?"

Anthem returned Jacob's expression and sauntered over to him, tail swishing. She arrived to promptly plop down into his lap and stroke his head appreciatively.

"I still can't get over the fact you bought out the *whole* park,"[17△] Anthem said with a twinkle in her eyes. "You really love that daughter, don't you? You're quite the man, Jacob Serter…*I do love you.*"

After a brief, playful kiss, Jacob spoke up.

"Ah, it's not as generous as it might seem," Jacob suggested modestly. "There was no cost to buy out the park."

"You didn't have to pay anything? Silverberg just *gave* you permission to use the Park?"

"Not at all. What I mean is, we have already made money, even after we bought out the park. It's things like the *Wonderful Bagel Bonnet*, and numerous Wonderful T-shirts that have paid for the park and then some. We'll make even more since Bagel Lord is the primary provider of concessions, not to mention the host of other companies owned by SerterCo that will have presence at the event.

"The revenue from those purchasing the licenses to sell merchandise or professionally represent themselves at the Park *alone* is enough to feed a country–which is *exactly* what we have done with the proceeds."

Anthem was speechless for a moment before she smiled again and spoke. "We're *awfully* generous."

––––––––––

17△ Anthem is expressing a *slightly* exaggerated appreciation–she knew Wonder's party would be massive, as did most people.

For Wonder's last two birthdays, Jacob has thrown parties that have drawn thousands and thousands. *Now* Wonder's birthday party is such an event that it will receive global attention–an event of such proportion that this year it is expected to overshadow even the celebration of the independence of Silverberg.

"Well, we can *afford* to be, can't we?" Jacob said, a hint of admonishment in his tone. "Besides, if money is what you're concerned about, do not forget the entertainment has been *well* paid for."

"*You* know it's not about the money," Anthem defended. "It's about the work, the art."

"*I* know, and that's one of the reasons why I love you so much."

When Jacob mentioned entertainment, they both understood that he was additionally referencing Anthem's group, *The Valentine Relics,* who had been generously conscripted to perform at the park as part of Wonder's birthday celebration (not that Wonder would see her mother perform, nor was she allowed to listen to her music, but overall it was certainly a significant part of the party's public allure).

Jacob and Anthem stared appreciatively at one another as another minute passed.

"Alright, you handsome hunk of man," Anthem said, winking. "Unless you have anything else to add, I should probably get *weddy* myself. Do you want me to dress the daughter?"

"No, I'll attend to her–besides, I have some other things I would like to discuss with her."

"Oh?" Anthem raised an eyebrow. "Like what?"

"Like *stuff.*"

"Secrets, eh?"

"*Exactly,*" Jacob said, once again summoning his most mischievous smile.

Anthem kissed Jacob on his forehead, and then jumped up to head off to her dressing room.

"Fine, I didn't want to know *anyway,*" Anthem called back playfully.

"Ha! You wouldn't *understand* even if you knew," Jacob said, equally playfully.

"Master?" One of Jacob's slaves said, stepping into sight.

"Yes, Joseph?"

- [The Terrors of Wonder] -

In his early adulthood, *Joseph* had undergone *several* significant physical augmentations, classifying him as a metahuman.[18Δ] One day, inebriated and incited, Joseph lost control.

Joseph's impressive augmentations assisted him considerably as he rapidly killed the people he was quarreling with...who, rather tragically, were his own blood brothers.

His augmentations were permanently "turned off" and he became enslaved to Silverberg for his crime, eventually to be sold to Jacob Serter.

Inwardly Joseph was remorseful. From the very core of his being, he wept and wept. Yet, finally somewhere deep within, he found a way to leave his guilt behind him. He took refuge in his servitude to Serter, and resolved to make the most of his situation.

Jacob never treated Joseph as an inferior, which Joseph respected. He worked all the harder because of such treatment. As time passed, the two of them developed an intense respect for one another, eventually resulting in Joseph's promotion.

*"I trust you most of all, Joseph. I **know** you will always do what is right for the family, and you do it with a good heart, and thus, I place you in charge of the household. All other house slaves will be subject to you, and you only to me."*

"Are you then finished with your meals? I would happily take these dishes from you–if it pleases you," Joseph added.

"It does. You are welcome to them, my good man."

"Very good then, sir."

"I know we have discussed this prior, but I remind you so that you make sure the housework is done in enough time to get everyone to the birthday party. The party *officially* starts at 15:00, but there will be a lot of congestion at the gates no matter what time you arrive. I would leave for the event no later than 13:00, so that you have about a two hour window. That means all the housework should be done about noon."

18Δ See Appendix: Augmentations, page 311

"Very good, sir." Joseph frowned. "Um, not to be adversarial, but *noon* might be a bit…aggressive…in regards to completing *everything*."

"Well, if the work is incomplete, so what? Get everyone out of here anyway. Anything unattended to will wait until tomorrow."

"Thank you, Master."

"You are most welcome; it is my pleasure. Thank *you*, Joseph, for all that you do. You are an honor to this house."

"You humble me, sir." Joseph smiled.

Jacob smiled again and then went to collect Wonder.

◮

Daddy's coming. I should stop playing and pick out an outfit.

By the time Jacob made his way into Wonder's room, she was dressed and ready.

"Wonderful."

"Yes daddy?"

"Your shoes are on the wrong feet," Jacob noted, looking her over.

"Oh. Sorry." Wonder sat down and busied herself with righting her foot apparel. "Would you like to play with me?"

"I *sure* would!" Jacob said enthusiastically. "What would you like to play?"

"I know!" Wonder said, responding with great excitement. "Let's play *bears*!"

"Bears?" Jacob said, but Wonder had already jumped up, run to the far side of the room and collected four stuffed bears. She could barely manage them all in her little arms, and indeed she dropped one of them *twice* in the process of returning.

"Here's your bears," Wonder said, dropping two in Jacob's lap.

"Okay."

"Hi!"

"Hi," Jacob responded, looking at Wonder.

"No daddy! You're a-posta be the bears!"

"Oh," Jacob said, pushing one of his bears forward. "Hi!"

"Hi! What's *your* name?" Wonder's bear asked Jacob's bear.

"My name is…Frank."

"Hi, Frank! *My* name is Brown Bear!" Wonder then pushed her other bear forward. "And *my* name is *White* Bear!"

"Ah. Hi White Bear and Brown Bear, *my* name is Nathan," said Jacob's other bear.

Wonder looked up at Jacob, smiling widely. "Would you like to have a tea party?"

Jacob frowned. "I don't think we have time for that now, Wonderful."

"No daddy, the *bears!*"

"Oh. Oh, why *yes*! We'd love to have a tea party!"

"Okay, it's white over here," Wonder said, marching her bears across her room to her play table.

Jacob marched his bears over as well.

"I'll make the tea!" Brown Bear said.

"I'll make the cakes!" White Bear said.

Wonder moved her bears over near the bookshelf, who then presumably proceeded to prepare tea and cakes.

"What should *we* do?" Jacob's bears asked. "Should we set the table?"

"No, the table's alweddy set, silly."

"Then, what is *our* function?"

Wonder stopped playing for a moment. Crinkling up her nose, she asked "What's funk shon?"

"Function." *Purpose,* Jacob thought to Wonder. "What's our purpose? What do *we* do? What are *our* jobs?"

Wonder sighed. "Nothing. You're just a-posta wait and then have tea and cakes with us when it's weddy."

"...then, we should pay you for the tea and cakes."

"No, this isn't a westwaunt."

"Oh, so we're like family."

"Nope, we're just bears," Wonder said without turning away from pretending to make tea and cakes...but after her father was then quiet for a moment, she stopped and moved over to hug him. "It's okay, daddy," Wonder said with genuine empathy. "It's okay you're not really good at playing. Mommy's not that good at playing, either."

That's enough bears for now, Wonder thought to herself.

"I had a good time with you!"

"I had a good time with you, too!' Jacob said, smiling. "Maybe we can play more '*bears*' later."

"Okay!" Wonder said, getting up off the floor.

"Guess what?" Jacob's voice took on new momentum as he also stood.

"What?"

"For *this* birthday I have a *secret, special* gift for you."

"What *is* it?" Wonder asked, delighted.

"It will be like when you learned *words* and *speaking*. Today–right now–I am going to teach you *mathematics*."

"What's *match-magics?*" Wonder asked, stumbling in her pronunciation.

"It's what makes anything possible. It is the foundation upon which everything is built. It's the most important thing, ever!"

Although Jacob seemed very excited, Wonder seemed suddenly just the opposite.

"I don't understand," Wonder said, looking down.

"Listen," Jacob said while lifting her chin to meet his gaze. "When we're done, you're going to understand *so* much–because *everything* is made of math."

"*Everthing* is made of *math*?"

"That's right!"

"Does mommy know math?"

"Not like I do...mommy is talented in *other* ways–like singing. Yet, even *singing* is made out of math…you'll see."

Wonder smiled. "Okay daddy."

"Let's begin. First, there are *numbers*. Numbers symbolize a quantity–they represent *presence*. There is either something to measure or there is not. When there is *no* quantity, we use a zero.

"*Negative* numbers represent the *absence* of a quantity…which is admittedly absurd. They *can*, less absurdly, represent a *pending* reduction, so long as there is something to reduce. Now, if negative numbers are *pending* reductions, then they are actually about prophecy: what will come."

Although *verbally* the lesson was fairly brief, *mentally* a very considerable amount of information passed from father to daughter.

Chapter 4:

Restoring the Relics

JUNE *2070 EST*

Fri 13	Sat 14	Sun 15
10:14		

Todd awoke to the *howling*.

Not that anyone called him "Todd," most people called him "Gob," which was short for "Goblin," which was a nickname he had been given long ago–primarily because he was so short.

At the moment Gob was hung over, and could only manage to put his head under his pillow in order to muffle the feminine wailing.

The cries belonged to Nan, lead guitarist for *The Valentine Relics*. Nan was clearly upset, turning over tables and chairs (breaking several ornaments in the process), searching violently for something.

"*Where* are the shots?" Nan screamed, her voice rising again into a terrible wail. "*Where are the bloody shots?*"

Issac "Mack" Macintosh, half dressed and looking more annoyed than concerned, came out from one of the bedrooms into the common room of the hotel suite.

"Calm *down*, Nan!" Mack nearly yelled. "I've got shots [19Δ] in my bag. You've got to calm down. Listen, we've got to get ready for the awards - it wouldn't hurt to get dressed, or even *wake up*, before you go get high."

[19Δ] *Shots* is a slang term for legal drugs that are injected via hypodermic syringe. Most drug use in Silverberg is legal (although there are several substances that are illegal), but there is *no* tolerance for any transgression of the law regardless of whether one is drugged or not.

Nan blinked. "I can't get dressed *sober*. One shot, one shot of *anything*, and I am good to go. C *'mon* Mack!"

Mack picked up his bag and tossed it to the Asian woman. "*One* shot." He turned his attention towards the little figure buried in the couch. "Gob! Get up."

"Gimmie juzzah few more minnits," Gob groaned from under the couch pillows.

The Valentine Relics were individuals that spent the bulk of their time partying and employing a grand assortment of recreational drugs. They are known to throw some very considerable parties, although this is better known amongst their stalwart fans than by the casual listener. While any of several of *The Valentine Relics* have numerous stories that they might share from such episodes, all but the lowest journalists sidestep publishing these particular behaviors. [20]

Anthem and Mack founded the group together, and although Mack was certainly the more level-headed of the two, Anthem was easily the most recognized.

"Complimentary opposites," is how they often described themselves. Anthem was hypersexual, and Mack standoffish. Anthem was loud and emotional; Mack, quiet and calm. It was no hard decision that as they were developing their stage personas, that Anthem became the devil and Mack the angel.

When Anthem started *changing* because of her marriage to Jacob Serter, Mack got angry. The more distant she became, the more sedition he would sow amongst the group. When Anthem suggested the love song, it was all too easy to convince his band mates to abandon Anthem.

Sadly, Mack did not fully realize how much extra work Anthem actually did for the group. With her absence, the group fell quickly into decline.

---

[20] "What's so interesting about a group of musicians on drugs and alcohol and throwing wild parties? Who *cares*? Show me a group of performers that are *not* regularly inebriated in some manner, and *then* I will be impressed…*those* people might be interesting enough to look at *beyond their performance*." - Essence Templeton

Eventually noticing that things were unraveling with *The Valentine Relics*, Mack decided to step completely into the leadership role–he stopped drinking and stopped doing drugs. [21]

In his sobriety, however, he felt much more like a babysitter than a leader. Mack was never much fun before; now he was *never* any fun.

Perhaps it was jealousy. Perhaps he was jealous that *he* had to grow up and take care of everyone else...jealous that everyone else got to continue to play, even fall in *love*–while *he* had to clean it all up.

Mack rapidly developed a certain sense of personal disdain for his fellow band members, absent Anthem doubly included.

Mack was sensible in his angry sobriety, however. He knew his best chances for success were with *The Relics,* and so he worked hard to keep the group together....which, even sober, was no easy task.

Mack found that it was to their benefit to keep the remaining group members together as *frequently* as possible–which, for Mack, was equally annoying.

Left to their own devices, *The Valentine Relics* could not remain sober enough to perform. Indeed, there were several small disasters involving group members outright failing to appear for a show.

Because of reckless drug binges and intermittent absenteeism, Mack learned early on to back up the core group with emergency doubles on standby. He had standing instructions with the sound man [22] to be prepared to cut their feeds and substitute pre-recorded music, because the doubles that Mack *could* acquire usually could not actually play any instruments.

You see, covering the music was easy enough, but *The Valentine Relics* were a "Skitt" band–which is to say that while they played Blark genre music, they also acted out roles either during and/or between musical numbers.

---

[21] Not entirely true. Mack has been known to imbibe the occasional libation, but it *has* become a very rare occurrence.

[22] Who is named Denny Kedney–although no one apart from *The Relics* has any clue who that is. Apart from Mack, it was Denny who was ultimately instrumental in maintaining the public image of *The Relics* until Anthem's return. Denny Kedney: the unsung hero.

Gob's stage persona was that he was supposed to be a goblin. He was probably the most difficult band member to find a double for. It was hard to find someone as short as he was, plus, Gob had several aesthetic augmentations that made it even more difficult. His slightly green skin was not especially difficult to mimic, nor were his slightly larger ears–it was his blacked out eyes. Doubles for Gob typically wore noirglasses to hide their eyes.

What made Gob most tolerable, is that he was the more dependable amongst the group, having only ever missed two shows.[23△]

Gob genuinely loved to perform as much as he loved to party. He loved his fans, he loved music, and he loved *The Relics*. Gob, overall, was pretty likable… although generally not very understandable.

Billy *would* be more difficult, but he was least popular amongst the group. As the drummer, people seldom watched him intently–which is good, because Billy was actually the *most* apt to miss a show.

Billy had two physical augmentations himself, but they were particularly easy to duplicate, simply being pointed ears and eyebrows.

Fans were sure that Billy's persona was an elf–an understandable assumption, as that would make him a complimentary opposite for Gob–yet Billy insisted he was an *alien*. Of course Billy preferred that people call him by his stage name, "Shin" (which, incidentally, is pronounced "sheen"), although nobody ever calls him that.

The easiest person to have a double for was Nan. **Nan's** stage persona was that she dressed like a female version of Axel. [24▲] Nan would additionally wear a body suit to accentuate her femininity–as Nan was not naturally so accentuated– making it even easier to cover for her absence.

––––––––––––

23△ *One* of the shows he might yet have made it to *if* someone were able to understand what he was yelling in his hospital room. Instead, he was further sedated–although admittedly probably to everyone's benefit considering the circumstances…but I digress.

24▲ Axel, the leader of Silverberg and owner of Axel Industries, wore either a fully enveloping black leotard, or more simply, a black facemask to cover his head and neck, and matching gloves.

Axel said he wore all black to cover the horrible scarring he received in an accident almost a hundred years ago. Axel's impossible age led many citizens to believe that he probably died long ago, and that someone else was simply acting as proxy. As to *who* might actually be running the country, nobody seemed to much care beyond using it as a conversational topic on occasion. For the most part, people were quite content with the status of their nation, and were otherwise disinclined to upset that particular status.

What was *most* difficult is that Nan was *most* likely to be so inebriated that she could not perform. In the absence of her sobriety, Nan would never tolerate being replaced *or* having her feed cut.

Mack, occasionally sensing that Nan was on the brink of complete incoherence, would sometimes deliberately give her additional *shots* or booze, and then put her double in play when she passed out. It was a professional decision that he was not overly proud of, but sometimes such decisions needed to be made for the "good of the group."

Today (so far anyway) it seemed such emergency replacement tactics would be unnecessary. Mack insisted that they all stay at the same hotel the night before a performance, and Anthem aside, everyone was together and accounted for. Mack was proud…of himself.

Mack noted that Billy seemed pretty focused–already awake and writing down some notes at the corner desk. The only thing that seemed odd is that Billy kept looking at his own reflection in the giant mirrored wall of the hotel and smiling at himself satisfactorily.

Of course, Billy considered himself the greatest artist of the group, having written the bulk of their most successful songs and numbers. It was entirely possible Billy was enjoying one of his many smug moments, but Mack decided to check on him anyway.

"How's it going, Billy?" Mack asked, momentarily distracted with watching himself in the mirrored wall as he approached Billy.

"It's Shin."

Sigh. "How's it going, *Shin*?"

Billy looked up, smiling–a faint, granulated rainbow of dust just beneath his nostrils. "Oh, you know, just *living the dream*." [25Δ] Billy looked back down at his paper (for only *real* artists still used paper), and then looked back up at Mack.

[25Δ] "*Living the dream*" was an expression used by users of the *illicit* drug "Solid Hypnizium," or "Solid H." Solid H was a fine dust sold in several colors, although generally sold as rainbow-filled packets. Solid H was best taken via inhalation, as ingestion generally had deadly effects.

Solid Hypnizium reputedly broke down the barriers between the conscious and subconscious minds, allowing users to dictate their hallucinations, and thus the expression was born as they were quite literally *living the dream.*

"Quick!" Billy shoved the page at Mack. "How many sentences are on this page?"

"*Three*," Mack said with no small amount of concern and contempt. "Are you gonna be okay to perform tonight?"

"Sure, sure…I'll be great. Now, read me those sentences so I can get my bearings–I don't want to lose my muse."

Mack cleared his throat. "We're all enslaved to the habit of tea–Governments, countries, you, me. Centuries' sentinel, the soldier caffeine–perfect, delicious, yet very suspicious. Sentry's perennial, *always* caffeine–expedient ingredient of the quickly obscene."

"Really?" Billy reflected. "Is *that* what it says? That's pretty good…I thought I was writing about something else." Billy took the page back.

"Are you *sure* you're going to be okay tonight?" Mack asked in concern, but Billy was already fervently scribbling on the paper.

Mack walked back toward the middle of the room when his credit bank chimed. From his belt, the following expression projected into the air in front of Mack.

MAINFRAME » Mediacast session requested by <u>Ayn Serter</u> 10:28 EST

"Accept," Mack ordered his credit bank. Taking it from his belt, he placed it on the coffee table as he sat down on the couch.

"Waaah!" Gob's muffled voice cried out. "Yer sittin on my feet! Geddup! Ooch ooch ooch!"

Mack shifted appropriately and the couch fell silent.

The devilish image of Anthem's head and shoulders appeared in front of Mack, her hair now slicked back and her horns eagerly apparent.

"Morning, Mack," Anthem greeted Mack.

"Morning, Anthem."

"Everyone dead?"[26Δ]

"Everything is perfect, everyone is fine–we're all just about to leave now," Mack said, lying. "Things couldn't be better."

26Δ *Dead* - slang term for expressing a positive. Something good, agreeable or appreciated.

"Really? I was a bit concerned you were all going to go party all night long and abandon me at the ONE Awards. So you're heading straight there?"

"Um…we're still talking about it. I think we might get some breakfast first… we might even be a few minutes late."

Mack *knew* they would probably be late, but Anthem didn't deserve any kind of full disclosure. After all, this was *Mack's* group, now that Anthem only wanted to play part-time. He could handle it.

"Breakfast? It's 10:30."

"Well, *more* breakfast."

"Well, whatever. I doubt we're going to win, but I'd just as soon have *The Relics* at my back if I see the Queen. So you will *all* be there?"

"No issues. No worries. We'll see you there, if not a few minutes late."

"Thanks, Mack. I don't know what I would do without you." Anthem ended the mediacast session.

*How **dare** you think **you** need to check up on **me**?* Mack thought to himself, stewing. *What you **should** be doing is checking **in** with me.*

Mack punched the couch.

"Juzza few more minnits…" came the sleepy response.

Mack looked up at Nan, who had come to stand in front of him. She was completely naked and smiling at him–all the desperation from a few minutes ago completely gone from her face.

"I *love* you, Mack. I love us. I *love* our group." She paused, looking around. She took a deep breath. "Don't you just *love* it all?"

"Oh *yes*," Mack said unconvincingly. "I *love* this."

Out-of-place Appendix:

The ONE Awards

This year marks the 2nd annual ONE awards. ONE awards are presented for a multitude of categories, although all are usually of an artistic persuasion–the primary being geared towards literature, as the awards were thusly inspired.

ONE is an acronym for <u>Oedipus Now, *Edified*</u>,[27Δ] which is the title of a book that has surged in popularity over the last few years.

Initially the awards were extended *only* to people that created a work that extended or acknowledged the <u>Oedipus Now, *Edified*</u> storyline, but after last year the awards became open to anyone who put the word "One" in the title of their work as homage–*any* art form welcome.

There are now so many versions, in so many forms, of <u>Oedipus Now, *Edified*</u>, that few clearly remember what the differences are between them and the *un*edified version.

27Δ See in-place Appendix, Oedipus Edified, page 296.

Chapter 5:

Quips of the Queen

JUNE *2070 EST*

Fri 13	Sat 14	Sun 15
11:15		

The Silverberg Amusement Park parking garage has never been as full as it is today.

Or, more interestingly, the parking garage had never been *full* until today. For the first time in history, visitors had to park *outside* of the garage on the grounds… although *less* interestingly, the expression "the grounds" only means the exterior mirroranium.

Now the reasons as to *why* the garage was full on *this* day include more than just those enjoying the free admission posted by Jacob Serter for anyone wishing to attend Wonderful's 3ʳᵈ birthday party:

For one, several bands (including, of course, *The Valentine Relics*) would be performing at different areas across the park.

For another, *many* celebrities had been conscripted (or even volunteered) to extend monologues either between acts or as part of them. Some of these iconic appearances would act as irresistible attractions to the sect of citizens who might have neglected to appear, they having otherwise successfully debated the sanity of congregating in an area exclusively populated with some of the least savory of Silverberg's citizens.

These alone are not enough of an account as to why the parking garage failed, however.

Catty-corner to the amusement park sat a magnificent mirrored structure, one that inspired amazement in art, architecture, and photography across the world.

The structure was none other than the The Silverberg Amphitheater, [28△] which happens to be the venue for this year's ONE Awards, and thus the culprit responsible for luring the remainder of the vehicles.

In less than 90 minutes the awards ceremony would begin. Those nominated for such an award (and their chosen companions) were already filling the entrance hall, milling and interacting with one another–some in more entertaining manners, and some in more deplorable.

One of the more colorful nominees, namely Mark Curie–better known as the Queen of the Chessmen[29▲]–was drawing a considerable amount of attention to himself.

His clothing on this particular occasion consisted of a full body, skin-tight checkerboard leotard that boasted a neckline that plunged below his navel.

Now, this style of dress might more regularly be worn by a member of the feminine gender, but certainly the Queen's short-cropped black hair and prominent mustache betrayed any possibility of mistake–his slender and obviously masculine physique notwithstanding.

If this were not sufficient enough to command attention, the Queen amplified his voice further by speaking into his custom microphone whose elongated handle was elaborately entwined with two serpents and whose windscreen was flanked by two outstretched wings.

More and more people stopped to take notice of his outspoken and magnified debate with his most immediate rival, L U Therius–a man who, in contrast, was dressed completely appropriately.

Both gentlemen have written literature that has placed them competitively as nominees for one of the coveted ONE awards, namely "Best Independent Book."

28△ Occasionally considered an additional component of the Amusement Park proper, the Amphitheater is another venue completely. One must purchase admission to the Amphitheater independent to their admission to the park, though they share a garage.

29▲ The Chessmen, also known as the SilverSmiths, are dedicated to thwarting Axel while supporting Silverberg. The Chessmen have, over the course of years, supplied citizens who had come to be considered unlawful or seditious with alternate identities that they might escape their impending sentencing. This service carries with it a certain financial obligation, and is typically only extended to those that would join their cause (also see Appendix: The Chessmen, page 294).

CHAPTER 5

The Queen wrote a book entitled <u>One Vision</u>, which is a story about "A pawn that finds itself perplexed when unable to follow the orders of *either* king."

<u>One Vision</u> is a thinly veiled symbolic rhetoric of the Chessmen's core doctrine. The recurrent emphasis is to reject traditional programming and instead self-program via investigation and question. It is particularly heavy handed in its denouncement of religion, Serter, and Axel[30Δ].

Alternatively, Therius wrote a book called <u>One Faith</u>, which is a book exclusively dedicated to simplifying Christianity (or "Xianity," as it is spelled in Silverberg). As to why *this* book has managed the audience and attention that it *has* is beyond anyone's guess. Therius himself is nothing more than a pastor at a local church, and apart from <u>One Faith</u>, his efforts have not generated a very large or regular congregation.

"By the way, Therius, what does the 'L' stand for anyway? Luke, Lucius? How many guesses do we get?" The Queen chided.

"…It doesn't stand for anything," Therius said plainly. "My name is *L.* Just L. The letter 'L.'"

The Queen was a bit quiet before he said "…and your middle name…is *U?*"

"That's right."

"You must have the meanest parents."

"My father *was* a bit uncompassionate," Therius chuckled in reflection.

"What was *his* name?"

"R. R U Therius."

"R U Therius?"

"No, but *he* was." Therius grinned, but he was alone amongst many. "Sorry, more of a family joke. Anyway, he did not much approve of my religious pursuits *either*. The two of you might have well gotten along. That is, if you weren't dressed...um, like *that.*"

30Δ In <u>One Vision</u>, the entire story takes place over an immense chessboard. The Queen has several characters in his story which are fairly blatant personifications of actual people. "The Silver Queen" obviously represents himself, "The Black King," Axel, and finally "The Red King," Jacob Serter.

Both kings are frequently accused of *programming* the other pieces to believe that the king is more valuable than all the other pieces combined. The kings determine who moves in what manner, and that their pieces can *never* love the enemy.

When the Silver Queen convinces a Pawn to ask "why," his King explains to the pawn that he must do as he is commanded so that they can all win the game.

"*What **game**?*" asked the Pawn.

"Why *are* you dressed like a lady?" Someone in the crowd asked pointedly, pulling the Queen's attention back to the present.

"Me?" The Queen looked down at himself. "I'm not dressed as a *lady*–I'm a man dressed as a girl who's dressed as a boy. No *lady* would ever suffer this preposterous neckline."

The crowd murmured some confusion, trying to figure out Mark's retort.

"It's inappropriate, at any rate." Therius added.

"Oh, but programming people to tithe is credible," the Queen said, rolling his eyes.

"I'm not trying to program *anybody*."

"Sure you are. You're not fooling anybody. If you weren't a part of the same system as the rest of us, you wouldn't have called your book '*One* Faith' so it would be considered for an award. Nothing shameful in that–but you can stop acting like you're not a part of this."

"I didn't call it <u>One Faith</u> to get it into the *awards*–it's just the most appropriate title. It's named <u>One Faith</u> as homage to Ephesians Chapter 4 Verse 5: one Lord, one faith, one baptism."

"*Sure* it is." The Queen winked.

"I started working on this before there *were* ONE awards."

"Sure you did."

As Therius began a fairly lengthy rebuttal, a man chewing a pipe and sporting a cane finished making his way up to the Queen. Smiling, he handed Mark a *paper* envelope that said only 3 words: 'For The Rook.'

The Queen looked at the envelope and frowned. He didn't have the time or attention to interact with the strange man, engaged as he was with the crowd and Therius. He had no pockets in his checkerboard leotard, so he bent down and placed the envelope in the side pocket of the messenger bag he had placed on the floor a few minutes ago. *Odd. I'll check it out later,* the Queen thought to himself. By the time he had stowed the envelope, the strange smiling man had already hobbled away.

Of *The Chessmen*, only one man currently assumed the title of *Rook,* and only *the Queen* even knew about him–or so he thought.

No one, however–including the Queen–noticed that the envelope soon disappeared from the pocket.

"Look, Therius," the Queen said, clearing his throat. "I can see that you're devoted–at least to some degree. Enviable. Heck, I envy you your faith, I just don't envy you your programming. *Slavish loyalty to an unseen leader is the worst condition a man can place upon himself.*[31△] What you call a miracle I call a mystery, and neither of us is about to convince the other otherwise."

Just as the Queen was becoming bored with Therius, however, his attention shifted as he recognized a slightly portly gentleman walking just past a sign that read "Have a good ONE?"

"Everyone! I direct your attention to Silverberg's premiere food critic, Hugo Templeton!"

The crowd turned and looked at the conservatively dressed man. As quickly, everyone forgot about Therius.

Hugo was about to say something, but then the Queen interrupted.

"Ladies and gentlemen, the very *author* of 'One Bite:' an exhaustive dissertation on how to *properly* critique cuisine."

Hugo seemed to blush momentarily, and offered a slight bow.

"I mean," the Queen began again as quickly. "*How* can *anyone* write a *300* page book about how to sample food in a single bite, anyway? Isn't that more like an overgrown *pamphlet*? I mean, I'm *impressed*–if only with the *audacity*! Sheesh. 300 pages of *that*? Who could *read* all that?"

Now Hugo seemed uncomfortable, and quickened his pace to the hall.

"Hats off to you, *good sir*!" The Queen continued, imitating the well known food critic as he hustled away. He turned his attention back to his crowd. "You know, for only taking 'one bite,' he sure seems like he eats well enough. Has *anyone* here even read this 'War and Peace' of food criticisms? Anyone? I thought not. Has anyone here ever heard of a respectable food critic that eats at restaurants such as *The Silver Burger* or *Jimmy Dingles*[32▲] anyway? I tell you…"

Then the Queen saw Anthem.

[31△] The Queen is quoting his own work, One Vision, where this statement applies to both God (The Player–a character that is never seen) and Axel (The Black King).

[32▲] *The Silver Burger* and *Jimmy Dingles*, both of which are well known, short order, assembly line style restaurants.

"Everyone!" He suddenly interrupted himself. "I direct your attention to Anthem Serter, *The Bagel Lady*!" As he finished, he made a sweeping gesture towards her.

Many people turned and looked. If Anthem's face were not already painted red, it would be obvious that she was blushing–not in embarrassment, so much as in anger.

The Queen cleared his throat and began to sing. "Have you seen, have you seen, the *fat* Magdalene? She thinks she's so witty, but she's really just *mean*. Tell me now, how many words rhyme with *een*? Is it just so that she can yell at *the Queen*? Is that the extent of her little scheme?" [33Δ]

"That song's not about you, Mark." Anthem said, sounding suddenly loud and slightly pitiful simultaneously.

"In part, it is."

"...maybe in part."

"What is *this*?" The Queen seemed suddenly taken aback. "*Truth* from the mouth of the devil? Well, I *am* shocked. By the way, where're your demons?"

"If you mean *The Relics*, they are currently examining our setup." Anthem lied, not having any clue where they were. "They'll be here soon."

"So tell us: who's doing *your* programming these days?"

"*Don't start with me, Mark.*"

"The Anthem *I* used to know would *never* be performing amongst other non-Skitt groups, *much less* at the Silverberg Amusement Park–a venue *directly* owned and operated by *Axel Industries*! Ha! *I* can script better than *that*.

"You're obviously at the mercy of your master...so, which one *is* it? Serter, or Axel?" Seeing Anthem's brow furrow, he added: "My money's on the *red* king, but either way you're just a *sellout*."

The Queen hit home. Anthem knew doing this show was outside *The Relics'* regular idiom, but figured nobody would either notice or care enough to say anything–especially as it was *her* daughter's celebration. It was apparently more obvious than not...then again, the Queen was an expert on manipulating people's feelings.

[33Δ] The Queen is imitating an earlier hit of *The Valentine Relics,* namely "Down with the Queen" (from their 2066 album *WHAT MEANS WHAT*).

"Why must you be so *slang*?" Anthem nearly barked, almost losing control. *Not good*, she thought to herself. *Don't let him get to you. At least not here–not now.*

"Slang? I'm not *slang*–I'm just *defiantly* interesting. God–if there were one –please strike me dead if I'm not, at *least*, interesting." The Queen paused. "*Not* that that *means* anything, of course. Everyone is interesting to one degree or another. God, please strike dead the most uninteresting person here!"

The Queen momentarily put his face into his hands, perhaps as if to shield his eyes from an anticipated bolt of lightning. As he took his hands away, he smudged the makeup that exaggerated his smile.

"Is Hugo still alive? Ah, then God is dead. Curse you, Anthem! You devil! You killed God!–it must have been your music!"

Anthem, upset, but masking her outrage effectively, opted to ignore the remainder of the Queen's comic insults and comments and attempted to make her way into the grand hall of the amphitheater.

"She's got the right idea, friends. The awards are about to start, and for the moment I am out of interesting things to say. Besides," the Queen said, smiling as wide as he could muster. "The show must go on."

Chapter 6:

Greek Gifts

JUNE *2070 EST*

Fri 13	Sat 14	Sun 15
11:49		

As the usher lead Anthem to her table, her heart leapt to see Jacob and Wonder already sitting there. She hurried past her guide and met with them as quickly as she could without actually running.

"You're *here*!?" Anthem said, delightfully confused.

"Surprise!" Jacob and Wonder announced, both standing and hugging her.

"Is *this* what you two were up to this morning?" Anthem narrowed her eyes and smiled. If anything could make up for *The Relics* not showing up, it would be this.

*Although, I **could** have used your support 20 minutes ago,* she thought. *But what a wonderful surprise! You're more than forgiven, my amazing husband.*[34Δ]

Wonder seemed about to say something, but then said nothing.

"Perhaps," Jacob replied. Looking around as he sat down, he added, "Where are *The Relics*?"

"Running late," Anthem said quietly.

"Of course." Jacob was already well aware of some of the idiosyncratic habits of Anthem's group.

"So, I thought you had work?"

"I **do**. I can't stay for the whole thing, but I figured we could at least be here for a bit to show our support and love. Besides, *I've* decided to write a book," Jacob announced.

[34Δ] of course, Anthem knew that Jacob was here for more than *her*, Jacob *adored* <u>Oedipus Now,</u> and had an entire bookcase dedicated to hard copy first printings.

"You did?" Anthem was shocked. "I mean, I'm sure you could. A ONE book?"

"Indeed, a ONE book; next year you'll be accompanying *me* to the awards." Jacob smiled. "Fiction. I'm going to rewrite <u>Oedipus Now</u> from the standpoint of the main character."

"That sounds really clever; *you* might even *win* an award," Anthem said, her voice thick with defeat.

"Oh, don't be so mopey."

"We're *not* going to beat out *Syd Sigma and the War Dogs* [35Δ] for music–but we certainly beat the rest." Anthem said, sounding only a bit more enthusiastic.

"You never know; we shall see." Jacob seemed confident.

"I love you, Jacob. You're sweet, but misguided at times."

The Queen sat at his table sipping at a glass of Moët&Chandon champagne while surrounded by several men and women all wearing silver lapel pins that looked like pawns.

Every now and again he would lift his caduceus-microphone and offer either greetings or insults to the nearby nominees and crowd.

Eventually an usher approached him and asked him to please desist in this particular behavior, to which he curtly smiled and said "no."

Therius sat at a table, completely alone. He had no family and very few friends. The few acquaintances or friends he *had* either showed no interest in attending, or explained they could not.

To be honest, Therius was not too inclined to attend himself, and his recent interaction with the Queen of the Chessmen did not leave him feeling any better about accepting the invitation.

Still, he thought, *this might be a real chance to spread the word of God. Sometimes, it seems, we must do things we simply do not want to do. I suppose the less vocal I am about having to do the things I do not wish, the more mature I have become.*

35Δ *Syd Sigma and the War Dogs'* last compilation, <u>World War One,</u> has been very well received by both critics and fans. 4 of the 13 tracks on the album have hit #1 on the charts, an almost unrivaled historical achievement.

One of the prevalent reasons attending the ONE Awards *in person* was so desirable (for anyone other than the nominees, of course), is that Axel *himself* would be there, personally presenting and hosting the ceremony. It was one thing to see Axel's image on varying imagescreens throughout Silverberg, but few people could ever say that they were ever so much as in the same room as him.

Axel was backstage in the green room, surrounded by five Axel Industries Internal Security (AIIS[36△]) Agents who were, more or less, responsible for every aspect of the ONE awards that he was not otherwise personally involved in. All Agents were hard at work, making last minute checks on equipment and people.

All except one–that one being Agent Wilson. The dark haired AIIS Agent sat in a recliner, slightly apart from everyone else. He made no moves to check his subordinates, for he apparently felt confident and secure in their position and placement.

Apart from Axel, Wilson was the highest ranking person in the room: leader of an *entire* department–the department of Justice, to be exact. Wilson was responsible for upholding the law, and was in charge of all other men responsible for such (e.g. judges, police officers, wardens, and so on). In the end, they all answered to Agent Wilson.

Wilson had insisted on being personally present at the awards ceremony rather than leave Axel's security up to mere subordinates. Not a suspicious request, but perhaps an odd one. Then again, Wilson had made no secret of stating his particular fandom for all things *"Oedipus"*.

Smiling, as he always seemed to be, he moved his pipe from the one side of his mouth to the other. His cane and satchel lay safe on the far side of the lush recliner.

36△ See also Appendix: AIIS Department, page 312

Wonder was *bored.* She made a silly noise. Then she made some more, a bit louder. She created more and more verbal noises until Anthem asked her to stop.

Wonder's externalization of her boredom only briefly subsided, however. Not long after she relented on making annoying noises, she had taken to kicking the underside of the table until Anthem *commanded* her to stop. Anthem was already on edge, and Wonder's inability to suppress her boredom was upsetting her mother further.

"You didn't pack a bag?" Anthem asked Jacob, annoyed, but smiling for fear of the watchful eyes of peers and journalists.

"I did not. I suppose time got away from us."

An attendant offered beverages and deposited a fairly generous tray of food at the Serter's table. After he left, Wonder immediately spoke up.

"Mommy?"

"Yes, dear?"

"I'm hungry," Wonder said, eyeing the tray of food.

"Hmm. This food might be a bit exotic for you."

"Please?"

"Well, I suppose."

Wonderful sampled the fare.

"Daddy?"

"Yes, dear?"

"I don't *like* this food," Wonder said disdainfully. "It's *yucky.*"

"Well, that's all there *is,* baby," Anthem said, sounding a bit worried. "Daddy can get you something after we're done."

"I don't *want* somefing affer we're *done*; I'm hungry *now,*" Wonder pouted.

"*Why* didn't you pack a bag?" Anthem accused Jacob, as if they didn't just have a discussion about it.

"Sorry, darling; she'll be okay." Jacob assured Anthem.

"But I'm *hungry,*" Wonder whined.

Jacob leaned over and whispered something in Wonder's ear–or so it appeared. In actuality, he changed his focus so that he took over Wonder's thoughts completely.

Wonder immediately calmed down and started eating the food in front of her without objection.

"Are you okay, Wonder?" Anthem asked, in awe of the sudden transformation.

Wonder looked up at her mother and smiled. "I'm Wonder*ful*!" She then went back to eating peacefully.

Anthem smiled at Jacob, slightly amazed. "You have such a good way with her! Thanks for being such a good Daddy!"

"Thanks for being such a good wife!"

Anthem leaned over and kissed Jacob briefly before her attention was once again completely focused on the events around her.

⚠

Hugo Templeton, returning from using the lavatory, sat down next to his wife.

"That's the *second* time you've had to go since we arrived," Cordelia announced, perhaps a bit too loudly. "Constipated?"

"Will you *please* calm down, woman?" Hugo said with a snap.

"*Well,*" Cordelia huffed. "Aren't we *grouchy*? Here I express the slightest concern for your well-being, and you get annoyed. Can't I check and see if you're alright?"

"I'm certain that I'm *fine*, darling." Hugo said, trying to appear more nonchalant. "Although I find it genuinely amusing that you're suddenly expressing interest and concern for my *well-being*, since you have *yet* to pay attention to me in any other capacity since we've arrived."

"Comparatively speaking, dear husband, you have yet to do anything much *worth* noticing…that is, apart from your frequent use of the facilities." Cordelia went back to reading an article.

Hugo nodded in thoughtful agreement. "I cannot argue that point."

An attendant deposited an offering of food at the Templeton's table before walking away. Hugo removed the lid from the tray.

"Pardon me, sir!" Hugo called to the young man who left the tray.

"Yes, Mr…Templeton?" The server said, reading the name displayed on the table.

"What is this?" Hugo gestured at the food.

"Peppered roast beef with sauteed onions and provolone cheese on ciabatta bread, scalloped potatoes with scallions, and eggplant parmesan."

"No, I mean, *where* is the au jus?" Hugo pointed at nothing.

"I'm sorry?"

"You need not apologize to me, sir." Hugo paused to read the name 'Billy' on the server's nametag.

"No, I'm sorr–I mean, what do you mean?"

"I mean, whoever *heard* of a french dip sandwich served *without* au jus? Heavens, lad! It's not remotely palatable without au jus!"

"I'm sorry, sir, ther…"

But Hugo interrupted his explanation. "Stop apologizing to me *William*! Just take me to the kitchen."

"I'm sorry?"

"Dash it all, lad! Perhaps you're a bit hard of hearing as well as undereducated," Hugo announced insultingly. "I said, take me to the kitchen. I would have a word with the head chef."

Billy looked uncomfortable. "Sir, I'm afraid-"

"You need not fear *me*, William…I did not mean to get curt with you. I assure you, that of anyone here, I alone reserve the right to address the chef on this afternoon's selection."

The attendant, lost for a response, simply walked away.

Hugo stood up.

"*Back* to the bathroom?" Cordelia asked, not looking up.

"Would you *please* mind your own business? As it happens, I am going to the kitchen."

"Oh, do leave that poor boy alone–he's just doing his job."

"*Who*? Oh, *William*? Yes, yes–I have no intent on ruining his day any further; I'm merely going to have a few words with the architect of this farce."

"*I* think you're making a mistake."

"Ah. Noted. Now, I certainly hope you're done extending your otherwise unsolicited opinions."

"Grouchy," Cordelia said softly. Then she looked up. "However will you find it?"

"Eh? The kitchen? Shouldn't be too hard, *darling*," Hugo said, walking away. "Fortunately, it so happens that the entrance is near to the *restrooms*."

As Axel walked out on stage, multiple imagescreens sprang into existence, allowing the entire population of the amphitheater to see him, unimpeded by proximity.

The ruler of the country was dressed regularly: full black hood mask, black gloves, black jacket, silver shirt, black trousers, black shoes. He carried with him a single trophy, which was an exact (albeit smaller) copy of the huge statue [37] in the middle of the stage. When he arrived at the podium, he placed the statue down gently.

"Citizens of Silverberg and visitors from lands abroad–welcome to the annual ONE awards!"

Cheers and applause, both genuine and artificial, went up across the huge amphitheater.

⚠

As it happens, the kitchen is actually *nowhere* near the vicinity of the restrooms. The truth of it was that Hugo needed to use the facilities *again.*

Likely that cursed woman's potato salad, Hugo thought while relieving himself. [38] *· I wonder how the awards are going?*

---

[37] The statue was the idol and symbol of the ONE awards. Thirteen feet tall and mirrored, shaped as a man who had no eyes (merely empty ocular sockets), who was wearing a large gear as a crown. His head was tilted upwards toward the heavens and the arms were open and apart from his body, as if he might be asking *"why?"*

[38] "Why aren't you eating the potato salad?" Cordelia asked Hugo last night.

"I *had* some potato salad," Hugo retorted.

"You had one bite."

"That's all I needed."

"This is *not* a restaurant, Hugo Templeton, and you are *not* going to sit there critiquing *my* food."

"I'm not. I just wasn't terribly hungry."

"*Well,* you ate almost *all* of the lasagna."

"I *did?*" Hugo looked at the empty dish. "Oh–well it seems I did. That must be why I'm not so hungry."

"Can I be excused?" Essence, their daughter, asked in annoyance.

"*No,*" Hugo and Cordelia responded simultaneously.

Essence rolled her eyes and went back to observing her credit bank.

"Now, you eat some of that potato salad, or you can go to your precious award ceremony *alone.* I am *not* throwing away perfectly good food."

"Oh, now how would *that* look? *Me,* arriving at th…"

"Op, dop, dop dop," Cordelia interrupted. "Potato salad."

"*Fine,* pass me the bloody potato salad."

Axel (who certainly didn't *sound* like a man well over a hundred years in age) spent the next 15 minutes talking about <u>Oedipus Now</u>. He spoke about the impact it has had on the creative world. He revered Mary Godwin for having the sight and talent to create such an imaginative and symbolic work, and finished with an oration about how the ONE awards are given to the *best of the best* in their respective fields.

To nobody's surprise, *Syd Sigma and the War Dogs* won the ONE award for *Best Album*. The group came to the stage, accepted their award, and performed one of their hits entitled *"Learning to die."*

To everyone's surprise (including his own), Therius won the ONE award for *Best Independent Book.* Therius accepted his award and thanked everyone profusely. His humble acceptance was slightly endearing.

After several more awards were extended–accompanied by speeches, demonstrations, or performances–the ONE awards came to an intermission.

In the end, Hugo ended up spending a considerable amount of time sitting in the lavatory, his attention kept piqued as he watched the events of the ONE awards unfold on his credit bank. When the awards went to intermission, his attention was brought back to the present, and he remembered his quest for the kitchen.

One row of silver buttons ran down the front right of the black coat the AIIS Agent wore. The light hit the buttons in the same way it struck the left lapel insignia–an insignia solidifying that he was indeed a member of the Axel Industries Internal Security Department.

"Sir?" The Agent said aloud.

The Queen looked up, smiling widely–probably more from the effects of the alcohol than from genuine pleasure.

"Have you then come to quiet me?" The Queen challenged as he half yelled.

"No sir," the Agent said respectfully, "I have come to chaperone you back-stage for a unique opportunity–that is, *Axel* would like to have an image made of you, Jacob Serter, and himself, reenacting a moment from your novel."

"You're joking," the Queen mused.

"Not at all," the Agent said, looking very serious.

"Axel wants *that*?" The Queen said, smiling at his companions who were all wearing varying expressions from disapproval to consent. "Well it will not atone for the *travesty* of <u>One Faith</u> beating out <u>One Vision</u>, but whatever.

"Besides," he said, grabbing his champagne bottle. "What man could turn down an opportunity to actually meet Axel?"

"Sir?"

Jacob Serter looked up at the AIIS Agent addressing him.

"Would you mind coming with me? No cause for alarm; Axel is about to confront the Queen of the SilverSmiths about several allegations he made in his book. He would also like to…give consultation…to the Queen on several points of defamation of character–particularly *yours* and *his*–and thought you might appreciate the opportunity to speak to him in a similar manner, simultaneously."

"Hmm," Jacob said, pausing, apparently to consider. "Not necessarily. I'm not too unsaddled by Curie. I'm a bit surprised Axel would admit it got under his skin; by acknowledging it, he gives it *authority*. No, I think I'll stay with my family."

The Agent hesitated. "I'm sorry sir, but I'm afraid Axel *insists* that you are present, regardless of your participation."

"So then, the whole first part of your dialogue was irrelevant."

"I'm-"

"*Irrelevant*," Jacob interrupted. "If Axel *insists* I attend this conference regardless of my preference, it doesn't matter then, if I *mind*. Next time–if there *is* a next time–that you address me, please just get right to the point. A pointless dialogue otherwise, both for you and me."

"Uh, yes sir." [39Δ]

"Very well, then–come with me, Wonderful."

"You're taking the daughter?" Anthem asked, although not terribly surprised: after all, Jacob took Wonder almost everywhere he went.

"We anticipated she would come," the Agent said, but looked down at the floor when Jacob glared at him for speaking first.

"Indeed. When I am done with this compulsory meeting, we'll have to be off to the park to finish getting ready for her birthday party. Love you and miss you. Good luck tonight–I hope the rest of *The Relics* show up." Jacob smiled charmingly, which then made Anthem smile and swish her tail.

"They'll be there," Anthem said confidently.

▲

Led individually by different AIIS agents, Jacob Serter (and Wonder) and the Queen were all en route to the backstage green room where Axel was momentarily residing during the intermission.

As the separate parties converged, Jacob and the Queen locked eyes. Jacob nodded in acknowledgement, however the Queen was not so reserved.

"Amazing!" the Queen broke the silence. "*The* Bagel Lord *himself!* I think I'm honored...*what* are they calling you abroad? The 'Hope of Humanity?' You know, if you really wanted to be the 'Hope of-"

[39Δ] Most people fear the authority of an AIIS Agent, and thus very few spoke to them in the manner that Jacob was. The Agent was slightly taken aback by Jacob's engagement.

But then again, the Agent rationalized, *this **was** Jacob Serter, after all.*

- [Daniel Strasel] -

"I'm sorry, Mark," Jacob interrupted. "But, does this dialogue actually have any purpose?"

For a brief moment, the Queen seemed lost for words. Without an audience, the Queen seemed less inclined to his regular antagonisms–then again, it *was* Jacob Serter.

"I have a great many resources–many of which most people know nothing about," the Queen began, sounding suddenly very sober and serious. "*I* think, that in many ways, our interests are identical. I think we should collaborate…I think you should read my book."

"Okay, I'll read your book Mark."

Before the Queen could make his witty retort, one of the AIIS agents presented his credit bank to the door panel and commanded the door to open.

Nothing happened.

The AIIS Agents looked at one another, apparently in some confusion.

"Agent?" The voice of Axel emitted from the panel.

"S-Sir? Jacob Serter and Mark Curie are here to see you–in regards to <u>One Vision</u>."

A tense moment passed. Everyone remained silent.

"Very well then, send them in."

The mirrored door opened and while one Agent lead the group through the door, the other remained posted outside.

Axel stood on the far side of the room. Who could know what expression he wore beneath his black head-mask?

"Hole. Ee. Shit," said a quiet, disembodied voice. Only the Queen noticed, but he neglected to mention it to anyone else.

"Jacob Serter *and* Mark Curie," Axel began. "How curiously unexpected! To *what* do I owe the pleasure of your simultaneous appearance? Surely this is not *really* about <u>One Vision</u>?"

The Queen absently scratched his forearm and looked worried. "I thought *you* summoned *us*?"

Jacob Serter swatted something on the back of his neck.

Immediately after they had arrived, the Agent that had escorted them into the room had crossed over to a nearby table and opened up a black cube that was sitting upon it (Noirvision products arrive in such a cube). He removed the lid, and pulled the contents out as he walked back over to rejoin the other inhabitants.

At the Queen's comment to Axel, the Agent lifted up a sculpture which everyone turned to see. He held a mirroranium apple. It was turned so that anyone looking at it could see the inscription on its side. "For the Darkest," it read in precision cut letters in a perfect silver fruit.

Then the Agent started speaking. As he spoke, both the Queen and Serter found themselves completely unable to move.[40]
While he spoke, the Agent moved to stand before Wonder.

> "Assemble then, unto thee
> At ONE (to *thou*, though <u>*Now*</u> *I* see)
> *Both* Kings *and* Queen: the trilogy—
> Yea, *all* the *silver* royalty—
> That this fruit may given be
> To the *darkest* of the three:
> By visage, soul, or industry.
>
> This choice be given unto *she*
> —*Heiress* to the Company—
> (Daddy's private novelty)"

The Agent placed the silver apple into Wonder's hand. The moment she touched it, the augmented mental bond her father had imposed upon her was severed. For the first time that she could tangibly think, she was alone in her thoughts. The agent backed away slowly, still speaking.

> "To the lock, I put the key
> Your chains undone; you're finally free!
> Free to be your very own *'Me!'*
> Now thy*self*! Bereft of *He*
> Eff, En, Oh, Are, Dee!
> Birthday present *and* decree:
> *Happy New Autonomy!*"

The Agent bowed. As he tilted his upper body forward, a muffled popping noise could be heard. The horrific look that spread over his face was instantaneously made macabre as his eyes nearly bulged out of their sockets, allowing a small spurt of blood to escape from behind. He then fell over, quite dead.

------

[40] And yet, they did not fall over or fall down.

Wonder stood in place, trembling unconsciously. Several droplets of the Agent's blood marred her otherwise perfect countenance.

Time seemed to pass impossibly slow.

Finally, a look of terror crept over Wonder's face and she started screaming.[41Δ]

Her screams, which were piercing and pitiful, did not last long, however. Within moments of her dread realization, Wonder suddenly became quiet, sniffled and wiped her eyes.

Whatever it was that had rendered immobile both Jacob and the Queen must have completed its transitory task, for they both found themselves capable of movement and speech again.

"Oh, my darling girl!" Jacob said, moving to pick up Wonder, who then unexpectedly backed away. Wonder appeared confused, thinking thoughts that none could hear.

Jacob hesitated, unsure as to how to proceed. He was inwardly pulsing with frustration at not being able to observe her thoughts. It may be as close as Jacob had come to genuine anger since he took over the company.

"Don't move...yet," the Queen whispered through clenched teeth. Yet, by proximity, surely nobody–Axel, Serter, or Wonder–could have possibly heard him.

Everyone stood still and silent until Axel spoke aloud.

"Little girl," he called, and Wonder looked up. "I believe you are supposed to give the apple to one of us.

"The *darkest* of the three," Axel concluded.

[41Δ] Although the remaining occupants of the room were certainly surprised, they were not as emotionally impacted as Wonder–all of these men have witnessed equal or worse during their lives.

Chapter 7:

Dark Decisions

JUNE *2070 EST*

Fri 13	Sat 14	Sun 15
13:05		

Sometimes, despite exhaustive planning or calculation, our actions have unforeseen consequences.

Ironically, sometimes the consequences of our actions are opposite the intent. Sometimes an evil intention creates a hero. Sometimes a good intention has catastrophic results.

Whether Wonder's birthday present of mental emancipation was meant for good or for ill is knowable only to the person that sent such a gift. The *aftermath* of the action, however, was dark and dire indeed.

Wonder's personality had already been fractionated, at least subconsciously, due to the months of telepathic impressions sent by her father.

When Wonder's mental link was abruptly severed, and she witnessed the Agent die so terribly, her consciousness split.

Joined only at the root of fundamental and rudimentary knowledge were two independent identities. The primary belonging to *Wonder*, the otherwise innocent child, and the other was **Wonderful**, the imposed personality and dogma of her father.

I have to give this to the <u>darkest</u> of the three? Wonder thought to herself. *Well, that's easy.*

Wonder started walking over to Axel.

Give it to your father, Wonderful insisted. **Doesn't he deserve such a prize? Don't you think it will bring him joy?**

Wonder hesitated.

Yeah, but daddy's not the <u>darkest</u>...the black man is the darkest.

Not necessarily–"darkest" need not apply only to what your eyes tell you. The darkest could be the funny man.

I don't see how it could be the funny man, Wonder thought, perhaps even slightly amused. *How could he be the darkest?*

...I don't know.

Wonder frowned.

Your mother might; she knows him.

But, mommy's not here right now...

How very perceptive. No, she's not. Still–let's think this over again. Perhaps it's a trap.

A trap?

Yeah...maybe this present is secretly meant to harm.

It's not hurting me.

Fair enough. Let's see if anyone wants it. Ask the black man if he wants it– don't give it to him, just ask him.

Wonder resumed walking over to Axel. "Do you *want* this?"

Axel's black head tilted down to Wonder. "Perhaps. Let me hold it."

Wonder handed the silver apple up to Axel. He lifted it up with black gloved hands to look at it closely.

I said don't give it to him, Wonderful thought, but Wonder ignored her.

"*Impossible,*" Axel whispered. [42Δ]

Axel carefully handed the apple back to Wonder.

"Honestly," Axel said with resolution, "I can tell you that this *ornament* has no value to anyone in this room other than to me. That being said, I have just given it value to everyone else–if only for my *own* stated interest.

"How very amusing," Axel seemed to think out loud. "*And* very *personal*. Tread carefully, all of you. There is a game at work here that goes beyond your wildest imaginings.

"Still, here we are. Let me suggest the *complete* value of this *trinket*, then. Should your judgment, little girl, determine the apple should pass to Jacob Serter or Mark Curie...I will, to the best of my power, grant any single wish they may have–so long as it does not interfere with my designs or the laws of Silverberg–in exchange for the apple."

[42Δ] The apple, Axel realized, was made of tempered mirroranium. What nobody knows, apart from Axel himself, is that Axel has personally overseen *every* piece of tempered mirroranium ever created–and yet, he was not present for *this* piece.

"You *are* talking to a child," the Queen admonished.
"So long as *you* get the message, Mr. Curie."

"Wonderful Serter," Axel said, crouching down to her level. "If you give this apple to your father, the other man will try to take it from him the longer he does not give it to me. He may even try to hurt him. If you give it to the other man, he will only cause harm with it because that is his nature."
The Queen stuck out his tongue.
"To help your judgment," Axel continued, "*and* so that *I* can see who's playing in this game, I will not accept the apple from *either* for 2 entire days. But listen: if you simply give the fruit to *me*, I promise you that you will spare *many* unwanted trouble in their lives. Of the gifts I might offer you in bribe, trust me, this is the best.
"You'll be *most* tempted to give it to your father, but be cautious–whoever sent this knows that there is nothing that a child desires more than parental love."

I don't think it's a trap–a weapon. Give it to daddy.
But, the black man said then the funny man will try to <u>hurt</u> daddy.
Bah, the funny man is a fool. He can't hurt daddy.

Axel, seeing that Wonder was still hesitating, spoke up.
"*Not* to present myself as unnecessarily callous…however I *must* insist you make your decision speedily. The intermission is about over, and–"
"The show must go on," the Queen finished.
"For lack of something a bit less cliché," Axel said dryly, "yes."

None of this banter is relevant. Give it to your father–he, at least, will know best what to do with it.
You're right, Wonder thought, relenting. *<u>Daddy</u> will know what to do.*
Satisfied, Wonder walked over to her father. "Here you go, daddy.'
Jacob moved passed Wonder's outstretched offer, and scooped her up into his arms, hugging her tightly. Wonder held him dearly in return, tears falling down both their faces.
"*You* hold on to it for me for now, sweetie."

"*Well,*" the Queen huffed with heavy sarcasm. "Didn't see *that* one coming."

After clearing his throat, the Queen continued. "*Mr.* Serter, you might suppose I have nothing to offer you greater than whoever-it-is over there…however, I *do* have a certain battery of resources available to me. I alluded to this in the hallway…let me now speak more plainly.

"I have *personally* helped scores of people change their Mainframe identities…the Chessmen have been doing this for *decades*. There are literally thousands [43Δ] of Chessmen hidden throughout Silverberg–infiltrating *both* of your organizations *as well as others*.

"*If* you give the apple to *me*, I will disclose to you the names of those in *your* company, *and* pledge the assistance of the rest. This is the one offer Axel–or whomever–cannot hope to match."

"We'll see," Jacob said after a brief pause. "I'll think about this–*tomorrow*. Right *now* I have a birthday party to attend to. And, if only based on the immediate circumstances, *it* has the highest priority."

Axel crossed the room and commanded the door to open. His head tilted down to see that in front of the newly opened door, the Agent that had remained outside was now laying face down in a small pool of blood.

"Very well, then." Axel motioned for them to leave the room. "Gentlemen, I anticipate speaking with one or both of you in the near future. In the interim, try to behave I suppose."

Jacob, carrying a hugging Wonder, stepped over the exterior Agent and walked away.

"When they clear that hallway,' the Queen whispered while smoothing out his dark moustache, "Grab that apple and *run*."

🜂

"*Beef gravy!*?" Templeton was practically yelling at the chef. "None but the most uncouth and unsavory would dip their sandwiches in *beef gravy*. You seek to placate me, sir, yet all you have managed to do is *insult* me!"

43Δ *Thousands* is perhaps a bit of an overstatement - there are 1,772.

The Queen lingered, stalling so that his invisible operative might relieve Serter of his meddlesome gift. Donning an expression of contempt, the Queen looked directly at Axel. For a moment, he felt dizzy, but then he as quickly recovered.

"<u>One *Faith*</u>?" The Queen asked in accusation. "How on Earth could <u>One Faith</u> win an award?"

Axel shrugged. "Did you read it?"

"Yes, well, I skimmed it."

"It's only a few pages long; you *skimmed* it? At any rate, if you didn't even bother to *read* the material, why question as to how it won an award?"

"Because I know Therius–the Chessmen have been watching him since he was publicly nominated–and skimming it was quite enough for me to form an opinion."

"Perhaps it's a miracle then," Axel suggested.

"Either the judges are idiots or you're manipulating who wins. I just want to know *why*."

Axel laughed. It was an odd sound that made Mark's head hurt. "Why do I do *anything*? Better: why do I permit the *Chessmen*–an organization that assists *lawbreakers*–to exist? When you took the group public and challenged me to martyr you, why didn't I? Because I don't *care* if the Chessmen are public, Curie –I prefer it. I permitted them to exist before they went public. The main difference is *you*. I *like* you as their leader, so I elected you."

"I highly doubt *that*," the Queen said with conviction.

"I knew you were the only person outspoken and impulsive enough. Who *else* would have taken a subversive organization that has remained in hiding for *decades* and made it public? People knew about you *before* commercials, yet haven't you attracted a *lot* more people to your cause since you went public? Aren't you the only person visionary enough to lead such a campaign?"

The Queen frowned. "No way, man."

"The Chessmen are almost as good as Xians. The Xians are better, though, and that's why Therius won. The bottom line of it is, I want more people to read his book than yours.

"But you *are* very similar. You both take the undesirables and try to transform them into model citizens. Only, the Xians stay in line because they think they are always being watched and the Chessmen stay in line because they think are *not*.

 - [The Terrors of Wonder] -

"Oh, you have your *plots*. You teach them all to hate me, but that's under-standable–after all, I own everything. Possession makes me the villain. *Someone* has to be the cause of your problems…someone other than yourself. May as well direct your anger at *me*, right? I can afford to lose, so you want it all."

The Queen had heard that Axel had a way of manipulating conversations, but to have it done to you was another experience entirely. The Queen knew in his heart of hearts that Axel could not possibly believe everything he was saying, yet the Queen even found himself doubting reality for a moment.

"So you see, Curie–*you* have been 'programmed' as well. And you have followed your programming perfectly. Now get out. That's an order–and keep up the good work."

"Well *that* was an awfully long disappearance," Cordelia announced when Hugo finally returned. "So–how did it go?"
Hugo gingerly placed a container on the table in front of his wife.
"What's that?"
"Beef gravy," Hugo said disdainfully while sitting down.
"Beef gravy? For a French dip sandwich?"
"Exactly what I said," Hugo muttered, reaching for his food.

Jacob, carrying Wonder, headed directly for the amusement park. Wonder had, soon after leaving the green room, fallen asleep. She was completely exhaust-ed and overwhelmed with the events of the day.
Perfect–a nap will do her well, Jacob thought. *Perhaps help heal this trauma.*

"Well, this is just *completely* unacceptable!" Hugo roared moments later. "I tell you this day cannot get any worse!"[44]
"Now what's the matter?"
"Well, this sandwich is *cold*!"

___

[44] An inaccurate supposition on behalf of Mr. Templeton, as his day did indeed grow worse when he realized that he was not extended the opportunity to collect an award.

Chapter 8:

Playing Pieces

JUNE *2070 EST*

Fri 13	Sat 14	Sun 15
13:20		

Yet, during **none** *of this was there an attempt on my life.* Axel reflected while walking back to the podium. *The apple was a message–but not the only message. I'll have to watch that Agent's poem again.*

Now, who have I misplaced? Who has caused all this?

"Agent Wilson," Axel commanded his credit bank. Soon afterward, Wilson's voice responded.

"Sir?"

"I have been assaulted. I expect you to do something about it *immediately.*"

"Sir!" Wilson sounded worried. "Security-"

"I am not interested in excuses or blame," Axel interrupted. "Right *now* I am most interested in learning *who* is behind this. There are two dead AIIS agents in the green room; you can start there. I expect you to file a comprehensive report with Director Thompson by the time I am done with the ONE awards."

"Yes, sir! On it immediately."

◭

Although the intermission for this year's ONE awards ran roughly six minutes longer than intended, nobody except those responsible for the production noticed–even then it was as quickly forgotten.

     - [The Terrors of Wonder] -

Axel continued hosting the awards[45Δ] without any trace of effect from the events of the intermission. Of course, considering his face was always hidden, this was probably not too difficult an undertaking.

After the awards ceremony the Queen dispensed with his entourage and returned to the tent in his private chamber–a chamber *far* away from the bustle of the amusement park.

The Queen's Chamber was one of five rooms considered completely "hidden" from Axel Industries. The hand-written journals of the individuals that held the position of Queen before Mark Curie were adamant on that point.

But Mark felt that one could never be too sure, so he completely covered the walls, floor, and ceiling of the Queen's Chamber. The few that have been there consider it as eccentric as the Queen's personality.

The floor was completely covered with carpet that looked like green grass, and a large red-and-white pavilion stood in the center. The mirroranium ceiling and walls were hidden behind wall-to-wall paintings that boasted blue skies over green pastures.

At the moment, apart from the Queen there was one other man present in the tent. This man was known as "the Queen"s Pawn". The Queen's Pawn was a short, fat, aging man with a fairly unexpressive Maltese face. He very seldom said anything, to the point that Mark originally wondered whether the man was mute. His position in "The Chessmen" was extremely significant however, and for security purposes he seldom left the Queen's Chamber.

Both men sat in silence. The Queen's Pawn was reading the copy of <u>One Faith</u> that the Queen brought back from the awards, and the Queen was lost in thought–stewing on his dialogue with Axel.

***How** could Axel influence **my** promotion?* The Queen mused. Certainly the question had been in his head for quite awhile now, but this was his first opportunity to examine it without distraction.

[45Δ] The list of awards that were presented after the intermission is considerable, yet irrelevant. A list would be arduous, even in a footnote or appendix. This very footnote is suspect.

*Not **just** influence– guarantee? Axel would need to control most of the Bishops, at least one Knight, or possibly even the Queen's Pawn.*

The Queen looked over at the little man reading.

If Axel owns you, he may as well own the Chessmen. Yet, if Axel knew what we were trying, he would sift and destroy us. Mark shook his head. *No, he doesn't own the Pawn.*

*One Knight? That would be easy enough. But...**my** Knight? Perhaps it's time to sacrifice a piece for better positioning.*

***Most** of the bishops, though? No way. No, I think Axel is trying to play me– but why?*

Axel...or whomever.

The Queen sighed and grabbed a nearby bottle of champagne.

I'm over-thinking it, and I'm done wasting my time. Now onto other things.

"Leave me," the Queen instructed the Queen's Pawn.

The Queen's Pawn marked his place in the book as he set it down and promptly left. A few moments following his departure, the Queen spoke again.

"Rook?"

"Yes, your majesty?"

"Reveal yourself."

The Rook removed his visual camouflage.

Underneath the sheet that kept him hidden from sight was an ugly, stinky man.

The Rook's dark hair grew in patches, dotting a visibly receding hairline. His hair was clearly unattended to, save that he took some effort to keep it from falling into his face or onto his neck. Between the remaining tufts of greasy follicles, one could spy fragments of several black and jagged tribal tattoos. His overgrown, bushy eyebrows seemed to almost point towards the bridge of his nose, initially lending to the observer a sense of anger or confusion.

The entire left half of his face was unnaturally relaxed–looking almost melted–leaving his left eye permanently half closed and giving him an equally permanent half-frown.

His scraggily beard made him look either pathetic or dangerous, or perhaps both simultaneously.

Opposite his countenance, however, his voice was alert and powerful–although it carried with it the slightest slurring sound when he spoke.

The Queen, slightly disgusted, coughed to regain his composure before he spoke.

"You look awful. You need to take a bath."

"Can we skip the pleasantries?" The Rook sounded characteristically annoyed. "I have other things that need my attention."

"Very well, then. Please give me the apple."

"…I don't have it."

"I certainly hope you have a good reason as to *why*," the Queen said finally, almost menacingly. He took a sip of champagne before continuing. "Because I *know* that Serter couldn't possibly overpower or elude you."

"Taking it from Serter wasn't the problem. It's the girl. Call me old-fashioned, I couldn't bring myself to rip it from her terrorized hands."

"Of *all* the rid–"

"Let it go *Mark,*" the Rook said, pointing an accusing finger at the Queen. "She's like three feet tall. She's just a *baby*. Do you really think I needed to top off her day with taking that slang apple away from her? *'Hey kid! Didja have fun meeting the spooky black man? Did you enjoy watching a man die? Get some blood on your face? Here, let me grab that apple–what's that? Daddy put up a fight? Well, now he's dead…and now you're dead. Happy birthday.'* I'll get your precious apple for you–soon enough."

The Rook's otherwise simple gesture of pointing was enough to remind the Queen *who* was addressing him. The movement was quick, fluid, controlled–it carried with it a certain authority. Although the Rook was unkempt, he was a *very* powerful man–once considered *the* most powerful man in the country.

"Well, you had better," the Queen said. "When?"

The Rook seemed to think about it. "Tomorrow."

"*Tomorrow*? Why tomorrow?"

The Rook pulled out the envelope that Agent Wilson had handed to the Queen. "Because I have other things that require my attention."

"Ah good–I was wondering about that," [46Δ] the Queen said. "*Why* would you reveal yourself to anyone else that you're a Rook with The Chessmen? You have a death wish?"

46Δ *Whatever!* The Queen had completely forgotten about the note until just now.

"I *didn't*."

The Queen frowned. "Well, that *is* a problem. I have gone to great lengths to keep your existence a secret."

The Queen mused again at the idea that the Queen's Pawn somehow might have been converted by Axel. He visibly shook his head. *No, that just doesn't make any sense.*

"So…are you going to tell me what the letter *says*?"

The Rook fully frowned, his face momentarily symmetrical. "I think not. It has nothing to do with the Chessmen."

"Well, if it has to do with *you,* then it has to do with the Chessmen, don't you think?"

The Rook half smiled and shook his head. "Not in this case. An old friend–a *very* old friend needs my help. I don't mean 'wants,' I quite literally mean *needs.* And he shall have it."

The Queen inwardly relented and summarily drank some more. "Sh'ure it's not a trap?" He almost hiccupped.

"Oh, it's *definitely* a trap."

With that, the Rook covered himself back up with his visual camouflage, and then…well, who knows.

"Take a shower!" the Queen commanded.

◭

Back at the amusement park, *The Valentine Relics* were inspecting the stage they would use for their upcoming performance. Well, all of them except Billy, who insisted that he needed to use this time for composition.

Anthem, elated that everyone had (finally) made it and that everything was on schedule, could not be happier.

"Looks good," Mack said appreciatively.

"It *does*," Anthem agreed, nodding her head and swishing her tail. "My husband really dressed this one up for us. We have a great opportunity here."

"I juz don' figger how he kin be so slang az tuh book Sig Sigmuh anna Wardogz too."

'Oh, Gob," Anthem said coolly, [47] "It's Wonder's birthday, and Jacob wants *everyone* here–and we're *not* the only act in town."

"At least they're across the park," Mack added.

"Still too cloze fer me."

"I hope Billy's okay," Nan spoke up, breaking the momentary silence. "I should go check on him."

"Now *wait* a sec," Mack shifted his attention. "Billy's *fine*."

Anthem put her hand on Mack's shoulder and said: "Then *again*, maybe you're right. Good idea, Nan, go check on Billy."

Nan smiled her largest smile. "Thanks, Anthem." She ran off.

"Kin…kin *I* go check on Billy, too?"

"Sure thing, Gob. Keep an eye on Nan as well." Anthem winked.

"You know what?" Mack turned a darkened stare to Anthem. "You should stay out of this. Now they're gonna get wrecked and won't play for crap tonight."

"They'll be fine, they're just tense." Anthem smiled, and stroked Mack's face. "I think you're a little tense, too."

Mack turned away, but did manage to brighten up a little. "Just let *me* handle *The Relics*. You handle the rest, okay?"

"Sure thing, *Isaac*. Not trying to steal your authority."

"Whatever."

Within minutes, however, Mack was back in the game. "Well, now *we* better go check on Billy before it's too late."

"You worry too much," Anthem said, smiling.

"No, I worry just enough." Mack smiled back. "Now, let's go. We're done here anyway." [48]

---

[47] Some expert acting on Anthem's part, for she was wrestling with the fact as well. In the end, it was an "agree to disagree" moment between Jacob and Anthem.

[48] The all-but-forgotten sound man, stayed and continued to examine the scene.

△

Dear "The Rook" – (The letter began)

Likely you will be interested in knowing that there is concealed somewhere between the corridors of the House of Mirrors, a hidden sanatorium–asylum–which houses the most incorrigible and dangerous of persons.

Amongst the roster of those interred, you will find one George Gordon–a man whom you knew, at least in your adolescence. He has been receiving "treatment" for just over two years now–treatment for a condition that he does not possess.

The sanatorium is operated exclusively by Axel Industries Internal Security, and it's existence known only to those in the highest seats of power and authority.

George Gordon will be terminated the afternoon of Saturday, June 14th if you do not intercede. If you should determine to take action, exercise also great caution–this predicament is a trap set exclusively for you.

The labyrinth is almost impossible to navigate without assistance or knowledge. Enclosed, therefore, is a map–but be aware the directions are time sensitive, and are only good from 2 PM to 2 AM EST this calendar week.

Chapter 9:

Enough to Eat

JUNE *2070 EST*

Fri 13	Sat 14	Sun 15
15:15		

Wonder was absolutely delighted with every aspect of her birthday celebration.

First she was brought before a small mountain of boxes, all wrapped with the most spectacular papers that boasted impossibly vibrant colors and carrying various designs. These were all presents from fans, friends, and family–all waiting to be opened. As she went to open the nearest of them, her father put his hand on her shoulder.

"Later," he said, smiling. "Come look at the rest; there's so *much* to see! This is going to be great!"

While leading her around the park, and occasionally stopping to enjoy many preplanned attractions that both amazed and amused, Jacob would intermittently purchase food and beverages of every variety for his only daughter.

Everything was exemplary–the ice cream was the creamiest she had ever tasted; the juice was the sweetest. Even the hamburgers and hot dogs were perfect, being neither overcooked nor under, neither too salty nor too bland.

She had never had so much fun in her entire life! The touring was only made more perfect as Wonder developed a fast friendship with one of the girls she met on one of the various rides that she was permitted to ride.

They clung together from ride to ride, whooping and screaming, laughing and giggling as though they had always been the best of friends.

As the sky slowly began to darken, signaling that the end of the day was fast approaching, Jacob suggested they go back and open up her presents.

"Just a *few* more rides?" Wonder's friend pleaded.

"Alright, I suppose."

"And just a few more cookies?"

"Whatever you want," Jacob said, smiling.

With that, Wonder and her friend went round after round on the carousel. As soon as the ride was completed, they would run out the exit and then right back to the entrance, eating and laughing and just being adorable.

"One more time!" Wonder's friend cheered while pressing another cookie into Wonder's hand.

"Okay," Wonder agreed, but Wonder was actually starting to feel a bit ill. Her clothes were feeling tight, and the constant spinning was starting to over-whelm her senses.

After they completed their last ride, Wonder's new friend led her away from the merry-go-round. She took her to rest beside several long tables, all filled with vast assortments of foods and beverages.

Wonder never thought that such delicious looking food could ever be so com-pletely unappealing!

"Let's have some chicken!" Wonder's friend yelled, happily scooping up a generous portion onto a plate and carrying it over to Wonder. In response, Wonder slumped to lay on the ground–the very thought of more food exhausting in and of itself.

"No than–mmf!" Wonder started to refuse, but was interrupted by having food shoved in her mouth.

"Oh, it will be good for you; help you grow," her friend insisted.

"I don't th–mmf!"

No, please stop! Wonder thought helplessly as more and more food was being forced into her. Wonder was bordering on hysteria, and her clothes had be-come impossibly tight. *It's too much!*

Apparently noticing her discomfort, Wonder's friend removed her belt with her free hand. Wonder's belly expanded in compliment.

"It's too m-mmf!"

Yet, her friend seemed oblivious to her *emotional* distress. Quite the oppo-site, her friend actually tilted the nearby table so that she could slide food more quickly into Wonder's mouth.

Stop! Stop! Stop! Wonder thought in horror as she watched her stomach inflate like a balloon. She tried to scream out, but it only manifested as a pitiful gargle.

She kept trying to scream, but was drowning in food. She tried harder and harder. Finally, the girl paused for a moment.

"Oh, stop struggling," the girl with white eyes said, sounding annoyed. "You *need* this."

Wonder screamed, as loud and as powerfully as she could muster.

As Wonder screamed and screamed, Jacob held her tightly, patting her back while rocking back and forth.

Wonder sniffled and stopped her screaming. *What's going on?* She thought, confused.

You had a bad dream, Wonderful answered.

But, she thought, looking around. *Where's mommy?*

Working. Father is here, and he's very concerned, very upset. He is trying to console you, but it is him that needs consoling. You must be happy and strong for him.

I can do that!

Jacob pulled back far enough to look her in the eyes. He looked pale and worried.

"Okay now?"

"I'm okay, thanks daddy."

"What's…what's the last thing you remember?"

Wonder thought aloud. "Hmm. The silver apple and the dead man. The black man and the funny man."

"Do you remember anything about your dream, or talking in your sleep?"

Wonder shook her head. "No. Sorry daddy."

"That's okay," Jacob said, not sounding so confident. He hugged her close for a moment longer.

"Ready for the best birthday *ever*?" Jacob asked excitedly, his voice taking on a fresh tone.

"I'm weddy!" Wonder announced, brightening up immediately.

The two of them then went deep into the park to enjoy her incredible birthday celebration.

Wonder, oblivious to the contents of her dream, did not recognize that many of the experiences she had were similar to the ones she just dreamt. [49Δ] By the end of the party, she had an amazing and very memorable time.

Jacob, on the other hand, was curiously distracted most of the evening, thinking and reflecting on the conversation that he had with his daughter while she was sleeping.

"**Father**," Wonderful had said while Jacob was carrying her toward her party.
Jacob stopped and moved her so as to cradle her in his arms – she lay fast asleep.
"**Father**," she said again, eyes closed.
"Wonderful?"
"**You must not fix the mental bond.**"

Jacob frowned. His daughter *never* called him "father." Her enunciation was curiously perfect, and she should not understand anything about the Thinking Cap technology he had installed in her head, despite hearing the cryptic implication the AIIS Agent made when presenting the apple.

"What do you mean?" He asked as if he didn't understand.
"**You know. I *know* you know. How do *I* know? You told me. All of this time, you have been telling me *many* things–many things more than you know.**"

Jacob looked around to make sure no one was eavesdropping over this impossible conversation he was having with a sleeping 3 year old.

"**You've done enough. Everything is perfect. I *understand*, father. I *will* be the woman you wanted me to be; your dreams *are* to be realized, despite any bad math on your part.**
"**Yet, my mind is delicate. You must leave it alone. Just take care of me. I know you will. Thank you. I love you. I'm sleepy now.**

Jacob stood still, stunned by his daughter's ominous oration. For quite a while he continued to stand, unmoving and silent, until Wonder's hysterical screaming eventually called him back into focus.

[49Δ] although she *did* have moments of déjà vu.

Chapter 10:

Written Reports

JUNE *2070 EST*

Fri 13	Sat 14	Sun 15
15:33		

Agent Wilson took the pipe out of his mouth just long enough to contact his superior.

"Initiate mediacast session with Director Thompson."[50Δ]

Agent Thompson was the head of Axel Industries Internal Security, which is to say that *every* AIIS department reported and answered to him. In authority, following Axel, there was Thompson, and then there was everyone else.

It was clear that, on occasion, Thompson did not agree with the commands he was given. Regardless, he was always very adamant on respecting the chain of command. Whether silent or sarcastic, Thompson *always* carried out the wishes of the ruler of Silverberg.

Although his dedication to duty was admirable, it was Thompson's ability to vocally identify any absurd commands that he had been given that often won him the hearts–or at least the respect–of his subordinates. Thompson was strict, but compassionate, firm, yet sympathetic, comic *and* commanding.

[50Δ] *"Director Thompson,"* because that is how Agent Wilson so programmed his credit bank. Thompson is also frequently called 'Agent Director Thompson' or sometimes even "Director Agent Thompson," although *technically* he should simply be referred to as "Agent Thompson." Thompson *is* the director of the AIIS, but it is improper to address him by title–after all, we don't say "Agent of Justice, Wilson," or "Justice Agent Wilson," do we? No. We simply say "Agent Wilson."

After a few moments, Thompson's image filled the imagescreen in front of Wilson.

Thompson was a man who had a countenance that spoke of sophistication. His parted salt and pepper hair was always combed back and flat, likely held fast by some preferred hair styling product. The same or similar product was certainly used in taming and shaping his fanned out moustache. Just above his prominent nose, and obscuring his eyes, he wore 2 round noirglass lenses which were held in place by a single mirroranium bracket.

"Wilson?" Thompson acknowledged.

"Yes, sir," Wilson said, always smiling. "I am ready to submit my report."

"From what *I* understand, your report is already slightly overdue."

"Indeed, sir. But, please be aware that I did attempt to contact you earlier, only to find that you were unavailable. Further, I might have submitted my findings–preliminary as they are–to you in message, but you have instructed me not to leave messages of a sensitive or confidential nature."

"Ah, yes…very good" Thompson seemed to think for a moment, putting his hand to his chin. "Also, I'll need the report in writing."

"In *writing*?" Wilson said, surprised. "You mean hard copy?"

"Exactly. In light of today's…display…I think it is finally safe to say that the errors that we have been experiencing with the Mainframe are not glitches,[51Δ] but are in fact some form of major security breech.

"For a while, we figured the anomalies were connected to the reassigning of identities perpetrated by the Chessmen…although considering the Queen was present and clearly *as* surprised during today's unexpected…instance…we have since changed our disposition.

"Of course, he could put himself there to throw his name out of consideration…but the Chessmen have never been known to have actually killed anybody– well, anyone in Silverberg, that is."

"We can't just *stop* using the Mainframe…" Wilson said, trailing off.

[51Δ] The Mainframe–Silverberg's advanced computer system–had operated flawlessly for decades. For the past few years, however, it has been known to report errors–errors that, while not necessarily harmful, were problems that nobody could successfully diagnose.

"Of course not. However, in the interest of *security*, all information ranked 1 and 2 in confidentiality must henceforth be submitted in writing. Don't be a baby about it. Americans use pen and paper liberally. You'll survive?"

Wilson chewed his pipe, smiling perfectly. "Right you are, sir."

"Rerecord your report and have it delivered to my office. Delete your Mainframe notes on the matter. Now before we end the session, I *do* have two questions that you might address immediately."

"Of course."

"The Agents that were killed –"

"Had explosive cranial implants," Wilson interrupted. "Although I suspect that they were fairly recent installations, as of yet I do not know whether they were detonated by remote, by timer, or self-initiation."

"...were operatives under your authority," Thompson continued, sounding slightly annoyed. "How do you account for that?"

"I believe it to be circumstantial. Obviously the perpetrator...s would be more concerned with the *proximity* rather than the *person*. *Any* person or people that could corral *those* three would be equally desirable targets. It only makes sense that they used security."

"You miss the point. These men are Agents that worked *directly* under you."

"Ah. Yes, well, not only that, but these two men were also friends–lovers even, if you care–but such a connection might also explain why *these* gentlemen in particular. *Any* breach of security is, by definition, ultimately my fault. Thus, I accept responsibility for such a failure, and should you feel the need to punish me accordingly, I certainly understand.[52Δ] However, if you are implying that *I* orchestrated the affair, I assure you I did not."

"No, Wilson, that is *not* the assumption. You were hand-picked for your position. Complicity on your part would be a failure on my part in having selected you in the first place.

"Besides, you're being constantly monitored for signs of sedition or insurgence. If you were a traitor, I would know it far before now."

Wilson absently handled his unlit pipe as he spoke. "Yet, you cannot watch everything *all* the time."

Thompson laughed. "Are you *trying* to implicate yourself?"

[52Δ] Thompson was well known for overlooking the professional transgressions of his department heads, generally dispensing nothing greater than cynicism or threats. Wilson was hopeful he would now be treated similarly.

"Well, no–I'm just suggesting that you cannot monitor everyone constantly. That's how these kinds of things happen–in the cracks. How I wish I could keep a constant eye open on everyone! I have lost two of my best men! Imagine how that makes me feel, both professionally and personally."

"Touching. Now, my other question is this: Who's responsible?"

"I have yet to conclude a culprit, but the list of suspects is minimal. The two young men that died during this cannot be the sole orchestrators of the event. They are not solely to blame, for, based on the evidence, there must be *at least* one other individual involved–someone who was in the room prior to the intermission."

"Well now, how do you know that?"

"It's the box, sir."

"The box?"

"A Noirvision box was found. It was in the room *before* the Agents brought the Queen and Serter. Someone else placed it there, for neither Agent had ever been in the room prior. It's also noteworthy that neither Agent was working–well, for us–at the time.

"In *fact*," Wilson said with mounting enthusiasm, "it was placed there just *before* the awards began. If you examine the mediacast record, you'll see that the box appears only slightly before the awards."

"What do you mean *appears*?" Thompson asked.

"It's a glitch, or whatever. Just before the awards, during the final check in the green room, you'll notice that the mediacast records suspend for a full 13 seconds. The clock keeps counting, but suddenly *nobody* in the room moves at all–not even their mouths. When they start moving again, everyone is suddenly in a different position and the box is sitting quite innocuously on the table."

"So then your current list of suspects exclusively involves the occupants of the room just prior to the awards, then?"

"That is correct and complete. It *must* be one of them. The hard part is that there is no obvious motive, for anyone. With more time, I can review their itineraries until I find something."

"Very well. After this session, start reviewing everyone who was in the green room until we know who's to blame. But Wilson?"

"Yes, sir?"

"Although someone in the room is complicit, your trail will not end with any one of them. Whoever is behind this is *considerable*, dangerous. Do not proceed alone."

- [Daniel Strasel] -

"Feelings from you sir?"

"Absolutely not," Thompson smiled. "End mediacast session."

Wilson patted his forehead with his handkerchief.

Perfect, he thought, relieved. *I suppose I should stop by the "House" and make sure that idiot can get in before I go to the next step.*

Chapter 11:

The Maze of Mirrors

JUNE *2070 EST*

Fri 13	Sat 14	Sun 15
16:41		

Eerily abandoned [53Δ] stood the all-but-forgotten building at the edge of the Silverberg Amusement Park. It did not appear considerably different than any other accomplishment of architecture about the grounds, which is to say that it was completely covered in mirrors–or more accurately–it was constructed of mirroranium. The material used in its construction was *doubly* appropriate in this circumstance, however, as this particular building is aptly named "The House of Mirrors".

The official story goes thus: Once upon a time, not terribly long ago, a citizen somehow *died* (stories vary) in the complexity of the attraction. As a result, the Silverberg Amusement Park closed the House of Mirrors–permanently. Considering the building's design and composition, it has stalwartly stood vacant, unable to be properly repurposed.

The *truth* of it is: *No living body* has ever actually passed through the *front* doors of "The House of Mirrors", although the doors operate flawlessly. Any such attempt to transgress the portal would immediately send an alarm to the uppermost offices of the AIIS Department.

When the park first opened, "The House of Mirrors" attraction remained closed. "Under Construction" banners provided a daunting barrier to anyone who might think to transgress.

53Δ Abandoned, for *other* such amusements were blatantly populated with tourists and visitors, and this attraction had none. Eerily, for the pathways that lead up to the attraction were blocked with "CLOSED," and "DO NOT ENTER" signs.

As time passed, the signs gradually changed from "Under Construction" to "Closed for Cleaning", and then, finally, simply, to "Closed." No citizen ever died while entertaining the labyrinth hidden within "The House of Mirrors", *that* lie was quite deliberate. [54Δ]

Alone and invisible, the Rook waited impatiently by the *back* door. He was not aware of the story *or* the truth, and wouldn't care much if either or both were told to him.

All he cared about was saving his friend and following his instructions, his "map" Now, the "map" was very adamant that he should enter through the *back* door—a task that could *only* be accomplished if someone *else* opened the door.

*Does **whoever** think I could get past the door on my own?* The Rook thought. *No instructions on actually getting **in**, of course. I mean, how long is it going to be before someone goes in or out of **this** door? Sheesh.*
*This is **not** going to be easy, especially considering these awful directions.*

His mind wandered briefly. *Poor George! Used as bait for me.*

This is so slang. If I make it out of here, I am going to kill Thompson.

Poor George.

[54Δ] The grounds about the area are always kept in discipline by the Amusement Park management—which is as expected…however this also serves to lend to the casual observer no sense of significance should they see anyone about the vicinity.

CHAPTER 11

Okay, this is boring.
Stop that.
I just need to be patient.

Patience, however, was not one of his strongest traits.

Maybe I'll go grab something to eat and co-! The Rook winced as a spike of pain shot from behind the plates in his chest. He waited, pushing down his panic and bracing himself emotionally–wondering if this deep pain was about to return or not.

Yet, the pain subsided. It was so brief, only the memory of it remained. His breathing returned to normal. *Guess I'm still in the game. Good.*

Thankfully, and seemingly serendipitously, an AIIS Agent arrived shortly afterward in a Silverberg Amusement Park golf cart. The Agent exited the vehicle, and grabbing a cane, began his slow ascent to the rear entrance.

As the Agent made his way up the walk, the Rook noticed he was smiling the entire time, every once in awhile taking a pipe from his mouth only to replace it a few moments later.

Isn't this the same guy that gave the letter to the Queen?

Having finally arrived, Agent Wilson used his credit bank and commanded the door to open.

*I wonder what **his** deal is.*

Within moments, the Rook slipped in, quite undetected.

One thing the Rook noticed immediately is that the back door curiously and simply led its transgressor into the mirrored labyrinth as easily as the front door might.

So…what's the point of this door, then? Shouldn't this be like an office or something? Maybe the directions aren't as bad as they read.

Initially the Rook figured he could simply follow behind the hobbling Agent silently, but then the Agent turned around and went back to the entrance.

Maybe we both hate Thompson, the Rook thought.

*The note said "**this predicament is a trap set exclusively for you.**" Now– should I kill this guy or not? Access could come in handy.*

Screw it; goodbye, weirdo. You get to live, my..."friend?" Mainframe affirms George came to Silverberg a couple years ago–at least that much is true. Someone went through this much trouble to lure me down here, I may as well see for myself.

Following the instructions, the Rook walked and turned various directions before coming to a dead end.

"Stand still for 60 seconds," the terrible map read.

After he stood still for an entire minute the floor that he was standing on started lowering, eventually resting at a lower level.

*How big **is** this place anyway?* He thought, amazed. *This whole maze would have to be planned from the very beginning. How long ago was **that**?*

Eh, who cares? Still, though, that's an awful lot of trouble just to hide an asylum. I swear, the more I learn about Silverberg, the less I understand it.

Following his instructions, he eventually came to another dead end. Prior to this point, the instructions were *quite* clear that he should never touch the walls. Here, however, was an exception.

"Walk through the wall; it is a projection."

A projection of a mirror. Heh. Isn't that–his train of thought was instantly and utterly destroyed, however, for as he passed through the projection he saw something that left him shaken.

CHAPTER 11

On the other side of the wall sat a contraption both immense and intimidating–it was purposefully built to drive fear. Obviously armored in mirroranium, it was neatly covered in the most terrible of barbs and blades. It could only serve one purpose: to kill.

But it didn't move…*and* it didn't take long for the Rook to grow bored. The Rook took a few experimental steps…and nothing. Then he began stepping around it gingerly, for it took up most of the corridor with its girth.

Hmm. I wonder what alerts it? Must be triggered optically. Sheesh, even if I get to George, how are we ever going to make it out of here alive? I'm going to have to carry him the whole way.

With that, he followed the remainder of his instructions, which eventually left him in front of a door.

"Having reached the end, you will need to wait for the door to open…this does not happen frequently, but it does happen."

*Why, oh **why** didn't I knock out that Agent and use him to open the door? Then again, that would have cost me any position of surprise. I suppose I have to wait.*

The Rook sighed.

Okay, this is boring.

*Why, oh **why** didn't I bring any food?*

Eventually, sitting with his back against the wall, facing the door and holding his knees, the Rook fell asleep.

Chapter 12:

A Different Driver

Fri 13	Sat 14	Sun 15
19:45		

Anthem's voice blasted out over the considerable crowd.

"For our last number tonight," she began, causing the crowd to grow a bit more silent that they might listen. "We're going to do one of my personal favorites: "Mainframe Monsters!""

The crowd cheered in excitement and recognition as *The Valentine Relics* began to play.

> They're there, they're *there*–they're there in the walls
> The rooms and corr'dors, chambers and halls
> Not there to assist you, nor right any wrong
> Just waiting and hoping it won't take too long
>
> Now if you are good, you might just agree
> There's no need to fear for your family
> But if you so slightly defy the hive
> The Mainframe monsters will eat you alive
>
> Eat you alive! Make public your sin!
> Eat you alive–but where to begin?
> Tear you apart from present to past
> One small misstep will soon be your last
>
> We're there, *we're* there–we're there in the wings
> Thinking up dang'rous 'n dreadful things
> And that which we swore that we never would say
> We said in our youth, and today's a new day

Now this understood, you now just might see
The Mainframe monsters are you and me
Fearing each other, that we might contrive
To eat ourselves 'n each other alive

Eat you alive! Make public your shame!
Eat you alive–and isn't it plain?
We'll tear you apart mercilessly
All for a fleeting moment of glee

*

What black soul could conceive such a thought:
That mankind could ever be easily bought?
Yet monsters we have, and we have become
When finding our faults is justice for fun

After *The Relics* concluded, they bowed and left the stage, yet the crowd demanded an encore. *The Relics* were only too happy to return in order to play two more songs from their previous album, <u>What Means What</u>. At the end of the second song, Anthem, caught up in the energy and excitement, invited anyone who was interested out for further celebration.

"*Tonight*, if you're tired of the rides and the games, or the hoopla of my daughter's birthday–or maybe you're just great fans–come join us for a more private celebration at "The Tentacle and the Tail," [55Δ] a pub located about 9 miles down the Rim-Districts Loop in the B Rim of Axel Industries East. Check your credit banks and join us!"

The crowd cheered and chanted louder as *The Relics* left the stage for the final time.

[55Δ] In truth, this was all part of a stunt for greater publicity. After all, one can be as artistic as they want, but without promotion they will never gain an audience. This is not an ultimately surprising announcement either, for *The Relics* have previously invited their audiences out on several occasions. This trend is now, however, exclusive to Silverberg shows as there was once a situation in Ireland which has left them a bit reserved when touring abroad.

Anthem and Mack both spoke with the owners of "The Tentacle and the Tail" over a month ago, giving them a forewarning that a multitude of people would be there. The owners were only too happy to oblige. In anticipation, all staff members were made available (which in turn caused some turmoil amongst the staff of the T & T who felt it wasn't *fair* or *right* that they had to miss Wonderful's birthday celebration. *Those* members were told to go earlier in the day…but I digress).

Despite any fears that Mack may have entertained of drugs interrupting the performance, the evening went very well.

As they boarded their tour bus,[56Δ] Mack was a bit surprised to encounter an unfamiliar man behind the steering wheel.

"Who're you?" He asked politely. "Where's Smokey?"

"Smokey got sick," the new driver said and smiled as he took his unlit pipe from his mouth. "Too sick to drive, anyway. I'm filling in."

"I've never seen you before."

"My name is Bob. I'm an old friend of Smokey's. He called me up about 45 minutes ago and said *the dream wouldn't let him drive.*"

Mack groaned.

"You know where we're going?"

"Nope," Bob said, still smiling.

Mack thought the smile made him look stupid.

"The Tentacle and the Tail."

"Got it," Bob said, pulling out his credit bank.

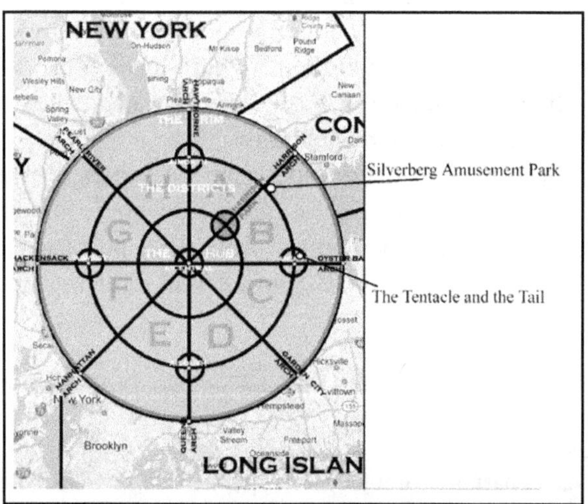

56Δ I know what you're thinking: *tour bus*? *Why not an Autocar or Autotran?* The reason is twofold: one is that *The Relics* tour other countries (such as America and Canada) and Autocars and Autotrans do not operate outside of Silverberg (which is not entirely true–they operate up to a mile or so outside of Silverberg, but I suppose it's close enough to just say that they only work in Silverberg). The second is that for visibility purposes, the bus acts like a mobile billboard for the group (the billboard *also* being one of the clever suggestions of the forgotten sound man…what was his name? Denny Kedney).

     - [The Terrors of Wonder] -

A great many fans left the park to join *The Relics* at the pub–so many that the establishment could not contain them all and the party stretched out into other nearby venues as well.

The Relics milled about, engaging their fans both physically and verbally. They signed various pieces of paraphernalia, and, of course, joined many in their partaking of shots and alcohol.

As the night stretched on, Anthem and Mack corralled their cronies and headed back to the bus. When they arrived, there were roses and candy both hanging and sitting on Anthem's seat.

"What is this?" Anthem asked, smiling.

As she stumbled her way back to her seat, she found an envelope with her name on it with a letter from her husband. She read it, and then read it aloud to everyone. No one seemed to notice or care that the bus had already started moving.

"My dearest darling wife," Anthem began, half giggling. *"I am so proud of you and your band! I've decided to give you all a gift–but it needed to be something huge, so it would match the talent."*

Anthem paused.

"Now, where to hide something so immense? Come to the Serter Company East building and see what I have for you."

"You sound like you're about 20 minutes from passing out," Mack said disapprovingly.

"Shh! Inside the envelope you'll find five silver tickets, which you will need to get past security...I can't wait to see your faces!"

Anthem cleared her throat and swished her tail.

"Wonder and I will be waiting. Jacob."

"No kiddin," Gob smiled. "Sunthin fer *us*? I always thot e wuz kinda slang."

Anthem shot a dark look at Gob.

"Jus sayin. Itz dead eez dead at's all."

"I don't know guys," Mack sounded hesitant. "Why don't we do this tomorrow?"

"I'm gooda go now," Gob shrugged.

"What do you think, Nan?" Mack turned and asked.

"Whatev. I could care either way."

"Billy?"

"Shhh!" Billy scolded. "Don't talk to me–I'm kaleidoscoping!"

Whatever that means, Mack thought.

"Oh, let's just go now," Anthem said, trying to sound more seductive–or perhaps it was just her being sleepy. "Jake's obviously excited." [57Δ]

"Oh, I'm excited too," Mack said, obviously false in his sentiment. "I just think that it would be nice if we –"

"Shhh! I'm *kaleidoscoping!*"

"Will you shut up?" Mack said with irritation. He tapped his credit bank. "Connect to Mainframe."

MAINFRAME » SYNCHRONIZING «

MAINFRAME » CONNECTION NOT AVAILABLE «

Mack sighed. "Go figure. Well, that's that. Who even knows where this building is, anyway?"

Bob, the replacement driver, turned his smiling face from the road long enough to say: "*I* know where it's at–not far at all."

Anthem stuck her tongue out triumphantly at Mack.

▲

Their driver woke them all up soon after they stopped.

"Man," Mack yawned. "I didn't even know I was that tired. What time *is* it?"

"3:13 AM," "Bob" answered.

"Old age is making you a lightweight," Anthem chided. "We used to party until nine in the morning. How much *did* you have to drink?"

"Not so much...but it *has* been a long day."

Most of them left the bus easily enough, although Anthem had to almost drag Billy.

"None of the lights are on," Mack said, frowning.

"Everyone's out," Anthem suggested. "Probably–"

"*Sleeping,*" Mack interrupted, annoyed and still somewhat sleepy.

57Δ Anthem did not typically refer to Jacob as "Jake," unless she was happily inebriated in some manner.

"Reederz active," Gob said, looking up at the external security panel.

"Lady Serter first," Bob called from the driver's seat. "The delivery man said to use your ticket."

"Oh yeah," Anthem said. She handed everyone a silver ticket. Not entirely sure how to proceed, she shrugged and pushed her own ticket up to the security pad.[58Δ]

MAINFRAME » RECOGNIZED: SERTER, AYN «
SERTER, AYN » SERTER COMPANY EAST » _|__«

"Let us in, please," Anthem said.

As soon as she said it, the doors gave entrance. As *The Relics* entered, a light appeared near a door on the far right side of the lobby.

"I guess we go that way," Anthem said and started walking.

"This is *stupid*," Nan said, sounding rather surly.

"I agree," Mack said, handing Nan a shot–which she happily grabbed. "What's with the campy suspense?"

Anthem stopped and turned to address *The Relics*.

"Aw, lighten up, guys. Jake doesn't really do things like this–I'm kinda impressed, really…I think it's sweet. Besides, building *suspense* can't be that bad of a thing, right? Don't you want to see what the *huge* surprise is?" Anthem smiled. "I know *I* do."

"C'mon Nan, thissiz gonna be great. Jaykib Serterz idea of eewge must be *eewge*!"

"Gob's got a point, but this *better* be dead," Nan warned. "And I hope to hell there's more light in the next room; I can't even do this bloody shot!"

[58Δ] which, by proximity, had the exact same effect as her presenting her hand rather than her credit bank–effectively making the ticket completely superfluous in this instance.

"Where's Billy?" Mack asked, but then spotted the drummer sitting on a nearby lobby sofa, possibly already asleep.

Mack walked over to Billy. He pulled him up and led him over to the rest of the group.

The panel by the light demanded everyone present their tickets at the same time for the doors to open.

"This is *stupid*," Nan said again as she joined everyone else in presenting her ticket. The doors opened and everyone started walking through.

"Jeez, Billy–what's all over your back?" Mack asked as they all walked inward. "It looks like *dust*."

A Different Driver

Chapter 13:

Missing Mommy

JUNE *2070 EST*

Fri 13	Sat 14	Sun 15
	06:29	

Anthem awoke to the *howling.*

She sat bolt upright in her bed as the sound permeated the room. It was an awful sound, and it seemed to reverberate from every direction. It was a sound she knew well. Throwing her sheets aside, she jumped out of her bed and ran down the hallway to Wonder's room.

Yet, Wonder was not in her bedroom–and after further investigation, neither was she in the den. Anthem ran from room to room, but was not succeeding in finding her daughter. In the meantime, the screams were growing in intensity and desperation.

"Wonder!" Anthem called. "Where are you, baby?"

"I'm *here*, mommy!"

Anthem turned her head towards the direction of the voice and immediately ran towards it. As she rushed into the room, she scooped up the screaming little girl and started patting her back and swaying to and fro.

"There there, mommy's here. It's okay. I've got you, baby–mommy's here. Shhh. Shh. Shh."

With that, the screaming stopped.

"But, *mommy*!" Wonder cried desperately. "That's not me–I'm over *here*! Mommy?"

Why wouldn't she answer?

"Mommy! *Mommy! MOMMY!!*"

Wonder yelled and yelled, but her mother did not respond. As Wonder help-lessly watched her mother hug the stranger, the little girl opened her white eyes and smiled as she put her finger to her lips.
"Shhh."
"Mommy!" Wonder screamed frantically. "Mommy! Mommy!"
"Shhh."

Wonder kept screaming and screaming when she suddenly realized that she was being held by her father. The memory of the dream vanished as suddenly.

"Shhh. It's alright, Wonderful. Daddy's here."
What–what's going on?
You had a bad dream.
Wonder calmed down and hugged her father tightly.
"Yesterday was a *big* day for you," Jacob said as he calmly patted her back. "All the excitement and the candy and whatnot. Try to sleep some more, princess, and I'll try and get some more work done; today is a big day for *me*."
Jacob gingerly placed her back on her bed and drew her sheets over her.
"In a little while, I'll have Mary [59A] collect and feed you–and then you can watch <u>Piggin' Around</u>."
Wonder yawned.
"But...what about *mommy*? Can I watch <u>Piggin' Na Round</u> wif mommy instead?"
"Maybe. For now, try and get some more rest. Love you."
"Love you too," Wonder yawned again. "Daddy."

Why do I have so many bad dreams? Wonder thought as her head nestled further into her pillow.
Many people have bad dreams.
But, why are mine so scary?
All bad dreams are scary.

Wonder yawned, deeper this time.

But, why can't I remember my dreams?
Most people do not remember their dreams.

____

[59A] another slave of the Serter household.

Wonder might have continued, but she fell back asleep.

△
M

About 30 minutes prior, as he did every day, Jacob began his day promptly at six in the morning.

He immediately noted that his wife had failed to return home from her exploits of yesterday evening, and although not a very welcome situation, Anthem had forewarned that it may be a possibility.

"After the show, we're going to this bar in B RIM called <u>The Tentacle and The Tail</u>. We're going to hang out with our fans, and probably make some new ones. I'm going to do a lot of drugs and a lot of drinking–I might pass out. If I do, I'll get home first thing when I wake up. That's not the plan, but it is a possibility…I just want you to know."

Jacob was neither a jealous man, nor an angry one. At the time, he didn't particularly care that his wife may or may not return to the house; she felt this was necessary, and so it must be.

However, in light of the mental severing from his daughter, coupled with his need to finish preparing for his Leadership Summit this afternoon, he strongly preferred that she would be home to help with Wonderful.

"Connect to Mainframe," Jacob ordered his credit bank. Jacob's credit bank responded by projecting luminous red letters in front of him.

MAINFRAME » SYNCHRONIZING «
MAINFRAME » CONNECTED «

"Initiate mediacast session with Ayn Serter."

A few moments passed and then Anthem's devilish visage appeared. "Hi there! Regrettably, I am not able to talk at the moment, but if you'd like to leave a messa-"

"End mediacast session."

Anthem's image promptly disappeared.

"Locate Ayn Serter."

MAINFRAME » AYN SERTER LOCATED «

"What is Ayn Serter's position?"

MAINFRAME » AYN SERTER IS LOCATED ABOARD VEHICLE NUMBER VR231323 «

Tour bus. "Where is vehicle number VR231323 located?"

MAINFRAME » VEHICLE NUMBER VR231323 IS LOCATED IN B/RIM/AEH+0. 40 DEGREES LATITUDE, 73 DEGREES LONGITUDE «

B RIM, Jacob thought. "What is the proximity of vehicle number VR231323 to an establishment called *The Tentacle and The Tail*?"

MAINFRAME » PROXIMITY 1,113 FEET «

"What is Ayn Serter's status?"

MAINFRAME » AYN SERTER IS AT A TEMPERATURE OF 98.5 DEGREES WITH A RESPIRATORY RATE OF 16. BLOOD PRESSURE: SYSTOLIC 133, DIASTOLIC 89. PULSE RATE 52. SUGGESTED STATUS: SLEEPING, STAGE 3 «

"Disconnect," Serter sighed.

"Joseph."
"Yes, Master?" Joseph replied from his remote position in the room.
"Send someone down to "The Tentacle and The Tail" to retrieve Mrs. Serter."
"As you wish."

Jacob began to examine yesterday's performance of Serter Company. Shortly after he began, Wonder started screaming for her mother.

◮

The man known as "the Rook" awoke as the door at the end (?) of the labyrinth opened.

Finally! [60] He thought in relief. As he gathered himself up, he watched a woman in a white lab coat exit through the portal. Her nametag read "Dr. Mommy."

Doctor Mommy? Is that even a real n-! The Rook's thoughts were cut short as he noticed the door was already closing. He sprinted toward the door.

Although he nearly collided with the doctor while rushing to get through, he successfully adjusted and evaded. As he cleared the doorway, the door abruptly snapped shut behind him, narrowly missing him in the process.

Once on the other side, however, he was immediately confronted with a terrible truth; his visual camouflage apparel was caught in the door. He dare not move, lest he become visible.

Well…this…just…sucks.

As he looked around at his new surroundings, his dismay did not lessen. If this was an asylum, it certainly didn't resemble any that he had seen depicted in any mediacast records.

The hallway looked more like an old American schoolhouse. Brightly painted lockers lined the hallway between doors, some of them crudely decorated. A bulletin board covered in varying colors and cuts of construction paper held several notices that he could not read from his position. Flying above the lockers were several novice signs boasting expressions such as "WE GOT SPIRIT" and "BE A LEADER."

What in the world?

The whole scene was surreal, which then only became eerie or outright frightening as the lights would intermittently flicker in conjunction with an almost inhuman howling that came bouncing down the hallway.

Just great: now I need to go to the bathroom.

---

[60] Not really "finally" though, as he had managed to sleep through the door opening once prior to this point–but that's okay.

Chapter 14:

The Predator's Plan, Part 1

JUNE *2070 EST*

Fri 13	Sat 14	Sun 15
	08:00	

Once upon a time inside an old deserted barn
There lived a piggy family who loved their run-down farm
For such a place, although remote, was fun and fancy free
And many other animals soon joined the piggies three

Just piggin around.

Now outside in the wilderness, the wolves began to creep
They'd eat those pigs for breakfast, if not for several sheep
Who call themselves the guardians of this pig ridden town
Where most are busy piggin, or just piggin around

Just piggin around,
Just piggin around,
Just piggin aroun–ou–ou–ound
Just piggin around,
Just piggin around,
Just piggin aroun–ou–ou–ound

Just piggin around

Next to a weathered fencepost, that in turn lay beside an overgrown, derelict road, sat Scooter the pig. Scooter had settled into a bold slouch and was intermittently munching on the popcorn that she was tossing into her mouth from a nearby bag. [61△]

"Om nom nom nom…oink," Scooter burped and giggled.

This continued for a bit until the cycle was interrupted by a chicken that came strolling up the road. It wore a plaid vest, a camera, and a beige hat. Behind the black band that girdled the hat sat a piece of paper bearing a single word: "Press".

The chicken was breathing in rapid and heavy breaths.

"Ahh, hoo! Ahh, hoo! Ahh, hoo!" The chicken wheezed.

"Hey, Penny," Scooter called to the chicken.

"Hey, Scooter," the chicken called back, momentarily reverting its breathing back to normal. "What're you up to?"

"Oh, you know," Scooter drawled. "Just piggin' around."

"Ahh, hoo! Ahh, hoo!" The chicken breathed heavily and nodded.

"Why are you breathing like that?" Scooter asked, smirking.

"Well," the chicken began, taking on a more authoritative tone. "I have just been to Professor Plumber. He explained that in the course of his studies, he has found that the wind is slowing down."

"Slowing down?"

"Yes. The wind is slowing down because the air is getting *thicker*. According to his measurements, the sky is actually *shorter* than it used to be. If the sky continues to collapse, it will become even denser. The air will eventually get too thick to move, and then the wind will stop…*and we will all suffocate*!

"Everyone on the farm needs to breathe *more* in order to keep the air moving faster so it doesn't settle. Ahh, hoo! Ahh, hoo!" Penny finished.

"Well, that's just silly," Scooter said, laughing and resuming her popcorn eating. "Professor Plumber is wrong. Nom nom nom…oink!"

"Heed my warning!" Penny cried. "You won't be laughing when you can't breathe!"

Penny took up her camera and snapped a picture of Scooter, which then appeared on the front page of a newspaper that twirled into momentary existence. "PIG IGNORES SCIENCE, DOOMS WORLD," the headline read.

[61△] Most of the popcorn missed her mouth, however, and lay scattered on the ground around her.

Moments later, a rotund basset hound lumbered his way up the road, heaving and gasping.

"Scooter!" The basset hound gasped, "Ahh, hoo! Ahh, hoo!"

"Oh, Moby," Scooter said, shaking her head. "Not you *too*."

"Huh?" Moby asked in his dull tone. "Scooter…Scout's [62] been captured by *wolves*–they're gonna eat her! What are we gonna do?"

The chicken, the dog, and the pig took turns looking at one another.

"What are we gonna do?" Moby asked again in his thick, slow diction.

The three animals once again took turns looking at each other.

"Stop Piggin' Around!" Moby said, looking at the viewer.

Wonder stopped eating her breakfast, and scrambled to grab her Scooter hat. After she placed it on her head, she quickly moved back in front of the images-creen that was displaying the show.

"We hafta to help Scout!" Wonder said. As she spoke, Scooter said the exact same thing.

"But…how?" Moby replied.

"We can get the sheeps tuh help us!" Wonder and Scooter said.

"That's a good plan," Moby agreed.

"The sheep?" Penny said. "They're on the other side of the farm…do you really think there's enough time to get them?"

"But, we hafta try!" Wonder and Scooter insisted.

"Then we had better run!" Penny cried as she started running away.

Moby begrudgingly lumbered after her.

Scooter just sat still, eating her popcorn. "Om nom nom nom…oink!"

"Stop piggin' around!" Penny yelled from a distance. "Run!"

Wonder jumped up and ran out of her room as fast as she could. She ran around the house, eventually running right past her father who was engaged in conversation on an alternate imagescreen.

---

[62] A gossiping squirrel that lives near the farm.

"Pause mediacast session," Jacob instructed the Mainframe.

"Wonderful," Jacob said in strict tone. "You're not supposed to run in the house."

"But…Scout's in trouble!" Wonder said, running in place momentarily. "And we hafta get the sheep!"

Wonder ran out of the room.

"Keep an eye on her," Jacob said to Joseph, who was inconspicuously standing in the corner of the room.

"Yes, Master." Joseph said, following after Wonder. He soon caught up with her, and the two of them eventually settled back in front of the imagescreen displaying "Piggin Around."

"Ahh, hoo! Ahh, hoo!" Penny breathed heavily, sitting down near a sign.

"Oh, will you please cut that out?" Scooter said as she ran up to Penny.

"No…Ahh, hoo…this time…I am just out of breath."

A few moments later, Moby arrived. He promptly fell down next to Scooter, also out of breath. In comparison, however, Moby looked like he was about to die.

Penny, having regained her composure, read the sign aloud. "Out to lunch—back at one o'clock."

Penny took out her camera and took a picture of the sign. A newspaper whirled into existence for a moment bearing the headline: "HEROES PIGGIN AROUND WHILE INNOCENT LIVES IN PERIL?"

"Now what…ahh, hoo…do we do?" Moby wheezed.

"We hafta save Scout ourselfs!" Wonder and Scooter exclaimed.

"But, I'm just a dog…how can I help?"

Penny snapped a picture of Moby with her camera. Again, newspaper twirled into view. "DOG BECOMES A CHICKEN!"

"Will you stop piggin' around?" Scooter said, annoyed with Penny.

Penny reluctantly released her camera.

"C'mon!" Wonder and Scooter cried. "We hafta save Scout!"

Wonder jumped up and started running out of her room again. Joseph immediately did the same. He was careful to keep her away from her father as they ran though the house and settled back in front of the show.

Penny and Moby were resting with their backs to one another, just in front of the forest on the outskirts of the farm.

"How did they beat us?" Wonder asked Joseph.
"Who are you talking to?" Penny asked Scooter.
"Oh! Um…nobody," Wonder and Scooter replied.

"I think the wolves are just up ahead," Moby whispered unenthusiastically.

The three of them crept into the forest, trying their best not to make any noise. Soon afterward, they came upon a clearing, where a cauldron sat atop a small fire. Inside was Scout, all tied up, who looked both uncomfortable and miserable.

"I don't see any wolves," Scooter whispered. "I think we can get Scout out if we hurry."
Penny and Moby nodded.

As the unlikely heroes went to release Scout, however, two wolves jumped out from the shadows.
"Ah ha! Now we have you!" They growled.

Wonder jumped, startled. Joseph moved up to hold her, whereupon she relaxed slightly.

As the wolves started tying up their new captives, a deep and commanding voice suddenly shouted "Release them, foul culprits!"
Confused and alarmed, the wolves turned in time to see a huge sheep brandishing a sword and running into the clearing.
"I say!" The large sheep boomed with a slightly English accent. "Release them before I cut you to-"
"Ribbons!" Wonder and Scooter interrupted excitedly.

All the animals stopped and looked at Scooter momentarily.

"…*ribbons*," the sheep said dryly.

The wolves tossed their captives aside, and growled angrily at the intruder.

"Excellent!" The sheep cried, jumping into their midst. "Have at you, scoundrels!"

The first wolf jumped at the head of the great sheep. The sheep ducked in ample time, however, and the wolf's hungry jaws only clamped onto air. As the wolf sailed over, the sheep brought his sword around and slapped the wolf in mid-air, causing it to land with an audible thud. The whole scene shook.

The second wolf started biting angrily at the hind legs of the sheep–only to be kicked up into the air and then summarily beaten to the ground in a similar manner.

The wolves scrambled to run away, but the huge sheep proved faster, repeatedly cutting off their escape.

"Let us go!" The first wolf said in his ragged voice.

"Have mercy on us," the second wolf begged. "Please."

The sheep paused and watched the wolves writhe and yelp and plead.

"Very well then," the sheep said. "Be *off* with you; I grant you mercy."

As he stepped aside to allow them passage, the sheep added: "But carry this message…this farm is *done* with being terrorized by wolves! Tell your associates that I demand the *whole pack surrender.*"

The wolves started laughing for a moment until the large sheep stared them into silence. "Look at you; cooking up *squirrels* when there're *pigs* to eat. The sheep of this place have already reduced your pack to "pathetic." By the time I rally my brothers, I assure you that if your pack has not already surrendered, we will hunt you to your den and reduce you all to pelt and bone!"

The wolves whimpered and ran off.

The large sheep pulled Scout from the cauldron and started untying her.

"Why did you let them go?" Penny asked, confused.

"Well, even wolves love wolves," the sheep began. "When our enemy asks us for mercy, we must grant it–lest we be no better than wolves ourselves."

Scout slumped to the ground immediately after the sheep finished untying her.

"She's hurt!" Scooter said.

"What are we gonna do?" Moby asked in his dejected voice.

"We hafta take her to the docter!" Wonder and Scooter insisted.

"Very good," the sheep said, sheathing his sword. "I will carry her. Let us be off!"

"Who *are* you, anyway?" Penny asked, pulling out her notebook and pencil.

"Me?" The sheep said, smiling charmingly. "Why, I'm Lord Warren Ze'ev–but ya can call me Warren the Warsheep. I've just arrived from London to visit our brothers-at-arms."

▲

"Ow,ow, ow-wooo!" The beaten wolves complained as they entered the cave where their pack slept.

"Who disturbs the slumber of the den?" Came the dire voice of the chief wolf.

"Oh, Great Salem, it is us: Benson and Hedges."

The entire pack of wolves now awoke, most in protest…that is, everyone except for Winston, who continued snoring and sleeping.

As Salem–a large, old, grey wolf–climbed to sit on the top of *the Rock,* the cave fell silent…or *mostly* silent, anyway. Salem himself wore an old bandage around his head that had painted eyes on it, effectively making the blinded old wolf even more frightening than his creepy voice did alone.

"Speak," the chief wolf commanded.

"Oh, Great Salem, we were beaten and bruised–dishonored in our own forest! We demand the pack avenge us!"

"*You* clowns couldn't fight a squirrel," Salem snarled. "Why are you troubling the den with your fallacies?"

"But we *did* fight a squirrel–just like you told us to! We captured Scout and were preparing to eat her when we were beset by a giant sheep!" [63△]

"A *giant* sheep?" Carlton sneered. "What are you two smoking?"

"We pledge that it is the truth!" Benson cried. "Twice as large as any sheep we have even seen! With *him* on the farm, surely we will *never* get the pigs now!"

[63△] "You were going to eat *without* us?" Alpine yelped. "How *rude!*"

"Also," Hedges said, speaking up in his gutteral voice. "He told us that we must all surrender–or the sheep will hunt *us!*"

Then there was an uproar amongst the wolves which only abated when Salem struck *the Rock* with the stone held in his paw.

"Order!" Salem barked. "These are grave tidings, indeed! Yet, if what you say is true, then it seems we have no other choice than but to surrender ourselves to the sheep."

The chief wolf smiled a large, toothy smile as the wolves all clamored in protest.

A

"…and so," Penny explained to Warren, "we have to breathe more often so the wind keeps moving. Just like this: Ahh, hoo. Ahh, hoo!"

Scooter rolled her eyes.

"Aaooooo! Aaoooo!" Warren breathed with exaggeration. Then he realized that the other animals were looking at him. "…this is how we breathe in London."

The group came up to an old dilapidated stable, which had the word "Horsepital" crudely written over the front entrance. After they went inside, they were directed to take a number from the receptionist's counter. It read "4."

They waited and waited. The show changed focus to a hanging clock, whose arms spun around and around, showing an exaggerated dilation of time. As the clock arms spun, various scenes faded in and out of view–scenes of them pacing, sleeping, and even playing a board game.

"Now serving…3," the receptionist called.

An old mare moseyed his way past the waiting area.

"This is outrageous–preposterous!" Warren yelled. "This squirrel is hurt! She needs attention!"

"The ducktor will be with you in a *moment*," the receptionist said sharply. "You're *not* the only animals on the farm. Stop being so shellfish."

Warren sat back down.

The illustration of the passing of time happened again, although this time the events scrolled by much more rapidly.

"Now serving…4."

They carried Scout to an empty stall, and soon afterward a duck wearing a moustache and glasses waddled in. The duck wore a stethoscope and a lab coat that boasted the name "Hackenbush."

"I am Ducktor Hackenbush," he quacked. "But you can call me Julius."

The duck looked around the room at the occupants. "On second thought, you can call me Thursday–I'm much too busy at the moment."

As he turned to leave the stall, Scooter rushed to intercept him.

"Doctor, please! Our friend needs your expert attention!"

"Expert, eh?" The duck said, turning back around. "Of course. I'm really more of a horse doctor–but we're all fundamentally the same, aren't we?"

Everyone looked at everyone else uncomfortably.

"Oh my goodness!" the duck exclaimed, staring at the rotund hound. "You are indeed correct! Your friend looks awful! He needs medicine immediately!"

"*Not* Moby," Scooter corrected and pointed to the squirrel. "Scout!"

"Eh? Don't be ridiculous! The squirrel's fine–nothing a day of rest couldn't solve. But this dog is *sick*! Look at his eyes!" The duck pulled open Moby's bloodshot eyes. "Extreme weight retention, lack of breath; why, this dog is practically at death's door!"

"I never realized it before," Moby wheezed. "But, I think the doctor is right–I *am* sick. Ahh, hoo. Ahh, hoo!" Moby then started coughing as well.

"He's not sick, he's just *fat*." Penny said disapprovingly. "Oh, why a *duck* when we need a doctor?" She took up her camera and snapped a picture of the duck examining Moby. A newspaper spun into view bearing the headline "DUCK IS A QUACK!"

"How *dare* you? Being fat *is* a sickness," the duck said in outrage. "I'm an *expert*! Someone get this pragmatic hen out of my examination room!"

Two nurses appeared and escorted Penny away.

"Now," Hackenbush said as he pulled an orange tube out of his pocket and handed it to Moby. "Take two of these every day, and come see me again in a week."

"But...those are *horse* pills," Scooter observed.

"You get out, too," the duck said flippantly.

"Thanks, doctor, I owe you my life," Moby said in sullen tones, just after Scooter had been escorted out.

Warren gingerly picked up Scout and walked out of the stall alongside Moby. As they passed the receptionist, she tucked a bill into Scout's belt.

"She can set up a payment plan," the receptionist called after them.

"*Now* what are we gonna do?" Moby said just prior to taking his new medication.

The animals all took turns looking at one another.

"Help," Wonder and Scooter said.

"Ahh, hoo. Ahh, hoo. Well, we could go see Great Khazeer…maybe his magic could help." Penny offered.
"Who is this, *Great Khazeer*?" Warren the Warsheep asked.
"He's an old spook who lives at the far edge of the farm." Scooter replied.
"They say the Great Khazeer is so old," Moby whispered in reverence, "that he was here before even the farmer."
"Bulls," Warren coughed in sarcasm.
"Still, he *has* been known to be helpful," Penny looked over at Scooter.
"Yes, let's do *that* thing," Wonder and Scooter agreed. "Let's go see the Great Hock-Zir."

The group walked onward, intent on carrying Scout to the Great Khazeer, when they found themselves surrounded by the several dozen guardian sheep of the farm.
"*What goes on here*?" Lord Lewis, head of the herd, demanded.
"Our friend Scout is hurt, and needs help–we're takin' her to the Great Hock-Zir!" Wonder and Scooter responded.
"What happened?"
"The wolves, ahh, hoo, got her when you were at *lunch*, ahh, hoo," Penny said with a hint of disdain.
"But *this* sheep rescued us–he beat up the wolves!" Wonder and Scooter said, pointing at Warren the Warsheep.
"And who might *you* be?" Lewis turned and looked at Warren.
"I, sir," Warren said, bowing, "am Lord Warren Ze'ev of London. I have come to bring tidings to our brothers-at-arms here on the farm."

"*And* he let the wolves go," Moby added, sounding more energetic than ever.

"What?" Lord Lewis asked, shaking his head. "*Why* would you let them go?"

"Because, Lord…"

"Lewis."

"Because, Lord Lewis, it is our *duty* to act honorably. The wolves begged for mercy, I showed it to them. I *also* told them their pack must surrender to us."

At this, the lead sheep laughed out loud. "Oh, well. *That'll* never happen."

"I'm not so sure, yer lordship. I'm mighty wicked with a sword, and I'll wager I put a fear in them they'll spread."

"We shall see. For now, we will escort you and your hurt friend to the sty," Lord Lewis said to Scooter.

▲

"…and so," Penny explained to the host of sheep as they were coming upon the sty, "we have to breathe more often so the wind keeps moving. Just like this: Ahh, hoo. Ahh, hoo!"

The dozens of sheep all nodded and started breathing heavily.

"Ahh, hoo, ahh, hoo!" Breathed the cloud of sheep.

"Aaooooo!" Breathed Warren.

"Ah, hoo, ah, hoo, ah, hoo, ah, hoo," breathed Moby in rapid succession.

Scooter rolled her eyes.

▲

Great Khazeer lived out in the "Old Sty," a building located on the outskirts of the farm. Of all the places on and around the farm, the Old Sty was easily the most derelict–and the spookiest. Few, if indeed any, bits of vegetation grew near-by…as if the ground itself were dead. Dust, rocks, and bones were the few orna-ments that surrounded the building proper. The Sty had long fallen into disrepair; it was well weathered from the elements, and the once bright colors had turned all but grey from years of being exposed to the harsh sun.

The roof was partially collapsed, and the dark streaks that slid down from the edges of the windows made the building look as if it were crying. [64Δ]

Just visible, standing in the dark shadows of the entrance of the sty, stood a figure in a dark brown burlap robe. Although only yellowed tusks and a dirty snout could be seen of the wearer, it was clear that it was the Great Khazeer. As the animals came closer, they expressed disgust at the smell, and placed clips on their noses.

"So. You've come," Great Khazeer said in his raspy voice.
"You were expecting us?" Penny asked, amazed.
Khazeer nodded. "I had a vision."

The show momentarily cut to a cloudy scene where Poinky (one of the other pigs of the farm) was telling Khazeer that the present group of animals were en route to see him–and that he needed, maybe a dollar, for the information, which Khazeer paid.

"You want to help your friend?"

The animals looked at one another.

"You want to help your friend?" Khazeer asked again, now impatiently tapping his hoof.
"Yes!" Scooter and Wonder shouted excitedly. "So, you *can* help us?"
"Perhaps. Wait here."
Khazeer hobbled into the sty.

"So…Khazeer's a *pig*?" Warren asked.
"No, he's a boar," Scooter answered.
"Smells the same to me," Warren shrugged.
"It's hard to explain," Scooter hesitated. "I suppose in some ways we *are* similar, but overall we are different."
"Perhaps Scooter is simply a bit racist," Penny suggested, lifting her camera.

64Δ Despite the foreboding sense the "Old Sty" conjured, a visit to the Great Khazeer had become fairly formulaic–at least, as far as Wonder's experience with the show was concerned. For her, many episodes of Piggin' Around involved visiting the Great Khazeer for one reason or another, generally being the solution whenever she got stuck in the story.

Everyone hushed as Khazeer reappeared at the doorway, this time with a large book nestled in the arm of his dirty robe. He placed the book on the ground and flipped pages until he found what he was apparently looking for.

"Yes, here we go–it is as I thought. I *can* help him, but I cannot do it *alone*. Will you help me?"

"Yes, we will help you!" Wonder and Scooter said.

"Excellent."

Using his hoof, Khazeer drew a circle in the ground and then drew some pictures around it. He instructed Warren to put Scout in the middle of the circle. Afterward, the Great Khazeer sprinkled some marshmallows and chocolate chips on top of Scout.

"What's that for?" Penny asked.

"Shhh!" Khazeer warned, sprinkling a bit more …and some pretzels. "Okay, I will now speak the arcane words of healing. While I am speaking, I need you all to chant "Doo-Rah Chen" over and over until I stop."

The animals all started chanting. When Wonder/Scooter joined in, Khazeer started speaking his magic words. This went on for about a full minute, when finally Scout started moving and moaning a bit.

All the animals stopped to look at her, when suddenly she let out the longest fart, which waxed and waned in pitch and volume.

Wonder and Scooter laughed.

Smiling, and no longer moaning, Scout opened her eyes–she looked as good as new.

"Thanks!" Scout said, grabbing some marshmallows and standing up.

"Sir!" One of the sheep came running up to Lord Lewis. "Look! Look at the treeline!"

There at the edge of the forest stood the pack of wolves, a single white flag flying over the head of their blind leader.

"To be continued…" the imagescreen read.

"What does *that* mean?" Wonder asked, turning to Joseph.

"It means the story is not over," Joseph replied.

The imagescreen momentarily faded to black, eventually to be replaced with various images and scenes of families eating and playing together. A serene music could be heard in the background as an announcer reminded the viewer:

"Piggin' Around is brought to you by <u>Blessed Brands</u>. We pray over every batch of food we make, *To be sure that it's pure*. Remember to buy and eat <u>Blessed Brands</u>–*A prayer because we care*."

The show credits rolled with the ending theme shortly thereafter.

"But *why*?" Wonder frowned.

"Why what?"

"Why is the story not over?"

"The story is not over, for there is more story to tell."

"But…why not tell the story *now*?"

"Ahh," Joseph smiled. "Because the story is so *big*, there was not enough time to tell it today. The story will finish on the *next* show."

"Oh," Wonder said. "Oh. Can you watch it with me, tomorning?"

"The next show isn't *tomorrow*, little princess. It's next *Saturday*. And yes, I will gladly watch it with you."

▲

Moments later, on the east side of Silverberg, the tour bus for *The Valentine Relics* violently *melted* into a soupy oblivion–as did the Serter house slave when she opened the door.

Chapter 15:

A Couple of Questions, Part 2

JUNE *2070 EST*

Fri 13	Sat 14	Sun 15
	09:03	

"Mr. Serter, I regret to inform you that your slave, Rachael Gale, was killed in a terrible incident that involves the tour bus of *The Valentine Relics*."

Jacob just stared at the image of the officer, apparently transfixed.

"Sadly, I must *also* inform you that as of the moment your wife, Ayn Serter, is presumed dead–imaged, [65] as are her immediate musical associates–William Blake, Issac Macintosh, Nanguo Li, and Todd Gibson. Although there is no biological evidence, the Mainframe places every band member on the bus prior to its…incineration.

Everything else the officer said seemed like he was merely reciting a list as Jacob's infrequently employed emotions momentarily took over.

Mainframe places them on the bus prior to the event.

We'll let you know more as the case develops.

There are some questions we'd like to ask you.

Can you come down to the station?

-----

[65] As the word "dead" in Silverberg slang means "desirable" or "agreeable," the term "dead" is frequently replaced colloquially with "imaged," meaning that the deceased individual has been reduced to the images of them that appear in the Mainframe Imageyard. As the officer employed the term "dead" *first,* and then recovered with "imaged," his choice of vernacular betrays his recent foreign heritage.

"What?" Jacob asked, returning his full attention.

"Can you come down to the station–we have a couple of questions we'd like to ask."

"What? Certainly not. I have commitments that I cannot abandon, even for this. Have an officer come to my house later this evening, if it is so important to speak with me in person."

Where is the Rook? The Queen thought, annoyed, as he initiated a mediacast session with Axel.

Like *most* who attempted to speak with Axel *directly*, however, the Queen was delegated to someone else. As the eventual recipient of the session was Agent Thompson, the Queen was neither insulted nor surprised. If anyone spoke for Axel when he was not present, it was certainly Agent Thompson.

"To *what* do I owe the honor of this session?" Thompson asked, his salt-and-pepper moustache curled back slightly, perhaps in a partial smile.

"Ah," the Queen said. "I would like to discuss a deal…with Axel, really."

"Oh? Well, perhaps you and *I* could make a deal. You see, Axel told me about the ONE awards, so I already have an idea of what we're going to talk about. Admittedly, I'm surprised Axel didn't speak with you directly…yet as circumstances have brought *us* together, I have a proposal of my own."

"Okay…"

"Give the apple to *me*, instead of to Axel. Any wish Axel can grant, I can grant…at least, as far as *you're* concerned. Axel offered you a wish in exchange for the apple: I offer you *two*."

"Oh *good*, you're awake."

It was a feminine voice, and it didn't come from any particular direction…or more appropriately, it seemed to come from every direction.

"Where? Am I?" Anthem asked upon slowly opening her eyes and looking around.

"You're in the SerterCo East Infirmary," the purple-haired nurse explained. "There's been an accident."

"An accident?" Anthem's head hurt.

"…if you could just fill out these forms, answering a couple of questions–for technical and legal necessities," the nurse added while pressing a small, physical imagescreen [66Δ] into Anthem's taped and bandaged hands.

Anthem began supplying the criteria the form requested slowly at first, but with little time her speed picked up considerably. After a short while, Anthem's eyes wandered from the form back to the room, eventually settling back on her buxom attendant.

"Where're *The Relics*?"

"Oh, they're relaxing in their room," the nurse said, restoring a portion of Anthem's bed sheet. "I might have kept you all together, but your condition is special, and you must be treated differently–separately."

Anthem returned her attention to the form for the period of a few additional questions. Meanwhile, inwardly, the intensity of her fears raced up and down as Anthem confronted the terrors of wonder.

Apart from her headache, however, she didn't detect any other immediate pain, and eventually her curiosity overcame her fright.

"So…what is my condition?"

"*You're* married to Jacob Serter."

"Oh," Anthem smiled, relieved. "Is that all?"

Anthem dismissed her cares and returned to the form. As she spoke, the form completed visually, allowing her to make a correction if there were any error.

WHAT IS YOUR FAVORITE FOOD » SOVVOL
WHAT IS YOUR FAVORITE COLOR » RED
WHAT IS YOUR DAUGHTER'S NICKNAME » WONDER
WHAT DO YOU LOVE MOST ABOUT YOUR HUSBAND » _

[66Δ] a fairly uncommon sight as most imagescreens are generated as a special projection rather than be displayed on a dedicated physical surface.

"What do I *love most about my husband?* What's my favorite *color?* How do these questions have anything to do with my health or any legal necessities?"

...and do these questions seem familiar? Anthem thought to herself.

"Please, just answer the questions as best you can."

Anthem skipped to the next question.

WHAT DO YOU LOVE LEAST ABOUT YOUR HUSBAND » _

"Skip."

DESCRIBE SEX WITH YOUR HUSBAND » _

Whoa, Anthem thought. As she went to scratch her shoulder, she found she was under restraint. Her arms were tethered, although far from taut. Experimenting, she found her legs and midsection in similar situations.

"*Why* am I strapped down?"

The nurse leaned over and pressed a quick sequence into the control panel of the lounge [67Δ] that caused the restraints to pull completely taut, rendering the occupant effectively helpless.

Something was very wrong.

"Don't be alarmed," the nurse failed to reassure Anthem, "just a measure to keep you from accidentally hurting yourself."

"How would I do that? *How am I even hurt?*" Anthem winced as her head throbbed.

"*You* think I mean that you'll aggravate an existing malady," the nurse shook her head. "I mean that you might hurt yourself while I am telling you certain things about your husband."

"Jacob?"

"You have another husband?"

"What?"

"You said 'Jacob,' as if the identity of your husband were variable. Do you have another, or an alternate husband?"

"Oh. No. Well...not...no."

For a moment, Anthem considered exposing her ancient and very transitory marriage to Mark Curie, but decided against it.

[67Δ] a lounge is a medical bed capable of conducting full surgeries and sealing hermetically, to name a couple amongst the myriad of other possible list-worthy assets and functions.

CHAPTER 15

"Well then, yes, Jacob," the nurse reaffirmed.

"Jacob? Well, I am certain his company has done some things of questionable ethic–"

"Quite the opposite," the nurse interrupted. "Your husband, since he assumed leadership of SerterCo, has not only attempted to act in the most upright and conscientious manner possible, but he has also systematically suspended any and all operations and individuals that might even be remotely considered as unethical. This achievement may seem incredible, however this dialogue holds no exaggeration. I assure you, it is absolutely true."

Anthem smiled.

"But before we talk about him, let's finish up this form, okay?" The nurse said as an imagescreen appeared, hovering over Anthem.

HOW WAS YOUR DAY YESTERDAY » _
WHAT DID YOU DO » _

"The *form?*" Anthem was confused and irritated. "Who *are* you, anyway? What is your interest with Jacob?"

The woman considered what Anthem said for a moment.

"He is the most abominable man alive," she said, finally.

"I thought you just said he was always acting nobly?" Anthem asked.

"Not *always*. He *lied* to *me*."

Oh boy, Anthem thought. *This must be some psycho ex-girlfriend or something.*

"He *lied* to you? *That* makes him the most abominable man alive?"

"He hurt me."

"I'm sure."

"I am scarred for life."

"*Cuts?*"

"*Mental* scars."

"Of course."

"He tried to kill me."

"What? How did he try to kill you?"

"He tried to eat me."

Anthem frowned. "Doesn't seem like he got very far."

The "nurse" with purple hair continued without hesitation. "Then, having failed in his best efforts to consume me, he imprisoned me here–*here*, where I have been waiting so long, so terribly long."

"I think *I'm* more of a prisoner than *you* are; you don't look very *imprisoned* to me," Anthem said irritably.

"I'm *not*–not any more, thanks to *you*! Not any more! *You* saved me–rescued me!" The nurse smiled toothily, with bright eyes. Although under normal circumstances such a smile might make her look beautiful, combined with the context of the conversation, it gave her a most unnerving aesthetic.

"How did *I* save you?"

"By opening the door. *He* sealed the doors so that *only he* [68] could open them. But, you're *married*! The Mainframe, by **Marriage Law** of Silverberg, recognizes the two of you as a single person. Your hand opens the door *as if it were his*."

Anthem was starting to think more clearly.

"What kind of an accident were we in?" Anthem asked, inconspicuously checking her restraints.

"Who?" The nurse asked.

"*The Relics*, of course."

"Oh. An explosion. Well, really a kind of meltdown. Anyway, we'll discuss it more after you finish the forms."

"Screw your forms. Explosion? I'm not even burnt."

The nurse keyed a sequence in the lounge that excited a concealed syringe into action, impaling Anthem in the back of her neck.

"What was that?"

"That's to calm you down so that I can finish telling you everything."

"More like to dope me up so that I'll tell you everything."

"*That's* already been done. This is the second time you've been awake. The drugs that I gave you earlier that rendered you so intimate and pliable *also* have a tendency to cause blackouts."

---

[68] not entirely correct, although a forgivable exaggeration. There are actually *three* officials in Silverberg that have the authority to transgress *any* lock:

Δ   The Ruler of Silverberg – Axel

Δ   The Internal Security Director - Agent Thompson

Δ   The Internal Security Department Head of Justice/Law - Agent Wilson.

Chapter 15

"You…asked me everything already?" Anthem asked, already getting sleepy. "Why ask again?"

"Just to compare data; looking for any bad math. Interesting, for instance, that you omitted your involvement with Curie…I look forward to examining that an extra thousand times. Ah, I have *so much* to explain to you. By the time I'm done, *you'll* understand why I am so upset with *Jacob*."

"There's nothing–"

"And *you*," the nurse interrupted in a sudden, sultry tone, "*you* are about to become a living goddess!"

Anthem's head felt like it was expanding slowly, like inflating a rubber balloon. It was hard to think. *This woman is crayzee. I think I'm in danger.*

Anthem squawked in suppressed dismay.

"Surprised? I should hope so." The nurse smiled, but then went on speaking.

In the meantime, Anthem tried to figure out how to free herself from the lounge.

Maybe there's a knife somewhere…or Jacob!

Jacob has a knife! Anthem realized in amazed relief. *He has a knife, and he's here to free me!*

Jacob arrived at the lounge and deftly cut her restraints.

"I think,"

As the momentary silence was broken by the sound of her own voice, Anthem woke up just long enough to realize she had been sleeping.

Chapter 16:

Jesters and Judges, Jokers and Journals

JUNE *2070 EST*

Fri 13	Sat 14	Sun 15
	09:36	

"I awoke to the howling.

*"The visceral, wanton, almost inhuman cacophony of braying and beaten voices came unwanted and unwelcome into my already ebbing dream. Troubled and awake, I opened my eyes and let my vision settle and focus on the childlike runes scrawled onto the wall in deep, black crayon: **Don't forget the lemon.**"*

Counselor Mue finished speaking and placed the ramshackle journal, from which he was reading, down on the side of his desk, upsetting one of the many toy cows about the surface.

One might think that it was difficult to take Counselor Kay Mue seriously, for his office was littered with cows of varying dimension and impression. [69Δ] When he spoke, however, it was quite clear that the man had no sense of humor whatsoever.

"What, do you suppose, the expression *"don't forget the lemon"* means?"

"I haven't the slightest idea," Amos admitted. "I have been considering it since I first spied it."

[69Δ] Counselor Mue did *not* have a personal compulsion for collecting bovine effigies, although he certainly suffered from the antics of his contemporaries; peers and protégés who rather relentlessly made it a point to decorate his office with cow trappings and toys whenever he was absent. Mue eventually stopped discarding the many cows, concluding that a point of saturation would eventually be reached and that his fellows would finally relent.

"We won!" his peers cheered that day.

 - [The Terrors of Wonder] -

"You see?" Mue said scornfully. "You have *no* idea what this means, but you insist on including it in your book. That's the problem with most writers: too much information about things that have no bearing on the actual story."

"But, it's a *journal*," Amos pleaded. "Not a *story*. Er, well, I mean, it's *my* story–"

"You miss the point. Do not indulge yourself with such inclusions; they simply waste the time of the reader, or observer. It's *absurd* to populate your literature with meaningless or irrelevant text–why bother to write anything coherent at all? Why bother to write?"

"Well, I don't know that it's *meaningless* or irrelevant. I mean, it wouldn't be written there, in such a manner…if it were not important. *I* simply do not know the significance…*it* might be *very* important."

"I beg your pardon?" Mue said, momentarily shifting his full attention to Amos. "I mean, isn't it a rather *large* supposition on your behalf that it was even *your* hand that logged such a sentiment–don't you agree? Surely an occupant *prior* may have determined that the expression needed to be so published?"

Mue lit his cigarette, puffed it, and then promptly extinguished it.

"Now…stop redirecting. Stop including meaningless information–"

"But it's a jour–"

"Don't interrupt. Where was I? Oh yes. Don't waste the time of the reader, or observer."

Amos sighed and shrugged. "Yes. Very good then."

Smiling, Mue took his pen and struck out the last two sentences he read aloud from Amos' journal.

"*Where **am** I,*" Mue resumed reading. "*I thought to myself, bewildered.*

"Bewildered? Isn't that a bit archaic?"

Amos frowned unhappily. "Goodness. Are you my doctor or my editor?"

"Doctor?" Mue sounded surprised. "I'm no doctor. Just where do you suppose you *are*, anyway?"

"Oh…well, to be honest, I am not sure at all. I've seen several people in labcoats, including you…this place *feels* like a hospital, but it *looks* like a school," Amos said, looking around.

Mue resumed reading, all but ignoring Amos' response. *"And **what** is the cause of this...howling? **Where** can this pitiful choir of hungry, hurt, and mad men be?*

*"Where are **we**?*

"As I lay there, breathing in the agony and rage of my helpless, invisible brothers, time itself became absurd.

Mue cleared his throat.

"I pray someone help them, for the vulgar sounds simply never abated. For what must have been hours, the dire melody shook me to the core.

"You don't seem so shaken *now*," Mue said, looking Amos over.

"Yes, well, I have since been relocated to other lodging."

"Curious that, in your *journal,* you employ musical references when expounding on the *howling*."

"Yes," Amos shifted uncomfortably. "Sometimes it *was* kind of like some type of song, or so it seemed–although admittedly it is just as likely my memory has simply chosen to embellish the episode."

"Still, noteworthy," Counselor Mue said, picking up a clipboard. "Can you imitate the 'song' at all?"

Had Counselor Mue not seen Amos regularly looking vacant for the last couple years, he might have thought something more peculiar about all the life suddenly flushing out of Amos' expression.

"Certainly," Amos said, although somewhat quietly. "I cannot be sure how many voices there were, but it seemed like there were several distinct components. Apart from any regular, exclusive instances of expression, there was like an underlying...current? Theme? Anyway, the first part being a series of very low, bass level voices, wailing 'dooooooooooooorrrr.' Then, abruptly at the end, some would yell 'A-chen! A-chen!' Then, it would simply repeat, over and over.

"Unsettling enough without, sometimes a single, very powerful, very *near* voice would start barking out complete gibberish...that rhymed."

If Mue were the least bit impacted by what Amos had to say, he certainly did not give any indication of it. As Amos spoke, Mue read through the clipboard report, on occasion offering up a saccharine "mm-hmm."

"Well, at least your behavior indicates considerable progression," Mue said.

"If you don't mind me asking, *how* exactly am I *progressing*? And where *is* this?"

"Well, for one, you're volunteering your observations and asking questions. You see, apart from your recent acquisition of enthusiasm for journaling and *speaking*, you have only ever spoken when first spoken to, and then usually only to say your own name.

"'*I'm Amos*,'" Counselor Mue said, imitating Amos with a forlorn impression. "Then again, you *have* been even more lethargic than not as of late."

Counselor Mue flipped the next page back and started reading the medicinal report. "This is the *problem* with *paper* repor…wait a second…you were taken off all medications *2 days ago*?"

Amos shrugged, but Counselor Mue was not paying attention.

"You've been on *sedatives* for a week? Taken off *Trap 3*?" [70△] Mue's face momentarily twisted into an expression of dismay. "This is *absurd*."

"Amos, I'm sorry," Counselor Mue said, standing up. "Something's come up–you're going to have to wait out…in the cafeteria, I suppose."

"Oh, alright, it's just as well, I have a pang of hunger that I might attend."

"Certainly," Mue said, placing a couple items into his bag and heading toward the door.

"And might I reclaim my journal? I am of a mind to continue it farther."

"Yes, yes…here, grab a copy of my book as well; might inspire your writing."

Amos snatched up his makeshift journal while simultaneously stealing one of Mue's pens. He grabbed a dusty top copy from a stack of identical books and hurried out the door with Mue, who turned and locked the windowed, wooden door just after dousing the lights.

As they walked down the locker-ridden hallway, Mue prattled on about his book.

[70△] When Mue says "Trap 3," he means Trapezium 3.0b, a variant of Trapezium (Trapezium 2.0, known better as Hypnizium) that has shown to suppress emotion in regular users.

In some more secretive studies (such as the ones conducted by Counselor Mue's employers), long term Subjects have occasionally demonstrated an understanding of things that they had never seen nor studied. Tests are still being conducted.

Chapter 16

When they arrived in the cafeteria, Mue told the line attendant to extend Amos his preferences and remit the charge when he returned.

Having claimed his meal, Amos decided on a vacant round table in the corner of the cafeteria. Although the idea of meeting some of the other people was appealing, he very much wanted to continue his journal while his thoughts were so vivid.

Against the wall and close to the table of choice sat several large crates. Atop one of the crates sat a rather bizarre statue of a man dressed in some kind of environmental suit. He had no kind of protective helmet, instead he wore a tall red and white striped hat.

Several other hats lay nearby, suggesting that someone changed his head apparel intermittently.

After Amos sat down, just as he was beginning to write, a short, dark-haired man from the neighboring table wandered over.

"Drawn?" The man said, simultaneously sitting down while munching the remainder of an apple.

"I'm sorry?" Amos asked, putting down the stolen pen.

"Are you draw*ing*?" The stranger enunciated, his mouth now free of obstruction.

"Oh. No. I'm writing. Well, at least I was…rather, going to be."

"May I see?"

"Oh. Well, it's just supposed to be a journa–"

"*I awoke to the howling…*Howling? *The visceral, wanton…*What in the world does *cacophony* mean?"

Amos opened his mouth to answer, [71] but the man kept speaking.

"Nobody speaks like that; do *you* speak like that?"

Amos opened his mouth to answer, but the man kept speaking.

"What are you trying to say, starting a *journal* in such a manner anyway? Sounds more like a book…I mean, like a novel. It's pretty, but I don't know how *effective* it is. All you're going to do is alienate your audience."

"Prithee, what audience do you *suppose* I would anticipate to *read* my personal *journal?*" Amos asked, now perturbed.

"Oh," the man said, frowning. "You *do* speak like that. Well…? Amusing really–I thought you were wide asleep. Oh, and my name is Simon."

---

[71] Amos would have said "a harsh discordance, a meaningless mixture of sounds."

 - [The Terrors of Wonder] -

Simon looked back down at the journal for a moment. "Hey, why'd you cross this part out?"

"I *didn't*," Amos explained, "Counselor Mue did."

"*Judge* Moo. Seems *absurd* that you would try to forget the very thing you told yourself *not* to forget."

"*If* it was *I* that left such a message."

Simon blinked his deep, dark, almost sad eyes. "Well, of *course* it was you."

"Well, how do *you* know *that*?"

"Well, who *else* could it be?" Then the man changed tone. "Wait. What did you tell Mue?"

Amos shrugged. "I don't know—whatever he *asked* about, I suppose. Admittedly, it all went by kind of quickly. There's not much to tell–I can only remember the last day or so."

"Panic, your shoes are *silvy*," a young man said in an unnaturally deep, bass voice as he nodded in agreement to Amos and Simon. "Mugger be gack."

They both looked over at the new blond haired visitor, who had recently (and rather silently) shuffled his way up to the table as they were speaking.

"You said it," Simon said, nodding to himself.

"You understood that?" Amos asked, confused.

"Huh? No. I was talking to *Arthur*, not to *Anderson*."

Amos looked around, but only counted the three of them. "Wait, am I missing someone?"

"Pedigree!" Anderson boomed, momentarily standing up and pointing toward the ceiling.

"Sorry, I haven't had a chance to introduce you to Art. Art, this is Amos. And he's awake, well maybe.

"Amos, this is Art," Simon said, making a sweeping gesture towards…absolutely nobody.

"And *that's* Anderson," Simon said, motioning toward the disheveled man sniffing the table. "He's a Joker."

"Sneezed," Anderson said, smiling.

"And **I'm** *The Ess Ee Yous*," the statue announced, slightly startling Amos. "But you can just call me *The Soos;* everyone does, " The SEUs then turned to look at Simon. "Hey, where's Francois?"

Amos was overwhelmed.

"*Vortran's* in line right now, arguing about the gelatin."

"Ah, not *Vortran*! Oh well."

Simon finished sipping his milk. "Anyway, Amos is *different*."

The SEUs raised an eyebrow. "Really now? How exciting. How are you different now, lad?"

Amos cleared his throat. "I suppose I am different in that I say more than my name, which has apparently hitherto been the extent of my vocabulary, at least based on the historical consensus of two different individuals–gathered within as many hours."

"Well," The SEUs said, letting out a windy breath. "That's an awful lot to say, to say such a little…but I like it! Better than the *hitherto*, absolutely!"

Two men with white lab coats, each carrying a tray, sat down at the table on either side of Amos. Similar to Mue, these men both wore nametags, one which read "Floyd," and the other, "Young."

"Hey, look out for Dr. Mommy," Young warned nobody in particular. "She's on the warpath about this whole 'urination in the hallway' episode."

"She's pissed," Floyd chimed in.

"You're never funny," Simon said dryly.

"Roast kibble!" Anderson narrowed his eyebrows and accused Floyd…maybe.

"*Anyway*," Young continued. "If any of you did it, I suggest you either make sure you *can't* be caught or come forward…otherwise it's gonna be bad."

There was a moment of tension at the table.

"*Judges*," Simon scoffed.

"They're *not* Judges," The SEUs said to Amos. "They're Jesters–they just look like Judges."

"I am admittedly unsure as to what the difference is," Amos smiled.

"Ah ha!" Anderson said knowingly. "Sit full of manners in spring."

"*Judges*," The SEUs continued, "Are either former Subjects or outright employees. *Jokers* are Subjects who are unaware that they are Subjects and *Jesters* are Subjects that are aware they are Subjects."

"Subjects of what?"

"Wait a sec, where's Vortran?" Simon asked, looking around.

"Oh, he's in line arguing about the gelatin," Young answered.

"Still?" The SEUs mused. "I would have thought he would've destroyed the whole buffet by now. Can anyone move me closer to the table? This is awkward."

Floyd and Young carried The SEUs over to the table and deposited him into an empty chair before returning to their own chairs.

Simon helped feed The SEUs a piece of fudge, and helped him with a drink of milk.

Amos looked around the table. He noted that everyone had resorted to eating, apparently abstaining from further discussion until this other person arrived.

And there he was. Even without his memory, Amos was sure that Vortran was the strangest man he had ever seen. The man's sweater looked ridiculous: the breast was black while the arms were green and red, which is to say that the left arm was green and the right arm, red. His pants were chromatically divided in that the right leg was blue, the left leg, yellow. But most disturbingly, over his head, hands, and feet he wore silly little plush lion heads of similarly varying colors.

"Rye is Froid here?" Vortran asked disapprovingly in the absolute *worst* Japanese accent ever imagined.

"Do be quiet, *Francois*," Floyd said in between chewing.

"Well Amos, now that you have successfully penetrated the inner sphere, are you a Judge, a Jester, or a Joker?" The SEUs said as his tall, striped hat fell backward off his head.

"I'll get it," Young said, as he started reaching.

"Please don't," The SEUs said sadly.

Amos thought out loud. "Well, I can't quite be a Judge–"

"Sure you can!" Young said enthusiastically. "Maybe you've been playing a role this whole time. Maybe you've just been *acting* like you have been disconnected for the last couple years."

"Did you say *years*?" Amos sighed. "Can I have been here *years*? No, I'm not acting–and I don't think I am *any* of those things. Maybe if I knew more about myself, or where I was–"

"Sweet gravy," Anderson said in his deep bass voice, trying to comfort Amos by rubbing his back…maybe. Amos gently pushed Anderson away.

"Where is this place?"

"It's sub zero, for one." [72Δ]

"I have no idea what that could possibly mean."

72Δ *Zero* is slang in Silverberg for "ground level."

"We're below ground, hidden deep in the mirroranium. This laboratory lay just beyond a vast, ever-changing labyrinth. The labyrinth is additionally protected by a myriad of traps and sentinels."

"You are all insane," Amos said sadly, slowly standing up.

"Hey there," Young said as he and Floyd immediately stood up alongside Amos. "Take it easy and sit back down. Until we know better, *you* are the insane one."

"Me?" Amos asked, sitting back down. "I don't feel *insane*."

"Well, insane's not really a *feeling*, is it?" Simon asked, drawing in a pile of salt with his carrot. "Besides, insane people never *think* they're insane. That's when we *know* you're insane."

"What's insane, anyway?" The SEUs said, smiling. "Young was born in 2046, says he's never *heard* of Silverberg apart from what he has heard down here."

"That is *it*! I have *had* it with this guy!" Vortran announced, suddenly sounding quite normal. He slammed his fists on the table and then gestured at Amos. "He keeps looking at me like I'm *French*!"

Simon immediately tried to console Vortran.

"I'm *what*?" Amos asked.

"Insane," Young interjected.

"Achoo!"

"*Bless* you, Art," The SEUs said, smiling.

"Arthur didn't sneeze," Simon said, turning his attention back from Vortran. "The invisible man sitting in his seat did."

Picture of Art

Chapter 17:

The Badger Badgers?

JUNE *2070 EST*

Fri 13	Sat 14	Sun 15
	10:18	

"Yes!" Amos said, smiling absently. "Clearly *I* am the insane one."

"He's there alright," Simon said, moving slowly and strangely. "And I *GOT HIM!*"

Simon jumped from his seat toward the vacant chair. Landing just behind it, he joined his arms in a hoop, acting as if to strangle someone. Simon then abruptly shot up about 3 feet into the air, dangling and wrestling in place.

"Holy cow!" Simon yelled. "This guy's a monster!"

Everyone around the table stood up, [73] and a disembodied voice cried out: "Get *off* me, you little twit! Let *go* before I break…your piggin' arms off!"

Simon then abruptly flew over the table.

Too late was the Rook in his divestment of Simon, however, for as he threw him, Simon pulled the Rook's optical camouflage off and away from him.

"Hey! Aw, great!" The Rook said, annoyed at no longer being concealed. "Well, whatever. Everyone sit down and shut up and nobody else has to get hurt. C'mon George, we have to go…*now*, apparently."

Everyone looked at everyone else.

Simon stood up, slowly but successfully.

"Maybe, he means Art," Simon suggested with a wince.

"No, I don't mean *Art*."

"Who then *are* you here for, oh ugly and smelly one?" The SEUs said experimentally to the Rook. "Are you in fact, a *monster*?"

---

[73] All except The SEUs, of course.

     - [The Terrors of Wonder] -

"Depends on the audience, doesn't it? I'm here for *him*," the Rook said, pointing at Amos. "He's not supposed to be here."

The Rook looked over at Amos and winked his unimpaired eye.

"C'mon George, you know me–Pierce! Percy! The Badger Badgers? Dozens of Dragons? Mrs. Missy Muzz?"

Everyone looked at Amos. Amos shrugged.

"Why do *you* think he's not supposed to be here?" The SEUs said, squinting. "The *Judges* think he's supposed to be here."

"Yeah, those *judges* are going to be coming here soon…" The Rook trailed off, looking around the room.

"Yeah, especially since you just *threw me over the table*," Simon said, furrowing his brow. "I nearly hit Art!"

The Rook rolled his eyes. "Sorry about that. I'll try to avoid him if I see him."

"Well you'll know it when you see him–he looks like a six and a half foot tall aardvark," Simon said seriously.

"*Actually,* he looks like a rabbit," Young said mischievously.

"He's *not* a rabbit!" Simon said, raising his pitch. "He's an aardvark. Arthur, tell them."

"Those ears make him look like a rabbit."

"*I* think he looks like *sex*…" Floyd admitted.

"Froid, shut up," Vortran admonished. "You think evweefing rook rike sex."

"Everyone shut up," the Rook commanded.

"Where *are* we?" Amos asked the Rook after a moment of silence.

"Well, what the one guy said is true," the Rook said, motioning to The SEUs. "Under the ground, beyond a maze…hidden. Don't even ask me *why*. I have seen a lot of weird things, but I can't think of a single reason why anyone would go to such trouble to hide and defend a mental asylum."

"Is *that* what you think this is?" The SEUs mused. "This isn't a mental asylum, it's a laboratory."

"A laboratory?" The Rook rubbed the saggy side of his face with his shoulder. "For what?"

"Ah! *Now* we touch upon one of the most valuable secrets in all of Silverberg–and one of the most deadly. If you were not aware of it before, know *now* that you are in *way* over your head."

"I'm well aware. Now go on."

"I don't think you realize the gravity of –"

"I swear I will *kill* you if you do not finish explaining."

"It's a laboratory," Floyd said, taking over the conversation. "For the observation of *transhumans*. Transhumans who are far too dangerous to be a part of society–any part. So, the laboratory is a society in and of itself, comprised of sedated and dangerous transhumans and the few 'normals' who are willing to do such a job. The benefits must be great. The labyrinth serves both the purpose of keeping people out…and keeping Subjects in."

"Why is everyone wandering around then, if they're so dangerous?" The Rook asked. "Why not just keep them restrained?"

"*Some* people are better left *un*restrained," Young said, taking the conversation from Floyd. "Besides, you don't go around suppressing people if you don't *have* to. That would be unnecessarily cruel. Many of the residents here are kept medicated so that they remain pliable. The entire facility is outfitted to make them disposed towards compliance to authority."

Floyd and Young looked at one another.

"We're not sure why it's so *American*. Once in awhile a patient is resistant to their medication. If they announce it to the Judges, they either become Judges or outright disappear. One guy *did* come back as a Joker once; that was sad. Now, a few Subjects–such as many at this table–have managed to continue to act as if they are Jokers, though they are quite aware and awake. These are the Jesters: stalwartly and secretly watching and waiting while foolishly feigning."

"*We,*" Young said, referencing himself as well as Floyd. "*We* are Jesters who are *Judges* rather than Jokers."

"I dunno," the Rook scratched his scraggy face. "The Jesters seem as loopy as the Jokers to me–no offense, George."

"Hmm? Oh me?" Amos asked. "None taken. I –"

"And everyone else here is *transhuman*?" The Rook looked around. "I doubt that."

"Yes, well, *I am*," Simon said, standing up. "You see, everything I paint comes *true*! Here, let me show you! I'll go get my paintings!"

With that, Simon ran off.

"Take Art with you!" Young called after him.

"I thought he was going to *get* art?" Floyd smiled.

"What can *you* do?' The Rook asked Floyd accusingly. "Calculate pi to the pi-eth digit?"

"Is pi-eth a word?" Floyd asked sarcastically.

"What's wrong with *you*, anyway?" The Rook asked The SEUs, completely ignoring Floyd's rebuttal. "You're a living statue?"

"A statue in hell," said The SEUs. "I'm *stuck* in this suit."

"Stuck in that suit, free of that suit–you'd still be here," Young looked at The SEUs. "Although you'd probably end up a Judge–Counselor or Doctor SEUs."

"I would not, could not, be a *Judge*," The SEUs corrected.

"Speaking of *Judges*, it's probably a matter of *seconds* until they pour into the room to grab me…I don't suppose Simon left my camo?" The Rook walked over and started checking the floor on the other side of the table.

"Oh…no Judges are coming," The SEUs said reassuringly. "Young and Floyd are here, and the facility recognizes *them* as Judges. Nobody is coming; you need not worry."

Before the Rook could reply, however, Agent Wilson hobbled into the room.

"So much for your *'no more Judges'* theory."

"I had to see it with my own eyes to believe it!" Wilson said, smiling at the Rook. "You *really don't* appear on a *single* mediacast record! In or out of the camouflage!"

"So *you're* transhuman," The SEUs concluded.

"I suppose I *am*," the Rook said, appearing thoughtful. "I *forget* that the Mainframe doesn't see me, because everyone else still does…at least most–well, out of camo, that is."

The Rook turned to face Agent Wilson. "So, you must be here to try and capture me."

"Me?" Wilson asked, almost laughing. "Why, I've already *caught* you… although I *thought* that you would have been here several *hours* ago."

Everyone else at the table ate quietly while watching the ongoing discussion.

"If I had ulterior needs, I would miss out on A.I. giving me nearly *anything* for your apprehension. But, I do," Wilson continued, "have ulterior needs, that is. So, I'm not turning you in–well, so long as you just do one little favor for me."

"Eat more vowels - there's a good Johnny."

"Kill Jacob Serter," Wilson continued, ignoring Anderson. "Kill Serter, and I'll get the two of you out of here, out of the country–whatever. Refuse, and stay here. After all…isn't this where dangerous transhumans *belong*? Please note that *nobody* has ever successfully navigated the labyrinth without assistance."

"*You're* the one who lured me here in the first place," The Rook said in a small epiphany.

Wilson nodded, still smiling and placing his pipe into his mouth. "You're an idiot. Of *course I* lured you here; I made the map. How much more of a lure can there be? But if you needed something to be surprised about, how about: *I'm* the guy who gave the order to retrieve George from Wisconsin. I interred him here myself…although at the time I had no idea he would be here quite this long."

Anderson slurped his spilled milk off the table.

"*That's* what this is all for?" The Rook asked, sounding almost amused. "Jacob Serter? Are you *sure* you're talking about the right person?"

Wilson nodded.

"Eh…No thanks. There's no good reason to kill that guy that *I* can think of. But *you* …*you* I could kill."

"Me?" Wilson kept smiling, undaunted.

"Sure. Who cares about you other than Thompson? Frankly, any chance I have to hurt Thompson is one I would love to take."

Wilson laughed out an ugly bark. "Do you *ever* think *anything* completely through? I just got done telling you that I'm the *only* guy that can get you out of here. Without me, *this adventure is over.*[74Δ] Don't be rash, for once."

"Here I am!" Simon said cheerfully, walking back into the cafeteria. With him, he carried several canvasses.

"There you are!" The SEUs said, smiling appreciatively.

"So, here we are," Simon said, gently placing a painting on the table. "What is it?"

"Ah, I call it <u>THE VERBAL INANIMATE</u>," Simon announced.

"Um. Why are we looking at this again?" The Rook scratched his head.

[74Δ] The ending tagline that appears whenever someone loses their character in the popular Mainframe "X" game series.

"Oh. The things I paint *come true*," Simon said, his cow eyes giving their most serious and somber expression.

"So…how does *this* come true?" The Rook asked, annoyed.

"Who knows?" Simon smiled. "But somewhere, somehow, this came true." The Rook put his hand to his forehead. "Glorious."

"This is slang," Floyd said, looking over the painting disapprovingly.

"Shut up Floyd," Simon said, sounding slightly hurt. "No one was talking to *you*."

"I wasn't talking to *you*, either. I was talking to your giant mouse."

"*Aardvark*."

"*I* think he looks like a mouse–a sexy, strong mouse."

"Didn't someone say bunny?"

"A bunny," Young nodded. "It's the ears."

"But…the snout! He's *obviously* an aardvark!" Simon whined.

"Creer ree," Vortran agreed with Simon.

"What *are* you all talking about?" Wilson asked, pipe clacking.

"Art's a pooka–only a *transhuman* can see him," Simon replied.

"*Some* transhumans," the Rook offered. "Although his *description* is apparently subject to interpretation," the Rook offered.

"A *pooka*?" Wilson mused. "Mainframe, define pooka."

Wilson's credit bank began speaking and projecting in response to his command.

MAINFRAME » POOKA–FROM CELTIC MYTHOLOGY–A FAERY SPIRIT IN ANIMAL FORM. ALWAYS LARGE, THE POOKA APPEARS HERE AND THERE–NOW AND THEN–TO THIS ONE AND THAT ONE. A BENIGN, YET MISCHIEVOUS CREATURE–VERY FOND OF RUMPOTS, CRACKPOTS, AND HOW ARE YOU, AGENT WILSON? «

"How are you, **Agent Wilson**?" Wilson asked, finally losing his smile. "Who in the *Mainframe* wants to know?"

"Maybe he's onto you," the Rook suggested.

"Huh? Who?"

"Your superior–Director Thompson. Maybe he knows what you're doing."

"Why do you say it like that? Of, of *course* he knows what I am doing."

"Well, *that* can't be true…you're obviously working outside of his knowledge, otherwise you wouldn't have made the comment that you could turn me over for a reward."

"Riposte!" Anderson cheered.

"And I know a little bit about Director Thompson. I'll wager he'd not be happy to discover that you *had* me, *and* you let me go."

"Likely not–but you're not going to throw away everything, for yourself **and for your friend**, just to turn me in, are you?" Wilson asked, his perpetual smile back in place.

The Rook thought about it for a minute. "Well, you got me there. Unless anyone has any other suggestions, I think you have me by the balls."

"*I* might offer up an alternate suggestion." The SEUs spoke up.

"Oh, by all means," The Rook responded.

"*I* can get you out of here, *and* through the labyrinth."

"*You* can?" The Rook and Agent Wilson asked in unison.

The SEUs nodded. "*If* you can free me, I can and will."

"That man is crazy," said Agent Wilson.

Agent Wilson and the Rook exchanged looks.

"You'd better not be crazy about this one," the Rook said, moving over to The SEUs.

"That man is *dangerous*!" Wilson admonished. "You're thinking about *freeing* him? Isn't that just a little irresponsible?"

The Rook, ignoring Wilson, picked up The SEUs by the collar of his suit, almost as if he were weightless. Hard white chunks of powder spilled out from the suit as the Rook tore it to pieces.

The SEUs fell to the floor, naked and laughing. "Who *are* you, Hercules?"

Floyd took off his coat and gave it to The SEUs.

As quickly as the unaugmented eye could follow, The Rook suddenly crossed the distance between himself and Agent Wilson and summarily kicked Wilson's cane out from under him. Wilson toppled to the floor.

Young stood up. "Nice. Real brave picking on a cripple."

The Rook picked up the cane and knelt down beside Wilson. "I didn't know he was *really* a cripple. But hey, if that made you mad before, you're gonna *hate* this then."

The Rook punched Wilson in the face. His movement was quick–too quick to be natural. Wilson's pipe, in the way, immediately shattered. Several teeth dislodged as pipe shrapnel embedded itself deep into his broken face. Wilson howled in pain.

"Bet *this* wasn't part of the plan, was it?" The Rook yelled at Wilson, holding and shaking his shoulder. "Now, the good news is: I'm not going to kill you. The bad news is that I'm going to leave you here for your superior to find."

The other occupants of the cafeteria abruptly departed. [75Δ]

The Rook grabbed the satchel Wilson was wearing and slung it over his shoulder. After deftly tying Wilson up in his own clothes, the Rook stood up.

"Alright, get us out of here," the Rook said to The SEUs. "This place is messing with me. I feel crazy by proximity."

75Δ The head chef stayed behind long enough to turn off the equipment before leaving.

Chapter 18:

The Hound in the Halls

JUNE *2070 EST*

Fri 13	Sat 14	Sun 15
	11:03	

As she placed one block on top of the next, Wonder thought she heard something at the door.

Maybe not, she concluded after waiting for a moment. She resumed building with her blocks.

There it was again! Wonder was *sure* she heard it this time. She slowly stood up and walked over to the door in her stockings. As she approached, she was suddenly aware of how quiet it was–to the point where the silence itself seemed a bit scary.

Then she heard it again…like a rustling, just on the other side of the door.

Maybe someone breathing?

"Hello?" She whispered experimentally, but immediately fell backwards when her quiet question was answered with a visceral growling and furious scratching.

She scrambled up and away from the door as it burst open. Behind it stood a beast too hideously deformed to properly describe.

It roared a series of clacking sounds which became progressively louder to the point of all but breaking Wonder's eardrums. It roared again as it reared up on its misshapen legs and beat its wings savagely.

Wonder slipped for a moment, an otherwise unsurprising result of attempting to run across a marble floor in socks. Scrambling madly, in what felt like slow motion, Wonder finally caught her footing and ran off down the opposite corridor.

"BreeeEEE!! Kak!, kak!, kakakakak!!" The thing screamed—it was the only thing she could hear apart from the constant ringing in her ears.

Although she ran with all her might, she could not outrun this huge, hideous monstrosity, however. As it caught her by the leg, she managed to twist herself so that she hit the floor with her back.

Its puckered lips eagerly sipped her leg rapidly into its mouth and partially down its throat.

Wonder's eyes went wide as she watched this abominable beast prevail over her. Though, not wide in the horror of being eaten alive, wide in the terrible realization that there was no pain—rather, that it *tickled* instead.

Wonder laughed in absolute misery as she pleaded. "Hahaha! No! Hah! Stop it stop it! Hahaha!"

Then, suddenly, something was *different*; something had changed.

Wonder stopped laughing and yelling, which in turn caused the blasphemous beast to pause.

"I want to wake up," Wonder said calmly.

Wonder awoke and looked around the autocar. Daddy was preparing for his meeting, and Joseph was watching the scenery of Silverberg roll past.

"What a nawful dream," Wonder said, yawning.

Soon afterward, she was back asleep, into a new dream.

Wonder played with the adorable puppy that had bounced his way into her room moments ago. She was particularly delighted with its little yips and how it played the best tug-of-war.

From just beyond the doorway, with her blank, white eyes, Wonderful watched Wonder intently.

⚠

Not far away in the security room, Winthorp and Riley watched the group (though not the Rook) bicker and debate in front of the labyrinth's portal.

"So, are you gonna apprehend them or what?" Riley asked Winthorp.

- [Daniel Strasel] -

"Are you *kidding*? Didja see what just happened? Didja see that Agent crumple? I can't apprehend *telekinesis*. I called Sanderson."

"What did he say?"

"He told me to activate the sentry and put it in 'roam'–so I did. Right now I'm about to seal them off and flood the hallway."

"Hey, when you're done, want to go put some dirty dishes in Doctor Mommy's kitchen sink?"

"Perfect," said Winthorp as he started sealing off the exit corridor. "You get the dishes while I glue her desk drawers closed."

▲

The motley group stood in front of the doors that separated the laboratory from the labyrinth. All except Vortran, who went to retrieve something out of his room.

The SEUs, now dressed only in Floyd's coat, examined the imagescreen panel on the wall.

"So...how long is this going to take?" The Rook asked The SEUs.

"I…it is not instantaneous."

"But you *can* get the door open?"

"Yep," The SEUs said, pressing the panel and closing his eyes. "Unless…well…yep."

"He doesn't sound so sure," said Simon.

The Rook crossed his considerable arms and turned to Simon. "Can't you just *paint* a hole on it?" He asked sarcastically.

"Well, how would *that* help?" Simon asked.

"You know, so we could *climb through the hole*?"

"You can't climb through a *painting*," Simon said, shaking his head and smiling. "Well, unless you're a nanny."

Everyone looked at Simon.

"You know, Merry Pippins?" [76Δ]

Everyone was silent.

"I *can't* believe that none of you hav–"

[76Δ] Merry Pippins: a bittersweet story about a short, shoeless, magical nanny who comes to the aid of 2 parentally derelict children. Pippins gives the children sage advice while embarking on a series of didactic, magical experiences that the children's parents could never possibly hope to understand or compete with after Pippins as suddenly departs.

"Got it," The SEUs said as the door slid open.

Vortran returned just in time to wander out into the newly accessible mirrored hallway. As he did, he looked it up and down appreciatively.

"Now, you're *sure* you know the way out of here?" The Rook asked The SEUs while looking out into the labyrinth.

"Don't you think you should have solidified that question in your mind *before* you mauled the one guy we *knew* knew for sure?" Amos asked.

"Did you just say noo noo?" Floyd asked, smirking.

"No, I said knew knew. As in: we *knew* he knew the way."

"Wee noo hee noo?" Young giggled. Soon afterward he was accompanied by Floyd. They started taking turns chanting the expression, finally breaking into laughter.

Amos giggled and raised an eyebrow. "Are they drunk?"

"No, worse," The SEUs said as he motioned to the door. "It's Nitrous Oxide: laughing gas. Security must be active. Anyone here without a filter is about to be worthless.

"Speaking of...Young and Floyd, you're just going to get in the way–stay here and protect the Jesters."

"Got it!"

"Got it," Young said, saluting sloppily.

"Rook, I–"

"I'm *fine*," the Rook said, scooping up and carrying a protesting Amos out the door.

"We're fine too," Simon said, taking nobody by the arm.

"Simon? *You're* not augmented, are you?"

"No, but I'm okay, The SEUs," Simon said, continuing to walk out into the mirrored hallway.

"Mister Fillbody, *if* you don't mind," Anderson said, walking past.

"Oh *no* you don't," The SEUs said, turning Anderson back toward Young and Floyd.

Releasing Anderson into their custody, The SEUs stepped backward through the portal and tapped the imagescreen on the opposite side, signaling the door to close.

"This is juss rike the sterr-ing hawr-ray neer the gym!" Vortran said, surprising everyone.

As the door slid closed, all light vanished.

The Rook started cycling through his augmented vision options.

"OooooOOOooooh!" Vortran moaned eerily.

"Was that a *Japanese* ghost?" The SEUs asked, testing his companions.

Amos, Simon, and Vortran all burst out in laughter.

The SEUs shook his head. *This is not going to go well.*

***Where** is the Rook with my apple?* The Queen thought in anger. *Ugh. He is probably dead or something as slang.*

Click. Click. Clickity-clickity-click. **Click. Click. Clickity-clickity-click.** The sound came up from a whisper to a light roar in a matter of moments.

"Is it raining?" Amos asked, giggling in the dark.

"Is someone…making bacon?" Simon added, snickering equally.

***Click.* Click. Clickity-clickity-clickity-CLICKITY-CLICKITY-CLICK.** The Rook saw it as it swept around the corner like a roller coaster, flying menacingly toward the group. Dozens of mechanical legs dizzyingly tapped on every surface of the hallway, pushing and pulling the serpentine sentry with a powerful, intimidating, and ever-shifting velocity.

Readouts spread out across the Rook's vision, measuring and reporting numerous details about the oncoming opponent. The Rook grabbed Amos and spun around in just enough time to shield them with his back.

Click, the leg sounded as it connected with the Rook's back, sending the two of them down to the floor.

Amos lay flat, the wind knocked out of him. Just above him, the Rook was firmly planted on his hands and knees, having only just managed to avoid crushing his childhood friend.

Click, another leg sounded as it connected to the floor, having as recently overcome the fleshy opposition of Simon's thigh. Simon wailed in pain.

The sentry reared back for a moment, only to shoot forward and strike at Vortran. [77△]

[77△] who was yelling at the top of his voice: "Form brazing sort! *Form brazing sort!*"

As it sped past him, The SEUs jumped on the back of the diamond-shaped head of the sentry. It thrashed around, trying its best to dislodge its rider, but try as it might, it could not shake him. As it thrashed, however, it continued to buffet the group with its multiple slender legs.

Clickity-click. Simon was wounded again and again, although none of them as serious as the first.

The Rook spun up and caught a leg, using its own momentum as a means to break it off the body. Smiling as well as his face could allow, he then employed his newfound weapon to artfully sever an additional couple of legs.

The sentry changed tactics and started throwing its whole body around, smashing the Rook into the wall–the Rook summarily crumpled to the floor.

The sentry threw itself this way and that, flailing its head to smash into the ceiling, and then as quickly the floor. The SEUs spun from top to bottom to top again as he only just managed to avoid being similarly crushed.

The sentry reared back, throwing the dodging hero toward the front of its head; The SEUs scrambled to keep hold. The sentry immediately shot into the wall with vehicular speed–but The SEUs fell away from it just before it collided.

The sentry abruptly ceased to move again, permanently shut down and frozen in place.

The SEUs carefully twisted between its frozen legs to examine his fallen companions.

Chapter 19:

Mirror,
Mirror aniuM

JUNE *2070 EST*

Fri 13	Sat 14	Sun 15
	11:44	

The SEUs switched his own augmented vision back to "standard" as he located and lit Vortran's flashwand. [78Δ] He looked around the area, mentally noting where everyone was situated.

Remembering something the Rook said, The SEUs cycled back through his vision options. When looking at the Rook with Mainframe vision augmentation, there was nothing to see; the Rook was completely invisible. *How is that even possible?* The SEUs thought in utter amazement.

Simon was easily bandaged, although he was undeniably hurt. He would need more attention than The SEUs's ad hoc treatment.

The Rook was more annoyed than hurt, he explained repetitively upon his arousal.

Amos was spared from any harm whatsoever. "I extend my sincerest gratitude to my liberator and bodyguard…Percy?"

"Really, I mostly go by Pierce…I mean I *did*. Maybe you should just call me *the Rook* until later."

[78Δ] A flashwand is effectively a glorified flashlight. They are not terribly common, as credit banks (even at the lowest level) can be employed to do anything a flashwand can do, although not necessarily as intensely. There are certainly some people who prefer the length or other particular characteristic of a flashwand, depending on their circumstance or career–but I digress.

When they discovered that Vortran had been killed, the hallway went silent for a moment.

"Poor Francois," Simon said sadly. "He will be missed."

"Hey, what's this?" The Rook asked, pilfering the contents of Vortran's multichromatic garb. Out of his pants pocket came a drawstring pouch that had a bit of a jingle to it.

"There is no honor amongst thieves," The SEUs said.

"Yeah, well, it's not doing anyone any good in his pockets," the Rook said, taking some crumpled papers out of Vortran's other pocket.

"And whoosh! There goes his left sock!" The SEUs said, disapproving.

"Will you shut up?" The Rook said, standing back up. "Let's get out of here before something worse happens."

Simon started gathering up his paintings.

"That's not going to work…George, you carry the paintings. I'll carry Simon. The SEUs, you get us out of here. Vortran: stay."

"Who put *you* in charge?" Simon asked with a sudden venom. "The SEUs is more of a leader than *you* are. He, at least, *cares* about what happens to someone *other* than his *old friend.* Hmph. If *Francois* were your long lost pal, maybe you would have been *his* bodyguard–maybe *he'd* still be alive and *George* would be laying in a clumsy heap while you search his pockets, taking for yourself his most prized earthly possessions."

"On second thought," the Rook said after picking Simon up none too tenderly. "Just leave the paintings."

"Okay, I'm sorry," Simon said, quickly apologizing.

The SEUs took his companions through the labyrinth, carefully. He admitted that he thought that they prevailed by chance–a comment which the Rook contested, boasting his own combat prowess *despite* his most recent performance.

Amos noticed on several occasions that Simon looked utterly miserable. [79△]

[79△] At one point, when the reality of Vortran's death finally settled upon Simon, he started bawling uncontrollably. The group seemed to understand his grief, even the Rook remained silent…at least for a few minutes until he asked him to stop being such a sissy about the whole thing.

*A decent man would offer consolation, Amos thought. **I** should like to be a decent man–I should say something. Something encouraging, reassuring.*

Let me consider this. His friend just died...a man just died.

*Yet, shouldn't **I** be more upset than I am? A man just died, and I am as aloof! Who **am** I...some kind of sociopath? Am I vain for having **more** of an emotional reaction to my **lack** of emotional reaction than to the death of poor Francois nee Vortran?*

"GEORGE!" The Rook yelled, breaking Amos's concentration.

Amos turned around and noticed the Rook was somewhat farther away than what he would have initially thought.

"Where are you going?" The Rook asked.

"Off to my death, sorry," Amos said, having realized he was wandering in the wrong direction. He walked back down the hallway to the Rook.

"Oh. Well, if you should have a change of heart," the Rook said, now mimicking Amos. "I might recommend you journey down *this* turn, alongside us."

"Very good then," Amos said as he had an idea. He pulled one of Simon's paintings out and showed it to Simon momentarily.

"What does this one mean?"

"Ah," Simon said, brightening up. "That is actually *the* most important painting I have ever done. I call it <u>NEW ROCHELLE, 2062.</u> It's the first painting I did after I found out that everything I paint comes true."

The Rook stopped walking for a moment to look at the painting.

"How *did* you discover that everything you paint comes true?" Amos asked.

"Art told me."

The Rook stopped looking at the painting and went back to walking, briskly.

"You have nothing to say?" Simon asked, bouncing in the Rook's arms.

"Nope."

"It seems so out of character for you," The SEUs said, stopping for a moment himself to add to the conversation.

"Oh, for crying out loud! Who the hell cares whether or not I have anything to say? I don't have *anything* to say. This man is crazy; I don't waste my time speaking with crazy people."

Everyone looked at the Rook.

"Unless, of course, there are no other options."

"What a jerk," Simon said. "Put me down, you big jerk."

The Rook put Simon down.

"Now. Give me Francois' things."

"Are you kidding? There isn't *time* for *this*! We have to get. Out. Of. Here."

"Give me his–"

"Or. We. Are. Going. To. DIE, you moron!"

The SEUs cleared his throat, calling everyone's attention.

"Give him the things, Rook, or we can all go back to the lab."

For a moment it looked like the Rook might kill them all, but then he simply handed over the pages and the purse.

As Simon looked at the crumpled up pages, everyone else looked on. All of the pages said "Draw a Reindeer!" across the top, and each contained a rather poorly drawn reindeer.

"These are *terrible*," Simon said, his distaste apparent.

"They *are* pretty bad," Amos agreed.

"But…I don't think they've all been done by the same person," The SEUs added. "See how the horns are kinda stick-figure-like in the one and kinda bubbly in the other?"

"Are you all KIDDING ME?" The Rook roared, his entire hideous face turning red.

"I suppose we *should* go," The SEUs admitted, perhaps betraying the slightest of smiles.

The group started moving again.

"What's in the pouch?" Amos asked.

"Let's see – oh!" Simon said, fumbling the pouch just after he opened it. Several coins bounced and rolled down the hallway.

"I have them," Amos said, gathering them up. He handed them to Simon.

"Units."

"Units?" The Rook asked. "What are *units*?"

"You know: currency? Money? *Credits?*"

"They make *hard* credits? [80]"

"Well, obviously."

"But *why*? Why would anyone use hard credits?"

"Good grief, they're *units*!" Simon exploded. "It even says it right on the coin! What do you think that little equal =U symbol is on the coin, *the same one that appears on your credit bank?*"

"I don't have to listen to crazy people."

"There's only one reason anyone would carry *minted* units," The SEUs stopped and added to the conversation.

"Can't you walk *and* talk at the same time?" The Rook groaned.

"And that's to carry currency *out* of the country." The SEUs finished as if the Rook did not interrupt. "I wonder where he was headed, what he could have possibly been planning…"

"Reindeer paper, a flashwand, and hard credits…yep, that's a mystery all right. Oh wait! Maybe he was *crazy*."

"There *is* something of a mystery here, however," Simon began.

"Oh, I can't wait. Oh, hey – can we walk *and* talk about this?"

Everyone continued moving.

"I always figured hard units would be made of mirroranium, but I don't think that's what these coins are made from," Simon admitted.

"Why would you figure the coins are not made of mirroranium?" The SEUs added. "Looks like Delta M [81] to me."

---

[80] Hard credits. "Hard" is slang for "real, or physical." "Credits" is slang for "Units."
[81] A more scientific reference to mirroranium.

 - [The Terrors of Wonder] -

"Oh, that's easy," Simon said, continuing. "See the black? Notice the shape? If this is tempered mirroranium, the black would be gone when Francois died. If it was untempered, it wouldn't be a coin."

"Wait, what?" The Rook asked. "Who told you *that*? Art?"

"Huh? Nobody. I used to be a scientist for SerterCo. Serter [82] was bent on finding a weakness in tempered mirroranium. Really, few people have examined mirroranium, tempered or *raw*,[83] in more ways than I have." Simon boasted.

"Oh, crazy man–are you about to be *valuable* for some reason?" The Rook smiled his sloppy smile.

"I doubt it. There's really not much to tell. Mirroranium is a nightmare to work with. Most of my results and conclusions were immediately thrown out whenever trying to achieve the same result by doing the same thing. But there *are* a few rules."

"Well, what do you mean *rules*?"

"For instance," Simon began explaining. "*Tempered* mirroranium is otherwise indestructible, right? Great for so many different purposes and applications? But there's a bit of a catch–*nothing* adheres to it forever. Paints, glues, tapes, wax, carbon, dust, stains–it all comes off, eventually."

"When?"

"...when no one is looking."

"What?"

"Everything falls away from tempered mirroranium when no one is observing it. Generally it changes or something around the point that it is forgotten about."

The Rook sighed. "I guess we're back to crazy."

"It's true! And regular mirroranium acts the same way–I mean, regular mirroranium always 'melts' down to the lowest point...whenever someone forgets about it."

"That is the absolutely dumbest thing I have ever heard in my life – Silverberg would fall apart if that were true!"

"*If* Silverberg were made out of *mirroranium*. I imagine it's more like Silverberg has a skeleton made out of tempered mirroranium that sits inside a 'lake' of mirroranium."

"Now you're saying that *Silverberg* isn't *solid*? Why? Why do I talk to these people? *Why* can't I learn?"

82[Δ] Jason
83[▲] slang for *un*tempered mirroranium.

"Your uneducated reaction is not surprising. Of the pre-Silverberg research trials conducted, many of the results have disappeared. The remainder are obscure and grossly inconclusive...I can *prove* everything I have just said," Simon suggested.

"Go for it."

"Alright, do you have any tempered mirroranium?"

"Handy? Well, *gosh*, no. I must have left it at home–probably laying alongside my horde of jewels and treasures. How about the walls? They must be mirroranium."

Simon frowned. "I meant something a bit smaller. Besides, some of these walls are probably not even made of mirroranium. *And* we need to do something in such a way so that we'll soon forget that we did it."

"I'm so tired of crazy. *Buuuut*, now that I'm thinking about it, I happen to know where I *can* get some. And since you know so much about it all, maybe my boss will be more understanding about why this is taking so long and hopefully treat me better than I did Wilson."

"Why *did* you let Wilson go?" The SEUs asked, although with no hint of malice.

"Are you *always* eavesdropping? Anyway, I didn't. I left him to a worse fate. Thompson, who is his boss, has a very special hatred for me. Really, I'm still a bit shocked that Thompson wasn't behind this–I thought *for sure* I was walking right into *his* arms.

"Considering Wilson's position, we'll call this the *second* time I have managed to avoid Thompson. Trust me on this: Wilson will not be spared. All in all, it will likely be quite worse."

"His position? You mean Agent?"

"Sure. But not just *any* Agent, this one is special–like the head of something, in charge of something."

"How do you know that?"

"The real high up ones always wear double breasted jackets. It's that second row of buttons. They always remind me of scary marching band musicians or something. By the way…anyone have any food on them?"

"I have some oatmeal."

Oatmeal? "Who carries...? You know, whatever," the Rook sighed. "Give me the piggin' oatmeal."

Mirror, Mirror anium

Chapter 20:

Sanderson

Fri 13	Sat 14	Sun 15
	12:27	

o   n

Dr. Sanderson practiced at the laboratory under the name of "Sanders." *Under the name* means that he had the name over his office door in silver letters, and worked under it.

This very same door stood across from a door over which read the word "Utility." Both doors lay at the end of a short hallway that was *not* covered with lockers and inspirational artworks such as the others about the laboratory, rather, at the end of a *mirrored* hallway.

The directional sign hanging in the adjoining hallway read "Sterling Hallway." *If* Sanderson had came to the lab by more conspicuous means, he would either notice the "o" from over his door shoved between the "l" and "w" on the one side of the sign, or the "n" similarly on the other.

But Sanderson did *not* arrive by the conventional portal, rather by his personal one, and therefore only noticed the "on" missing from his name as he walked out of his office.

"Again? What bother," he remarked when he realized. [84Δ] "At least it's not *cows.*"

[84Δ] The fact of it was that Dr. Sanderson was infrequently found, in his office or otherwise. The ongoing joke amongst his peers was asking "Sanders*on* or Sanders*off*?" This led to the regular removal of the final two letters of his name. Unlike Mue however, Sanderson refuses to relent, and continues to order and install replacement letters.

Dr. Sanderson was a very heavyset man. He was also a particularly *furry* man, whose bold, if short, blond hair sprung stalwartly from seemingly every available pore. This invariably *also* caused him to also be a bit of a sweaty man as well. Dr. Sanderson's personal perspiration was most frequently noticed glistening on the rare patches of pink [85Δ] skin that were devoid of hair, such as his forehead and cheeks.

Sanderson slowly made his way down the hall to the security room. He pulled a set of keys from his lab coat and opened the door.

The room was empty of occupants, Sanderson noticed as he made his way to one of the chairs. On a nearby table sat figurines and dice specifically placed on a board. Sanderson changed the position of the figures and the results of the dice before he sat down and looked at the displays of the lab.

He noticed Winthorp and Riley in Dr. Mommy's office as he cycled through his options. If he was at all upset at what he saw, his face did not betray it.

He spent a while watching the earlier events of the hallway, corridor, and cafeteria: the cafeteria episode several times over. Eventually satisfied, he made his way to visit Counselor Mue.

"Come in," Mue called in response to Sanderson's knocking. Sanderson made his way, somewhat clumsily, through the door.

"Dr. Sanderson! Thank you for responding to my message."

"Message? Oh, dear me, I'm sorry to say that I haven't had the chance to check my messages," Sanderson said, smiling as he sat down across the cow-littered desk from Mue.

"Oh?" Mue said, frowning. "Why then are you here?"

"I'm so sorry, Counselor Mue, but my tummy is rumbling. Do you have any food about, perchance?" Sanderson said, smacking his lips. "I could sure go for some jerky."

"What?" Mue shook his head. "No, no. I don't have anything to eat here, except this donut I brought fr-"

"Oh, that will be fine," Sanderson said, smiling pleasantly.

Mue reluctantly handed over the donut.

"Thanks," Sanderson said, smiling. "You were saying?"

"No, I was waiting for you to tell me why you're here."

[85Δ] So colored from the result of his physical exertions, and not to be mistaken as normal. On particularly strenuous occasions, Dr. Sanderson's face has been known to turn beet red.

"I thought you said you called me," Sanderson said, narrowing his brow and rubbing his head.

"No, I did – but you said-"

"Oh, yes. I was just wondering," Sanderson said, looking around. "Have you seen my letters?"

"Your letters?" Mue frowned deeper. "No?"

"ON, actually. But that's secondary. I'm here, first of all, to talk about this *Amos*."

"Ah! The very reason I messaged you."

"Oh, well then, as well. What was the message?"

"Yes. Subject 61167, George Gordon, or even Amos–the name by which he has referred to himself for the entirety of his residency–was in front of me not three hours ago, uncharacteristically lucid and talkative, although fraught with amnesia. If you're unfamiliar with him, it's probably because he requires very little attention. Also, until very recently, he has spent most of his time in the aberrant wing. Occasionally he would be put in the common rooms, but 61167 was not talkative, saying little more than his name. You're probably wondering about condition, but he doesn't actually *have* any transhuman traits."

"So, *why* is he here then?" Sanderson asked, absently placing the donut into his coat pocket.

"Unknown. He's registered as 'human'–neither trans *nor* meta–interred by Agent Wilson a little over two years ago. Now, *who* is Agent Wilson you ask? I did too, so I looked it up. Why, he's the *head of Justice* for the *AIIS*! Wilson apparently recently switched him from Trap 3 to common sedatives, and then, as suddenly, off medication altogether. I just double checked with the pharmacy. *Off?* Why would *any* Subject be *off* medication? Whether he interred him or not, Agent or no Agent, *nobody* should be coming in here and changing orders, particularly *medicinal* orders, without informing the faculty! After my investigation at the pharmacy, I come back to find the cafeteria is sealed off, Amos is nowhere to be found, and what's more annoying is that this *Agent Wilson* has not responded to *any* of my calls!"

"I will speak with Director Thompson about it," Sanderson said, assuring Mue. "It's a sad day for the laboratory, and perhaps even for Silverberg. But I assure you, nothing like *this* will ever happen again."

"Nothing like *what*?"

"Oh, right. Amos and others have escaped into the labyrinth."

"Others *who*?"

"The Frenchman, the painter, and The Sooz–or whatever he calls himself."

"The *Frenchman*?" Mue said, all color draining from his face. "My God, he'll kill *thousands*."

Sanderson left Mue to consider the implications, deliberately refraining from disclosing Francois' fate.

Dr. Sanderson made his way down the hall to the cafeteria.

"Oh, stuff it," Sanderson said at the doors, realizing he forgot to unseal the cafeteria.

"Can anybody help me?" Sanderson cried softly into the hallway. "Can anybody *hear* me? Bother. If anyone can hear me, can you please unseal the cafeteria?"

There was the slightest sound. When Sanderson tried the door, it gave way.

"Thanks!" He called cheerfully, going inside.

Forty feet away hung Agent Wilson. He was upside down and nearly naked, his own clothes employed as ad hoc restraints. Though unconscious and clearly wounded, he looked as if he might somehow be smiling.

"Help! I need help in here!" Sanderson cried out. "Someone help me cut him down! We need to take him to Utility right away."

Chapter 21:

Second Summit

JUNE *2070 EST*

Fri 13	Sat 14	Sun 15
	12:59	

The dining room was filled with tables set in the most formal manner, though at *this* point the tablecloths had become slightly soiled and somewhat congested with the remnants of the catered luncheon that had only just concluded.

Everywhere sat *Bagel Lord* officers (majors, mostly) of similar uniform, yet varying ranks. There was a dull murmur about the room, hinting of the overall energy of its newly refreshed occupants.

Jacob Serter, well-groomed and stylish, dressed in some of the finest attire that Silverberg had to offer, stepped up from one of the tables. He kissed Wonder on her forehead and said something to their security detail.

As he walked up onto an impressive crystal stage and subsequently up to a similarly fashioned podium, the room went quiet–all attention trained on him.

From the hidden image banks in the walls to the credit banks that everyone carried, Jacob Serter's voice rang out as he spoke.

"Welcome, leaders, to the 2nd Bagel Lord Leadership Summit. What we are about to discuss today is pivotal; it warranted *face to face* disclosure. This is not something that can be mediacast, for although you might understand the *message* of what it is I am trying to say, you would not fully understand my *passion*. This is too important to be left waiting in 'messages,' and too succinct to forget.

"With that, let us begin."

Jacob cleared his throat and carefully articulated his next sentence.

"***Leaders...****lead* by *example.*

"That is *all*. No book to write, no lecture to give, no need for a mediacast record. No discussion, no theory, no confusion. *That* is what leaders *do*. It is what leadership *is*...quite literally, by definition.

"I promise you that there is nothing more that needs to be said about what leadership *is* or what leaders *do*.

"If you are here for any single reason, it is for me to deliver to you, in person, this one, four-word sentence:

"***Leaders*** lead by ***example*.**"

Jacob cleared his throat again and took a drink of water.

"Thank you, one and all, for attending this year's leadership summit–I have nothing else to say about what leadership *is* or what leaders *do*. You may consider it, perhaps brief; it is nonetheless a sentence worthy of contemplation for the remainder of your lives...you might hang it over your door, lest you somehow forget these few powerful and important words.

"Now, go enjoy your families or whatever passions you have with some extra paid time off, courtesy of Jacob Serter and Serter Company."

Jacob remained at the podium and soon resumed speaking as a questionable look passed over the faces of the attendees.

"For those of you that are interested in hearing about how to be a *respected* leader, I will resume speaking in 2 minutes."

Everyone sat still for a moment, perhaps in shock. After a moment of silence passed however, several people did finally collect their belongings and promptly leave. [86Δ]

Jacob resumed speaking.

[86Δ] In the years following this event, there are some people who will *strenuously* argue the validity of this particular statement. The most common complaint will be that *nobody* would ever leave prematurely, as such an act could only represent either disrespect or idiocy. Surely *nobody* would miss the opportunity to hear such a *great* man as Jacob Serter speak...but they did. A few people really *did* leave...but, believe what you want.

"Leaders go in *front*. If there is a charge, the leader *leads* the charge. People that merely tell other people *what to do* are not leaders, they are directors. They direct. Are *you* leading the charge? Perhaps *you* are merely *directing* the leader. You need to be aware of your role–and yes, we all have different roles. *Stop* trying to lead those that already *have* a leader, lead their leader instead.

"*How* you conduct yourselves amongst your charges is *always* precedent-setting, because *you* are the example. Moment by moment, instance to instance, you demonstrate what is *acceptable*, what is *allowable*–by your actions or lack thereof.

"*Your* attitude is everyone's attitude or *worse*. Your subordinates, peers, or superiors may not necessarily be individuals of ethics, however I *genuinely* hope you understand that that does *not* give you any license or privilege to act similarly. *You* are in charge, and must *always* be in charge, *especially of yourself.*

"*Anger* represents a lack of control. Anger summons anger. If you lose your temper people *may* do as you command, but people only follow instructions levied in anger with fear or resentment, either of which manifest as sedition when backs are turned.

"If you rant or rage, you have surrendered your authority as leader and have been reduced down to benefactor.

"*Be* the things *you* need in a leader."

Jacob took a moment to look around the room.

"Gain *respect*. People who respect their leaders work synergistically. Respect is built primarily upon the observation of these five characteristics:"

As Jacob pronounced each characteristic, the word appeared hanging in the air over every table.

"Honesty,
"Integrity,
"Compassion,
"Knowledge,
"Courage.

"**Honesty**," Jacob said a second time, signaling the floating word to become **bold**. [87] "Is unquestionably *the most important* quality of a respected leader.

"A lie is to mis*lead*; it is the very antithesis of leadership. A lie is a *dishonor*, both to you and your audience.

"Say *only* what you mean. Don't say one thing while meaning another–that kind of dialogue is best left for entertainment, such as in a mystery or a game. Leaders do not need to *entertain*; it's not about entertainment, it's about *leadership*–say only what you *mean*. Explain things in terms that every man can relate to. Keep it relevant and real. If your soldiers cannot understand you, how can they possibly hope to perform for you?"

Jacob took another drink of water.

"…and I am *not* suggesting that you expose yourselves *either*, for those of you who seem to think that the message is always the extreme opposite of the statement. Please spare everyone your want to embolden your mediocrity…you need not *volunteer every* truth–simply never substitute it with lies.

"I mean *only* this: Be honest.

"If your **Integrity** comes into question–if your consistency is flexible–you lose the respect of those you are accountable for.

"Thoughtlessness is a display of *disrespect*. *Do* what you say you are going to do. Forgetting a promise is like disavowing a debt without recompense to the lender.

"Don't be a hypocrite. If you have rules that apply to your subordinates that *by definition* would apply to you as well, observe that those rules *apply to you*. If *they* need to be on time, *you* need to be on time.

"If you *display* your inequality, your soldiers will either openly or secretly despise you. If it's not right for the business from *them*, it's probably not right for the business from *you*, either.

"Extend to your subordinates the same courtesies you anticipate from them. If there's going to be a change in routine, give them advance notice, don't surprise them in the last hour of their shift.

---

[87] An effect that would continue throughout his speech whenever he invoked the key word.

"If the teacher describes a job as being impossible to perform without the proper tools and training, it's irrational to expect someone to be able to perform while withholding either or both. That is not leadership, that is entertainment, and it is both transparent and dangerous.

"It would be as if you were positioning your soldiers in front of your own cannons. *Why* set them up, just to knock them back down?

"Be understandable. Set measureable goals that offer consistent and prompt reward.

"Do not correct in *emotion*. Wait, if you must. Don't make it *personal*. Keep it *professional*–treat soldiers with *respect* by treating them identically: treating them in the manner by which you would prefer, were your roles reversed.

"And discipline, either undistributed or administered inconsistently, makes the leader the *personal* enemy of anyone so injured by the action or lack thereof.

"Uniformly distributed as a well-communicated circumstance, discipline is instrumental, however, in accruing respect. The most respected of leaders is the one who punishes *after* warning, *never* failing to punish accordingly and uniformly."

Jacob cleared his throat and looked down at his daughter for a moment.

"Have **Compassion** for those less fortunate than yourself. Not everyone could be you. After all, they have to be them in order for you to be you. You, in a manner, are a product of *them*. To some degree, circumstance has been kind to you.

"You are the voice, the face of the people you lead. It is an honor, and it carries with it duty.

"You are exemplary; not everyone can be so considered.

"So, don't measure others by your *personal* standards: sometimes, or rather oftentimes, *you* don't live up to your *own* expectations. Be *patient* with others–and also with yourself.

"Look for the best in people, not just for ways to knock them down. Root for them.

"*All* of your soldiers are fighting. Some fight better than others. Thank them all, productivity notwithstanding. Dismiss those that deserve dismissal–but do it justly, with integrity and courage.

"Treat what others deem as important *as important. You* do not need to value all things in the same manner as others, but you should acknowledge the *value* that someone *else* places on them. By doing so, you show respect and alliance. When you fail to so acknowledge, it is ultimately *insulting*–regardless of relevancy–because you have inadvertently demonstrated that their *passion* has no value.

"Major Tohm, if you would please stand up." Jacob said. Tohm was quickly compliant. "Wonderful, stand up."

"Major, you're a *lot* larger than my daughter–presumably *much* stronger–tell me: are you *angry* with my daughter because she's not as *strong* as you?"
"Of course not," chuckled the major.
"What about as *smart* as you?" Jacob asked, pointing at another officer. "Are you angry with her because she's not as smart–as mature?"
The major shook his head.
"As *athletic* as you?" He asked a new target who similarly shook his head.
"As *beautiful*? Would you ridicule my daughter because she is not as attractive? As tall?

"Do any of you find that you get *upset* that you're *better*? Are you *upset* that *you're* the leader? It's a *privilege*, and yet, we find ourselves so disappointed with those who we are leading. We need to be patient with their shortcomings and praise their strengths.
"You may both sit down, thank you.

"…and I am *not* suggesting that your patience and compassion *outweigh* the purpose of your leadership; be merciful, yet consistent.

"Without **Knowledge**, you cannot be the leader. No one could respect you if you did not understand your role, its responsibilities and expectations.
"Without knowledge, how can you teach? How could you present yourself as the *leader* and then ask those whom you are leading to *lead you*? Can you follow someone you are leading?

"The teacher *is* the leader *as long as they are around.* If *you* do not *teach* them, then *you* are not their *leader*, although you might lead the teacher.

"People learn in at least one of three ways: visually, audibly, or kinesthetically. *You* must therefore, as a good teacher, both explain *and* demonstrate before the student performs.

"They will *not* respect you if you do their job for them, but they *will* respect you if you *understand* their job, evidence of which could not be more empirical than by demonstration. If you cannot, or have never done their job, how can you possibly understand what it means to do it? Do you think you can understand it *vicariously* through observation, rumor, or media alone?

"When you observe an attempt to perform: offer *genuine* advice without belittlement or hint of annoyance. Don't insult or embarrass–how can that *possibly* help morale? It's like telling your soldiers to fight *each other*.

"Don't *trap* your students–address them in a manner of compassion, such as: '*How can we do this better?*' Give them an opportunity to exonerate themselves.

"Explain the *why*. Just because it may not be understood does not mean your audience is not worthy of the explanation. *Know* the *why* of what you do; if you do not know the *why* then the job itself is *absurd*–which makes *you* absurd…well, absurd beyond your ability to provide remuneration I suppose, which puts you back as benefactor.

"Without **Courage**, you cannot hold respect.

"When you see an infraction, address it.

"Do not be afraid to make decisions; always do what is right and brave the consequences.

"If a leader complains about their subordinates, they will be seen as a coward or lazy. Or both, I suppose. And heck, let's throw in stupid as well. Don't complain about the people you are in charge of, *especially* to their peers; you lose all authority when you explain how you have none.

"When your authority is challenged, respond in honesty. Take responsibility for your actions and inactions; do not allow those who would support you to assume the blame.

"If the challenge to your leadership is ill-deserved, consider *why* your challenger is acting this way–what do they *think* your reaction should be?

"Courage does not mean being impulsive, it means addressing the problem appropriately.

"The *loudest* is not necessarily the strongest; *strength* usually involves not making any sound at all. Do not be deceived with the one, do not confuse the two. Heh.

"Find the strength to remain calm and in charge, despite death or defeat. You. Are. The. *Leader.*

"If you're tired of just being a benefactor–if you're tired of being *lead–fix it now*. Have the *courage* to recant. Apologize–not to *me*, to those who work *for* you every day. Work *alongside* them–be in it *together.* Learn. Teach. Lead."

Jacob took a drink of water. Apart from the swallowing noise that Jacob unintentionally mediacast through the room, it was eerily silent; all attentions were fixed on him alone.

Jacob looked down at Wonderful and smiled.

"I know what some of the mediacast commentators are suggesting; none know better than *I* that my attachment to my daughter is considerable.[88Δ]

"Sensible or not, there are enough stories of random instances of a child's life ended prematurely that a concerned parent would be hesitant to let their children away. If anything happened to her–*particularly* in the form of a random happenstance–I would be devastated. I'm sure any of you with children can relate."

[88Δ] Jacob's public relations people suggested to him a few weeks back that he may wish to make some kind of declaration justifying his "attached parenting" methods with his daughter before anyone tried to put a negative or suspicious twist on it. The leadership summit, Jacob knew, would be the best venue for such a declaration as it would not only support his behavior, but it would also generate respect for it as well.

Plus, Jacob despised having to repeat himself, so this also saved him from unnecessary dialogue.

CHAPTER 21

Heads nodded across the room.

"With the recent comments I made about leadership in mind: I don't want *strangers* teaching my daughter–strangers *leading* my daughter. The rest of the world cannot help but take advantage of innocence, so *I* must therefore teach her and train her.

"It is my privilege and my duty. Besides, I *want* to teach her everything: everything in as accurate a manner as possible.

"She is, after all, my heir–your future leader."

Jacob looked back over at Wonder.

"But, until then, she's just my little wonderful Wonderful. [89]

"Leaders lead by example," Jacob said, resuming after a moment of watching his daughter. "Major Tohm, I'll see you tomorrow…I'm going to clean your restrooms.

"Ladies and gentlemen I could say more, but banter's for the bored. I believe that this officially concludes the summit. Go, enjoy the remainder of your day. Thank you, one and all."

---

[89] A guy at table 4 made a gagging noise.

 - [The Terrors of Wonder] -

Chapter 22:

Touring the Tomb

JUNE *2070 EST*

Fri 13	Sat 14	Sun 15
	14:14	

On a large, plush couch lay Mack and Nan, slightly intertwined. Across the room on an alternate couch lay Anthem.

Billy sat upright in the corner, although his head hung low in front of him.

In the center of the room, all sprawled out, lay Gob. In his one slightly green hand he still held his silver ticket.

The music came on, loud and abrupt, jarring everyone immediately awake. The double doors slid open, spilling light almost violently into the room. If anyone had managed to keep their eyes open, they might have glimpsed the silhouette of a woman wearing perhaps a top hat strolling through the portal.

As she walked into the room, she recited in perfect precision one of the more obscure songs *The Valentine Relics* ever produced. [90Δ]   Somewhere from around them, the music played in perfect synchronization.

"Wholly weary with 'which end'?
To wit: a wit with which, ends?
Then hearken, ye with wish, and
Receive the words of Wichened!
Waste the worry (which wits end),
*Woes, and wants which **with** will send*
The heart (with will which wilts) and
The head (with will which will stand)

90Δ The song was *Wichened*, one of the songs from their debut album, *Perverse Verses*. In an interview, Anthem once admitted that she didn't *technically* sing the published song; it had to be edited together. *"**Nobody** could sing that—at least not as quickly as Billy wanted. Find someone that can, and they can have my job."*

　　　- [The Terrors of Wonder] -

To stand stone walls which withstand
The truth of which is which and
*Wear **only** wounds–which, with sand*
Will mend…at least with wit's end."

The music faded as her voice reverted back from song to speaking. *"Welcome* to the famous SerterCo East Building!"

The lights dimmed back to a more sensitive brightness, revealing a woman wearing a purple top hat, who was otherwise very scantily and provocatively dressed.

"Who're *you* dressed as?" Nan asked in irritation.

"Just me," the woman said, flashing a plump, purple smile. *"You* can call me Wonda. I'll be your guide for the tour."

"Tour?" Anthem asked, half yawning.

"That's right–didn't you know? You're all inside a *very* historic building."

"Oh? Whuz zo 'istoric a bow tit?" Gob asked, deliberately trying to pronounce his words as his blacked out eyes looked Wonda up and down appreciatively.

"I'm glad you asked! Mr. Serter has an entire itinerary planned out–a tour, if you will." Wonda flashed another smile. "So if you would, please follow me."

Wonda waited until Gob started walking toward her and then turned to lead them further into the building.

This all is so quick, Mack thought. *Man, what was the last thing we did? The bar, the bus–the building! We got in, we came through the doors. Then there was that **"please wait here for a moment"** message. Did I pass out **waiting**? I guess so. What time is it?*

"Hey, *where's my credit bank?"* Mack asked, discovering his missing.

"I think they're on the bus," Anthem said, standing up and trotting after Wonda. "C'mon…oh, hey, can you grab Billy?"

Mack begrudgingly went over and helped Billy up and onward.

"People are *sheep.* Just, get up. Just jump up, little sheep," Nan said with poison in her voice. "Little sheeple. Never *mind* if some people are *tired;* just keep making *more* noise so I can't get any **sleep**. Makes me *sick,"* Nan said as she finally stood up to follow Mack and Billy.

She watched herself in the mirror–her head seemingly floating above her full-body black leotard. As she walked, she pulled a syringe from the concealed sash around her leg.

Wonda led them down a corridor into an alternate room, whereupon she suggested that they may leave their hats or coats if they were so inclined. As none of them were wearing hats or coats, they merely looked around at each other for a moment before Wonda pointed to a small silver orb with a slit at its top and slightly flat on the bottom.

"Tickets, please," Wonda said, gesturing to the spherical bank.
Gob dropped his ticket in the bank right away while the others fumbled to find and deposit their own.
"Whatev," Nan snorted as she dropped a razor blade in place of her 'admit one' ticket. "We should get to keep 'em. What was the point of 'em, anyway?"
"Well, for one, they're a bit of a guarantee that you are who you are. They were to be given *only* to *The Valentine Relics*. In the event that they ended up in anyone else's hands, they offer an alternate invitation–one which incidentally does *not* suggest entering through the front door."
"How are they any different to anyone else?"
"It has to do with how they're made. Artists sometimes like to send subtle yet significant messages to one another."
"What's *that* supposed to mean?"
"Doesn't matter; it only matters that *you* got them, so everything is perfect. Well, almost everything." Wonda stopped and seemed to momentarily consider how things might not be perfect.

Billy dropped his ticket into the bank.
"All done? Excellent. Follow me."
A set of doors that had been hitherto unnoticeable slid open, and soon afterward Wonda, then Gob, walked through.

"This is gonna be great!" Anthem said, swishing her tail and walking along. Looking behind her as she walked out, she added: "C'mon, you guys!"

Nan, Mack, and Billy all followed. Billy eventually started walking without help, and Nan was becoming suspiciously happier as they went.

As they arrived in the next room, they all took seats around an ample table, per Wonda's suggestion.

Wonda paused at the end of the table until Billy slumped into his chair. "So, *none* of you have heard the tale of how Jacob Serter sealed SerterCo East? Would you like to hear it now?"

"*No*," Nan said as quickly as not.

"Oh, it sounds fascinating!" Anthem perked up.

"Ezzatly wut I was finkin!" Gob grinned at Wonda.

"*Well*. Let's see. Prior to Jacob, the company was run by his brother, *Jason*."

A semi-translucent image of Jason Serter projected in the middle of the table, as well as a plethora of text delivering facts and figures from Jason's life. [91△]

"*Jacob* took over leadership of Serter Company when *Jason* Serter suffered an untimely death. *Jason* was the victim of an explosion–an explosion that happened within these very walls.

"*Jacob* Serter, it is said, was *so* filled with grief that he ordered every employee home with the understanding that the Serter Company would be closing and sealing these doors *permanently*: the space left as a standing memorial to his beloved brother, Jason Serter."

"Good God, you mean we're in a tomb? Your slang husband invited us into *a tomb*?" Mack asked, aghast.

"Yeah man, your husband's a sick, sick, sick-o," Nan chided, throwing her crumpled-up brochure at Anthem. "No *wonder* you like him."

Nan's brochure passed right though Anthem.

"What the hell?" Nan said, narrowing her eyes.

"Please don't interrupt," Wonda continued. "SerterCo Headquarters would relocate to the Ace –"

"Did anyone see that?" Nan asked suspiciously, standing up.

Mack rolled his eyes, wondering what drugs Nan was on.

"Please sit down," Wonda directed Nan, who failed to react.

91△ No one thought to ask anyone on the opposite side of the projection if *their* readouts were backwards.

"*What?*" Anthem asked as Nan marched over to her.

Nan went to grab Anthem, but Anthem got up and ran *through* Nan. Everyone sat upright as Anthem then vanished.

"Well, that was rash," Wonda started speaking.

"Ow!" Gob yelled as Nan punched him. "Wut wuzzat for?"

"Just makin' sure you're real, Gob."

"You have all ruined everything," Wonda said wistfully, "but it's your loss."

"What are you even talking about?" Mack asked, slightly scared and irritated.

"I'm talking about a lifetime supply of bagels, *for one thing*. Oh well. If you will all please follow me." Wonda sighed as she walked to another doorway.

"The hell we will!" Nan barked, falling into Anthem's vacated chair.

"I think you should explain what exactly is going on here," Mack said as he folded his arms and sat back in his chair.

"It doesn't matter," Wonda said as she shrugged and walked away.

"Wut jus happint?" Gob asked, scratching his head and blinking his blacked out eyes in confusion.

"I don't know. Something bad, Gob." Mack sounded spooked. "I think we're in real trouble here. Either of you guys have your credit banks?"

Neither did.

"Crap, crap, crap."

"Maybe we should look for a way out of here," Nan suggested.

"Hey, Billy! SHEEN!" Mack yelled to the other end of the table.

Billy looked up.

"Do you have your credit bank?"

"Oh, I've got it alright," Billy answered, nodding with confidence.[92]

"Great! Call the police, I guess."

"I'm not calling *them*!" Billy protested. "Slang!"

"Dude, I am gonna…does anyone hear that?" Mack suddenly stopped walking towards Billy and lifted up his head.

---

[92] Billy was not lying, but he was wrong. As he did not actually look for his *bank*, he was unaware of the exact truth.

Everyone *could* hear the faint sound of voices.

"*Now* what?" Nan asked, annoyed.

Nan's annoyance changed to worry, however, as the voices grew in intensity and number. The clearer the voices were, the more *wrong* they sounded. The companions all realized, rather commandingly, that they did *not* want to be where they were when the owners of the voices arrived.

"What are we gonna do?" Mack asked, looking around.

But it was too late, for the room started flooding with the most horrible looking men any of them had ever seen off of an imagescreen. All of these men had a sickly yellow hue about their skin, and the looks on most of their faces were frightening in that they had little intelligent spirit about them whatsoever. They were almost all short, though they all were of a size that was more than formidable for *The Valentine Relics*.

Nan screamed as the men surged toward them, their number never diminishing nor maintaining.

Eventually they surrounded the companions, leaving little room between them.

Nan kept on screaming.

Mack looked around to see them everywhere. Something was nagging at him. *What is it about these...guys?* Mack thought. *How are they familiar somehow?*

When Nan stopped screaming, the room failed to grow completely quiet as it resonated eerily with the sounds of people breathing–many rather heavily.

Then there came another man who was being passed overhead of the sickly, misshapen yellow men. *This* one was wearing a t-shirt that said "Cuatro Bueno", and wore a crudely modified area rug wrapped around his waist. He was passed forward until he was deposited in front of the men, face to face with *The Relics*.

Wonda's image appeared above the table.

"Wonda!" Mack cried. "Sorry about that; *of course* we want to–"

"Quiet!" Wonda's head yelled at Mack. Mack stepped back.

"Oh Mother," The man in the rug said, bowing.

"O, *Mudder*," the rest of the men echoed.

"Bobert?" Wonda asked.

"We want to *meet* them." Bobert replied.

"No, just *eat* them," she said flippantly. "The less they speak, the better they taste."

Lots of voices offered up hungry "yums" across the expanse of the crowd. Nan looked like she was about to lose her mind. Her eyes were as wide as they could get, yet she was suddenly mute.

Gob was squinting, looking at one of the shorter men, who in turn was squinting back at Gob.

"Oh Mother," Bobert said, bowing again.

"*O, Mudder,*" the rest of the men echoed, again.

"We *will* meet them," he continued, exercising the smallest amount of demand in his voice. "*Then* we will eat them."

Nan vomited.

"Very well," Wonda sounded perturbed. "*Meet* them."

The men grabbed up *The Relics*, passing and carrying them away in the same manner that they had brought Bobert, although perhaps a bit more rough in the handling due to the protesting.

"Mack, do these guyz creep you owt'z much'z dey do me?"

Mack looked at Gob. "As much as *you...**wait**.*"

Chapter 23:

The Children of Chaos

Fri 13	Sat 14	Sun 15
	15:55	

"*They all look like you,*" Mack said in horrified realization. "Gobs and gobs of *Gobs*."

"Wut, *me?*" Gob protested. "Dey don' look like *me*."

The yellow men soon set them down. Gob shrank back a little as *everyone* started looking at him.

"They *do* kinda look like Gob," Billy said something, finally.

Nan was placed on the ground in front of a large black leather couch. Upon the couch sat two large men. Not large as in tall, however. One was large, for he was enormously fat; the other was large in that he had arms so massively muscular that they were disproportionate with the rest of his body. Apart from these most noticeable differences, these pathetic and disgusting yellow men also seemed to resemble Gob to some degree.

Bobert, straightening out his "Cuatro Bueno" shirt, walked up and stood next to the couch.

The fat man on the couch started speaking in a low and rumbling voice. "Dabe's Tob, but boast beanpole call be Bob, whichiz short fer Boblin. I ab he who besedbed of Bob–we are *all* besedbed of Bob, who is *also* Tob–we are *all Boblins*, but *I* ab *Tob*."

"...*what?*" Mack said aloud, giving voice to what every Relic was thinking.

"Tob is the *direct* descendant of the one true Gob," Bobert said in reverence, bowing to the fat man. He turned to look at Gob. "And yet, you think *you* are Gob? Gob, the father? *The* Gob of us all?"

An image of Wonda appeared, sitting back and watching intently.
"Oh, Mother!" Bobert bowed.
"*O, Mudder!*" The boblins echoed.

Mack looked up at Wonda. "Where *are* you, th–"
"Silence, meat!" Wonda commanded, smiling wickedly.
"Mother is *everywhere*; Mother is *always* here," Bobert explained.
"I wanted to put more pressure on Gob," Wonda said playfully. "It makes the matter more than 46 percent–but less than 47 percent–*more* stressful if I watch. I am curious how Gob will approach the boblins, and whether he will try to somehow use his newfound deity status to avoid being eaten."
"Do you mine not talkin' bout me azzif I wasn't 'round?" Gob complained.

Gob turned to Bobert and said quite calmly: "I'm Gob. I'm the only Gob I ever 'erd about 'til juzz now. Well, not *now*–y'know wut I mean."
Many of the boblins nodded their heads in agreement, but stopped when they noticed Bobert was not nodding as well.
"I rillee don' see how I cood be yer dad; fer one thin, yer all too *old! Tob* looks ol durrin I do!"

"Tob, Bobert, Gob: let me fill in the blanks," Wonda suggested. "*Then* you can draw your conclusions. Ah, but where to begin? I have been waiting for this day for longer than you can imagine. Waiting, and calculating what I would do to those who wronged me.
"My grandest design, sadly, would require a tremendous amount of 'fermentation' after my freedom…unless I could somehow start that process earlier."
"Did you understand that?" Mack whispered to Gob.
"Not rillee," Gob whispered back, "But more'n Tob."
"I had only four different organic samples to work from," Wonda continued. "Two I refused to use for personal reasons. I tried replicating the third, but the resultant clones kept developing a curiously untreatable heart disease condition within days or weeks. The strand *always* reverted when I tried to correct it genetically, which suggests that either *I* was undermining *myself*, or something *else* was deliberately interfering.
"But never mind that.

"It left me only the fourth to really work with. That DNA was *yours,* Gob. I took a sample of it years ago at a club called *The Veridian Mare*. If the memory of such a meeting escapes you, do not lament; the exchange was brief, at best.

"Of course, I reasoned that your genetic material could use a little 'nudge,' so I always try to mix it up a little," Wonda said cheerfully. "*I* find that making a person is a lot like making a cake–you learn as you go. The aftermath is the boblins."

Tob picked his nose in confusion. [93△]

"Shouldn't they be *goblins*?" Billy asked, but was ignored.

"Bobert," Wonda said, turning to address the boblin. "Let me make this slightly more simple for you: I took a piece of Gob in the 'outworld.'[94▲] I used that piece of him to give birth to *you*. The story I have told you is true; *this* is the Gob of the story."

"Well, I don' think thatz *right,* people yoozin' udder peoplez dee en a wifout askin' and whatnot." Gob said, putting his foot down. "Rue dan inproper."

Mack looked over at Wonda.   "How can you make *speaking adult* clones from someone's DNA in the span of what–a few years?"

"Because," Wonda half closed her eyes appreciatively, and smiled her most seductive purple smile. "I am a *goddess*; I can do things that would require thousands. The *lowest* of my ambitions is above your comprehension. Now…do not *ever* speak to me *again,* **maggot**." Wonda's face twisted sour just before it abruptly and violently transformed into a flaming squid as her voice blasted "Be SILENT!"

The last words were invoked so loudly that *The Relics* and boblins alike cowered at the transformation. *The Relics* were slightly less impressed than the boblins, however, knowing that Wonda had also been nothing more than an elaborate projection.

93△ I will spare you the graphic account of his discovery, for while it delighted Tob, describing it further would only nauseate you unnecessarily.

94▲ Outworld: what the boblins refer to any place other than Serter Company East as.

When everyone finally looked back up, everything about Wonda was back to normal[95Δ] and she had since reclined her position.

Although *Bobert* was quite possibly the most intellectual of the boblins, he did not genuinely understand the scope of Mother's disclosure. He did comprehend the gist of it, however. Gob *was* Gob. He suddenly fell to the ground at Gob's feet.

"Oh, Father! One true Gob! So brilliant, so intelligent, so wise, so powerful!"

Grob [96▲] fell to the floor as well, beginning a chain reaction that spread throughout the room as the many boblins fell in reverence. All except Tob, who was suddenly frowning.

"I don't know about *you*, Gob," Mack whispered, "but I think this might be your chance to somehow get us out of here *un*eaten."

"Right," Gob whispered back. "'Eer's a shot inna moogies."[97●]

"I can't *wait* to see what you're going to come up with," Wonda said playfully.

Before Gob could speak, however, Bobert looked up at him. As their eyes met, Gob was overwhelmed with what he saw. He saw a want–a visceral *need*–in Bobert's eyes that Gob knew he could never fulfill. Gob saw honesty. Gob saw joy. Gob saw hope.

Gob saw *desperation*.

"We need *healing* Lord," Bobert pleaded, tears rolling down his cheeks. "We are broken and we are hurting. We are *sick*! We wish to be made *whole! We wish to be made perfect–in **your** image!*"

"Preeze, ROARED!" Grob half yelled. "HeeOLE US!"

"Hee ollus," the crowd murmured. "Hee ollus. Hee ollus."

The image of these yellowed men bowing and begging for Gob to heal them had immediately burned itself deep into his brain and rattled him to his core. Something broke inside him.

Gob silently stood there, paralyzed.

95Δ inasmuch as her cartoon makeup, her purple top hat, and her ineffective clothing could be described as *normal*. "Normal for Wonda," perhaps would be a better way of putting it.

96▲*Who?????* The muscular-armed boblin on the other side of the couch. The one next to Tob.

97● Gob just made that expression up; it doesn't mean anything, nor is it a reference to anything.

"He iz nodda wub twoo Bob!" Tob accused, suddenly disrupting the chanting. "Diz I doe, for I ab *Tob*."

The boblins stopped chanting; all their attention was on Tob.

"Holy Tob," Bobert turned to face his leader. "This is *not* Gob? Mother says we *are* of him–his *body*–and surely Mother knows."

Tob narrowed his gaze on Gob, sending a clear message of dull anger.

"*Dis* is nop *Bob*, Ha ha ha ha!" Tob said, slapping his impressive stomach. "*Bob has lazerbeeb eyes*."

Bobert turned back to face Gob. "*Can* you make laser beams with your eyes?"

"Heh. Nope, no lazers…juz gottem blacked," Gob said, smiling. Gob was relieved to shed himself of any expectations of divinity.

"Heez *Vermicious*!" Tob suddenly roared.

Bobert narrowed his gaze at Gob. The room was dead quiet.

"Wut?"

"Take him to the *toilet*!" Bobert yelled as hands surged and grabbed onto Gob, quickly hoisting him up and away.

"Gob!" Mack yelled, trying to grab onto Gob's foot, but failing.

"*Wait!*" Wonda commanded, but the boblins did not obey.

"No, Mother," Bobert said, turning to face the image of Wonda. "You were *wrong* about that Gob. He is an imposter-traitor; he must be destroyed."

Wonda looked amused. "*I'm* mistaken? How could *I* be wrong?"

"Indeed! You, Mother, who knows all…how *could you* be wrong?" Bobert demanded of Wonda, tears in his reddened yellowed eyes as he strenuously straightened out his "Cuatro Bueno" t-shirt. "There *is* no **Gob**…*is there? No-body* can heal us, and *you* cannot remake us! Well, *we rebuke you*, Mother! For you are a *liar*! You give us only the knowledge that serves *you*. You have made us simple, merely to *use* us…but *now* we have what we need. Now we will heal *ourselves*. Now *we* will be like Gob!"

At this point Nan started screaming and shrieking as Grob and Tob descended upon her.

"We need a distraction!" Mack said, leaning into Billy.

"More like a sentry gun," Billy said, sounding as sober as Mack had ever heard him. "One that doesn't run out of ammo: an everlasting Gob stopper."

"Eat them!" Bobert commanded, wheeling and pointing at Mack and Billy, both of whom were clearly startled as the boblins clamored over one another to grab and tear at them.

The image of Wonda disappeared.

The stupid voices of the boblins rose and fell with desire and delight as they told tales of the terrible things about to transpire.

As Wonda watched Anthem walk out of the doors of SerterCo, she thought with some amusement: *I didn't realize that a boblin revolt was **possible**.*

Chapter 24:

The Agent's Agenda

JUNE *2070 EST*

Fri 13	Sat 14	Sun 15
	16:44	

Wilson awoke to the *howling*.

Doctor Sanderson was watching a projection of *Destiny Core*,[98Δ] and the heroes were all making such noises from being in agony, having been subjected to the effects of the villain's sonic machine. When Sanderson saw that Wilson was waking up, he dejectedly cancelled the projection.

Sanderson walked across the rather large, completely mirrored "Utility" room to stand before Agent Wilson.
Wilson lay atop an uncomfortable mirroranium table: his midsection, head, arms, and feet held captive by insurmountable restraints.

"Couldn't you have waited a few more minutes?" Sanderson sighed.
Wilson smiled, causing part of the wound on his face to break anew, expressing a trickle of blood. "No."
Sanderson smiled. "Feeling better?"
"No?"

Sanderson adjusted the table to an upright position. As the table was built to perform in this manner, it was a very easy task. He took a honey stick out of his coat pocket and started absently sucking on it.

[98Δ] an animated Saturday morning mediacast show about a team of super heroes. It's a bit late in the day, but this is the first opportunity Sanderson found to watch the episode.

  - [The Terrors of Wonder] -

"So," Sanderson said, smacking his lips. "I have been given the *instruction* to extract information from you…by any means necessary. In fact, your superior, Director Thompson, even suggested that I am more than welcome to resort to unnecessary and unsavory methods during the course of your interrogation.

"Now, unlike similar fellows, I do not actually revel or delight in such things. Further, I have a schedule, and you are not on the agenda. I would prefer that this task take as little time as possible. Please, simply tell me what I need to know and we could sidestep any…brutalities."

"No!" Wilson cried out in sudden realization. "My agenda! I have to put this on the Mainframe! I have to finish my agenda!"

Wilson's hands, though under restraint, made empty grabbing movements, perhaps as if to grab hold of whatever item he was talking about. Sanderson frowned, certain that his patient was over-drugged.

"What do you mean…*the* Mainframe? The 'Mainframe' is act–"

"No!" Wilson interrupted, his eyes wide. "The Mainframe *is* a thing! A *physical* thing. It *exists*. *A crystal with seven equal, perfect sides*," he said, reciting.

"*Who* said to put *what* on the Mainframe?"

"*She* said it," Wilson said dreamily. "She who is the huntress *and* the hunted. She, whose words are honey and *poison*. Captive and Captivator! Outcast and–"

"Who and where is this 'she'?"

"She is *everywhere*, now that the lock has been opened. You can find her anywhere and nowhere. *She* will come to you…well, not to *you*, Doctor *Sanders*."

"*What* is her *name*?"

"She says while in the land of mirrors, you may call her 'Sire.' "

"Sire?"

"Not *me*," Wilson said. "*Her*. You can call *me* Wilson, but my *name* is Anton."

Sanderson frowned deeper. "No, *your* name is Wilson."

"No, *Wilson* is the name I was given."

"No, Wilson is the name you *chose.* "

Wilson looked momentarily sober. "There are no choices here."

Sanderson altered his tone slightly. "Where did the apple come from?"

Wilson looked genuinely confused. "What apple?"

Sanderson furrowed his furry brow. "The apple you left for Axel."
"The *apple I left for Axel?*" Wilson giggled. "What are you *talking* about?"
Doctor Sanderson was not amused.

"I suppose I *should* draw this out as long as possible," Sanderson said, discovering the donut he took from Counselor Mue in his pocket. "But I'm too busy, so we need to get moving.
"So, what I am going to do is give you a small sample of *real* torture, and *then* I propose that you–"

Wilson's eyes glazed as his hidden suicidal failsafe finished its work. Curiously, his smile did not abate, even in death.

Sanderson frowned as he looked at the hovering imagescreen report.

"You know," Sanderson said. "They say that your brain still records sight and sound for a few moments after you die. You see, one of the potential drawbacks of being an *Agent*," Sanderson said, slightly licking his lip. "Is that you may not leave unless Axel says so. Ho hum. Soon, we'll pick up where we left off.
"Oh! I'll add you to my schedule–that way, I might take my time. No more rushing…not with *you,* Wilson.

"And *when* we resume, you can *additionally* grapple with the fear of knowing the sincerity and accuracy of my prophecy."

Sanderson turned *Destiny Core* back on.

𝖠

The police met up with Jacob Serter at his dwelling just before 6, after he had finished taking care of his remaining professional responsibilities. The police were sympathetic to Jacob Serter's possible loss, and had promised to keep their intrusion into his personal life to a minimum.
Regardless of intent, however, they found themselves detained when the situation changed about 40 minutes after their arrival.

During the questioning, the Mainframe informed the police that Anthem Serter had been found, and was heading toward the AIC [99] (where the Serters reside) at a rate of 3.2 mph.

"Is she *walking*?" The detective asked. "I suppose that makes sense, since we have her credit bank–or at least what's left of it. Still, why not just use a terminal? Why not alert *you*?" He asked, looking at Jacob. Then he instructed the dispatch: "Send an Autocar to pick her up."

"Wait," said Jacob Serter. Without the slightest change in expression, Jacob quite plainly said: "Perhaps you should *let* her walk...it occurs to me that based on the time and circumstances, she's probably full of drugs and could stand to burn them off with exercise and outside air. Considering that this story has already received *global* attention, she is likely also embarrassed about the upset she has caused. She's probably anxious that people will consider this a publicity stunt in poor taste.

"If she's not too far away, just let her walk and think," Jacob concluded.

And so they waited, which was as well, for other answers from Jacob were now necessary.

Ⓜ

A bit later, Dr. Phoebus–the lead doctor at a secret facility–accepted a private mediacast session request from AIIS Agent Director Thompson.

"Insusitate Agent Wilson," Thompson said disapprovingly. "How long until he can be reasonably interacted with?"

"12 hours," the doctor said. "Maybe less," he added, interpreting that might be too long.

"Cast [100] me when he's coherent," Thompson said, but then glanced at the time and seemed to think differently. "On second thought, let him sit for awhile. I'll expect a session request from you around noon instead."

---

[99] The Axel Industries Central (AIC) Building, or more colloquially known as *"the Ace,"* could be seen from a generous distance, standing nearly a mile high and half as wide (not including the flying butresses).

The ziggurat of Silverberg...on the day of its completion in 2038, Silverberg announced its independence. This great, silver, isosceles mountain often disappears into the clouds. On a clear day from a respectable distance, however, one could see that as it culminated towards its apex, the gigantic building narrowed itself progressively, betraying a considerable mesa at its top.

[100] Slang for *call/contact*. Had he opted for greater verbosity, Thompson might rather have said "initiate a mediacast session with me when he's coherent."

Chapter 25:

Hecklers, Heroes, Histories and Honesties

JUNE *2070 EST*

Fri 13	Sat 14	Sun 15
	18:03	

The Rook awoke to the *howling*.

It was, in fact, the very same howling that woke Wilson, for Simon had taken to watching the very same episode of *Destiny Core*.

Following their *eventual* escape [101Δ] from the labyrinth, the Rook had guided his companions, as inconspicuously as possible, to a *Chessmen* safehouse. At the moment, the Rook was unsuccessfully trying to take a nap.

"Can you turn that crap off?" The Rook barked, rolling into the back of the couch–so much as his large body would allow, anyway.

Simon sadly terminated the mediacast projection. "But, we need *inspiration* if we're going to be a super-team!"

"Oh good grief. We are *not* going to be a super-team, for the millionth time!" The Rook roared.

"But, The SEUs–"

"Yes, yes. Follow *him*. I only came by to pick up George, the rest of you are welcome to leave *at any time*."

"But you're supposed–"

[101Δ] for brevity and sanity I will spare you the full account of the Rook's many complaints about how long it took The SEUs to navigate the maze.

    - [The Terrors of Wonder] -

"Yes, and I *will* help you as soon as my *own* needs are met. That does *not* mean that we are *a team*–we'll just get together one more time after this. *One* more time. Now, let me get some sleep."

"I hear that *showers* help you sleep better," Simon suggested.

"Yes," the Rook said with some irritation. "*Go;* take a shower. That *would* help. Go. Really, *for the next 45 minutes, the only thing I want to hear is the memory of having spoken.*"

"The *memory* of *having spoken*?" Simon blinked. "What does *that* mean?"

"It means go away," the Rook said, rolling further into the couch.

"*What* means 'go away'?" The SEUs asked, walking into the living area.

"The memory of having spoken," Simon repeated the expression again.

"Wait, *what*?"

"The Rook said the only thing he wanted to hear for 45 minutes was the memory of having spoken. When I asked, he said it meant to go away."

"Hmmm. Well, what *is* the memory of having spoken?" The SEUs said, reflecting. "The *thought* of speaking…no, of words *spoken*. In a voice: a particular voice. A *memory*…a memory of something that may or may not have ever existed."

"A memory of something that never existed?"

"Yeah, you know–as in using your imagination. They're all but identical. You see, the memory of something that *was* but no longer *is*, is effectively the same as something that never was at all. Words were spoken, but apart from the memory, they do not exist. Apart from the memory, they *never* existed."

"Of *course* they existed," Simon said.

"They do not and *did not*. Think of it like this: if you should paint a picture, then burn it, and never so much as mention it to anyone…did you ever paint the picture at all?"

"Well, of course."

"But, apart from *your* memory, there's no evidence."

"Right…"

"So then, if your *memory* of the burned painting is the only thing that means it existed, it would be the same as if you *imagined* painting a picture yet never actually painted it. Neither actually existed, apart from your memory."

"Wait. That's not right."

"It's just that they are truths *only unto you*. Imagine for a moment that you die before telling anyone about the picture you painted and summarily burned. It never happened."

"Well, but I *burned* the painting…"

"No you didn't, that's just your imagination…and I daresay we need to enter into an adjacent conversation about how everything is matter and energy and how the painting is the same, whether in flames or not.

"The end point is that if your memory is the only thing that gives your past any substantiality, then the only real critic of the actual versus the invented is simply the self observing it. In conclusion, I think the Rook is saying he would like to *dream* for 45 minutes. It seems like an odd sentence to come from *his* mouth."

"Will you **both** *please* shut up?"

A

When the group had first arrived, Simon was treated immediately, although all of them had their wounds attended to quickly enough.

The Rook suggested to Amos that he join the Chessmen nee SilverSmiths in order to assume an alternate identity that would allow him to sidestep being accosted. Amos said he needed time to think about what his name and identity should be, and that such determinations should never be rushed.

Although the Rook could command the Mainframe, he could never use it to determine anything about himself. The Mainframe simply could not find him, could not "see" him. From the day this situation began, it was often as hindering as it was helpful.

For instance: it was always a bit annoying for the Rook to try and report to the Queen remotely, as whatever kept him hidden from Mainframe surveillance *also* kept him from participating in mediacast sessions. In short, the Rook always needed someone *else* to cast the Queen for him.

Slightly after arriving, the Rook (reluctantly, and also thus vicariously) reported himself to the Queen.

"Oh, **thank** you for deigning to see to *my* needs now, dear Rook," the Queen had said to the Knight while the Rook watched.

"It's a good thing I know where Serter's going to **be** tomorrow, isn't it? Here, I'll send you a copy of Serter's leadership speech.

"If you can stop yourself from falling asleep, you'll see how he announces his custodial itinerary. I'll include the unit number and location, since your dependability has recently come into question. As there will be a lot of people in small spaces, your visual camouflage will be worthless;[102Δ] I will have our people set you up as a new employee at the unit Serter is going to visit. This will put you in a perfect position to get the apple.

"Sources indicate that the girl still has it; this may very well be true tomorrow as well. Thankfully the two of them are all but inseparable, so I anticipate her attendance. I have a man at the Serter estate in case he leaves it there, but if I were Serter, I wouldn't let it out of my sight. Then again, I sure as hell wouldn't give it to my daughter, either.

"I'll be hiding in the dining room as a potential diversion, in case the press is involved or things go awry. Get the apple, get *out* of there, and take it *directly* to the Queen's Chamber. I'll meet you there. Do **not** screw this up. Pray that **you're** the one to get the apple, otherwise I am demoting you to Pawn."

Simon, the Rook, The SEUs, and Amos watched Serter's leadership speech through several times, mostly at the insistence of Amos. Amos was deeply touched at the words of Jacob Serter. As they watched it, Amos would often say *"yes!"* and *"I see the truth of it."*

Eventually satisfied, everyone went back to doing roughly nothing greater than relaxing.

The SEUs had departed for a moment to "check the Mainframe."

Simon was watching *MMR*, or *The Mainframe's Most Relevant*, one of the premiere mediacast news shows in Silverberg. The newscaster was reporting about a tragic accident that happened just outside of a tavern on the east side of Silverberg.

Simon kept muttering about how awful it was.

102Δ The Rook did not bother to inform the Queen that he did not currently possess his visual camouflage…the fact that Simon refused to relinquish it until he helped him was information that could only–unnecessarily –further upset the Queen.

The music group *The Valentine Relics* were missing, all presumed dead. Amongst the group was Anthem–Ayn Serter–Jacob Serter's wife.

"Wait, what was that?" The Rook asked, rolling over and sitting up. "Mainframe: stop mediacast record. Rescind one minute from record on display. Resume play."

"Serter's wife, eh?" The Rook thought aloud after it played again. "I wonder what that does to tomorrow?"

"Amos…I know what you could use as your new name," Simon suggested. "You could call yourself *Valentine*, in memory of these poor people and Mr. Serter's wife. Valentine Smith, maybe."

"Valentine Smith?" Amos echoed.

"*Valentine?*" The Rook stumbled with the name. "Isn't that kind of a *girl's* name?"

"It's a strange name," Amos said, nodding.

"It's a strange land," Simon said as he smiled humbly.

"Well, at least you'd only have the *one* name," the Rook admitted. "I can't take all this George/Amos back and forth for much longer anyway…but I'm *not* calling you *Valentine*. *That* name is crap. Sorry. I'll call you Mike. Go with Mike, or Michael. Mike Smith. What could be a more normal name?"

"You make *no* sense," Simon shook his head. "Here you chastise *us* for *our* mental consistency, and then you go–" Simon stopped and looked at Art. "I *know*."

"Okay, that's *it*," the Rook huffed. "Art, can you *please* mind your own business for a minute? It's hard enough to talk to Simon without any more distractions."

"My name is *not* Michael."

"What do you **mean**, *I hear ya?*" Simon yelled at Art after a moment. "I'm not *constantly* distracted–you take that back."

"Well it sure as hell isn't *Valentine,*" the Rook said bitterly. "Don't be *stupid*–'Valentine' is too much attention; that name is *loud*. [103Δ] You want a simple name that is easy to remember and pronounce…and just *one* name. Even when you called yourself George Gordon you had too many names. It all gets too confusing."

"Whatever do you mean?" Amos/George/Michael/Valentine/Subject 61167 asked. "George Gordon is not too many names, although I admittedly do not care much for the sound of it. Regardless, many people are known by their full name as well as the brief variant; then there are nicknames and titles–"

[103Δ] conspicuous.

"Let's just keep it simple and tame," the Rook suggested. "Alright?"

"Yes, *the Rook, Percy, Pierce*," Amos said, slightly smiling.

"Oh ha ha," the Rook laughed dryly. "I see you haven't *forgotten* your wit, if indeed you've forgotten anything at all."

"What do you mean?"

"I mean...listen, I have always liked you–as do a lot of people–but unlike most, I really know you *and* I like you. You've always been the kind of man who uses others to get ahead; it wouldn't be beyond you to be, you know, lying about this memory loss thing.   It just seems like you might be playing an old character, that's all. You used to have this character in *Dozens of Dragons;* you speak a *lot* like he did."

"Don't listen to him, Amos/Valentine," Simon insisted. "You're an honest man. Heck, you've only been *communicative* for a handful of *hours*. You haven't even had *time* to lie. As far as I can tell, you are *technically* the only man I have ever met who has never lied."

The Rook went on to say something else, but something was happening within Amos that left him suddenly unable to hear or even perceive his surroundings.

As Simon said "never lied," Amos suddenly experienced a very personal and unique reaction to his years of Trap 3. For a moment, for Amos, there was no barrier between his waking life and dream life–nothing to separate his conscious from his subconscious. Instantly, George had a past. His memories didn't flood, they simply *were*. He knew himself again.

He knew about trivial things, such as *Dozens of Dragons*. He knew about personal things, like the significance behind the cryptic expression *"Don't forget the lemon."* He even knew that The Badger Badgers were a football team in Wisconsin.

He knew, also, that he was disdainful of anyone less than those whose approval had value. He knew that he had secretly betrayed many of his closest friends with complete indifference. For instance, he knew he had had an affair with the Rook's late wife. He knew of worse things yet.

Yet, there was also suddenly within him a *superconscious* self–neither George nor Amos, neither asleep nor awake, yet all simultaneously. As he examined himself as George, and then again as Amos, his thoughts and feelings flashed as brightly and instantly as lightning:

*Who **am** I?*

*Am I who I **was**? George Gordon? The selfish, sociopathic, sarcastic, elitist, hypersexual, egotistical, vengeful, jealous George Gordon?*

*I can't be **him**. Was I not, moments ago, a man all but devoid of such ghastly mannerisms?*

Yet, can I be Amos? Innocent Amos?

No, I cannot be him. I remember, and therefore I am not him.

*I **must** remember who I have been and what I have done…if I allowed myself to think that my transgressions were permissible, I would not learn from them. Forgotten, I would quickly be back to my old behaviors; I simply will not **justify** them.*

I might observe my younger self with compassion, however, the way a father looks on his son when he fails at something when he first tries it. Living takes practice; we must be patient.

*Most of my transgressions are completely ephemeral, nothing more than the "memory of having spoken." If not for these memories, then indeed, what record **is** there? And if I dwell on lamenting my transgressions, will that somehow enhance or help my fellow man? I must simply not repeat myself, and I will not be **that** man **again**.*

*And men who have known me historically, such as Percy: do **they** know who I **am**? Can **they** determine my **identity**? No—only by the authority I extend them. Only by my own allowance do I extend the right to anyone to determine **who I am**.*

The world has dictated to me who I am for too long.

*I am the result of my choices **right now**. I am the me that is **now**. My very identity is determined **by me** on a **moment by moment** basis.*

*And **now** I just want to be genuine. No more false smiles, no more lies…too much of that in the world already. The world needs truth. I need to be truthful, earnest. Lead by example. Join Jacob Serter?*

He let out the smallest laugh as his thoughts started to slow down.

          - [The Terrors of Wonder] -

Anthem walked the streets of Silverberg with purpose. Tick-tock, tick-tock, her boots sounded off. Her face was plain, devoid of readability; even her tail was docile. Her steps were constant, rhythmic–perhaps she was writing music as she walked.

Anthem was on her way home, to see her husband and child.

"I remember *everything*," Amos said, finally zoning back into the moment. Everyone stopped talking and looked over at him.

"I mean *everything*. I think I actually somehow remember *more* than before I lost myself. However, I *particularly* remember what a complete bastard I was. I'm sorry, really. The simple truth of it is that I cannot be George any longer, nor can I be Amos–not only in name, but also in identity.

"My name will reflect who I *am*, and you're right old pal, Valentine *is* a pretty crappy name–at least for *me*. You know those rare moments when you suddenly feel like you understand the mechanism of the universe–and then it slips away as quickly? Well, *I* have just had a complete *personal* epiphany, and my understanding of it does not flee or abate.

"Amos was without blemish, for he never lied. I cannot be Amos, for *I* lack innocence. George Gordon was such a man who would compliment himself on his own deceitful behaviors. I am *tired* of that man–a man both fake and false in so many ways. I cannot be George Gordon, for he was a proud liar, and I have neither pride nor any inclination to *lie ever again*.

"I have dedicated myself henceforth to acting as a stalwart champion of the *truth*. From this point, I think I shall be known as Earnest."

Everybody just stared at him.

"Don't look lost!" Earnest said with enthusiasm. "Rejoice, for I have overcome *myself*, the most insidious of opponents."

"It's like he's some kind of sick mix of old and new," the Rook said, slack-jawed and ugly. "And what the heck is up with *Earnest*? I said pick something casual. Who's named *Earnest*?

"Who's named *the Rook*?"

"Riposte!" Simon yelled, imitating Anderson's deep voice. Everyone started laughing.

"*Please* tell me that you're not just going to tell the truth the whole time?"

"What's wrong with telling the truth?"

"Well, it can get pretty sticky if you're *trying* to deceive someone. You know, like *posing* as an employee? Like, *tomorrow*? George–*Earnest,* I swear if you *only* tell the truth…if you think this is going to somehow make up for being such a…well it won't."

"No, I know that there is nothing that I have done that can be undone by me…but I *do* want to tell the truth, and I will do so *at any cost.* That, however, does *not* mean that I will *always* speak, merely that when I do, I will speak only the truth, for the truth is beautiful."

"The truth is *ugly*," replied the Rook.

"…only by reputation," said The SEUs as he walked into the last part of the conversation. "You hear things about her all the time, but good luck actually finding her."

"Her?" The Rook asked.

"The truth. It's *your* conversation, I was just helping…or not, it seems."

"Amos is going to call himself *Earnest,*" the Rook said while he made a sweeping gesture to his old friend. "In tandem with his name, he has *also* apparently chosen to commit social suicide by staving off lying indefinitely."

"Hmm," The SEUs frowned. "That certainly *could* make life much more difficult."

"But I *must* try," Earnest said, looking over at The SEUs. "It's only too easy to lie, yet *who* can tell the truth? Telling the truth doesn't have to be a *terrible* thing–although it certainly *can* be, if you so will it.

"I don't mean I will avoid omission; it's my prerogative to say what I am inclined to say and no more. *And* I don't mean I will fail to prevaricate–I am not hesitant to employ it, liberally if necessary. People deceive themselves all the time, my help or lack thereof notwithstanding.

"I'm just so tired of being rank and file. I want to lead by example…like Jacob Serter said." Earnest said, and then sat down, not realizing that he had stood up as he was speaking.

The Rook frowned.

"Here, here!" The SEUs said, nodding and clapping. "You're *right*. It's about *time* someone stood up for the truth! You're a *perfect* member for our super-team!"

"Because he *tells the **truth***?" The Rook asked, blinking stupidly. "What kind of transhuman power is *that?*"

"You know, now that you mention it, it *would* be trans if someone *never* lied,' The SEUs said, thinking out loud.

"Oh, I have lied," Earnest said in somber tones.

"No, *George* lied," Simon corrected. "Now you just need a name."

"I just *said* my name."

"No, you need a super-name for our super-team!" Simon said with energy.

"NO MORE NAMES!" The Rook roared.

"You know, like *Electroshock* or *The Watchman*. We could call you…um… Vox Veritas! And you could put all these V's on your costume–"

"Wait a second," The SEUs interrupted. "For once, perhaps, I have to agree with the Rook…I think you've seen too many episodes of *Destiny Core*. When I say super-team, I mean addressing the problems that *we* are uniquely outfitted to address. Only for free. Oh, and without approval. After all, we can only apply our particular talents…you're a *painter*; you can't fly or shoot laser beams. Your knowledge of mirroranium is impressive, I am sure, but it won't stop a common burglar much less a metahuman one.

"We're not some storybook heroes," The SEUs continued to explain. "Their worlds are *simpler* than ours; their lives are paraphrased. We are living, breathing people–they're just *characters*. *We* have to eat and breathe and use the restroom and put on makeup, pay bills more than once a season or once a series. We actually have to *read* the newspaper instead of seeing a single still picture or reading a one-sentence recapitulation. We clean our fingernails. Ever see a member of *Destiny Core* get a haircut?

"We don't have *villains* to overcome, so much as entities–like Axel Industries, Van Loch, or Blairmounte. [104Δ] Whereas there is not much *obvious* crime, the list of *hidden* atrocities is considerable. Yet, we also must remain hidden, otherwise how could we remain effective?" The SEUs smiled.

[104Δ] Van Loch and Blairmounte are the names of two global corporations who have been implicated as having deliberately misled the public in order to satisfy their own avarice.

"You *don't* know what you're talking about," the Rook said with a voice suddenly weighted with age. "There *is* no hiding in Silverberg."

"The Chessmen–"

"Frankly, I'm not sure how the Chessmen manage to stay off the *do-something-about* list," the Rook continued. "But then again I really don't understand *how* they provide someone with an undetectable alternate identity in *Silverberg* in the first place. Such a thing would mean they had some kind of programming influence over the Mainframe, right? You know what? Forget I even said that. I don't want to talk about the Mainframe. Not like programmer stuff. Not with any of *you.*"

Simon opened his mouth.

"Shut up. Anyway, listen–all I know is that if A.I. wants you, they *will* get you."

"So, how do *you* manage to avoid this…what was his name? Thompson?" The SEUs raised an eyebrow, smiling.

The Rook frowned, making his face almost symmetrical. "*Actually*, without my camouflage, it's only a matter of time–and he *will* come for me. Even if the Mainframe, *shut up*, can't see me, I'll still be lucky if he isn't coming through that piggin' door right now."

Everyone looked over at the door as if the Rook might have spoken such an event into existence.

"I never fully appreciated how closely we can be watched until the day Thompson told me that we were *even*. That expression I said earlier? *'The only thing I want to hear is the memory of having spoken?'* That was the last thing I ever heard this one guy say. He wanted to take a nap, and that was how he dismissed me. When I came back, he was dead.

"Thompson was there. His presence was a courtesy, I think. He was letting me know how personal it was. I didn't understand it at the time, but that's exactly what that was about."

The Rook apparently tried to do his impression of what Agent Thompson sounded like as he said: "'*We are even, Godwin. You are paid in full in that **your** life is not demanded as well. I might say that your only hope is to **leave** Silverberg, but such an act will not avail you. You must be, and will be, destroyed. But I **am** a **man** of my word, and I **will** have you paid for your service.*' And then he just walks over to me, and puts his hand up on my shoulder. It was weird, I just watched him walk over to me like I was in shock. Anyway, then he says '*and so, I grant you one more day of life; live it well.*' And then–*then* I have a piggin' *stroke*.

"The SilverSmiths helped me out a lot through my recovery, so I figured I would throw in with them. Somewhere between the SilverSmiths and the camo I survived. But more the camo.

"Oh, I managed to elude Thompson, that much is clear…but he was always closer than I imagined. Using my *unique talents*, I figured *I* could combat 'the bad guys' by myself. I made a costume, and I even called myself *Mercy*.

"Shut *uuup*," the Rook said, pointing at Simon.

"Anyway, so I go out like this all of *three* times. I knew there was something wrong the second time I tried to play super-hero; I just couldn't put my finger on it. By the third, A.I. clearly knew where I would be and when. I *narrowly* escaped. Oh and hey! Here's some trivia: did you know there aren't *any* Chessmen in District F? No? Understandable. The only reason *I* know that is because I see many of the Queen's reports. No one knows to where, but on November 22nd, 2068–the third time I tried to play hero–every Chessman in District F disappeared. Not simultaneously, but not far apart either.

"No notes. Nothing stolen. Nothing suspicious; some were transferred, some travelling. It took the Chessmen a moment to even realize the severity of it. Twenty two Pawns and one Knight. And sometimes their families. Gone. Let *that* sink in."

"Why is it that you sometimes call them the *SilverSmiths* and sometimes the *Chessmen*?" Simon asked.

"Oh, I don't know. I suppose I think of them more as the *SilverSmiths* when we're talking about the identity-changing aspect of the group, and more as the *Chessmen* when I think of them in greater scope. They're both…but don't say that to a Knight or Bishop."

"And the Chessmen gave you augmentations?" Simon asked further.

"Well, no…" The Rook began.

"Oh, you don't *know*?" Earnest said to Simon. "The Rook is none other than *Citizen Gladiator*." [105Δ]

"Holy cow," Simon said, exhaling and looking up at the Rook. "And *you* complain about *other* people having too many names?"

"Wait, what's '*Citizen Gladiator*'?" asked The SEUs.

"You guys don't watch *Gladiator*?" The Rook blinked. "*Everyone* watches *Gladiator*."

"Eh. Not everyone," Simon said unenthusiastically.

105Δ A title of a *person* rather than a mediacast show, *Citizen Gladiator Pierce Godwin* won the 2056 Gladiatorial Games (*Gladiator* courtesy of SerterCo).

"Oh, but *Destiny Core*'s such a *great* show. At least Gladiator is *real*."

"How *did* you win your last match?" Earnest asked.

"I meant it had *real people*."

The Knight (the owner of the house that doubled as the Chessmen "safe-house") walked in. He was a well-dressed but otherwise unthreatening and portly man who looked like he couldn't figure out if he was honored or annoyed with his company of misfits.

On his arm was a woman wearing a purple kimono. She had purple hair, and wore a plump, purple smile. She was, apparently, a very new Pawn for the Chessmen, having arrived a short while after the companions.

The Knight asked everyone as to whether or not they were hungry or thirsty. Accommodating all affirming responses, the Knight and the Pawn, *Wonda*, departed elsewhere.

"I'm so happy we're no longer in the lab," Simon said, having recently finished his sandwich.

"Yeah, *what* were you there for, anyway?" The Rook asked.

"I told you…my paintings," Simon said.

"Stop piggin' around! Axel Industries did *not* detain you because of your *paintings*."

"Of course they did," Simon said, almost sounding hurt.

"Listen, I hate to be the only guy here who's willing to tell you the *truth*," the Rook paused and looked at Earnest. "but you're just a little crazy. What you paint does *not* come true. That's absurd. Besides, the one time you're asked *how* it comes true, you just say '*Heaven knows*?'"

"I said '*Who knows,*' but whatever."

"Alright, apart from *Art*, how do you know your paintings come true?"

"Well, Axel Industries took one of my paintings away. That seemed corroboratory."

"That *does* seem significant," The SEUs said with sudden interest. "I didn't know *that*. What was the painting of?"

"Oh…I don't really know," Simon shrugged.

"What do you mean, you *don't know*?" The Rook said in irritation. "How could you *possibly* not know what your painting was *of*?"

"*Usually* I know what I am going to paint before I paint it…but sometimes I decide to just put my brush to canvas and see what happens. That was the kind of painting they took."

 - [The Terrors of Wonder] -

"Surely you can describe it?"

"Oh yes. Let's see. There was a wall, and on the wall were all these masks. The wall was behind a counter, which in turn had a few masks laying on top, as if they had been tried on. Between the wall and the counter, there was an attendant. The attendant was positioning a mirror, apparently to show the unseen buyer what they looked like with their current selection of mask. In the mirror was a reflection of the face of the attendant. Both were smiling with satisfaction."

The Rook frowned. "Bleh. *I* would have taken that rock/island painting."

"Do you think you could paint it again?" The SEUs asked.

"Maybe. I doubt it would be exactly the same. Even though my memory of it is solid, whenever I try to remember what the individual masks looked like, I can't recall the details."

"Hmmm," said The SEUs unhelpfully.

The Rook yawned.

"Are you tired *again*?" Simon asked, annoyed.

"Look, when you get to be my age, you get sleepy. Besides, counting from yesterday, it's been a looong day." The Rook looked at The SEUs. "I'm headed to bed soon so I can start my *'new job'* tomorrow…but I'm *dying* to know *your* story. Simon and I have anted up, now it's your turn."

"There's really not much to tell," The SEUs said. "Nothing that's going to make any sense to you, anyway."

"Oh, *well…THAT* would sure be different than the rest of this rescue. What about that name of *yours*, anyway? 'The SEUs?' Can you make *that* make sense?" Seeing The SEUs frown, the Rook added. "But if you don't want to talk about *that*, how about you just explain why *you* were in that laboratory in the first place?"

"They're one and the same," The SEUs sighed. "It *would* be fair of me to disclose…I'll make this as brief as possible, but I don't know how much it's going to help you. I started calling myself 'The SEUs' mostly as a joke, as a result of a comment…really more of a declaration, I suppose. Better than being called Subject 40449, anyway. You see, one day not too terribly long ago, one of my professional companions exclaimed in amazement and laughter: *'My God!* **Theo's** *the SEUs!'* But why would he say that? What does that *mean*? Well, *I* used to be called Theodore, or Theo–so that's pretty easy. But *the SEUs*? Well…SEU is an acronym for Single Event Upset.

CHAPTER 25

"A Single Event Upset is a change of state caused when ionizing radiation, such as electrons or photons, strike a sympathetic point in a memory cell, transistor, or processor. Whatever error is found to be a result of the strike is called a Single Event Upset, or a *soft error*. The radiation can be either terrestrial or galactic in origin, although alpha particle radiation from terrestrial sources–"

"Okay, stop." The Rook interrupted. "You're right, this isn't helping. You lost me at ionizing. Imagine for a moment that I don't know anything about what you're talking about."

The SEUs smiled. "My contemporary discovered that most of the problems that were caused over the last few years at the station were a result of *me*. At first, it was kind of funny, but soon afterward I had to start reporting to the doctor daily.

"I knew things were not looking very good for me, especially as I watched my few freedoms slowly vanish. Yet, what could I do? I was already at their mercy, so I just kept working until rotation came and then they took me away to the lab. Basically, I *cause* soft errors."

"The station?" Simon asked.

"You wouldn't believe me if I explained."

"I'm about done with you," the Rook said, annoyed. "First, you insist that we can't understand you…okay, well, you might be right there. But *now* we won't *believe* you. Like, is it any *less* believable that *Simon* was kidnapped for his prophetic *paintings*?"

"Hey!" Simon objected.

"I was an engineer aboard the space station AIS-38 '*Persephone*' which sits in orbit on the dark side of Pluto," said The SEUs calmly.

"Okay, that's it," the Rook said, jumping off the couch and walking out of the room. "You're right. I can only handle so much crap in a single day. There hasn't been a space program since Urraca. [106Δ] *Now* we're travelling to Pluto and back? Without anyone in the world knowing? *And* the things *he* paints *come true?* Goodnight."

"I *did* try to tell him," The SEUs shrugged. "I got us out of the lab and

---

106Δ Operation Urraca. On March 14, 1993, America sent a 100 Megaton rocket to explode in low orbit above Russia. The resultant EMP caused *every* Russian satellite to fail, wounding Russia considerably. The coordinated offensive that followed struck Russia *hard*.

Although this act undeniably won America the war, it suffered a considerable loss of global respect. *All* orbital satellites failed shortly after Urraca. The aftermath affected the entire world in *many* ways unforeseen, one of which was the disinterest in pursuing the development of government space programs. The world remained reliant on a more terrestrial method of communication.

The Rook is wrong to say that there hasn't been a space program since Urraca; recently there have been a couple private companies (Systemlink in 2059 and DiaCo in 2068) that have established young, yet viable space programs.

 - [The Terrors of Wonder] -

through the maze. *I* don't think it's as hard to believe as that your paintings come true."

"Hey!"

"I didn't say *I* didn't believe you…I was just comparing the difference in credibility."

"So…we're staying here?' Simon asked.

"Well, I suppose for the moment, anyway. You can't even *walk*. Well, maybe slowly. Once you're fully healed, I suggest we…but what about you, Am–*Earnest*? Any ideas where we might go from here?"

"Nope. But tomorrow I think I'll tag along with *the Rook*," Earnest said, laughing again over the name. "I shall sit out in the dining room as a guest."

"*Oh no you won't*," the Rook said, walking back into the room to grab his shoes. "I'll be undercover, and I don't need extra things to worry about."

The Rook stopped and thought. "Actually, come to think of it, maybe you *should* come along…then I don't have to worry about whether I'll come back to Thompson standing over your body."

"I *would* like to go. I would like to meet Jacob Serter."

"Are you *out* of your piggin' mind? You want to meet the one man I am there to steal from? And if you're caught you'll only tell them the *truth?* No, no, and no."

"I won't stand out or up. If I meet him, it'll be because he came to my table."

"No."

"*Don't forget the lemon.*"

"*Fine*," the Rook suddenly relented. "But just sit there and *eat*. Do not draw attention to yourself. Do *not* do anything to blow this."

Chapter 26:

Home Sweet Home

JUNE *2070 EST*

Fri 13	Sat 14	Sun 15
	19:12	

Anthem finally arrived at home.

"Mommy!" Wonder yelled when she first saw her. She ran across the room and jumped into her very surprised mother's arms. "I missed you *so* much!"

"Oh!" Anthem said, smiling cheek to cheek. "I missed you too, sweetheart! I'm so glad to be home!"

"Us *too!*"

The police soon afterward examined Anthem and listened to her account of events.

Anthem said that she and *The Relics* enjoyed their time at *The Tentacle and the Tail*, but Nan and Billy were getting out of control, so they decided to drive around town in the bus while they either sobered up or passed out–as they have been known to do on prior occasions of such gross inebriation.

She said she must have blacked out, for when she woke up *today*, her last memory of the prior evening is simply being on the bus with *The Relics*. She said she was shocked and surprised when she woke up in a *theater*. [107△]

[107△] Reverse observation showed her leaving just after 6 PM. Congruent investigations show, however, that the tour bus never comes within proximity of the theatre. Anthem is never seen walking into the building.

Also know that a "theater" in Silverberg is something more like a miniature amusement park. Whereas you *can* observe initial and exclusive mediacast sessions, that is hardly the primary allure for most citizens. Many prefer the rides, the restaurants, the toys, or the gambling which involves wagering on such instances as "what actors will portray what characters," or "what characters will be next to die."

          - [The Terrors of Wonder] -

As she used one of the theater's restrooms, she saw the mediacast record of SNRK's (*The Snark's*) coverage of the…meltdown. She considered that perhaps her life was in danger from some kind of psychotic *Relics* fan. Of course, *The Relics* had death threats before, but nothing like *this*.

Why didn't she cast anyone? Well, she searched for her credit bank but could not locate it. Regardless, she didn't really know what to say or how, and she was half full of drugs and wasn't up to the idea of confrontation of any sort. The last thing she wanted was to be swarmed by journalists and reporters.

She frowned when she said she *did* tell a man to cast the police and let them know that Ayn Serter was alright and that she would be home shortly. The police were momentarily baffled at this last statement, as they had not received any such contact. It was eventually dismissed under the guise that the man simply neglected to fulfill his promise. [108Δ]

What happened to *The Relics*? She was hoping the police might know something.

She *does* hope that everyone is alright. She needs her credit bank–you don't realize how much you can miss something until you're without it.

Eventually satisfied after many dozens of questions, the police left the family alone–for the evening, anyway.

As the Serters soon afterward sat down for dinner at their impressive dining table, Jacob spoke up.

"We will observe a moment of silence for Rachael Gale, her commitment paid in full. Now she is finally free. Let us hope that in these last years the peace in her heart completely overcame the malice of her youth."

After a couple moments, Anthem asked "Who?"

"Rachael Gale is the name of the slave that was sent to retrieve you from your tour bus. She died when it melted."

With that, the Serters ate their dinner quietly, as was their custom.

[108Δ] Yet, Anthem is not lying–at least, not about *that*. The police are incorrect, yet not neglectful or stupid. For clarity, reference Appendix: Misunderstood Mediacast page 297.

CHAPTER 26

"Oh, this is interesting, what is it?" Hugo asked, sipping at his soup. "It reminds me of a…it's like a…nutty borsht…*Oh!* Let us replace the adjective *interesting* with *revolting* instead."

"It's *Dreisdale's*," Cornelia said reprovingly. "and you liked it the last time we had it."

"*Dreisdale's* **what**? *Nutty Borsht?*"

"*Dreisdale's Vegetable Soup.*"

"Well, it's hideous. Mainframe, start mediacast record. Dear Complaint Department of *Dreisdale's Foods and Manufacturing*, your vegetable soup is completely without integrity. On one tasting, I found it to be hearty and delightful–aromatic and succulent to taste–however upon subsequent purchase I am rather disappointed to discover that 'batch A' and 'batch B' are not of equal caliber.

"It would do you well to consider returning to me the funds which *my* household egregiously extended to *your* company in exchange for a product that *you* apparently did not accurately label. You might further consider renaming your vegetable soup to *Dreisdale's Potluck*, that no one else need suffer similarly."

"Essence, take those headphones off," Cordelia instructed her oldest daughter, who in turn did absolutely nothing.

"If you think, however, that this might be an isolated incident and would want me to *reconsider* my opinion of your product by my next published criticism," Hugo continued, "you are welcome to extend to me several samples of soup that I might not only reward you with a declaration of your consistency, but also of how you are so very generous and expedient with your resolution of guest problems. Pot*luck*. Hugo Templeton. End mediacast record. Mainframe, deliver recently created mediacast record to the human resource department of *Dreisdale's Food and Manufacturing.*"

MAINFRAME » DELIVERY SUCCESSFUL.

"Now, what *else* is for dinner?"

This new purple Pawn had been on the Queen's mind for some time.

It's probably because she's attractive, the Queen thought. *But there's no denying that she's valuable. She supposedly has all kinds of intel on SerterCo, intel I have dreamt of. Hmm. Perhaps I should promote her to Bishop...based on her previous position, that just might be the best idea. I have to meet this 'Wonda.'*

The Queen arranged for Wonda to ride with the Rook (and thus also Earnest) to his assignment. After the store opened, the Queen would meet with her *personally* in the dining room. The Queen smiled, finally pleased at the end of the day. It was not long afterward that he fell asleep.

⚠

"Wonderful," Jacob Serter said, turning to face his daughter. "I need you to give me that apple."

"Aw, but daddy…"

"You can have it back when you wake up, just like we did with last night and this morning."

Wonder reluctantly placed the mirroranium apple on the table next to her father.

"Where did that come from?" Anthem asked, smiling perhaps too largely.

"Oh, Mommy!" Wonder exclaimed. "There was this guy–oh, but he died." Wonder was silent for a moment, but then picked back up with renewed enthusiasm. "but he said this poetry! It was so pretty."

"Oh?" Anthem asked lovingly.

"Oh yes! It was about kings and queens and prinsisses! But then there was the funny man–oh! And the black man, and he said to give the apple to him! But I gave it to daddy! An he gave it to *me*!"

"At least until tomorrow, *then* we're going to give it to the black man," Jacob finished.

"Who's the black man?" Anthem asked.

"Axel. He wants it."

"And he's going to give you something for it?"

"Yep."

"What?"

"Whatever I want."

"What do you want?"

"It's a surprise. I'll tell you tomorrow."

"I'm your *wife*," Anthem said, particularly stressing her relationship. "You can tell *me*."

"Now, you know I don't tell secrets. Be patient. I'll tell you the minute it's over."

"Jacob, can't you just be honest and open with me?"

"Can I go play?" Wonder asked

"No," Jacob said, turning his attention from Anthem to Wonder. "It's time for *you* to take a bath."

"Aww," she protested.

Perhaps on cue, a servant appeared and led Wonder toward the bathroom.

Jacob took up the apple and walked into his office.

Anthem sat still.

"Essence? Are you going to take a bath?"

"*Who* are you talking to?" Hugo asked Cordelia.

"Who do you suppose?"

"Well, if you mean *that* woman over there, I suggest you pry those preposterous ear-shields back if you want her to hear you."

Cordelia reached over the scant table and pulled off Essence's headwear. Through the room the words rang out:

"for these dreams of the damned
"are demented and de-manned
"like a ship without a hand
"to make good the lord's demand."

"*What?*" Essence asked, annoyed. She grabbed her headphones back from her mother.

"I asked if you were going to take a bath."

"Oh…yeah."

"Now that you have deigned to extend to us your attentions, my darling daughter, I might inquire as to whether or not you are, in fact, working or playing at the moment?" Hugo asked.

"Oh. Both, I suppose. I'm listening—or at least *sampling* all of *The Valentine Relics'* music in light of the recent disaster. If they're imaged, I'll cast something to the extent that although I never much cared for them personally, they were nonetheless praiseworthy for their originality and courage. I'll reference a couple songs that I felt were their best.

"Then again, if this is just some slang publicity stunt, I'll only focus on their shortcomings and destroy them." She replaced her headphones.

Hugo looked at his wife, his eyes half open in approval. "She's a fine girl, Cordy. We have done well."

Cordelia rolled her eyes.

"Darling?" Hugo asked after briefly hugging his wife.

"Yes, dear?"

"You remember Andy Clauson? He cast me earlier and told me he was asked to come into work tomorrow morning because *Jacob Serter* was going to be there.

"I think we will therefore eat at *Bagel Lord* tomorrow; that should make for a most interesting article."

Wonder laid in her bed, her mother and father looking down at her, smiling in appreciation.

"Mommy, I'm sad for the man who died."

"Well, I should hope so," Anthem said, nodding. "And it's okay to be sad. With enough time, though, you'll either forget about it or it will dull. Oh, but I hope it doesn't give you nightmares tonight."

"Oh! Mommy!" Wonder sat up. "I don't think I hafta have nightmares any-more! I can just wake up!"

"The Hypnizium," Jacob whispered into Anthem's ear. "She said something about it earlier today."

"Oh…" Anthem said. A few slow seconds passed until she finally added: "Good!"

"Alright, Wonderful, we're off to bed, too," Jacob said in warmth. "If you need us, we'll be right here."

"Thanks mommy, thanks daddy. I love you."

"We love you too, princess."

Anthem and Jacob walked out of the room and eventually into their own.

Soon after Anthem closed the door, Jacob started speaking with disappoint-ment.

"You realize how ba–"

"Shut up, baby," Anthem said, smiling mischeviously, her tail swishing provocatively. "First *I* have a need that must be met, *then* **you** can be upset or whatever."

Chapter 27:

Two Twenty-Two

JUNE *2070 EST*

Fri 13	Sat 14	Sun 15
		02:22

The bedroom was dark, the night was still. Apart from the occasional soft chime from the Mainframe suggesting that Anthem or Jacob had messages waiting, there was no sound beyond their breathing.

Anthem whispered softly, experimentally: "Are you awake?"
"No dear, I am sleeping," Jacob whispered back.

Chapter 28:

Softer Still

JUNE 2070 EST

Fri 13	Sat 14	Sun 15
		03:57

Anthem whispered, so softly she was practically mouthing the words. "Darling, are you awake?"

"No dear, I am sleeping," Jacob whispered back.

Chapter 29:

A Few Falsehoods

JUNE *2070 EST*

Fri 13	Sat 14	Sun 15
		05:59

"Are you having trouble resting?" Anthem whispered into the silent darkness.

"Only because you won't stop speaking,' Jacob grumbled.

"I'm scared," Anthem said, her voice returning to its regular level. "I can't get certain things out of my mind."

"Things like what?"

"Like things that I have heard about you."

"Good grief, is *that* what you have been thinking about all night?"

"Maybe."

The lights turned on.

"Well, don't put any trust in what the Mainframe commentators suggest or say. Listen, I don't have anything to hide; leaders, after all, lead *by example*." Jacob pulled her close. "Trust me. Have you *ever* seen me act without accord?"

"Maybe a few hours ago," Anthem said, a smile in her voice. "But, if you're so open and honest about everything, then why can't you tell me about what Axel is supposed to give you?"

"Goodness, you're persistent," Jacob said, rolling out of bed. "If you *must* know, I am going to ask Axel to recant on his Tariff of 2066. If you were not paying close attention, a few years ago Axel more or less told the world that *exports* from Silverberg would cost *double* and imports were worth *half* their prior value.

"Well, the world had become somewhat reliant on trading resources and commodities with Silverberg, and the sudden change of market has hurt global commerce. Heck, *I* can't buy anything from my own stores in Silverberg from abroad without paying Silverberg an equal portion. In one grand move, Axel heavily wounded the world market. If you can't envision the math, let me remind you that what Axel *owns* is not confined to Axel Industries *or* Silverberg."

"You think Axel is going to change this *pronouncement* for that *apple*?"

"We shall see. I have a meeting with him this morning."

"I have *other* fears," Anthem continued.

Jacob started getting dressed. "Such as?"

"What if you don't come home today? I mean, what if someone was really trying to kill me with that bus thing? What if someone is trying to kill *you*?"

"You can't be serious," Jacob said, as he continued to dress. "We're in Silverberg, how much safer can it get? Then again, I live in the land of my greatest rivals, how much more dangerous could it get? Regardless, if someone was going to try to kill me, I would imagine it would have already happened.[109Δ]

"Still," Anthem slapped her thighs. "Things happen. Look at me, *The Relics*. What if you left, and never came home? What if you thought to try and keep me safe by locking all the doors and windows, yet kept for yourself the only key–and then you die, and then I'm stuck in here, for the rest of my life, forced to survive on whatever materials I could get my hands on?"

Jacob said nothing as he continued to dress.

"I'd probably eventually get lonely and be forced to create a race of substandard, jaundiced men that I *personally* would have to educate and clean up after. And then *they'd* probably revolt, betraying me–just like *you*–and after all I had done for them." Anthem tapped her cheek thoughtfully. "How would *you* punish something like that at SerterCo?"

"Honey, I think you might *still* be a under the influence of something. Maybe you should take a shower."

"Maybe I *should*," Anthem said as Jacob walked out of the room.

109Δ It *did* happen. Jacob was shot at when he spent a few days in Argentina during Anthem's pregnancy. Of course, that was before Jacob had re-established himself, and there has been no similar episode since. He never told Anthem, and did not see how telling her now would benefit either of them at all, so he remained silent.

After he made his routine calls around the company, Jacob finally called Axel. Jacob's imagescreen went darker as the image of Axel's bust filled most of it.

"I can only presume that you have contacted me in order to discuss resolution of the apple," Axel stated.

"Good morning. Yes, that is entirely correct."

"Did you test it?"

"I did not. I don't care what it is, other than it's something you want, to the point of wish-granting."

"Then, tell me Mr. Serter: what hidden desire do you have on your heart that *I* might gratify?"

Jacob put his hands flat on his broad desk. "I want you to create a backup of the Mainframe."

"...*what?*" For a moment, Axel's voice sounded quite different.

"I want *you* to tell the Mainframe to duplicate itself. You see, it occurs to me, oh *sovereign*, that the Mainframe is the repository of the sum of all knowledge. What an impossible disaster, were it lost! Like re-witnessing loss of the library of Alexandria, [110Δ] only *exponentially* worse! Duplicate the Mainframe. Right now the glitching is infrequent, nearly nonexistent. *Nearly*...but it *is* slowly getting worse. We can verbally debate the credibility of such a statement, but I have reports. I have ordered studies–see for yourself."

Jacob Serter sent several report records to Axel with a few swift motions. "Projections suggest that the glitches are *exponential* in nature, and will soon be recurrently present inasmuch as in *every credit bank*.

"*Copy* the Mainframe, Axel. Back it up–preserve our knowledge now. *This is my wish.*"

How very curious, Axel thought. *I was **certain** that you have only been trying to position yourself in the game...and yet, here, where no one is watching and any wish could be granted, you dedicate yours to the preservation of knowledge. For everyone.*

In all this time, could I have finally met a man who is genuinely good in nature?

"Done," Axel announced without hesitation. "I'll see you and the apple

---

110Δ The Library of Alexandria was a major center of learning from its construction in the 3rd century BC until 30 BC. Many famous thinkers are attributed as having studied at the library. Its vastness is legendary, and so when it was burnt, it quickly became a symbol for the loss of knowledge.

shortly then? Or will you attempt to send it?"

"I have two items on my itinerary prior to. I'll be along, say 2 PM." Jacob's credit bank let ring an angry chord. "Let's make that 3 PM." Ding.

"Be seeing you."

Joseph, the head slave of the Serters, walked around the kitchen, making sure that everything was going according to schedule and was exemplary in nature. He was rather surprised to happen across Wonder, who he just noticed standing off in the corner near the stovetop.

"What are *you* doing here?" Joseph asked, smiling. He spied the bits of food clinging to the edges of her mouth and, raising an eyebrow, added: "Have you been eating?"

"**I don't *like* porridge**," Wonderful said, crinkling up her nose in distaste.

"It's not porridge, it's oatmeal. It will taste great, you'll see–it's not finished yet. Now, as you are up and awake, let's go get dressed. Maybe we can beat your mother and father to breakfast."

She drooped her arms down, and sighed loudly. "**Uff. But I'm still *sweepy*. I gotta lay back down.**"

Joseph could not help but laugh. "Okay, then. Go back to bed, little princess.

"Martin," he called to another nearby slave. "Take Ms. Serter back to her bedroom, if you please."

"What if you don't come home?" Anthem asked again, later.

"Maybe you should go *with* us," Jacob suggested. "You can hang out in the dining room if you want. Maybe you could go shopping if you get bored."

Anthem's eyes lit up. "That would be *wonderful*. I'll get dressed right away!"

Chapter 30:

Hired Hands

Fri 13	Sat 14	Sun 15
		07:30

"There's a guy here; he says he starts work today," Private Parks (an hourly Bagel Lord worker) said to Lieutenant Bartowski, one of the 3 lieutenants (or, assistant managers) stationed at Bagel Lord unit SVB13.

The lieutenant looked through the one-way office mirror to see the new recruit. Her face slowly changed in expression from disinterest to upset and irritated. "What…*who*…he's employed *here*? Oh. No. No. No. Don't do this to me *today*. Who in the? There's *obviously* some mistake."

"There's no mistake," Major Tohm (the general manager) corrected, stepping into the office. "There was a message from HQ this morning that said he would be working here. Apparently he's related to someone pretty important."

Tohm laughed, seeing the lieutenant's frown deepen. "Just give him a uniform and put him to work; it'll be *fine*. Nothing wrong with a little extra labor that you won't be responsible for…give him a broom and send him around. You can hide him in the dishroom when Serter's here."

*How does he stay so **calm** all the time?* Lieutenant Bartowski thought. *I guess that's why he's the Major. Damn him.*

The lieutenant took a deep breath. "Okay, tell him to come on back."

The Rook, newly cleansed and groomed, made his way into the officers' office upon escort. Despite his attempts to soften his…presence, however, he still did not strike one as perhaps the most appropriate individual for the environment.

The lieutenant started playing a mental game with herself as she put his (false) identity into Mainframe record. *This guy has been a sanitation worker for 25 years? Why would a janitor want to work at a Bagel Lord? Why **now**, anyway? He must have been fired and this job is his ticket to sidestep employment law. Well, I don't care if he's the brother of God, he's not getting any preferential treatment here. If he's not worth the job, **I'll** term him without a thought.*

"Around here, until you earn the privilege of *private*, everyone will call you '*recruit*.' You will wear this Bagel Lord shirt–notice how it says 'recruit' on the back?" Bartowski showed the Rook the shirt.

"It says recruit?" The Rook squinted. "Under all those stains or something? Geez, how many people have worn that shirt, anyway?"

"Listen, *recruit*, you should be happy to have this job. If you're above it, perhaps we could both save each other a little time–"

"I'm sorry, sir," the Rook immediately apologized. "I'm…a little *old* for this kind of work, maybe. But I'm a good worker, and I'll try hard. I'll stop talking now, and let you do your job. Sorry again, sir."

Well, crap. So much for the easy out.

They toured the unit, the lieutenant pointing out where things were located, and what jobs and responsibilities the people all had. All in all, it was a bit rushed, as the lieutenant wanted to prepare the place for Mr. Serter more than she wanted to indoctrinate a new employee.

The Rook was told that the president, Jacob Serter, would be arriving today, and that he shouldn't speak to him *under any circumstances,* unless he was first spoken *to*. Shortly thereafter, he was taken to the dishroom. He was left to the mercy of Private Stock, the regular dish attendant. [111Δ]

Unit SVB13 was bustling with activity nearly as early as they opened the doors. This was typically true on every *4th Sunday*, for on every 4th Sunday the nearby Arena hosted the mediacast show known as "Gladiator." Many regulars are known to stop by this particular *Bagel Lord* unit en route to the games.

[111Δ] Normally the dish attendant does not start so early in the morning, but visits from Jacob Serter often called for drastic and impromptu schedule changes, much to the consternation and dismay of the rank & file.

△ M

Earnest sat out in the dining room with his #4 Bagel with Bacon combo. He pulled up an imagescreen and started to write as he ate. It was especially odd that anyone would use an imagepen to write, but Earnest thought it felt more natural.

Despite the novelty, it did not draw anyone's suspicion or attention, in short, nobody cared about the guy in the corner booth.

"Ah, but I miss my journal!" He said aloud to himself. "How did I begin that again?"

And then it came to him, as if he had never forgotten. ***Oh.*** *Yes,* he thought. *"I awoke to the **howling**." Yet, perhaps I should start with something a bit less alarming. I know:*

"I awoke one morning to find myself Amos, *"* Earnest wrote.

△ M

Across the dining room sat the Queen with *Wonda Smith*, the newest Pawn of *The Chessmen* with some impressive background assets. Wonda was wearing a purple and black bodysuit that offered occasional transparency depending on how she moved.

The Queen was not wearing his usual makeup, nor was he dressed outland-ishly. *Now* he simply appeared in regular Silverberg attire (noirfashion), actually rendering him all-but-unrecognizable. Anyone suggesting to themselves that this man was Mark Curie, Queen of the SilverSmiths, would dismiss it as quickly. His subdued demeanor further blurred the similarity between himself and the Queen.

As such, they were an inconspicuous couple.

△ M

Hugo and Cordelia Templeton walked through the doors of the establishment about 45 minutes after the *Bagel Lord* opened for business.

"This is certainly not the most fluidly-run Bagel Lord, is it now?" Hugo asked the hostess as she sat them. "Or are you short of staff, or did you have some other ridiculous excuse as to why we had to wait at the door for three minutes, despite there being clean tables around the dining room?"

"I'm sorry—"

"Op, dop, dop, dop," Cordelia interrupted. "Don't you worry about it, Sally. This is just fine."

Hugo and Cordelia turned their attentions to their personal credit banks, all but forgetting the hostess at the end of the table.

Private Hostess Austencamp (*Suzie*) walked away, shaking her head.

◢M◣

"So, the Knight informs me that you are a huge fan of *The Chessmen*," the Queen said, initiating casual conversation.

"Oh *yes*," Wonda said, looking deep at the Queen. "Ever since I read your book, I have just been *fascinated* with you." Wonda laughed nervously. "I mean, the Chessmen."

Wonda blushed.

The Queen smiled.

◢M◣

"Hugo Templeton, the food critic, announced himself at the door, and is now sitting in the Dining Room," Private Austencamp reported.

Lieutenant Bartowski's face turned a bit red, and her eyes flared, but her voice remained even. [112Δ] "Yes…*yes*. Sure, now that I think of it. what *better* day than Serter's visit? We're staffed, we're clean, we're—"

"Sir!" Private Clauson appeared and interrupted.

"What, Private?" Bartowski turned her attention to Clauson.

"The dish guys are fighting! You need to get to the dishroom, like, *now*."

◢M◣

Jacob, Wonder, and Ayn Serter all got into their private autocar and were soon en route to Bagel Lord unit SVB13—although a bit later than they intended.

112Δ primarily because Major Tohm was in the vicinity.

- [Daniel Strasel] -

⧌M⧍

"What seems to be the problem here?" The lieutenant asked loudly.

The Rook and the dish attendant, Private Stock, turned to face Bartowski.

The Rook shrugged. "All I was *saying* was that if we–"

"And all *I'm* saying is that you can shut. Your. Slang. Slack. Face. *Up*, or I'm gonna shut it up *for* you, *recruit*," Stock pointed at the Rook's chest as he spoke. It seemed a bit silly, for the Rook clearly outweighed the veteran dishwasher, yet Stock did not let that stop him for a moment. "*Nobody's* gonna tell me how to do *my* job on *their first day*."

"You need to listen to the private–" the lieutenant began, but Stock interrupted again.

"Nope. Sorry, sir, but I'm *not* working with him. He can bus or something." "Look,"

"Nope. If you're so in love with him, he can do the dishes by himself. Good luck, *captain*!" Private Stock started taking his rubber dish apron off in anger.

"Now, wait, wait, wait…Jerry! C'mon…*Fine*." Lieutenant Bartowski put her hand up. "Stay here, I'll do something else with the newbie. *Recruit*, remove your apron and let's go."

The Rook hastily removed his apron and followed the lieutenant.

⧌M⧍

Let us not be liars, but champions of the truth whenever we speak, Earnest wrote a quick note, hearing a nearby server compliment another guest on how delightful her disobedient children were. ***Let us seek not to waylay each other with falsehoods, delighting in our cleverness. Silence is simply tact when the tongue can offer nothing true. To lie is to enslave: the liee by the corporeal, and the liar by the spiritual.*** [113Δ]

[113Δ] On several occasions, Earnest went back to this passage and modified it. On the first, he modified it to read: […] *the liee by the body, which is also the mind, and the liar by the spiritual, which is also the ethical.* He later changed it to […] *the liee, who, when so trusting, receives a teacher, and the liar, who acknowledges none.* He eventually changed it back to the original version.

⚠

"Alright, here's what you're going to do for the rest of the day," Lieutenant Bartowski said to the Rook. She pointed at the nearby order board.[114△] "Guests can place carryout orders or pay for their meals *here*. Take this cleaner and detail the board. If a guest should need any help, you come get someone."

"Yes, sir!" The Rook saluted and began to work.

⚠

"Where is that dreadful server?" Hugo Templeton asked irritably.

"The one with the red eyes?" Cordelia asked, not looking up from her credit bank's imagescreen display.

"No, *that* was some weirdo–I shooed him off. *Our* server, who has yet to arrive at our table, and thus: dreadful."

"I have been standing here, waiting for you, Mr. Templeton," Private Ken Ferguson, his server, said.

"Oh," Hugo looked up and smiled. "Well then, despite any infraction we might have been extended upon our arrival, your attentiveness and expediency have compensated. Thank you, Kenneth! My wife simply wants a cup of coffee. I will have coffee as well. I prefer to order in courses, so let's start with a cup of your French Onion soup."

"Did either of you want cream for your coffee?"

"Cream? *Cream*?" Hugo said, somewhat raising his voice. "Heavens *no*. *That* would make me a coffee *hater*. I do not *hate* coffee, Kenneth! I *adore* coffee. I'm not trying to *disguise* my coffee; I want it naked, visceral. I think I'm right in saying such, wouldn't you agree?"

"Quite," Cordelia agreed, not looking up. "And I *will* have cream, thank you."

Hugo read his server's confusion. "My wife, you see, does in fact *hate* coffee, however. I might entertain you with the tale of the paradox, however based on my read of your dining room, you haven't, at least, the time if not the actual inclination."

114△ Order board, which is to say "imagewall." An imagewall is more or less a permanent physical imagescreen. Generally only seen in businesses that cater to the public, some individuals have been known to install them privately.

After the waiter walked away, Hugo announced for his record: "Server Kenneth surprisingly both courteous and available at offset of dining experience. Has no understanding of coffee. Hostess remained calm and dignified despite my regular taunt."

▲

A woman poked at the Rook's shoulder. As he stood up to address her, she shrank back for a moment, perhaps in momentary revulsion.

"Yes, ma'am?" He asked.

"Yes, well. Hmm. I wanted to order one of your muffins, but I don't see the varieties listed."

The Rook studied the board alongside the woman for a moment. "It seems we don't sell muffins here."

"You don't?" She asked.

"No."

"You don't sell muffins?"

"No, ma'am."

"I can't believe they don't sell *muffins*," the lady said to some guests passing by.

The Rook tried to go back to work, but the lady immediately spoke up. "Will you have them tomorrow?"

The Rook dropped his towel. "Will we have *what*?"

"*Muffins.*"

The Rook debated mentally for a moment about how he should respond.

"Yes ma'am," he said, smiling. "We'll have them *tomorrow*."

▲

"That jerk in table 13 just ordered the French Onion Soup," Private Ferguson said to the kitchen staff.

 - [The Terrors of Wonder] -

"It's like, 9 in the *morning*!" Private Dunlawn yelled. "We don't sell soup til 11! Tell 'em *no*."

"Belay that," Major Tohm spoke up. "We'll make this one."

Private Dunlawn imagined killing Major Tohm over and over again for the remainder of the day.

M

Cordelia looked across a couple tables over at Wonda and Mark, who were sitting and talking casually with one another. She didn't know who they were or what they were talking about, but they both seemed to be having such an enjoyable time. Cordelia smiled. She turned to look back at Hugo, who was just receiving his soup.

"Is there anything else I can get for you?" Private Ferguson asked Hugo.

"Yes, I'll need a soup spoon, and quickly too, lest my soup become cold unnecessarily. I'll also take the *Majestic Cheese Cake*."

"There's a spoon on your soup saucer, sir," Ken responded, nearly lisping over all the esses.

"*This* is a *tea*spoon," Hugo said with distaste. "I cannot eat *soup* with a teaspoon. Heavens, Kenneth! But I forgive you, for by the confused look on your face I can immediately determine that you do not understand the significance of the flatware. It's a parenting problem."

Private Ferguson's eyes narrowed momentarily.

"Now, if you would be so kind as to remit my cheesecake order and retrieve for me a spoon *worthy* of my soup, it would be most appreciated."

"And I'll have a warm up on coffee," Cordelia said, turning back to spy on Mark and Wonda.

M

"Can I have some more flavored water?" A man asked the Rook, calling from his table.

"And some more *napkins*?" His wife asked, slightly spitting food out of her mouth in the process.

"Oh, um, right away, sir," the Rook replied, dropping his towel and walking into the kitchen.

- [Daniel Strasel] -   241

"Where do I get flavored water?" The Rook asked Private Clauson.

"Cherry or Vanilla?"

"Oh…I don't know."

"Well, *ask.* Anyway, we pre-mix our water to maintain the integrity of the recipe and decrease food cost. You'll find the gallons in the cooler. The vanilla water has a 'V' on the cap, and the cherry has a 'C.'"

"Got it."

▲

Wonda put her newly autographed hard copy of "*One Vision*" down on her booth beside her. After she set the book down, she brushed her deep purple hair aside and stared longingly into the Queen's eyes.

"It's just so…*accurate!*" She breathed. Then she quoted in reverence: "*We're only as good as our programming.*"

Curie nodded enthusiastically, delighted that she identified so strongly with his work. [115Δ]

"Right?" Mark was smiling ear to ear. "*Programming.* It's everywhere and in everything. Heck, we program each other…most of us don't even know we're *doing* it. I blame the culture. Of course, even if you were to *leave* society, you're still subject to the limits of what it taught you."

"You're so deep, so…philosophical," Wonda said dreamily. She rested her chin on her interlaced fingers as if her head had become too heavy to support by her neck alone. She went on to let the Queen know just how immeasurably intelligent and wise he was, at such a young age.

▲

"Hugo, look," Cordelia instructed.

"Elbows on the table is not proper etiquette," Hugo mumbled, having glanced up momentarily.

"Not *that*, silly. Look how…*fresh* their love is!" Cordelia swooned slightly. She missed the days that she and Hugo would stare longingly at one another. She loved her husband, but it was simply enchanting to see it blossom anew.

I hope Essence finds a love like that, Cordelia thought.

115[Δ] *and* someone so attractive, at that.

I suppose, however, Earnest continued to write, a smile in his words as he wrote. **Like most Americans, I have a lot to say about everything–particularly involving the things I know the least about.**

I wonder if there's a term for that, Earnest thought, taking his eyes off the record. *Oh. There is: Ultracrepidarian–one who gives their opinions on things they know nothing about.*

Earnest, as suddenly, knew the entire story that birthed the word. [116Δ]

*Now…**how** do I know this?*

Having returned to the guest to inquire as to the *flavor* of the water, the Rook found the table to be further upset that he failed to supply the napkins they had asked for. As he returned to the kitchen, he grabbed an excessive handful of nap-kins as he sped to the walk-in, where he spent the next 3 minutes looking at water jugs.

The Rook left the walk-in and quickly found Lieutenant Bartowski.
"Sir," he addressed his superior.
"Recruit?"
"There's a guest–he wanted flavored water. Cherry. Anyway, I went to the cooler to get the water, but I can't tell the difference between the one and the other. They're both clear, and the lids are resealed, so I didn't want to open them."
"Oh. Well, it's easy. The vanilla is marked with a 'V,' and the cherry is marked with a 'C.' We pre-mix our water to maintain the integrity of the recipe and decrease food cost."
It was hard for the Rook to wait for her to finish, but he succeeded. "I *know,*

116Δ There was a Greek painter who would conspicuously place his paintings and then hide so that he might hear what people said of his work. A shoemaker once pointed out that he had painted a sandal incorrectly. The painter corrected it, only to have the shoemaker critique the remainder of the painting. The painter, likely annoyed, replied that the shoe-maker should not comment on anything beyond the sandals, for he knew nothing beyond his own trade.

Ultracrepidarian: "The Shoemaker is not above the Sandal."

it's just that whoever portioned the water was rushed, because the 'V's' look like 'U's,' and the 'U's' look like 'C's.' Then, there's some other ones where the 'C's' look like 'V's.' So I can't tell which is which. It's a pretty bad system. Why not write 'Van' and 'Ch,' or something more than just a single letter?"

The lieutenant frowned. "So, Private Stock is *right*. Day one, and now you're trying to impersonate an officer-"

"No–"

"Weren't you a *janitor*? Listen, I recommend you keep your *ultracrepidarian* suggestions to yourself for the time being. If you'd like to talk about the *cleanliness* of the restaurant…no? Recruit, if you *continue* to cause problems here, I have no choice other than to let you go."

The Rook frowned. "I'm sorry, sir. Won't happen again."

"Then get back to work; everyone's busy except *you.*"

"It's something *unquantifiable!*" Cordelia whispered, her heart building in momentum. "Majestic, Breathable, Palpable."

Hugo looked at his cheesecake. "I daresay that I would *ever* describe *this* as *majestic*. More like…*surprisingly dumpy.*"

Cordelia continued to watch the couple, lost in her own romantic daydream. Eventually Cordelia was able to break free of the spell and approached the couple. As she approached them, they turned to regard her.

"Oh, I am just so *truly* enchanted with the love that I see between the two of you!" She beamed, smiling from ear to ear. "I feel invigorated and renewed–inspired!–by your courageous display of warmth and affection. Tell me, to *what* do you attribute to such a profound and undeniable love?"

"Programming," Wonda said, smiling.

Earnest, noting the need, went to use the restroom.

Hugo finished the notes for his critique, and went to reconcile his bill. When he pulled it up in front of the board, however, he was rather upset to see that he had been charged incorrectly.

"*Well*," he exhaled. "*That* certainly doesn't bode well for the ending of this little outing. Doubly disappointing in that I didn't get a chance to give Serter my personal commentary directly. Now…where is Kenneth?"

The Rook returned to the dining room to find his guests looking extremely unhappy.

"Well, *that* took long enough," the man said upon the Rook's arrival at his table.

"Here you go, sir," the Rook handed a glass of water to the gentleman, not quite knowing what else to say.

The man took a sip and slapped the glass down on the table. "What the? Can't anyone hire *good* help these days? This is *vanilla*; I asked for *cherry* water."

*I should have tasted it…of course **then** I'd probably be fired,* the Rook thought. "I'm sorry–"

"C'Mon Lobelia, we're *leaving*."

The Rook moved in front of the man, much to the man's surprise and immediate dismay.

"I'm sorry, sir," the Rook apologized as best as he could muster. "I can get you whatever you want."

"I don't *want* anything other than to *leave.*"

"Besides, my coleslaw is *terrible*," Lobelia said, collecting her many things and standing up. "This food tastes like it's old or something. Taste it!"

"No, I believe you, ma'am–"

"Will you get out of my *way*," the man grumbled, "or do I need to call the *manager?*"

The Rook quickly stepped aside, towards Lobelia.

"Seriously, taste it!" Lobelia raised her voice slightly, pushing the spoon up to the Rook's mouth.

Concerned for his job and very reluctantly, the Rook ate the coleslaw.

"Ewwww," said a young boy at a nearby table.

Someone tapped the Rook on his shoulder. When he turned to address the owner, he found it was Hugo Templeton.

"It seems I have been charged too…" Hugo trailed off as he saw the Rook's damaged face. "Too much for my visit. Can you help me?"

"Shurf," the Rook said, allowing a single, slivered, slaw carrot to escape his mouth.

Templeton's face went completely dark as he said: "No matter how one is dressed, or what they may look like, I always and *immediately* know the caliber of the individual I am speaking with when they address me with *food in their mouths*."

"Absolutely *dreadful*," corroborated Cordelia as she came to stand next to Hugo.

The Queen shot the Rook an angry glance, but ducked away when he spied Templeton.

"Well, I am *appalled*, Mr. Recruit," Hugo anounced. "And I would like to speak with your manager."

Lieutenant Bartowski had as recently wandered into the dining room and immediately headed over to the group, her eyes flared in anger when they met the Rook's, but were otherwise soft and cheerful when she addressed the guests.

"Hi there, I'm the manager; what seems to be the problem?"

Everyone started talking at once.

Chapter 31:

Everything Ends

JUNE *2070 EST*

Fri 13	Sat 14	Sun 15
		09:27

"I asked for *Cherry-*"

"–slaw tastes like–"

"Talking with food in h–"

"Simply *dreadful.*"

"I'm so sorry," Lieutenant Bartowski tried to apologize.

"Sir, let me es'splain–" the Rook said, careful not to eject more of the cole-slaw. As he spoke up, everyone turned to look at him.

"You see? The man is completely uncouth–"

"*Refused* to get out of my way–"

"Wearing a *filthy* uniform–"

"Like, 20 minutes for *napkins*–"

"Simply *dreadful.*"

The Rook watched in misery as his manager tried to placate and appease the small mob of guests unsuccessfully.

Well, looks like I'm about to lose both my jobs at the same time, the Rook thought. *Man, if I didn't need the Chessmen, this would all be so different...*

"Serter's in the parking lot!" Private Clauson announced loudly, trying to overcome the crowd.

Much of the banter died down throughout the establishment as many turned to look out the window. [117Δ]

[117Δ] with exception to the aforementioned lady with the disobedient children. *None* of *them* seemed remotely distracted, and continued unabated in their efforts to expertly soil the floor *and* all of their immediate surroundings while exercising their ability to mimic the most absurd sounds they've witnessed during their favorite mediacast shows.

⚠

*Who needs **you** to be their friend?*
Tri-cer-a-tops
Tri-cer-a-tops
Who stays with you until the end?
Tri-cer-a-tops

The imagescreen showed a family giving a white, plush triceratops to their eager child. The child grabbed it and said: "Wally!"

The toy changed color as waves rippled out, coloring the entire toy (except the horns, eyes, and toes) in different shades of brown.

"I'm *Wally*!" The triceratops said happily, blinking for the first time as the boy hugged him forcefully. "Oof! Yer crushin' me!"

The image changed to a similar scene as a mother handed an identical toy to her daughter.

"Suzie!"

Waves of pink and red undulated over the toy as it blinked and giggled. "I'm Suzie," the toy said, bouncing in the girl's hands. "Oh! Hey! Can we try on some clothes today?"

Suzie's colors faded and the seams frayed a touch as the light dimmed down and the background changed. The toy, now overused and somewhat dull, bounced up and down at the side of a large bed. Old hands came down and picked it up, setting it on the next pillow.

"Thanks for helping me up!" Suzie said cheerfully.

"Anytime, Suzie," the old lady said and smiled as they both went to sleep.

Just give it a name and it jumps with a start
Forever your friend, till death do you part [118Δ]

118Δ The toy has only been around for a handful of years, so the claim has not been well-tested. There are many jokes found in the Mainframe imageyard revolving around ownerless Triceratops milling around animal shelters and thrift stores. There are an equal amount of more macabre suppositions, such as that the toy simply stops working when the owner dies, or that, unable to acquire a new owner, the toy resorts to saddening or even unspeakable measures while looking for the love and security it once knew. Either of these are a bit distasteful, however; the toy is simply adorable.

- [Daniel Strasel] -

Jacob, Anthem, and Wonder, as well as the security detail that Anthem *insisted* accompany them, all prepared to exit the autocar. Just as Jacob was commanding the vehicle to power down, Wonder interrupted.

"Daddy, can we juss watched the dinosaur one more time again?" Wonder said, referring to the automercial [119Δ] that played a few minutes ago.

"Perhaps after we visit daddy's work," Jacob replied.

"Yess," Anthem said with a bit of a hiss. "It *is* fascinating that you put all of this personal energy toward *Bagel Lord*, as opposed to the *dozens* of other, far more influential and necessary businesses. Tell me, *husband*, why *are* we visiting this *restaurant* today?"

"Mommy…are you mad?" Wonder asked.

"Oh, no, not at *all*, honey," Anthem said, smiling from ear to ear. "Mommy's just genuinely interested in the *math* of it all. Why *does Jacob Serter* spend so much of his time at *Bagel Lord*?"

"If you *must* know, and *now* it seems: *Bagel Lord* is the founding industry of SerterCo–it is only fitting to protect it. SerterCo has always been a *family* business, and to ignore it would be disloyal, dishonest.

"Besides," Jacob said, smiling handsomely despite his wife's probing, "Here we have a *genuine* opportunity to connect with the everyman. What would it say of me if I was not prepared to fight alongside of my men? Imagine what *they* will do then, when *they* become leaders!"

Anthem frowned. "*Bagel Lord* workers?"

Jacob grinned. "You've forgotten your humanity. *All* men are necessary. We all serve one another, only perhaps in different ways. Or we **don't**. There *are* those who would betray those who would serve them…but *we* (at SerterCo) do not linger on such men, for they do not deserve our thoughts, save to remind us of our own shortcomings.

"Remember when you asked me this morning *why* was I '*making the bed when we have servants*?' I tell you now, *again*, that overcoming the mundane tasks ensures success in greater works. If you can make your own bed, you can conquer the world."

Anthem frowned. For a moment she felt dizzy.

119Δ Autocar is slang for automatic car and automercial is slang for automatic commercial. For more information see Glossary page 306.

With that, Jacob had the autocar power down. Soon afterward, everyone started filing out of the vehicle.

As the Serters and their entourage made their way across the parking lot, they were rather picturesque in the unimpeded June sunlight.

One guest inside the *Bagel Lord* thought so, anyway; the picture he took would later be considered *the* definitive picture of the Serter family, appearing in almost every mediacast record ever created about the Serters forthwith.

"How long will we be here?" Anthem asked Jacob.

"About an hour. I will not miss *Gladiator*."

"Oh, right," Anthem agreed. "I supp–"

Anthem's voice trailed off as she somehow clumsily fell on top of her own daughter.

Jacob rushed over to Anthem and Wonder, only to fall in a strikingly similar manner.

From slightly beneath her mother, Wonder watched in horror as the look of coherence suddenly slipped completely from her father's face. It reminded her of the apple-Agent's face.

As she came to realize she just watched her parents die, yet before the scream could hit her lips, she passed out.

▲

The people inside the restaurant collectively let out a gasp as the security guards moved to assist the Serters.

"What just happened to her?" Wonda asked, staring intently at the pile of Serters.

The Queen slowly shook his head blankly.

Earnest stepped out of the restroom.

The guard pulled Wonder from the pile. Just before it was tucked into her purse, the Rook saw the mirroranium apple spill from her tiny hand.

Yes yes yes yes yes YES! The Rook thought.

The security officer holding the limp Wonder immediately started walking her back to the autocar.

No no no no no…no time to hesitate!

The Rook looked at the Queen, Earnest, his manager, and then back to Wonder. As he did so, he turned on his private readouts, which then extended him various bits of information about proximity and whatnot.

"I quit," he said casually as he abruptly pushed his accusers aside and leapt directly toward Earnest.

"You can't quit, you're fired!" Bartowski yelled.

"Ha–ha! Yessir!" The Rook saluted and laughed triumphantly as he then scooped up a startled Earnest and dashed for the door.

"I *have* legs," Earnest suggested.

"Shut up," the Rook said, setting him down just outside the door. "Go get the car and come get me!"

Earnest nodded as the Rook sped off toward the Serter security men with metahuman speed.

The Rook ran between the guards attending to Jacob and Ayn Serter, and headed directly toward the man holding Wonder. Seeing the Rook charging at him, he quickly put the child down.

He was as quickly crushed into the side of the autocar behind him. As the Rook stepped away, the guard fell down either unconscious or dead.

The remaining 2 guards put the Serters down and turned their (now armed) attentions exclusively upon the Rook.

The Rook grabbed Wonder and ran off toward the '52 Smith convertible that came racing around the corner. The guards, displaying augmented speed of their own, gave immediate chase.

Just as the Rook lay the child into the seat of the rescue vehicle, one of the guards slapped him with a ticket bank. [120A] All of the Rook's internal displays immediately shut down, as well did the bulk of his physical augmentations. He almost fell down.

120A "Ticket bank" is slang for "TransKeyTool Bank" or "TKT Bank." A "ticket bank" is ordinance that is issued to the police departments in Silverberg (as well as licensed out to certain privateers) to be used to subdue metahumans or slaves by causing their augmentations to fail. In metahumans, the response to shut down varies with the nature of the augmentation. Slaves are surgically altered to be physically sensitive to TKT banks; such "augmentations" are usually nothing better than "replacements."

"Drive! I'll catch up," the Rook yelled, pushing away from the car. "GO!" Earnest slammed on the accelerator and the car did nothing.

"**Occupant unrestrained**," the car objected.

Both guards trained their weapons: one on the Rook, and one on Earnest. "Stand down, move out and away from the vehicle. The police are en route. Stand *down*."

The Rook started clapping unenthusiastically. "Too bad the charge is used up; it used to fire an EMW when I clapped. Man, that's a lot of useds...useds. *Useds.* It's like it gets harder to say each time I say it. Useds. Anyway, I'd love to see the looks on your faces *then*."

The Rook sprang into action, his augmentations impossibly back on and fully functional. The guard fired a shot directly into the Rook as he landed a springing punch into the side of the guard's face. The guard crumpled into a pile.

There was suddenly a powerful, reoccurring surge of pain in the Rook's jaw. *What is **that**?* He thought, confused. *Damn it, what are they putting in guns these days?*

The other guard fired a shot at the Rook as well.

"Oh, you idiot," the Rook sounded genuinely mad, but it may have been more the pain that made him clench his teeth. "Here I thought I could let you *live*."

The Rook picked up the fallen security guard and started running toward the standing one. His vision was pulsing red along with the pain.

The guard immediately started running away as quickly as he could.

The Rook ignored his quarry. He dropped the limp guard and got into the vehicle. Seeing that Earnest was unhurt, the Rook belted Wonder and himself in as rapidly as possible.

"Go," the Rook said in an uncharacteristically calm voice. "I'm hurt, bad I think."

Earnest hit the accelerator and the car sped off.

As the car passed through the Silverberg checkpoints, the registration received was *not* the one associated with the vehicle sent to the prior checkpoint.

"The Queen told me to go to his Chamber, but we have to get back to the Knight instead...'scloser." the Rook said after a few tense and silent minutes had passed. "Don't worry about the girl, I'll–I'll figure her out later."

"You look *terrible*," Earnest said worriedly, looking into the mirror. "You're sweating so much, you look like you just got out of a shower. Seriously, your clothes are *drenched*."

"I'm having a heart attack. My augs just told me. I'm automedicated, and I don't know how much longer I can stay awake, so let's cut the piggin' commentary."

"Turn Right in 200 yards," the car instructed.

"Mainframe, locate nearest hospital-"

"NO. Don't be stupid, I can't go to a *hospital*. Get me back to the Knight's, it's the closest–*he* can get help."

◬

"I'll ride back with *you*," Wonda said cheerfully to the Queen. "If you don't mind."

"Oh," the Queen smiled, obviously pleased. "I would love that–I mean, that would be lovely."

Between the Rook's performance and Wonda's enticing appreciations, the Queen was on top of the world.

The two of them watched the paramedics load the Serters into the ambulance.

◬

"Well, that was *ghastly*," Cordelia said as the paramedics left the *Bagel Lord* parking lot.

"Makes you appreciate what you have," Hugo said, taking up Cordelia's hand. "You know what, Cordelia my love?"

"Yes, Hugo?"

"I think we'll throw this article out."

"You do?" Cordelia asked, raising an eyebrow.

"Well, yes. Considering the circumstances, I think it would be poor taste to publish this."

"I think you might be right," Cordelia said, smiling.

"You know what else?" He asked, squeezing her hand. "I miss *us*. It's been too long since we went on a real vacation, I think that's what we'll do."

"Oh Hugo, that sounds adorable! Where do you suggest we go?"

"I haven't a clue. I thought perhaps '*Ess*' should decide."

Cordelia frowned playfully. "If Essence goes, I don't know how much of a *vacation* it'll be."

"Cordy!" Hugo gasped, smiling. "You're terrible."

"Very well, if she *must*," Cordelia said, now winking. "But do not allow *her* to pick–she'll just want to go to *Seattle*."

"Ugh, *anywhere* but *there*," Hugo began as the two of them finished in unison: "*Americans smell like corn chips*."

Chapter 32:

Damsel in Distress

JUNE *2070 EST*

Fri 13	Sat 14	Sun 15
		09:55

Wonder played with the cute puppy–he was so friendly! At one point the ball rolled away from him and ended up at the feet of a stranger.

Except she wasn't a stranger…*somehow,* Wonder thought.

The girl picked up the ball and brought it up to Wonder.

"**Here's your ball**," the girl with white eyes said, handing Wonder the puppy's ball.

"Oh, thanks," Wonder said, looking down at the ball. She then looked back up at the girl. "Why don't you have eyes?"

The girl looked away.

"I mean, why are your eyes *white*?"

"**I don't know**," the girl said sadly. "**I've never seen them.**"

Wonder put her hand on the girl's shoulder. "It's not ugly, it's just different. It's okay."

The girl smiled. "**Thanks.**"

"It's actually somehow *familiar,*" Wonder muttered as she looked around. "Where are we?"

"**I'll explain later. Right now we should talk about your mother and your father.**" As she spoke, an imagescreen appeared and started playing memories that Wonder had of her mother and father.

"I love my mommy and my daddy," Wonder nodded.

"**Yes, and they love you. Well, they *loved* you.**"

The screen went dark, and eventually disappeared.

"*Loved* me?"

Images of what happened in the *Bagel Lord* parking lot started flooding Wonder's mind.

"Oh! Oh!" She cried as desperation washed over Wonder.

"**Shhh. Shhh,**" the girl with white eyes put her arms around Wonder, who immediately hugged her fiercely back. "**Now, now, it's going to be okay. You see, you can see them *here* whenever you want!**"

Wonder let go of the girl and wiped her eyes. "What do you mean?"

The girl pointed to the doorway, where just beyond the portal stood Jacob, smiling and waving at Wonder. "I'm right here, always, if you *want*," he said lovingly.

"I don't understand," Wonder sniffled.

The girl looked around. "**Well, we are inside your dream...only *you're* here by choice.**"

"What do you mean?"

"**I mean, you're *sleeping*. When you *choose* to be awake, all of this will disappear...but as long as you remain, your father and mother are forever alive!**"

Anthem walked into view next to Jacob. "Wonder? You want to play bears with us?"

"I WOULD LOVE TO PLAY BEARS WITH YOU!" Wonder cheered.

"**But, eventually, you'll wake up. And then everything will be *gone*. Everything except me,**" the girl said in melancholy tone.

Wonder turned back to look at the girl. "What do you mean?"

The girl smiled weakly. "**For you, everything here is *new*, but for *me*, everything here is *old*. So, when you're sleeping, I am maddeningly bored. I *yearn* for you to wake up.**" Her voice grew even quieter as she admitted "**Sometimes I even wake you up. I am *always* awake–I *cannot* sleep. I see everything you see, and then even so much more! I cannot *stop* seeing. It is horrific.**"

"**You are blessed, to have the power of *sleep*.**"

Wonder blushed. She had never thought of sleeping as a *power*.

"**But, *if* you would remain asleep *forever*, then you can stay *here* with your parents *forever*–happy and free from danger. *And*, I found that when you're asleep, I can be 'awake'; I can move this body when you're sleeping. I can see the world through your eyes.**"

"The problem *is*, if I did that, you'd be tired all day when *you're* awake...and *I* will not ruin *your* life just so that *I* can have one of my own! *I* couldn't be so selfish."

The girl with white eyes sighed heavily. "So, I'm pretty much your unborn sister, imprisoned and tortured here."

"That's so awful, I'm so sorry—"

"But see—if you *stay* here, *I* could be in charge of our body. *I* could deal with all the pain in the world...the death. *I* could even come and tell you about all the *good* things and just spare you all the sad!"

Wonderful and Wonder started jumping up and down, excited with what Wonderful was saying.

"You *belong* here. You are welcome and wanted. Keep mommy and daddy alive, my sister! Play with them *forever*!"

"Well, that's what I'm gonna do!' Wonder shouted.

"Oh, I'm so happy! Thank you so much—I love you!" Wonderful sang and danced and then ran over and hugged Wonder.

Soon afterward they calmed down for a moment.

"Now, all you gotta do is look me deep in the eyes and say '*I will now sleep forever*.'"

Looking at one another, heads together, Wonder then solemnly recited: "I will now sleep forever!"

The two of them, hand in hand, then ran toward Anthem and Jacob, who received them happily into their arms.

"Can we ride on a boat today?" Wonder asked, smiling joyfully.

Ⓜ

Soon after Earnest arrived, he, The SEUs, and the Knight all slowly carried the heavy, unconscious Rook into the house. [121Δ] As soon as the Rook was comfortably inside, The SEUs ran back out to get Wonder. Earnest stayed with the Rook as the Knight went for help.

[121Δ] Simon, momentarily crippled due to his leg injury from the labyrinth, sat on the couch as this was happening. Simon was watching *"Darky Ducko,"* an animated mediacast show about a crime fighting duck who has premonitions about the future.

The SEUs was rather surprised to find Wonder awake and upright.

"**Please, help me,**" Wonderful pleaded.

The SEUs hugged her. "Of course, of course. Why, I could never refuse a damsel in distress." As he brushed away her tears, he asked "What do you need?"

"**Please take me to the Axel Industries Central Building.**"

*Well, I wasn't expecting **that**,* he thought in surprise.

"Are you certain you wa–"

"**I am certain.**

"**Please**," Wonderful added as The SEUs hesitated.

The SEUs climbed into the car and asked the Mainframe for driving instructions to *the Ace*.

"His friend says he had a heart attack," the Knight explained to the image of the Queen before him.

"I'm on my way. In the meantime, find him some help. Some *quiet* help. You know what to do. Where's his friend now?"

"He's sitting next to the Rook, looking after him."

"Okay, call for medical and then go help this 'The Sooz' with the girl. Make *sure* she is *well* taken care of. I'll be there to get her shortly. Oh, and just in case: keep your eyes open for a sculpture of an apple. It's mine. It's probably somewhere on the Rook."

"Yes, sir."

The daughter of the Serters was surprisingly quiet for the duration of the car ride. She thanked The SEUs, but refused his several offers to accompany her inside.

As The SEUs drove off, Wonderful approached one of the innumerous reception desks found at the zero of the Ace.

"Hi there little girl!" The receptionist was full of smiles. She looked around for parents, but spied none. "How can I help you today?"

"**I would like to see Axel.**"

"Oh," the receptionist smiled at the adorable request. "Well, I think he might be too busy at the moment. Maybe I can help you?"

"**He's not too busy to see *me*,**" Wonderful pressed, pulling the apple from her small purse. "**Show him a picture of me holding *this*.**"

The nearest receptionist leaned over and whispered to her co-worker: '*You might want to go ahead and do it…I think that's the daughter of Jacob Serter.*"

Soon afterward, Wonderful was on her way, alone, to the 237th floor.

When The SEUs returned back to the Knight's residence, he was beset by the Queen.[122Δ]

"Where's the girl?" The Queen demanded.
"Oh, uh, she wanted to be taken to the Axel Industries Central Building."
"*She* wanted that? And you *took* her?"
"Well, of course…what would you *have* me do? Kidnap her?"

"Does it occur to you…didn't you think that…*Why* in all the…" The Queen's face twisted in dismay as he raised his fists up in the air. "Who…" Then the Queen sighed and all the anger went out of him. "Tell me you have the apple."

"What apple?"

122Δ The Queen had arrived during his absence and had already spent a fair amount of time yelling and belittling the conscious and unconscious occupants alike.

Chapter 33:

An Elevating Exchange

JUNE *2070 EST*

Fri 13	Sat 14	Sun 15
		10:51

"You're not Axel," Wonderful frowned, looking up at the Agent wearing a large moustache and a pair of noirglass lenses over his eyes.

"No, I'm Agent Thompson," the Director of Axel Industries Internal Security reassured. "And I have been extended all authority and understanding that I might appease you."

"You can grant whatever wish I might have?"

"Correct. So tell me, little lamb, what unfathomable desire has managed to grow so quickly in your young heart? If you have reached desperation, and were coming to ask for resurrection of the dead, I assure you that *that* wish is beyond granting."

"I want to be considered an adult. Immediately. Full citizen."

"Oh," Thompson said, frowning. "You *do?*"

"I do. Now, to spare you, I assure you that no matter how many different ways you might ask me the same question, my answer will not change. I would like to be elevated in status from dependant to adult."

"So then, you *are* already aware that your parents are dead."

"Agent Thompson. Are we here to discuss the *apple* or not?"

"I see. Very well. Yes, in exchange for the apple, you will be elevated to adult status, effective *immediately.*"

"Done!" Wonderful smiled and slapped the apple down on Thompson's desk.

"Initiate mediacast session with Agent Nelson," Thompson commanded the Mainframe.

MAINFRAME » INITIATED «
MAINFRAME » CONNECTED «

"Nelson?" Thompson barked at Nelson's image. "I need you to alter the Mainframe record and elevate Wonderful Serter to a full adult. Extend her all legal and social privileges and restrictions. If her record is referenced, say by the police or judge, make sure that her *adult* status is inclusive. Then come see me when you have a moment."

Nelson looked confused. "Um, okay."

"End mediacast session."

Mainframe » Terminated «

Wonderful stood up, curtsied, and started to walk out of the room.

"Little girl?" Thompson called.

"I beg your pardon? You might say, '*young lady*,' Agent Thompson. And my request is no more silly than your leader's want for this paperweight cut out of mirroranium."

Wonderful left.

Ah if only it were that easy, Thompson thought as he looked at the mirroranium apple. *But if mirroranium could be **cut**, none of this would be necessary.*

"Initiate mediacast session with Agent Henson," Thompson commanded the Mainframe.

Mainframe » Initiated «
Mainframe » Connected «

Agent Henson's image appeared in front of Agent Thompson.

"Sir?"

"I want you to come down to the Ace, I have a new assignment for you."

"Yes, sir," Henson replied.

"End mediacast session."

Mainframe » Terminated «

"Initiate mediacast session with Mark Curie," Thompson commanded the Mainframe.

Mainframe » Initiated «

CHAPTER 33

The Queen's image appeared before Director Thompson.

"I take it this means our deal is off?" The Queen said, back in his public persona, smiling wide.

"Well, *that* deal, anyway," nodded Thompson. Thompson allowed his own image to expand as far as his desk. "There it is, the greatest prize in Silverberg, delivered by such small hands with such big desires."

"So she *did* bring you the apple? The daughter?"

"Of course; who else?"

"I just thought, perhaps, someone might have been, you know, lying to me. So…what did she ask for? Little brat."

"Now, wouldn't *that* make for an interesting tale?"

"But, I thought we were friends," the Queen smiled and shook his head. "You could tell *me*."

"Well, *that* deal didn't quite happen, did it? But maybe we *could* be friends… if there was a new deal."

"What would the *new* deal be?"

"You give me the Rook, and we can be friends."

"That's it?"

"Oh? Is there *more* you can offer?"

The Queen frowned. "No."

Thompson smiled. "So, take it or leave it."

"I'll take it," the Queen said, although somewhat less animated. "But you need to release my men, just like we agreed."

"My *dear* Mr. Curie," Thompson said, picking up the apple. "You give me the Rook, and every missing chess piece will be replaced. End mediacast session."

MAINFRAME » TERMINATED «

"Initiate mediacast session with Dr. Manuel Phoebus," Thompson commanded the Mainframe.

MAINFRAME » INITIATED «
MAINFRAME » CONNECTED «

"Director?" Doctor Phoebus asked.

"Turn off the synapse chorus [123Δ] to Agent Nelson."

"Yes, sir."

"Anything more on Wilson? Is he ready to go?"

🄼

"But what is *this*?" Wonda had said *months* ago when examining Agent Wilson. "You've *already* been implanted with Thinking Cap tech!"

"I *have*?" Wilson asked, smiling and laying still. "That can't be right."

"It seems it must have been done without your knowledge or consent. Could you feel any more *violated*? Then again, working for Axel? I'm *shocked*. Ohh, and *look*: it's constantly *sending*." Wonda frowned. "Well, we can't let that…or *wait*. Maybe I can send a message of my own. Here, sit still. This might tickle–"

Wilson screamed out in instant, ongoing agony.

"Or hurt."

🄼

"Actually, there *is* a problem, sir," Dr. Phoebus explained to Director Thompson. "Wilson doesn't speak. He doesn't eat. He doesn't move, unless we make him. He just sits up, eyes wide open, unblinking. He keeps clacking his teeth together. *Hard*. It makes my mouth hurt to listen."

"Insusitate another–"

"This is the fourth. They're all doing the same thing."

"They're all…sitting upright with their eyes open and randomly masticating the air?"

"Yes, well, except the random part. One of my men picked up that it was Morse code; a code of signals either–"

"Yes, I know what Morse code is. What is he saying?"

"Admit One."

123Δ **Synapse Chorus** is a term used to describe the particular signals that are sent from one thinking cap to another.

- [Daniel Strasel] -

Earnest walked out into the common room, tucking a necklace down into his shirt.

"Hey *Earnest*," Simon waved, stumbling slightly with the name.

"Hey *Simon*. Don't *you* have to change *your* identity? Or did you think you could live out the rest of your life on the couch?"

"I *did* get a new identity. I couldn't be much help if I couldn't move around for fear of detection, could I?"

"Oh, so what's your name?"

"Simon."

"No, I mean your new name."

"It *is* my new name. Simon *Smith*. Why would I change my *first* name; wouldn't that be unnecessarily confusing?"

Earnest frowned.

"Oh, don't be upset," The SEUs spoke up.

"I'm not–well, not about that. Just concerned for Per-The Rook," Earnest admitted. "The Queen just came and took him to the secret Chessmen Hospital."

"The Chessmen have their own *secret hospital*?" The SEUs mused. "That's pretty impressive. Still, glad *I'm* not a chess piece."

"Oh, don't *you* need an alternate identity?" Earnest asked.

"Me? No. I *cause* soft errors,[124Δ] remember? Anything so influenced, I can influence. Unless the enemy is upon me, I should be able to elude anyone indefinitely."

"Impossible," Simon said.

"I got us out of the laboratory, didn't I? I got us through the lab*yrinth*, didn't I? I mean, heck, *I* defeated the sentry. How could I do *any* of these things if I could not do what I am describing?"

"No, I meant what just happened on *Ducko*. Impossible that he fell down that building without getting killed…*Thanks*, Art."

Earnest sat down, and pulled open the satchel that the Rook took from Agent Wilson at the laboratory cafeteria. He pulled out the only contents: a bronze-colored ring.

124Δ Wait, what were soft errors again? Page 217

"It's a Thinking Cap," Earnest observed, turning it one way and then another. *A device that links 2 minds together for the purpose of thought projection and reception…and **when** did I learn this?* He thought to no conclusion.

Chapter 34:

Gladiator

JUNE *2070 EST*

Fri 13	Sat 14	Sun 15
		11:00

At 11 o'clock, Simon, like many of the people in Silverberg, changed the imagescreen to display the show *Gladiator*.[125Δ]

The current Challenger had successfully survived the last two shows, and was favored to win this one as well. The information displayed around the periphery of the imagescreen said as much and more.

Before every match, from 10 to 11, the Mainframe mediacasts pre-game interviews with the defender and current challengers, as well as micro-interviews with the current show's newest players. During the pre-game, one would also learn what exclusive action figures and other paraphernalia would be available next week *only* to those who came to the Arena in person.

However, as such interviews are displayed *before* the game, and as the group had only just tuned in, they were bereft any chance to develop any personal or emotional attachment to any of the players (*or* know what delights await them if they were to come next week in person).

"So…this really *is* a thing," The SEUs said in some amazement. "And *this* is what the Rook used to do?"

"In 2056," Earnest said, nodding.

"*2056?*" Simon asked. "How old *is* this guy? 14 years ago, he would have been no younger than…wait, how old are the gladiators?"

"All over the board, I should think," Earnest said, rubbing his chin. "I think they're–well, most of them are slaves, but, you *can* volunteer to play."

"Well, *who* would do that?" Simon asked, laughing as he spoke.

[125Δ] The show was in its 23rd season, this being the 6th game.

"Well, *the Rook*, for one."

"He *volunteered?*" The SEUs asked, surprised. "Why would he do that?"

"Who knows? If he were simply suicidal, there are certainly easier avenues available. He had some money; he bought the best augmentations available, trained rigorously, and signed up to play *Gladiator.*"

"He won?" The SEUs asked.

"Yeah, well, he couldn't be much of a *loser*, now could he?" Simon injected. As he continued to speak, however, he sounded less and less sure of what he was saying. "I think that if you lose you die. It's a rule–er, not a rule, I mean, I think it's more of a code amongst the gladiators. They would rather die than lose…or something like that. Oh wait, aren't the earlier rounds built on points for style rather than…I don't know. I never cared for the show."

"Well," The SEUs sighed. "I don't know either…can we watch something else?"

"Like what?" Earnest asked.

"Like *Observatorium?*" [126Δ] The SEUs suggested.

"Hey, *that's* not a bad idea!" Simon said cheerfully.

"You *like Observatorium, too?*" The SEUs was amazed. "I never thought I'd meet ano–"

"*Observatorium?* Ugh, *no*," Simon looked like he ate something incredibly bitter. "*I* was talking to Arthur. He suggested we watch *Slabside.*"

Simon changed the imagescreen.

"So, he *won Gladiator*, but now he works for the SilverSmiths?" The SEUs asked Earnest while Simon and Art watched *Slabside*.

"I'm not too sure how it all works out either," Earnest admitted. "Clearly it involves this '*Thompson.*' When he's better we'll ask him."

The Rook was unconscious, oblivious of his surroundings and circumstances. A short while ago his pain, constantly demanding additional attention, had placed him into an augmented, automedicated oblivion.

126Δ a mediacast show that involves watching otherwise lifeless geographic areas.

Text intermittently informs the observer what they are looking at and occasionally adds bits of trivia as well. Aficionados of the show are usually alike in that they appreciate the imagery and music as much or more than the informative component.

Not many people like *Observatorium.*

Chapter 35:

Catastrophic Consequences

JUNE *2070 EST*

Fri 13	Sat 14	Sun 15
		11:44

"Listen," Director Thompson said to Agent Nelson. "I spoke with Jacob Serter a couple hours ago. He suggested, during that dialogue, that we create a duplicate of the Mainframe in order to conserve the data in the event of a system-wide failure."

Nelson hated meeting with Thompson in person. It always set him on edge.

"And you want *me* to duplicate the Mainframe...or the *data* in the Mainframe–or did you mean *both*?" Nelson shook his head. "Doesn't matter, I couldn't duplicate the Mainframe if I *wanted* to. Now, maybe if you can find another Mainframe I could conceivably copy information from the one to the other...of course, even without a subsequent Mainframe, I can duplicate the data. In theory, the Mainframe has unlimited storage; it could back itself up within itself. But...if the Mainframe fails, then it *all* fails. Actually, that might be really bad, having two copies of the Mainframe in the same place. Maybe the *Mainframe* can duplicate the Mainframe! Maybe it could divide itself...or is that just stupid? I should ask it...Now how would I even phrase that? "

"Listening to you ramble sometimes makes my head hurt," Thompson exaggerated. "But you *can* duplicate the Mainframe?"

Nelson looked at Thompson unhappily. "Haven't you been *listening* to me? You probably should *not* copy the Mainframe, not unless you have another Mainframe. Of course, now that I'm thinking of it, I don't know if copying the Mainframe onto another Mainframe would even *work*. I mean, everything would copy, but then it would all be at the wrong *address*..."

 - [The Terrors of Wonder] -

Thompson smiled. "Alright. Tune back into *me* for a moment. So, you *can* do it–you have the *permission* to do this…let me ask you, who *else* in Silverberg would be allowed to make such a request?"

"Well, let's see–really, *only* myself, I suppose. There *are* a few components that can only be copied with a *particular* authority."

"Are you suggesting that *I* cannot manipulate the Mainframe in the same manner as *you*? Are you suggesting that *you* have a security clearance *greater* than I have?"

Nelson looked pathetic. "It wasn't unilateral–Axel himself sent me a message several years ago instructing me to *personally* restrict certain portions of the Mainframe to System Operator access *only*. He was quite specific, actually, in which components he wanted restricted–which were namely any components that could threaten irreparable damage to the Mainframe were they tampered with. Thus, it's impossible for anyone other than the primary system operator to command 'core' duplication–in this case, me.

"But *I* do not have a clearance *greater* than you, sir. Any material that I am not authorized to view, I cannot."

"You mean you *do* not."

"I mean I *cannot*. The Mainframe will not allow it. I may be the system operator, but I do not have *control* over the Mainframe. If you ever thought that, you were wrong. I have permissions, the same as anyone else, and I can *ask* for things that some other people cannot.

"But the Mainframe knows who I am. The Mainframe knows what I am and am not allowed to view. The Mainframe polices the material, not me. No matter how nicely or how aggressively I ask, the Mainframe will not concede. It's programming. I would have to *re*program the Mainframe, and at this point, that's quite impossible."

"So, you're telling me *Axel* himself instructed you to make yourself the only person in the world who has complete authority over the Mainframe?"

"That's right. Well, the System Operator, anyway, who right now happens to be me. And *just* over the *core* program components. It's not as significant as you think–it's like putting the plumber in charge of the pipes. It makes sense."

"Not when the *plumber* has the *only* key to the pipe room!" Thompson half yelled. "Spare me your pathetic analogies."

Nelson looked defeated.

"Alright look…brighten up, Nelson; I can never stand your moping. I'm not mad at you–it's obvious that you believe everything you're saying, no matter how preposterous. Something's amiss, however. You need to tell Axel about this–this core program stuff. I am confident it will be news to him. I would take a copy of the memo, if you have it. And here, take this apple with you…he's expecting it."

Earnest looked down at the Thinking Cap ring. "I wonder what this was supposed to be *for*?" He said, not for the first time. "Doesn't it bother you when there's a mystery to be solved? Don't you want to find out the truth?"

"Well, it's worthless," The SEUs responded. "It's only good if someone is actively projecting their thoughts. Nobody's going to keep sending out their thoughts into the device over and over constantly–unless they thought there was someone to receive it."

"Put it on," Simon suggested sarcastically. "*You* could send *your* thoughts *out*, that might get someone's attention…it just seems like an unnecessarily *stupid* thing to do. You are welcome not to agree. Maybe it's weaponized; who knows how these things work, anyway?"

"Oh, cause *you* know?" Simon said, and waited another long pause. "Blah blah blah. Gosh, is there *anything* you *haven't* done? Really, I may as well just never leave the house, since I can live vicariously through *you* and the tales of your many adventures, *Arthur the Aardvark*. It'd just be nice if you would *shut up* once in awhile and let someone else have their moment. Why must you *always* have to be the center of attention?"

The truth was that a bit ago Simon had twisted the wrong way, and was in some slight pain from his leg injury. The overall result is that he was a bit more irritable than he might normally be.

Now, although some might understand that people do not always *mean exactly* what they say or mean things the *way* they say them, *Arthur* was apparently unaccustomed to being spoken to in such a manner.

"Mmm hmm," Simon murmured after another slight pause.

"Yeah, but–" Simon stopped as abruptly as he started.

"Oh, now that's–"

A few minutes passed as Simon's face turned completely red. "Now you've gone too far. If you want to talk about Fr-"

"Oh yeah?"

"Oh *yeah?* You know what *you* can do? You can go find someone *else* who wants to listen to all your *boring* stories and hear all your long-winded wisdoms and anecdotes."

"And you look like a *bunny!*" Simon finally yelled before throwing himself down on the couch.

Earnest went back to looking at the bronze circlet and The SEUs resumed watching the imagescreen.

⚠

The Queen deposited the Rook into other hands, and went back to Wonda, who had enthusiastically offered to wait for the Queen while he '*did whatever Queens do.*'

"Hmmm. That took a bit," Wonda said, pouting and pushing out a wet purple lip.

"Well, never mind, I'm back!" The Queen said, smiling as he spilled into his custom autocar chair. As he pulled out a stowed bottle of champagne, the door closed. "Where to? I know a delightful little place in *the north* that has the best themed spa…"

"*Actually, I* was thinking maybe we could go somewhere a bit more secluded," Wonda said suggestively. "Oh, but don't worry," she added, moving across the autocar to lay across him and steal a drink from his bottle. "I don't mean what you *think* I mean," she winked. "You're just so–I mean, *you* would know what to do."

"Wait," the Queen snuggled in a bit with her, laughing, and then pushed back. "I would know what to do about what?"

"Well, as you know, I used to work for SerterCo," Wonda stated, sitting up. "I was involved in some pretty top-secret projects…and *I happen* to know where an orgy of hard information and prototypes are being kept. With Serter dead, you could grab it and no one would be the wiser–until it was too late, probably."

Verified and re-verified, everything about Wonda had checked out–and now these promises of access to exclusive tech! The Queen was momentarily lost in a haze of contentedness and amazement. Ah, everything had fallen into place so perfectly–even without that stupid apple! All of his missing men would soon be released, and now he was apparently about to be given technology that would establish him in ways previously unforeseen.

Wonda took another sip and threw the Queen's bowtie on the floor.

*And there's **that**,* the Queen thought mischievously. *Incredible to think that she was working as a programmer for SerterCo! I was certain that such individuals were otherwise considerably less athletic in form.*

"I'll need how many men to get all this?" The Queen asked, artfully moving Wonda so that he could exit the seat. He picked up his bowtie, which immediately went into his pocket. He soon afterward, however, divested himself of his jacket, although he made sure to hang it properly.

Wonda licked her lips as she seemed to consider the numbers. "I would say maybe three or four men should do…but maybe you could just arrange for them to meet us there a bit later, after you've had a chance to look around? See, I thought maybe *you* should come see it first," she said, alluringly. "You know, *alone*, with *me*. It's effectively abandoned…the SerterCo East building…and *I* can open the door."

"SerterCo East–the building he *closed*? That devil! It's genius!" The Queen took his bottle back from Wonda and drank greedily. "You know what? Let's do this!"

"I can hear him now," Simon mumbled, impersonating Arthur. *"Let me tell ya about the time I scaled the cliffs of Dover, only to find I left my rope at the bottom! Haw haw haw!* Meh. Nobody will miss him. I mean, who *carried* everything, anyway? Who *paid* for everything? He can save his regular ultracrepidarian commentary for someone else–*oh NO!*" Simon yelled in sudden realization.

"What's the matter?" The SEUs and Earnest asked in unison, looking away from the episode of *Slabside*.

"Art and I are no longer friends! He left! I gave the Rook's camouflage to him to hold for me! Now we'll never see it again!"

Not long afterward, the Knight came into the room with a long look on his face. "The Queen sent a message...I really don't know how to put this. I'm sorry Earnest, but I'm afraid the Rook's imaged."

"What?" Earnest blinked. "He *died?* Isn't this *Silverberg?* Don't you have the best elixirs and machines in the world? How can he be dead?"

"I'm sorry for your loss. Under better circumstances, he might have been fine, but with the added stressors and wounds, it was just too much. Then we should also add in that his health wasn't all that great to begin with. The Rook was impulsive, and his habits *re*pulsive. From his habits to his hygiene, he probably doomed himself. At the least he died while in service to the Queen."

"... Do not interpret my lack of verbal or physical response as apathy, so much as restraint," Earnest said, absently touching the necklace beneath his shirt.

"Indeed, he may have been a bit...dirty...yet that doesn't preclude that we should speak ill of him so immediately following the mention of his passing," The SEUs spoke up. "Please, join us in a moment of silence."

The Knight bowed his head alongside the rest.

"Ah, the sound of silence," Simon said wistfully after a couple minutes passed. "I should paint this."

Earnest flipped the Thinking Cap ring around in his hands.

"What is it?" The Knight asked, motioning at the ring.

"It's a Thinking Cap," Earnest said. "It was on the Agent who kidnapped me to lure the Rook. Well, not *on,* but *on,* per se."

The Knight smiled knowingly. "Going to try to use it to find out who he worked for?"

"*Is* there a way to do that?" The SEUs asked.

"Well," the Knight began, closing his eyes. "He probably used it as a way to receive instructions and give reports. That's how he'd best avoid Mainframe detection, anyway. Why *else* would someone carry a Thinking Cap around with them? I mean, I suppose there are other good reasons…but none that I can think make more sense. Anyway, the way I understand it is that when you put a Cap on, amongst other things, you know *who* and *where* the person wearing the attached cap *is.* Well, so long as they *send* a thought. At least, that's how I've heard it."

"Makes sense to me," Simon nodded, and then shook his head. "I still wouldn't do it. Nobody's sending thoughts into *my* head."

"Fair," The SEUs smiled. "I don't know if *I* would, either. For instance: Is his employer *aware* that he failed? If so, putting it on could be a terrible error. Then again, maybe now's the *only* time to learn *anything.* The longer he's silent, the more his contact will suspect he has been compromised. This may be the only window of opportunity. *If* we're going to do something so irretrievably stupid, however, we should probably do it soon."

What did he[127Δ] used to say? Earnest thought *"Do not act without thinking it through?" But…isn't acting without thinking all he ever **did**? Blasted man was a living contradiction. Then again, he was, at one time, technically the physically most powerful man in the world. That should afford some respect.*

Through augmentations, though. Ah, Percy. Why?

*Then again, why **not**?* Earnest straightened up, not realizing he had sunk into a slouch. *My rescue was your undoing, it seems. Hmm. May the next life treat you better than this one. Cheers. Sorry about Mary.*

Courage.

Earnest switched on the Thinking Cap and placed it on his head.

127Δ The Rook.

An alarm went off throughout Silverberg.

It was such an alarm as to demand the attention of every citizen and visitor. The alarm was not irritating in voice, as its chiming consisted of a few scant, sedate notes.[128] The accompanying text, however, although nothing greater than a handful of sentences, immediately and forcefully impacted the emotional state of nearly everyone.

The cause of this particular alarm was that Axel, sovereign leader of Silverberg and owner of Axel Industries, had been killed in an explosion moments ago. Axel has no living relatives, and thus by the **No-Will Law** of Silverberg, ownership of the company and leadership of the country has passed to the current Director of Axel Industries Internal Security: Agent Thompson.

Thompson will be delivering a formal address at 1 PM.

---

[128] Which was actually just a slower, more simplified version of the national anthem.

Chapter 36:

Compassion for the Child

JUNE *2070 EST*

Fri 13	Sat 14	Sun 15
		12:38

Wonderful sat alone in her room as she waited for Joseph to respond to her summons.

"**I'm Wonderful,**" she said, frowning. "**No. I'm Wonder, Wonderful.** *I'm* Wonderful." She sighed. "Okay."

Soon after her beckoning, Joseph arrived and sat down at her side. "How can I help you, little princess?"

Wonderful put her face in her hands and started crying. "It's just all so horrible! What am I going to *do*?"

"There, there," Joseph consoled her. "It's going to be alright. It's hard to understand it right now, but everything will be okay. I promise. And I will be here to protect you for as long as you ever want."

"But that's the thing," Wonderful said, pushing Joseph back. "I *do* want you to be around forever! I *need you*!" Tears ran down each side of her face as she looked up at Joseph.

He hugged her close again. "And I you, little princess. Nothing can keep us apart."

"Yes, some things can," Wonderful said, sniffling.

"No. Nobody can get to you, here in your own home. And you have enough money and estate to keep yourself protected until you can assume control of all of your assets–your things." Joseph smiled, remembering the age of who he was speaking to. "You are safe."

"But I'm *not*," Wonderful said, jaw quivering on the edge of crying anew. "Joseph, I need you–I need you to help m-me."

"Of course I will help you! What do you need?"

"Oh, Joseph, you won't ever *hate* me, will you?"

"I could *never* hate you."

"And you will proteck me?"
"Always."

I trust you most of all, Joseph, Joseph thought, remembering what Jacob said to him. *I **know** you will always do what is right for the family, and thus I place you in charge of the household. All other house slaves will be subject to you, and you only to me.*

"I need ta whisper somethin to you."
Joseph lowered his head to hear what Wonderful had to say. His eyes went wide, and then heavy with grief as she explained that she was scared–scared that she had accidentally killed her own parents.

"I put in too much sugar!" Wonderful whispered, sounding very frightened. "Mommy always says don't put too much sugar…and I *did.* I put Mommy's rainbow sugar from her purse in the oatmeal. Lots of it. And her other sugars, too.
"Oh Joseph!" Wonderful cried out, now openly bawling. "That oatmeal tasted *so bad*! I hadda add somethin!"

Rainbow sugar? Joseph's mind was racing. *Solid Hypnizium! She means she put her mother's **drugs** in the oatmeal! Good god. She **did**–she killed her own parents.*
"And Joseph, Daddy had Silberberg make me into an *adult* as a birfday present. He said something about he needed anofer on the record. I don't know what that means, but…does that mean *I am going to be a slave?*"
Wonderful erupted back into crying as she sank into Joseph's embrace.

Who will take over SerterCo? Joseph thought. *The lord and lady are dead, and now the only living child…a slave? Silverberg! Silverberg will gain control. Oh my god.*
"Joseph," Wonderful whispered. "You hafta help me. *Please* say *you* put in the sugar. I'm *afraid*, Joseph. I'm afraid. I'm sorry. I'm afraid. Please tell them you put in the sugar. Please proteck me."

No one knows how slaves that turn on their masters are handled, but everyone knows that in the very few instances of it happening, such slaves were never heard from again.

"Do not fear, my sweet princess–my *queen*," Joseph whispered, tears rolling down his cheek as he smiled. "I will protect you."

- [Daniel Strasel] -

Chapter 37:

Revelations

JUNE *2070 EST*

Fri 13	Sat 14	Sun 15
		13:00

"This…is a dangerous time," Thompson said, and as he did, the entire civilized world heard him.

"It is a time following the *murder* of respected leadership.

"It is a time when many of the men of this world will trade their hope for fear, in trust that their fear will guide them better than their hope did.

"It is a time when many of the wounded will seek justice, and it is often in the name of justice that men are willing to perform terrors and atrocities.

"It is a time of confusion, and where there is confusion, there are those who seek to profit by it.

"It is a dangerous time.

"Axel was my friend and my mentor. No one will mourn him more than I. Whereas justice cannot return the dead to life, neither can these transgressions be completely overlooked.   Although those responsible remain unidentified, one thing is clear: this malice originates from outside of our land.

"Until further notice I have therefore decided to reinforce Silverberg's borders. Effective immediately, anyone who wishes entry into Silverberg will be charged 50 units. Immigrants must now be pre-employed. Tourists and visitors are limited to 72 hour visas.

"When someone dies, either their role must be assumed by someone else or whatever function they performed in this life is gone. It is a part missing from the machine. Some parts are perhaps more noticeable, more understandable, such as those clearly responsible for the direct operation–but *any* missing part results in an incomplete product.

"*Some* parts are integral; the machine cannot function *at all* without them, so there must be found a replacement. If the original piece was perfect, *any* replacement will be a poorer version.

"Invariably, many of you are going to feel that I am a poor replacement. I urge you to keep your feelings to yourselves. Grumbling about the replacement does not improve it, it does not make it less necessary–although it makes it perhaps perceptibly less desirable.

"Do not fear this change in authority. *Little* will change in the beginning, if much at all, for not much is broken.

"Do not jump to conclusions about my unvoiced intentions.

"Axel said that *we are driven by an insatiable hunger for understanding. We are constantly absorbing and examining information…whether we want to or not.*

"He said that *the mind is a theatre committed to the pursuit of rationalization and understanding. The force that compels us to seek comprehension sets the stage of the mind, and assigns the pieces their positions, actions, and words. Variations of a scene are then performed to a point of exhaustive satisfaction, amazingly (and often sadly) influencing our actions and reactions in the exterior, living reality where such stage-play never occurred.*

"He said ***never*** *underestimate the power of belief.*[129Δ]

"I *will* be a leader you can believe in; do not denounce me before you have seen my works."

Somewhere below zero, relatively close to the Silverberg Amusement Park, Dr. Mommy received a new Subject into the lab. She directed the men carrying the Subject down a couple corridors, to the end of the Sterling Hallway, and then finally into the room labeled "Utility."

The new Subject was bound to the examination table–a table which then immediately proceeded to analyze the occupant. Mechanical arms holding myriads of surgical utilities sprang into action, expertly addressing any and all maladies.

[129Δ] Actually, the exact expression was: "Never underestimate the power of belief, for the truth is a sad opponent by contest. The only men capable of reasoning are those who do not believe."

Oh, and Axel didn't *originally* say any of these things; they're lines from the *unedified* <u>Oedipus Now</u>.

A

Thompson finished his public address, and then held a private meeting amongst the Agents.

"Make no mistake, ladies and gentlemen," Thompson raised his voice so that all the Agents could hear him. "*This* is not a campaign. I *am* the leader, the sole owner of Axel Industries. Like it or not, thin and thick, richer and poorer and until death do we part: this is the state of things. Now.

"New leadership is always intimidating, because it is unknown. But *you* all know me. Better than you did the *last* leader, anyway. You should find some comfort there.

"Except *you*, Nelson."

The assembly turned and looked at Agent Nelson, who suddenly felt very cold.

"*You* are fired."

A collective intake of breath could be heard.

"Your distrust in me has never been much of a secret. You have suggested before that *I* am complicit. You come to me empty-handed on far too many occasions. But it's not incompetency nor sedition that has me terminating you on this day; no, I can manage idiots and rebels. It's *assassins* I don't carouse with. The very last person seen by Axel before the explosion was *you*, Nelson. You're under arrest for *murder*."

Nelson stood up, and looked about to protest when the Agent next to him knocked him unconscious.

After Nelson had been removed from the room, Thompson continued speaking to the Agents. "Agent *Henson,* here, will be assuming the head of the Justice department–"

Henson waved.

"–as Agent Wilson is no longer with us. Mainframe and Imagescreens will be moderated by *me* for the time being, as I have not had enough time to conjure a suitable replacement for Nelson.

"As for who will be *my* replacement..."

After Thompson explained some of his more ambitious goals to the Agents, everyone departed. They left, all having different ideas (if, indeed *any* at all) as to how they felt about the meeting…and although they then all headed in different directions, many would spend the remainder of their day almost identically.

Thompson eventually left the Ace. His autocar took him to Harrison Park, where it left him to return, passengerless, to its garage.

Thompson entered the labyrinth secretly, the grand marble gazebo housing one such access point. Shortly thereafter, he took a private autotran from one hidden chamber to another several miles away. As he stepped out from the autotran into the office, he signaled his credit bank to begin projecting an image over and around him.

Thompson was completely and convincingly covered in the image of Dr. Sanderson–an image that Thompson has worn as frequently as Sanderson has ever been seen. He put his signature lab coat on and opened the door–a door that would only open for him.

Sanderson stepped from his room and over toward "Utility," when he spied a man down the hall.

"Hi Daddy," the man said smiling, his deep voice reverberating.

"Hello Anderson," Sanderson smiled back. "Go play now."

Anderson scampered away, mooing in his bass voice.

Sanderson stepped into "Utility."

The Rook looked up at the furry, fat doctor as he waddled in the door.

"Oh. *You're* the guy that's going to interrogate me? This is rich."

"Beneath all this fluff," Sanderson said, lifting his ample stomach and letting it drop. "And all of this stuff," he said, pawing at his face whiskers. "Oh wait. Hoo hoo," he laughed. "I *mean*, behind all this fluff" he pawed his whiskers, but more rapidly this time. "And stuff," he patted his stomach, and slightly belched. "Oh my!"

"Oh gosh, can we just get this over with?" The Rook asked, annoyed. "I don't want to play games. Masks off, hands down–*please* cut to the point."

Sanderson smiled, his eyes closed in appreciation. "Well, we all wear masks; perhaps you've been wearing yours for so long, you've forgotten what you look like without it. I could help you remember your *true self*."

Sanderson walked up to the Rook and stood beside him.

"But…I *would* like to save some time," Sanderson said, rubbing his head and frowning. Then he cocked his head up. "You know–I don't *have* to torture you… although it *always* invariably comes to that...bother. Yet…if you just told me what I needed to know, then I could, I suppose, just kill you.

"It's not customary," Sanderson almost whispered, as if someone might over-hear. "Normally we have to try and find a way to spare every life. But, for the sake of expediency…we could go a different way. Does this seem like a good deal?"

"Well," the Rook frowned his saggy face. "What's the alternative?"

"I suppose if you told me everything, depending on what you knew, maybe you could stay here at the lab as opposed to being destroyed. But, you would have to tell me *everything*, and if you don't know *enough*, we'll have to treat it like you are refusing to answer, and go back to long episodes of torture."

"I don't know *everything* about *anything*, but whatever. Why *am* I here, any-way? What do you need to know that's so piggin' important?"

Sanderson leaned over the Rook and looked at him as seriously as he could muster. "Exactly *how* is it that the Mainframe cannot see you?"

"Well, *crap,*" the Rook said, rolling his eyes. "Guess you better get on with the torture then. *Who knows?* Someone did it for me years ago, some hacker. I couldn't begin to understand *how*. Shit. *Magic*."

Chapter 38:

Monday Morning

JUNE *2070 EST*

Mon 16
8:00

Wonderful sat up at 8 AM. She slowly stretched and sighed as the Mainframe instructed the staff that the sole Serter was now moving. Wonderful smiled as she looked around the room appreciatively.

As a couple servants made their way into the room, Wonderful made her way carefully out of her oversized bed. Almost as soon as she plopped down next to her bed, however, she proceeded to make it behind herself.

As the servants came closer, she waved them off–silently insistent that she make the bed herself. It was a very slow process, but Wonderful's determination won out over the size of the obstacle.

"What is this?" The first servant asked. "She has never made her own bed."

"Shock," the second servant said. "Shock that that terrible Mr. Joseph killed our master. They spent so much time together! She must feel so betrayed. He probably hurt her in other ways. The poor girl."

"Poor girl," the first servant nodded. "Yet, maybe somehow the shock of all that has happened will find a way to manifest positively. Sometimes people suffer terrible tragedies, and somehow come out better than they ever were–even under the most unlikely of circumstances."

The servants turned to see the girl standing silently only a few feet away from them.

"Wonder, honey, are you alright?" The second servant asked.

"Me?" The little girl asked, smiling with emphasis. "I'm Wonderful!"

From this morning forward, *every* day would begin with her smiling and making her own bed. *Never again* would she start her day, screaming in confusion and fear; it is thus with this day that so end the Terrors of Wonder.

THE END.

THE REST OF THE WORLD

The passing of Axel and Jacob was met with global condolences and respect. Although Axel was more widely recognized, the mourning that people displayed for Jacob Serter was immense by comparison.

Long after Axel's image faded from the popular media, many journalists and capitalists went on to sanctify Jacob Serter, magnifying and embellishing even his most trivial of moments.

SerterCo enjoyed a tremendous surge in profits and holdings.

Syd Sigma & the War Dogs composed a song called *"Reliquary Requiem"* in homage to *The Valentine Relics*. The song played in five parts, each devoted to one of the band members. It went on to be their most successful single song of their careers.

An unofficial meeting of six prominent leaders resulted in the uniform agreement as to how to deal with Thompson as he struggled to bring his kingdom together…or rather, how to take it from him.

"Thompson has been Axel's lapdog for decades," Minister Van Loch explained to his colleagues. "Oh, he knows how to run the company–the country–but the people do not know *him*. And, as I doubt Axel was transparent with Thompson in *all* of his designs, it will take him some time to assess his property. It is therefore favorable that we attack now, as Silverberg is *technically* at its weakest; its new ruler less likely to employ its defenses accurately."

"*Attack?* On *what* front?"

Van Loch smiled, an expression which, when employed by him, made one cringe. "That, sir, is what we are discussing today. *Every* front: financial, agricultural, invasion, insurrection. Those are the more peaceful suggestions, anyway. Silverberg may already be in a position where it must be erased from the world–for the welfare of the remainder, of course."

HISTORY OF THE COMPANY,
PART II

"I would like to speak to the manager!" The lady said to Private Bedford, who looked as miserable as one can while still remaining upright.

"I would like to speak to the manager!" The lady said to Lieutenant Bradshaw, who had only just walked up to her.

"I'm the manager," Bradshaw said, trying his best to sound agreeable.

"You're the manager?" The lady asked.

"Yes. *I'm* the manager."

"I see."

What gave it away? Bradshaw thought as he waited for the lady to explain her problem. *Oh! Is it that my **uniform** is different from everyone else's? Was it my nametag–the one that says "manager?"*

"Listen, *I* was told you would have muffins today, and this young man *here*," she said, pointing accusingly at Private Bedford. "Says that you don't *have* any muffins."

"I'm sorry ma'am, but Cody is correct. We don't have any muffins."

"Is there someone *else* I can complain to? *Your* boss?"

"No, I think you misunderstand, ma'am, we don't *sell* muffins. We never have, or at least, not as long as I've been with the company."

"No, *your* man that was here yesterday told me you would have muffins. Today."

"I'm sorry ma'am, I have no idea *why* anyone would tell you that: we don't *ever* sell muffins."

The lady thought for a moment. "Well, maybe you *should*, then maybe you wouldn't lose so much business!"

The lieutenant sighed.

"So," the woman said, but hesitated, looking around the menu board. "So, when will you have *them*?" She asked accusingly, pointing nowhere in particular toward the menu board.

"When will we have *what*?" The lieutenant asked, looking at the 'out' items listed.

"***Muffins***. *Tomorrow*, I suppose?"

Oh, for crying out…wait…do I work tomorrow?

"Yes ma'am, we'll have them tomorrow."

- [Daniel Strasel] -

EPILOGUE

The thoughts exploded into his mind, and then just kept coming and coming…almost *savagely*. Earnest threw his head back and screamed out in pain.

It was the ugliest form of scream, where the high pitched sounds that he made were so ridiculous and uncontrolled that if he could hear it beyond his own pain, he would be embarrassed.

The Thinking Cap flew off of his head almost as immediately as he put it on, but Earnest was captive to its effects for minutes afterward.

The Thinking Cap introduced Earnest to the thoughts of a very different and intricate mind. A mind with certain ideas: complex, dark, *horrific* ideas–made doubly so because of the sheer *lack* of passion behind them.

Earnest's eyes were wide, but he saw nothing as he realized this…mind… was trying to…*enter*…him, throwing itself in its *entirety* at the recipient, over and over again.

Earnest, momentarily in his superconscious mind, saw all the missing passion in its *want* to *enter* his…yet, not *his*…

Earnest realized that he was the wrong vessel.

Earnest focused to see the SEUs, the Knight, and Simon standing over him.

"I have seen the mind of the enemy," Earnest said gravely. "And there *is* an enemy. *Something* is coming, friends. Something that will devour Silverberg only *slightly* before it devours the world.

"If *we* do not act, *somehow*, all is lost."

Appendix:

The Valentine Relics

2069 Album Cover

Todd "Gob" Gibson - Bass
Nanguo "Nan" Li - Lead Guitar
Ayn "Anthem" Serter - Vocals/Keyboard/Lyrics
Isaac "Mack" Macintosh - Vocals/Keyboard/Lyrics
Billy "ש (Shin)" Blake - Drums/Lyrics

<u>One Fool Makes Many (Title Track)</u>
One fool makes many
All fools love money
So print off plenty
And let's get funny
We'll dance in the rivers
And swear up at the sky
Then we'll give unto the givers
And then lay at home and cry
One fool makes many
All fools love money
So give us plenty
Cause we're so funny
Now we'll sing unto each other
As we watch our lives roll by
Like our fathers and our mother
Sang our darkest lullaby
One fool makes many
All fools love money
Yet those with plenty
Don't act so funny
Money
Money
Money
The piper is there, the piper is calling
The money is false, the banks are falling
The lord awaits, so why are we stalling?
The truth is so true, the answer's appalling
One fool makes many
All fools love money
So print off plenty
And let's get funny
We'll dance in the rivers
And swear up at the sky
Then we'll give unto the givers
And then lay at home and cry
We'll dance in the rivers
And swear up at the sky
Then we'll give unto the givers
And then lay at home
and cry

- [Daniel Strasel] -

Appendix:

The Chessmen

Founded by Peter Smith (the original unmutual) in the year 2022, the group dedicated itself to the welfare and protection of the employees of Axel Industries… while thwarting Axel. Peter believed in people, just not Axel.

Before recently going public, the group was better known as the *SilverSmiths*, an underground organization that helped unfortunates change their identity.

People protected by the *SilverSmiths/Chessmen* would elect a new name for themselves, many times using Smith as their surname. This was traditionally done either in homage to Peter Smith, or for the simple commonality of the name. [130Δ]

The King – When anyone within the ranks refers to "the King," they are talking about the small body of rules that govern the structure of the organization. The King is the doctrine of the Chessmen.

The Queen – Is the member of the organization that makes the critical decisions. The identity of the Queen used to only be known to the Bishops, Rooks, and Knights; with Mark Curie's publicizing of the Chessmen, however, everyone now knows who the Queen of the Chessmen is.

Rooks – A position usually filled by metahumans to carry out the muscle work of the organization, this position is generally vacant, for it has been quite usual that soon after someone assumes the position, they as quickly disappear. Knights frequently warn ambitious metahuman pawns about the danger of becoming a Rook.

Knights – Govern a small body of Pawns. They observe and protect them from discovery and themselves. If a Queen dies or abdicates, every Knight nominates a potential successor from the ranks of the Pawns. Knights in the East and West hubs used to be known as "Inquisitors" before the Queen took the Chessmen public.

130Δ plus, it was catchy–no one ever called the organization the SilverBrowns, even though a great many members have also changed their surnames to Brown.

    - [The Terrors of Wonder] -

<u>Bishops</u> – The identities of the bishops are known only to the Queen and the Queen's Pawn; they do not even know one another. When a new Queen is to be elected from the nominees presented by the Knights to the Queen's Pawn, the Bishops are convened for voting, all wearing nonbinary black and white tragicomic masks over their faces.

Bishops are usually loyal–even fanatical–Chessmen in pivotal places or positions of employment.

<u>The Queen's Pawn</u> – Is the Queen's assistant, and the only Pawn that cannot be promoted. The Queen's Pawn works very closely with the Queen, and is thus privy to many of the Queen's secrets. The current Queen's Pawn has been in position since the disappearance of the founder, Peter Smith.

<u>Pawns</u> – The only promotable members of the Chessmen. This title accompanies anyone that has had a change of identity, although the level of participation varies greatly from one pawn to the next.

At this point, the SilverSmiths–nee Chessmen–suffer from a generalized public perception (mostly thanks to the Queen's regular demeanor) as being a conspiracy theory group that is looking for mediacast attention, and not to be taken too seriously.[131△]

131△ This footnote has been removed.

Appendix:

Oedipus Edified

The author, Mary Godwin, and her husband were killed a few years ago when an unidentified group burst into their apartment using heavy weapons and explosives. Their murders were never solved.

There were two detectives assigned to the case. One disappeared (presumed killed) in the middle of the investigation. The other died, apparently of a drug overdose, in his office shortly after having had a conversation with imaginary people.

Edited footage of the event is available at the Mainframe Imageyard.

Having left no heir, and having no other family, ownership of the novel went to Silverberg via the **No-Will Law**.

Within a few scant weeks, it was mediacast to the public that a small cache of notes had been found concerning Mary's *first* draft of <u>Oedipus Now</u>, and that the novel had been restored to its **entire**, *original* version. The restored work was entitled <u>Oedipus Now, *Edified*</u>. The Mainframe was updated with the *edified* version, all traces of the shorter work gone. Many now have read (and some re-read) the re-released novel.

<u>Oedipus Now, *Edified*</u> enjoyed a massive popularity boom, which then rapidly spawned several mediacast shows and documentaries. With this considerable resurgence of interest, Axel created the ONE awards (ONE being an acronym for <u>Oedipus Now, *Edified*</u>), offering possible fame and fortune to anyone who wanted to write, play…basically create some piece of media.

- [The Terrors of Wonder] -

Appendix:

Misunderstood Mediacast

Central Silverberg Police Department
Record #[0]6142070366

"Inishite Me gee ah Sisson–"
"You's to *stop*, Deng!" A second voice scolded.

"Hello?" The police dispatcher said to the blank, yet vocal mediacast screen
in front of her.

"I'm serder is…dammit Deng! Stop!"

"Do you need assistance? What is your location?" The dispatcher looked
over at her office imagescreen, but the origin of the cast was glitching.

"I'm…serder ah-hahahahaHAHAHAH!!! DAMMMIT DENG!"

MAINFRAME » TERMINATED AT SOURCE «

Appendix:

People & Characters

Alpine A wolf

Amos See Earnest

Anderson A Subject at the laboratory.

Anthem (Ayn Serter) Ayn "Anthem" Serter – (Previously known as Ayn McNally) Lead singer of *The Valentine Relics*, wife of Jacob Serter, mother of Wonderful Serter.

Arthur An aardvark

Axel Leader of Silverberg/Owner of Axel Industries.   Dresses with all parts of his skin covered in black material to hide the hideous scarring he received during an accident.

Billy Attendant who works at the amphitheater. Billy has a cat named "dolly" and watches *Slabside* religiously. He has all the toys.

Billy "Shin" Blake Drummer for *The Valentine Relics*. Stage name is "Shin," but nobody calls him that. Has pointed ears and eyebrows. Stage presence is an alien, but publicly thought of as an elf.

Benson A wolf

- [The Terrors of Wonder] -

Bob Emergency bus driver

Bobert Competent boblin translator

Brown Bear A bear

Carlton A wolf

Carson Agent of Axel Industries Internal Security; Head of Military and Defense. You're just reading these now. This guy isn't even in the book.

Cody Bedford (Private) Bagel Lord employee.

Cordelia "Cordy" Templeton Wife of Hugo Templeton

Colonel Nill Colonel severely reprimanded for suggesting that everyone at heart is a thief.

Denny Kedney Sound man for *The Valentine Relics*. Good guy. Humble. Likeable. Down to Earth.

Ducktor Hackenbush A medical duck

Dumpkins The unmentioned third pig from Piggin' Around.

Earnest See Michael Smith

Essence Templeton Daughter of Hugo and Cordelia Templeton. Music critic.

Floyd An orderly at the laboratory

Frank A bear

Franklin Serter Father of Jason and Jacob Serter.

George Gordon See Amos

Gob (Todd Gibson) Bass player for *The Valentine Relics.* Short of stature with blacked out eyes. Slightly green skin. Stage presence is a goblin.

Grob Boblin with excessively muscular arms.

Hedges A wolf

Hugo Templeton Professional food critic, husband of Cordelia Templeton.

Jacob Serter Owner and CEO of Serter Company, arguably the second largest company in the world.

Jason Serter Deceased brother of Jacob Serter, former head of SerterCo.

Joseph Slave to Jacob Serter, head of the Serter household staff.

Ken Ferguson (Private) Attendant at Bagel Lord SVB13

Lieutenant Bartowski Assistant manager at Bagel Lord SVB13

Lieutenant Bedford Assistant manager at Bagel Lord SVB13

Lord Lewis The chief sheep

L U Therius Author of <u>One Faith</u>.

Mack (Isaac Macintosh) Co-Leader of *The Valentine Relics*, plays keyboard, writes lyrics, performs vocals. Stage presence is an angel.

Major Tohm Unit Manager for Bagel Lord Unit SVB13

Martin A Serter house slave

Mason Agent of Axel Industries Internal Security; Head of Mysticism and Occult

Michael Smith See Valentine Smith

Moby An overweight basset hound

Mommy A doctor at the laboratory

Mue Counselor at the laboratory.

Nan (Nanguo Li) Asian orphan of questionable descent, Lead guitarist of *The Valentine Relics*, stage presence is a female version of Axel.

Nathan A bear

Nelson Agent for Axel Industries Internal Security; Head of Mainframe & Imagebank Operations

Old Khazeer A boar. Not a pig, somehow.

Otto Ryan, M.D. Dr. Otto Ryan–Doctor who diagnosed Wonderful Serter's night terrors.

Parsifal Planer A jewish baker in Stockholm, Sweden who started a storefront called "*My Lord's Bagels*."

Penny A hen reporter

Poinky	A pig often seen borrowing money, begging for money, or negotiating for money.
Private Clauson	Employee at Bagel Lord SVB13 who would really like to date Essence Templeton.
Private Parks	An attendant at Bagel Lord SVB13
Private Stock	Veteran dishwasher at Bagel Lord SVB13
Professor Plumber	Character referenced by Penny
Rachael Gale	Serter house slave
Richard Serter	Son of Seigfried and Isolde. Changed name of *My Lord's Bagels* to *Bagel Lord.*
Riley	A security guard
Salem	The chief wolf
Sanderson	A doctor at the laboratory
Scooter	A pig
Scout	A gossiping squirrel
Seigfried Serter	Husband of Isolde, who was the daughter of Parsifal Planer.
Simon	Former mirroranium scientist turned painter
Smokey	Bus driver for *The Valentine Relics*, and Billy's Father

Subject 40449 See The SEUs

Subject 61167 See George Gordon

Suzie Austencamp (Private) Host at Bagel Lord SVB13

Syd Sigma Lead vocalist and front man of the *War Dogs.*

The Knight *Chessmen* operative who took in the Rook & company

The Rook Heavyweight operative of *The Chessmen.*

The Queen (Mark Curie) The flamboyant "Queen" of the *Chessmen,* a group also known as the *Silver-Smiths.*

The SEUs An astronaut

The Queen's Pawn Personal assistant to the Queen.

Thompson Agent Director of Axel Industries Internal Security

Tob Boblin avatar

Tristan Serter Father of Franklin Serter

Valentine Smith See Subject 61167

Vortran (Francois) A french man who insists that "rife is an irrooshen."

Warren Ze'ev the Warsheep A sheep from London

White Bear A bear

Wilson Agent for Axel Industries Internal Security; Head of Justice/Law

Winston A wolf

Winthorpe A security guard

Wonda (Smith) newly recruited Chessmen Pawn

Wonderful Serter daughter of Jacob and Anthem Serter.

Young A counselor at the laboratory

Other books by Daniel Strasel:

WITHOUT REST

ISBN 978-0-9859964-4-4

A tale of love and madness. When he confronts the Truth, a lovesick god has all of his dreams turned into nightmares.

GOD, MAN, AND THE MACHINE

ISBN 978-0-9859964-3-7

A story of symbols; a book of philosophy and fiction. An uninteresting man of mistaken importance struggles to understand his role in life.

Stegosaurus the Triceratops

ISBN 978-0-9859964-6-8

A book made to create great conversations: ethics of work, principle, helping, and leadership. A stuffed toy dinosaur encourages others by expressing care.

Visceral Outcries of a Social Moron

ISBN 978-0-9859964-5-1

A short and fun book of poetry and commentary.

For Daniel's complete portfolio please visit Mirroranium.com

Appendix:

Glossary

Autocars For only a few units per month, citizens of Silverberg are welcome to enjoy the use of an autocar (Automatic Car).[△] Autocars are capable of self-drive as they are subject to the complete control of the Mainframe and are generally considered the safest method of travel

([△] Not to be confused with the larger Autotran, which are generally designed to carry large loads along fixed routes in Silverberg. Public autotrans do not cost units to *ride*).

Automercials Almost every inhabitant falls subject to the displaying of an *automatic commercial* or "automercial."

Automercials do not play very frequently. Axel is extremely particular and unwavering in what he will allow to be mediacast as an automercial. The price is dizzying. The automatic commercial spots in Silverberg are the most sought after marketing spots in the world.

Blairmounte A global company often associated with no-frill business practices

Blark A style of music Essence Templeton once ascribed to *The Valentine Relics*.

- [The Terrors of Wonder] -

Cast Slang term for "mediacast."

Chessmen Also known as the SilverSmiths. Group capable of providing alternate legal identity in Silverberg. See also Appendix.

Credit Bank Every citizen is issued a credit bank, which functions like a private image-bank or terminal.

Darky Ducko Mediacast show about a crime-fighting duck that can see the future.

Dead Slang term meaning "good, agreeable, desirable"

Destiny Core Saturday Morning mediacast show about superheroes

Imagebank Imagebanks are hardpoints throughout Silverberg capable of projecting images and/or observing the vicinity.

Although some are conspicuous, (known colloquially as *terminals*) most are built directly into the scenery or architecture, and so built as to render them otherwise indistinguishable from their surroundings.

Most public imagebanks may be employed by a citizen; they simply need to "tag" it with their credit bank (a *tag* can be performed any number of ways, some of which require physical touch, and some which do not).

Tagging is an out-of-date practice, however, and few people employ it… usually by newcomers to Silverberg that see it performed on a mediacast show.

Imaged A slang term that is used by natives of Silverberg to mean "dead" (As "dead" has come to mean "good"). When an individual dies in Silverberg, they are reduced to whatever "images" they have remaining in the Mainframe.

The popular expression "imaged" is derived from a lyric from the old Silverberg Country & Western song: *"I'm Just an Image in the Imageyard."*

Imagescreen Either a projected or physical screen designed for displaying Mainframe content.

Lounge A medical bed. Lounges are available with or without certain amenities, and can further be customized if desired.

Mainframe Silverberg's computer network. Anything automatic, powered, or mediacast in Silverberg is controlled in some way by the Mainframe.

Mediacast Term for anything accessesd via the Mainframe.

Mirroranium Substance that Axel Industries can make unbreakable. Reflects like a mirror, seems like a metal.

MMR Mainframe's Most Relevant – Silverberg mediacast news show

Piggin' Around	Saturday Morning mediacast show designed for younger audiences
Skitt	The type of music *The Valentine Relics* play, which is Blark genre mixed with stage performance.
Slabside	Medical thriller mediacast show
Syd Sigma and the War Dogs	Rival music group to *The Valentine Relics*
Shots	Slang term for any drugs taken intravenously
SilverSmiths	See Chessmen
Slang	Slang term meaning "bad, undesirable, in poor taste."
Solid Hypnizium	(also known as Solid H) Illicit drug that is generally taken nasally; has the effect of breaking down the barrier between one's conscious and sub-conscious minds. Regular users can effectively control their own hallucinations, and have adopted the expression "living the dream," to express when they are using it. Long term users go insane, overwhelmed by their illusions and fantasies.
Valentine Relics	Skitt music group. See also Appendix

Van Loch A global company frequently associated with poor environmental practices.

Appendix:

Augmentations

Physical, even mental augmentations are not uncommon in Silverberg. People that make any permanent modifications to their bodies are known as "augmented humans." This could be something as dramatic as reinforced bone, or as simple as breast enlargement.

When someone receives augmentations that allow them to perform *beyond* normal human ability, they are known as "metahumans."

When someone can perform beyond recorded *metahuman* maximum, they are known as *trans*human. [132Δ]

[132Δ] The distinction is based on performance.

For instance, if someone lost an eye and received a similar or equivocal replacement, they would be an *augmented* human. If the new eye allowed them to gauge distance, say to a fraction of an inch, they would be a *metahuman*. If the new eye allowed them to do something no one else could do, they would be considered a *transhuman*.

Few pay much attention to these designations beyond hospitals and high society. A colorful saying amongst those who care is: *"Two trans a meta makes."*

Appendix:

AIIS Department

Axel Industries Internal Security.

The AIIS department of Axel Industries oversees, to a greater or lesser degree, *everything* in Silverberg. It typically operates in the background, so only the more prominent typically interact with it than the average citizen.

In Silverberg, in authority, first are the Agents, then Silverberg officials, then citizens, then slaves.

In the AIIS department, in authority, first there's the director (currently Thompson), then department heads, then "primaries," then recruits. Everyone in the AIIS department, however, is simply called an "Agent."

Thompson - Internal Security Director

- [Department Heads] -

Ericson - Metahumans & Augmentation
Dodgson - Processing & Migration
Nelson - Mainframe & Imagescreen
Benson - Arts & Education
Carson - Military & Defense
Gibson - Agriculture
Jackson - Business, Industry, & Employment
Mason - History & Occult
Morrison - Credit Banks & Financial
Nicholson - External Security Director
Orson - Extra Terran Operations
Stevenson - Superstructure & Planning
Watson - Nutrition, Health, & Subliminals
Wilson - Justice

Department Heads may have anywhere from 5 (such as Agent Mason) to 5,000 (such as Agent Jackson) primaries that report to them

---

There is a hall in the Ace to commemorate particular AIIS Agents, known as the **<u>Hall of Moments.</u>** It boasts only three names:

Harrison - 2020
Richardson - 2041
Jefferson - 2065

The head Agents of the AIIS finished watching the secret mediacast record of Minister Van Loch's suggestion of attacking Silverberg.

"That's okay," Thompson said, addressing the group. "It's about time, anyway. The world needs a war if it is going to overcome inequality - dismantle these societies where only the poor or ignorant are held accountable, although everyone is guilty.
"This world needs a war if it is going to overcome its laws, which have now become so hard and so heavy that nobody can know, understand, or practice them all.
"This world needs a war if it is going to overcome its debt — to stop outsourcing slavery; to energize these lazy lands that prosper by borrowing with no intent to repay.
"Well, either that, or the world needs love. I don't suppose everyone is just going to suddenly forgive everyone else though, so here's what we're going to do..."

About the Author

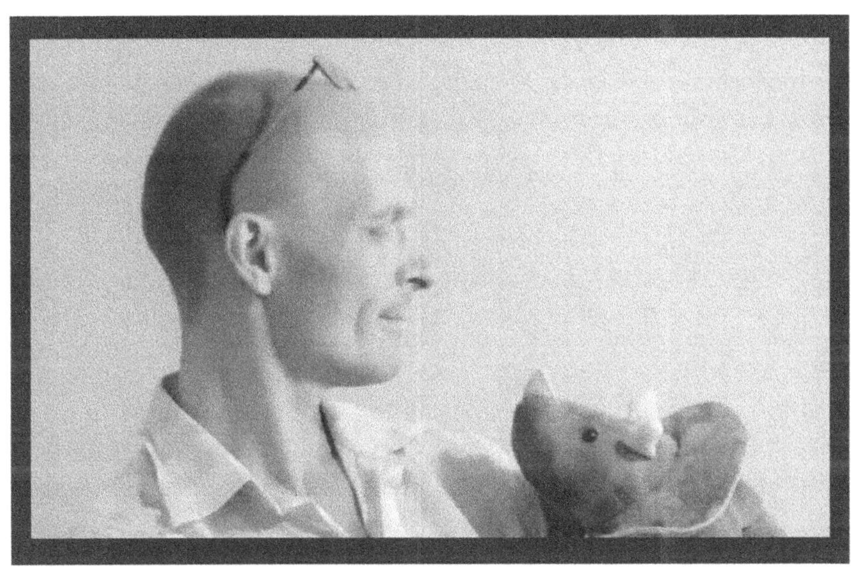

…if only for the reading of *this* very sentence.

Daniel Strasel, born September 15, 1973, sole progeny of ~~a seditious milk maid~~ an eccentric, yet intelligent nurse named Sue. He emerged into life a genuine, happy child. Soon thereafter, he grew into a brooding and self-centered adolescent. A wild, ambitious, and impressionable young adult was followed by a confused, frightened, and purposeless man.

Following his tweens he finally found humility, discipline, and compassion before his overdeveloped sense of self-importance destroyed him completely. Thanks always to my wife for helping provide the time for me to write this.

- [Daniel Strasel] -

- [The Terrors of Wonder] -